Beneath
the
KEEP

www.penguin.co.uk

ALSO BY ERIKA JOHANSEN

The Queen of the Tearling
The Invasion of the Tearling
The Fate of the Tearling

BENEATH THE KEEP

A NOVEL OF THE TEARLING

ERIKA JOHANSEN

BANTAM PRESS

TRANSWORLD PUBLISHERS
Penguin Random House, One Embassy Gardens,
8 Viaduct Gardens, London SW11 7BW
www.penguin.co.uk

Transworld is part of the Penguin Random House group of companies
whose addresses can be found at global.penguinrandomhouse.com

Penguin
Random House
UK

First published in Great Britain in 2021 by Bantam Press
an imprint of Transworld Publishers

A CIP catalogue record for this book
is available from the British Library.

ISBNs
9781787632356 (hb)
9781787630659 (tpb)

Printed and bound in Great Britain by Clays Ltd, Elcograf S.p.A.

The authorized representative in the EEA is Penguin Random House Ireland,
Morrison Chambers, 32 Nassau Street, Dublin D02 YH68.

Penguin Random House is committed to a sustainable
future for our business, our readers and our planet. This book
is made from Forest Stewardship Council® certified paper.

For Dorian Karchmar, my Captain of Guard

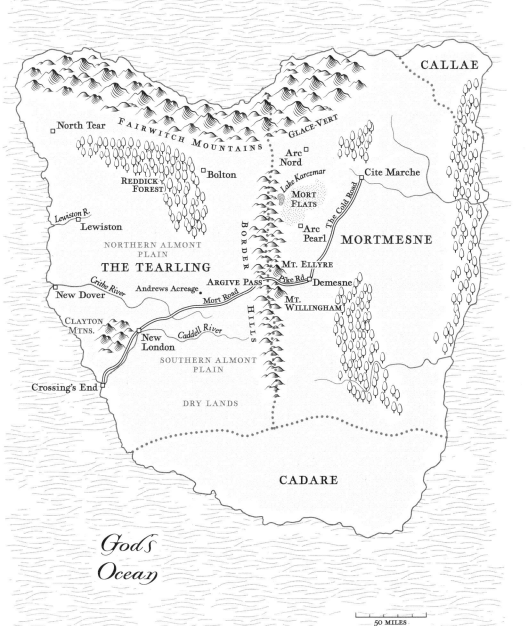

Fairwitch
Sea

CALLAE

North Tear

FAIRWITCH MOUNTAINS

GLACE-VERT

Arc
Nord

Cite Marche

REDDICK
FOREST

Bolton

Lake Karczmar

MORT
FLATS

Lewiston R.

Lewiston

NORTHERN ALMONT
PLAIN

THE TEARLING

B
O
R
D
E
R

H
I
L
L
S

Arc
Pearl

MORTMESNE

The Cold Road

MT. ELLYRE

Andrews Acreage

ARGIVE PASS

Pike Rd.

Demesne

Crithe River

New Dover

Mort Road

MT.
WILLINGHAM

CLAYTON
MTNS.

New
London

Caddell River

SOUTHERN ALMONT
PLAIN

Crossing's End

DRY LANDS

CADARE

God's
Ocean

50 MILES

Map Copyright © MMXX Springer Cartographics LLC

Is God willing to prevent evil, but not able? Then he is not omnipotent.
Is he able, but not willing? Then he is malevolent.
Is he both able and willing? Then whence cometh evil?
Is he neither able nor willing? Then why call him God?

—Epicurus

BENEATH
THE
KEEP

PROLOGUE

B oy! Over here now!"

Christian looked up from his meal, a well-picked-over rib of beef that had been left in the tunnel outside. There was still meat on the bone, and before he acknowledged the man who had entered the room, he was determined to gnaw away the last bits.

"Boy!"

Christian looked up again, resigned. There was no light here but a single candle, its thin illumination barely enough to reveal the shadowy figure in the doorway. But still, Christian knew the man: a portly figure whose muscle had long since run to fat, his thick jowls and bright red nose revealing an overfondness for drink. He would know Wigan anywhere. He would know him on his dying day.

"Come on. It's time."

Casting the stripped bone into the corner, Christian popped to his feet. Some days he got enough to eat, some days he didn't, but either way, he always had his reflexes. They had spared him several beatings at Wigan's hands when he was much younger. But Wigan rarely tried to hit him anymore. He was too valuable.

He followed Wigan out into the corridor, their footfalls echoing off the stone walls of the tunnel. From time to time they would pass open doorways, other entrances, and Christian could see people inside, could see everything they were doing. Most of the dens on this level were full of whores, their pimps, their customers. Even down here, most promoters had better accommodations, but two months before, Wigan had made a disastrous bet on a dogfight, and the two of them had been stuck in Whore's Alley ever since.

"I hope you've got your best game today, boy," Wigan grunted. "Ellis brought that giant idiot of his, and he can swing a haymaker like no one's business."

Christian said nothing, but he could already feel his blood warming up, drowning out his handler, thrumming with the pulse of the ring. Nothing mattered there, not Wigan, not the hunger, not the dark warren of the tunnels. The ring was clear, well-defined. The ring was easy.

"Did you hear me, boy?"

He nodded.

"Swear to Christ, half the time I think *you're* a fucking idiot. Speak when you're spoken to!"

"I understand," Christian replied tonelessly.

"Well, why don't you say so?"

Christian shrugged. He was only eleven years old, but he had learned long before that every time he opened his mouth, he gave a piece of himself away.

They climbed a poorly carved stone staircase, reaching the second level. Christian could hear the low roar now, and although it was muted, still several twists and turns away, that roar pulsed in his blood like alcohol, like morphia. He had been given morphia once, years before, when his injuries were so bad that he could not sleep or stay quiet, and he had never forgotten that night: a long, snaking dream in his head, an epic journey through a world filled with light. It was seductive, the scale of that mindlessness, and for that very reason Christian distrusted it. He had never tried morphia again, but there was no need; he already had his own narcotic. The ring resonated in his very bloodstream.

"Have you stretched your arms?"

He nodded again, though he hadn't. Wigan liked to brag that Christian was a physical marvel, and perhaps he was, for he never needed to stretch, never needed to condition, never needed to go through any of the hundred little routines that the other boys apparently did. He was always ready to fight.

"By the way, I thought of a name for you."

I have a name, Christian nearly replied, but he remained silent. It didn't matter what Wigan chose to call him in the ring. Creche babies generally knew nothing about their parentage; Christian had been sold to a handler when he was only a few days old. His name seemed an important thing to keep, since he'd been born with nothing else.

"We'll try it on tonight, see if it sticks."

The roar had grown now, filling the tunnel, echoing off the stone walls to thrum inside Christian's head. A good crowd; that would please Wigan, but Christian hardly cared anymore. Even the people, their yelling and screaming, the stench they brought with them—tobacco and body stink and cheap piss-watered ale—even they didn't matter once he was inside the ring.

They rounded the corner and entered a room that blazed like a bonfire, lit by dozens of torches on the walls and an array of lamps set into the ceiling. Men suddenly seemed to surround Christian, all kinds of men: nobles and beggars, merchants with the embroidered insignia of their guild visible on their shoulders . . . even a couple of frocks from the Arvath, their white robes conspicuous among the dark mass of the crowd, gold twinkling around their necks. The men shouted encouragement, pounding Christian on the shoulder, breathing ale in his face. Wigan bared his brown teeth and bathed in their approval, shouting greetings to those he knew, as one would to friends, but Christian knew that Wigan was nothing to them. Christian was the prize, the object of value, and the reason was simple: he never lost.

"Crush him, boy!"

"Kill that idiot!"

Peering through the crowd, Christian saw that it was indeed Brendan Maartens standing in the ring, his face white in the torchlight. At age fourteen, Maartens was already approaching six feet and had arms like great slabs of stone. But he was also slow, and not just in speed. Maartens barely knew how to talk. Like Christian, he had been in the ring since earliest childhood; years before, he had taken a bad blow to the head that had left its mark. Christian did not want to hurt Maartens, but he knew he would. Money was heavy in the air; mostly pounds, but he spotted Mort marks changing hands as well. Wigan pushed Christian forward, and he tried not to wince as men slapped and punched him in the back.

"He's so small!" a child's voice piped up to his left. "How can he win?"

Christian halted. Amid all the things in flux in this world, one fact held firm: he would win. It was the only thing he knew for certain, and it was enough to sustain him through the small wounds brought by each new day: Wigan's drunks and his heavy hands; the knowledge that Maura, whom Christian thought he might love, was fucking men old enough to be her grandfather; and the blood of other boys, no older than himself, soaked into the skin of his knuckles. This certainty, the knowledge of his own abilities in the ring, was all he had.

Whirling to his left, Christian found a dark-haired child, perhaps two or three years younger than Christian himself, a thin, sickly boy with a narrow, pointed face. He was well-dressed, in thick wool and a black cloak—from topside, clearly—but it was his eyes that stayed Christian's hand. They were bright green and hungry, and although this well-fed child couldn't be more than eight years old, Christian sensed that the boy was fundamentally unsatisfied, constantly seeking something he did not find. Christian had never seen his own reflection, but somehow he knew just what his own eyes would look like: neither hungry nor content, but filled with a vast distance of nothing.

"Back away, Tommy, or he'll have you too!" a man shouted over the child's head. The man was well-dressed also, with manicured hands.... A rich man, Christian thought, bringing his son down to the Creche for a taste of the wild side. Losing interest, Christian turned away, but as he did so, the well-dressed man stroked a hand along his bottom. Christian stiffened, but then an iron grip descended on his shoulder.

"Do nothing!" Wigan hissed in his ear. "It's the Prince and his handler. This is a fight you can't win, boy. Get a move on."

A fight he couldn't win. Wigan might think so, but Christian had already marked the handler, engraving the man's face on his memory. He might never see the man again, but then again, he might run into him, find him all alone in one of these dark tunnels....

"Go on, boy," Wigan growled. "Don't go getting too big for yourself. They're all waiting. Go on."

Christian went, rolling his shoulders, leaving the Prince and the rest of the world behind. He was in the ring now, and in the ring there was only the opponent across from him, who would present no challenge at all. Christian could smell weakness, even well-hidden weakness, and he perceived that the huge boy-man in front of him was frightened, too frightened to make full use of his enormous biceps, hopelessly cowed by the reputation of a small, quick boy who did not lose.

"Christian! Christian!"

Turning, he saw Maura on the far side of the ring, leaning over the gates. She wore a low-cut green dress that sat absurdly on her child's body. Mrs. Evans often let a few of her girls out on fight nights, so that they could go trawling through the crowd for johns. But Maura had not been at one of Christian's fights in months, and he suddenly found that he did not want her here, did not want her to see what was about to happen. But he waved to her, smiling, ignoring the men who crowded around her, hemming her in.

"Christian! Here!"

She was holding something out to him. Reluctantly—for he knew that many eyes watched and marked such things—he moved toward her, crossing the ring.

"What is it?"

"I made it for you. For luck."

She dropped something into his open palm, and Christian stared at it stupidly for a moment before he realized that it was a bracelet of some kind, woven of many different-colored threads. The design showed a bright orange circle that Christian recognized as the sun, sitting over a blue line: water.

"Thank you," he told her. "It's a pretty thing."

"Do you want me to help you tie it on?"

"No. I can't wear it in the ring."

Maura's smile dimmed for a moment. She was older than Christian, by perhaps a year, but he often felt that he topped her by five years, or ten. She retained a strange innocence that this place had barely touched, and he hated to puncture it, to watch her smile fade. But after a moment, she cheered.

"Well, put it in your pocket, then. For luck."

Christian tucked the bracelet deep into the pocket of the short trousers he wore in the ring. It would likely get ruined in there, stained with blood and sweat, but somehow he could not ask

Maura to take it back, or even to hold it for him until the fight was done. Either request, he knew, would hurt her. He put a light hand on her shoulder.

"Let's go, boy!" Wigan shouted behind him. "Time enough for that later!"

Christian turned and saw the promoter waiting on the sidelines. Someone offered Wigan a shot of whiskey, and he downed it, then gave Christian a quick grin, a comradely grin, as though they were partners. Christian closed his eyes, feeling a wintry chill descend upon him. He took his hand from Maura's shoulder and moved back toward his corner.

"A perfect fighter!" Wigan cried over the din, nodding this way and that, his face gleaming with drink. "He cannot be bested!"

He waited a beat, until the crowd quieted down, and Christian felt an unwilling twinge of admiration; drunk or sober, Wigan was a solid showman. He always knew how to play a crowd.

"I give you ... LAZARUS!"

Ignoring their howls, Christian waded in. A circle, quiet and cool, seemed to close around him, sealing him off from the world. Only when the opponent lay dead would there be anything else. Christian lashed out with his right fist and broke Maartens's nose, sending him toppling backward against the ropes. He had already forgotten everything: Maura, Wigan, even the well-dressed Prince and his leering guardian. But Christian never forgot anything, not really, and years later, when he saw Thomas Raleigh again, he would recognize those hungry green eyes with no trouble at all. The Prince had aged, yes, but that was only chronology. Whatever he sought, it still eluded him.

But now there was only the ring, another fight that was over before really beginning. Brendan Maartens had begun to sob now, but Christian was beyond caring. Deep cold had descended upon him, for he already knew that there would be nothing for him but this ring. There was a different life elsewhere, he knew, high above the stinking tunnels of the Creche, but that life was not for him, and as Christian lunged forward and began to kick his opponent to death, he never thought of the world above, not even once.

BOOK I

CHAPTER 1

THUNDERCLOUDS ON THE HORIZON

In retrospect, the seeds of rebellion in the pre-Glynn Tearling are easy to see. The divide between rich and poor was monstrous. More than one million tenant farmers labored in subsistence for the pleasure of some thousand noble families. The Tear had an entrepreneurial class, but it was only a tiny fraction of the population. Economic mobility was almost a myth. The Raleigh ruling family was chronically disengaged, making no move to check the deepening progression of social ills in the kingdom. God's Church was widespread, but the Church kept its wealth carefully hoarded; Arvath priests offered only salvation in the hereafter, not material assistance in the here and now. In the cities, the unemployed begged; in the country, tenants starved. Looking at the entire map, one sees a kingdom ripe for revolution.

—The Early History of the Tearling, AS TOLD BY MERWINIAN

Miles, Lord Marshall, had never wanted to come down here in the first place. He'd heard enough about the Creche to want no part of it, and most of the others seemed to feel the same; looking around the dim, crowded room, Miles saw expressions of boredom, exasperation, disgust. But no one made a move to leave.

Lord Williams had produced the crone off of one of his tenant patches. Even Miles, whose acreage was more than fifty miles away in the Almont Plain, had heard about this woman: Orra, the Eye of the Crithe. They said she could foretell the weather, and though Miles did not quite believe in such things, it could not be denied that Williams had been extraordinarily lucky. Bumper crops, averted floods . . . Miles had even heard that Orra had helped foil a plot by the Blue Horizon to rob one of Williams's caravans on its way to New London. Several lords from the northern Almont had tried to steal the old woman once, Miles had heard, but she had seen them coming, and her entire village had beaten the would-be kidnappers off with sticks. Miles didn't know if the rumor was true, but it made a good tale, and he loved a good tale.

What am I doing here? he wondered again, looking around the dingy room, an incongruous background for the crowd of well-dressed nobles that filled it from end to end. Miles was by no means young, but he was certainly the newest lord here; his father had died unexpectedly four years before, launching him into the family lands and titles at the age of thirty-eight. Miles had never been to the Creche before, for his vices were minimal—cards and an occasional drink—and they could be well serviced in the Gut. As the group traveled through the endless warren of tunnels and intersections—Miles praying, all the while, that they would not get lost, for he could think of nothing worse than wandering directionless in this dark, dank hell beneath the streets of New London—he had begun to understand that the Creche was another animal entirely. He tried not to look, but he had never had that gift some had of turning away from degeneracy entirely, and so he saw them: children, rooms and rooms full of them, their eyes big and dark with want. Some of them were skinny to the point of emaciation, and many looked as though they hadn't bathed in weeks. In one room, Miles had seen a girl no older than his youngest daughter, doing a strangely sinuous dance for a group of men, and that single glimpse had convinced him that all of the stories about the Creche were true.

Now there was a shuffling and murmuring at the far end of the room. The crowd of nobles parted to admit the old woman, who walked with one hand on a cane and the other wrapped around Lord Williams's arm. As she came closer, Miles saw that she was blind, both of her eyes milky with cataracts. As her sightless gaze passed over him, he shuddered.

"Ellens!" Williams deposited the old woman gently into a chair that had been placed beside the six-foot slab of stone in the center of the room. "You have the girl?"

Ellens came forward, leading a slight figure in a hood and cloak. When Ellens pulled back her hood, Miles saw that she was very young, surely no more than fourteen. She had a peasant's simple face, her nose dotted with freckles. Her eyes rolled vacantly toward the ceiling.

Drugged, Miles realized.

"Well, let's get on with it!" someone barked from the back. Miles thought it was Lord Tare. "I don't want to spend a moment more in this shithole than I have to!"

"No one begged you to come, Tare!" Williams snapped back. "In fact, I seem to recall lifting a hundred pounds from you for the privilege."

Tare muttered something inaudible but venomous. Ellens removed the girl's cloak and helped her to lie down on the stone slab. Now that Miles's eyes had adjusted to the light, he saw that the slab itself was covered with odd symbols that had been etched into the stone: sun and moon, the crude rendering of a ship, even a five-pointed star. That last was a pagan symbol, Miles knew, and he wondered—not for the first time—what Bishop Wallace would say if he could see Miles here, in the Creche. In this room.

Best not to think about it. Best to just get it done.

"Light," the old woman croaked, froglike. She wasn't really so old, Miles saw now; it was only her sight and the cane that gave the illusion of age. She might be as young as fifty. She stood patiently, waiting, while three of Williams's men brought torches and stationed them in the stands around the slab, creating a bright circle of light around the young girl in the center of the shadowy room. The girl wore a thin white dress, little more than a shift, and Miles had the unwilling thought that she must be cold, drugs or no. It was early April, warming outside, but in this dank, mold-dripping hell, there was no warmth.

"Go ahead, Orra," Williams told the old woman, his voice deep and solicitous, and Miles felt a sudden, poisonous envy. Williams wasn't even a good Christian; he went to church, certainly, as they all did, but that didn't stop him from keeping two mistresses in his manse. Rumor said that Williams was so brazen about it that the mistresses slept on the same floor as his wife.

He will get his reward in the hereafter, Miles thought, feeling a grim satisfaction at the idea. *And there won't be any seers to grease the skids there.*

The old woman had bent over the younger one now, pulling her arms from her dress. She rolled the bodice of the dress down to the girl's waist, revealing her breasts and the milk-white skin of her torso. Miles crossed himself and looked away, but a moment later his eyes had gone back, almost unwilling.

The old woman began murmuring, low words that Miles could not hear, and the young woman began to writhe. As she twisted on the slab, her eyes rolled up into her head, showing the whites. Miles was growing more uncomfortable by the second, and he didn't think he was the only one; there was an almost imperceptible movement in the crowd of nobles, shifting and fidgeting, as though they all wished they were anywhere else. When Miles first heard about Williams's offer, it had seemed a downright bargain: one hundred pounds to find out the year's forecast! His acres had been devastated in the drought, and the hundred pounds would bring the family treasury down to its last thousand, but a man who knew the year's weather could make ten times that much, not only by planting the right crops but by hoarding his own long-term stores to create a shortage. Paying Williams had been the easiest decision that Miles had ever made; only now, in this dank room, did he understand that there might be an additional price. His fellow nobles knew it too; they shifted uncomfortably, none of them willing to look at each other, all of them trying not to look at the girl. She had arched her back now, lifting her torso off the table, and her eyes continued to gaze whitely at the ceiling, almost as whitely as those of the old woman who stared down at her, her palm placed flat between the girl's breasts. The woman's other hand emerged from the shadows, and Miles saw that she held a dagger.

"God save us," someone muttered nearby, and several of the lords who stood opposite Miles crossed themselves. But none of them moved to interfere, not even when the old woman made a shallow vertical cut along the line of the girl's breastbone. Blood welled immediately, a red river cutting a ravine between mountains, almost shockingly scarlet in contrast to the girl's white skin. Several of the lords in the audience cursed, and behind Miles, someone drew a shaking, hissing breath. As the old woman removed the dagger, the girl stopped writhing and lay still, so still that Miles could not even see her breathe.

"Is she dead?" Lord March asked timidly.

"Shut up, March!" Lord Williams hissed, his eyes focused on the old woman.

My God, Miles thought, *he has seen all of this before. How many times?*

"I come to speak before you now," the old woman said, and her voice made Miles jump. It was not the voice of an old woman, or even of a woman at all. The words were hollow and cold, less than human. That night, and for many months afterward, Miles would wake gasping from dreams he could barely remember, dreams in which that voice spoke to him, taunted him, stalked him, coming closer and closer in the dark.

"The stars change," the old woman intoned hollowly. "The moon falls. The tide surges, then ebbs."

Miles blinked. He had expected this to be a simple business, though he didn't know why. Just a few straightforward words: would the drought continue, or not? But this was prophecy; of course it would not be straightforward. For a moment he wondered whether the old woman were milking it, building suspense as a good carnival palmist would . . . and then he dismissed the thought as that lifeless voice spoke again.

"Seventeen ships went over the horizon, all of them bound for the better world. One ship sank; innumerable sorrows arose. Sixteen ships landed, and the Tearling was born."

"The Crossing," someone muttered behind Miles. "Who gives a toss? Just tell us about the weather."

"William Tear fell," the old woman continued. For a moment her milky eyes seemed to look right at Miles, and he froze, unable even to breathe until her gaze had moved on.

"William Tear fell," the old woman repeated.

"We know!" someone shouted from the back. "Just get on with it!"

"Shut up!" Lord Williams snapped again. But he looked uncomfortable, and Miles realized uneasily that the process was not going the way it was supposed to. Something was wrong.

"William Tear was the True King," the old woman intoned. "The one who saved them all. He fell, and the kingdom fell with him."

The entire room was muttering now; even Williams could ignore it no longer. He grabbed the old woman's shoulders, giving her a gentle shake.

"Orra! The harvest! The drought! What of the drought?"

In a single fluid movement the old woman whipped around, jerked the dagger upward, and sliced Williams across the face, jaw to forehead. Williams screamed, clasping his hand to the cut, and even before he fell backward the woman was up and out of the chair, leaping, almost springing, like a frog. Miles too jumped backward, knocking several men over behind him. The old woman's milky eyes seemed not blind now, but malevolent. Her mouth was lifted in a hideous grin. She jumped again, three quick springs to the far end of the room.

"Stop her!" Williams shouted, one hand clasped to his bleeding cheek. "Don't let her get away!"

"The harvest," the old woman croaked happily, her white eyes gleaming in the dark. "Yes, you will reap. The moon falls, the stars rise. They shift and change!" Her voice was rising now, almost into a scream; Miles clapped his hands over his ears, but it was no good. He could still hear her, even over the blood that thudded in his ears.

"The True Queen comes!" the harridan shrieked. "I see her! The queen who will be! The one who saves us all!"

"Shut her up!" Williams howled.

But no one in the room seemed to dare. The dagger had fallen from the old woman's hand, but now she began to twitch madly, almost to dance, her body rolling wildly against the wall, her white eyes disappearing and reappearing in the shadows, and that was so horrible that Miles shut his eyes, praying silently. But her screams went on.

"The queen of spades! The victory of ships! She comes! I see her! I see—"

Her voice cut off abruptly, leaving a silence so loud that at first Miles thought someone was still screaming. He drew his hands down from his eyes, but for a long moment he didn't dare open them, not wanting to see. Someone put a hand on his shoulder, and Miles almost screamed himself, but when he looked up it was only Lord Gelland, using him as a support to get to his feet. He thought of saying something, but then a gagging sound from the corner brought him back to where he was.

The old woman lay on the floor, bleeding to death; her throat had been cut. Lord Carvel stood over her, wiping his blade with a red cloth. Of course it would be Carvel. The old lord was well past sixty, but he was former Caden, an assassin who had attained his unlikely lordship by helping old Queen Elaine net a ring of Mort spies. Carvel wasn't one to be frightened by an old woman, even one who spoke in the voice of the dead. For a long moment, no one said anything, and Miles had time to feel relief that—with the exception of Carvel, of course—they had all been as frightened as he was.

"What the fuck was that?" Lady Andrews demanded, pushing her way through the crowd. She was the only woman among them, but the group of nobles parted before her like the Red Sea. Rumor said that Lord Andrews lived in mortal fear of his wife, but he was hardly alone in that; no man in the Tearling wanted Lady Andrews's notice, let alone her enmity. She stalked toward Lord Williams and planted herself before him: a pretty woman, if no longer young, with her hands on her hips.

"I paid good money for a read on the harvest, Williams. Is that what I paid for?"

"I will reimburse you," Williams said, almost humbly. Lady Andrews continued to stare at him for a long moment, and Williams added, "Plus twenty pounds for your trouble."

She nodded coldly and then turned to her two retainers.

"Let's get out of here. This place stinks."

They went off through the crowd. Several more nobles left in their wake, but most of the group simply stood there, staring blankly at the dead crone who lay beside the wall. Williams bent to examine the corpse, then turned to Lord Carvel, his eyes blazing.

"I told you to grab her, not kill her! Why in God's name did you do that?"

"These tunnels echo. She was making too much noise."

"But where am I going to find another seer? She was worth her weight in gold!"

Carvel shrugged, unmoved.

"Perhaps all is not lost." Lord Gosselin had moved up now, putting a soothing hand on Williams's arm. That was not surprising, either; Gosselin was always the placator, the peacemaker.

"It's well known that the sight runs in families," Gosselin continued. "Did your seer have any children? You might—"

"She did," Williams muttered. "But I sold the baby, years ago, long before I knew what Orra was. They were looking for girls, paying well—"

"She's gone!"

Miles spun around with the rest. The stone slab stood empty, a bright circle of light in the middle of the room.

"The whore!" Williams shouted. "Christ, she saw it all! Find her! Check the tunnels! Go!"

Nobles scattered in all directions, drawing swords as they went, and Williams followed them, one hand holding a sword and the other still clasped to his bleeding face. Miles, who had no intention of charging off into that lightless labyrinth, was left behind. He thought he was the only one, but after a moment he realized that Lord Gayel had stayed as well. Gayel was a neighbor in the central Almont, owner of vast tracts of wheat. He was by no means a friend, but not an enemy either. They stared at each other across the stone slab.

"What a cock-up," Gayel remarked, fastening his cloak. "I should have never gotten involved with this business."

"Nor I," Miles admitted.

"Well, at least Williams will not have the advantage over us any longer."

They turned toward the corpse. The floors in the Creche were nowhere near level; blood had run from the seer's cut throat to end up almost halfway across the room. Her white eyes stared at them, truly blind now, and yet Miles did not like to meet her gaze, any more than he had before.

"Do you think they'll find the girl?" he asked Gayel.

"I don't think it matters. She was poppied out of her mind, and even if she did remember anything, who would believe her? She was just a pigeon from the Alley."

"But surely someone will want her back."

"No. Ellens bought her outright."

Miles nodded, relieved. His only worry was that the story might get back to Queen Arla somehow, but Gayel was right; no one cared about the words of a Creche whore.

"Come on, Marshall. Let's get out of this place. The Andrews bitch was right about one thing: it reeks."

Miles nodded. But he could not resist a last look back at the body on the floor. The seer's head was thrown backward, her eyes still seeming to stare across the room. Miles turned quickly, following Gayel into the tunnels.

Gayel knew his way; he came down here to watch the fights, and Miles followed him confidently through the tunnels as they branched, met, and then branched again. The two of them talked of home, of the drought, of Lord Doleran's problems with his new wife, who was known to have an eye for young servingmen. But even as he gossiped and laughed, Miles was thinking of the old woman, trying to remember exactly what she had said. She had talked about the True Queen, he knew that, and about ships, and something about the queen of spades. Miles was a good poker player, and he knew the spade queen well . . . but somehow he did not think that the crone had been talking about cards. He and Gayel climbed the great staircase and emerged into the sunshine—early-morning sunshine, bright and cheerful—but Miles did not feel it, for his entire body had gone suddenly, inexplicably cold.

"Thunderclouds on the horizon!" his father had liked to shout toward the end of his illness. "Right there on the horizon, Miles!" And Miles could not calm him, not with whiskey or books or the foul-smelling medicine from the local apothecary. Until the day he died, Robert Marshall remained convinced that the storm was already upon them, a storm so strong that it would shatter the kingdom in two.

Right there on the horizon, Miles repeated to himself. The familiar landscape of the Gut passed around them, pubs and card hells and brothels, but he was not comforted, for he could only think of the seer's milky eyes, her gloating mouth. Beneath the raucous life of the Gut around him, he could still hear her voice.

"The True Queen! She comes now! I have seen it!"

She wasn't talking about Arla, Miles thought. Queen Arla was a ruler like her mother, Queen Elaine, and Elaine's mother before her, a queen who did what was expected . . . and with a sudden start, Miles wondered whether the woman might have been talking about Elyssa. The Crown Princess was already a subject of some unease among the nobility, for she did not mingle with them, not even with the noblewomen her own age, preferring instead the company of servants. Rumor said that Princess Elyssa had sympathies for the poor; Lord Dillon, who spent plenty of time at court, even claimed that she believed in redistribution of wealth. The Princess was young, only twenty-one, but stubborn. Even Queen Arla had not been able to tame her. A collectivist on the throne would be a disaster for the Tearling.

And for me, Miles thought. And then, looking at Gayel beside him: *For all of us.*

Then he told himself not to be ridiculous. Queen Arla had many years to live yet, and the old woman had only been a village seer. Good at forecasting the weather, perhaps, but telling the weather and telling the future of a kingdom were two very different things. Miles was out a hundred pounds, but Williams had made Lady Andrews whole, and having done so publicly, he would have to reimburse everyone; in the end, Miles would have his hundred back as well. The drought would end soon, and the crops rebound, but even if not, there were still fortunes to be made in a time of need. All would surely be well, but even so, Miles could not stop thinking of stars rising and moons falling, of prophecy, and though he was a good Christian who lent no credence to such things, he could not repress a chill.

Distantly, not with his ears but with his mind, he seemed to hear thunder.

CHAPTER 2

THE WOMAN IN THE CLOAK

Elyssa Anne Raleigh–Sixth Queen of the Tearling. Also known as the Shipper Queen. Mother: Queen Arla Raleigh (Arla the Just). Father: Lord Devin Burrell, fourth lord of the Burrell seat (predeceased).

—The Early History of the Tearling (INDEX), AS TOLD BY MERWINIAN

E lyssa hated her mother's court.

She supposed she should be thankful that this wasn't a full audience. More than six hundred people crowded the Queen's throne room, but that was only a fraction of the number the room could hold. It was late May, but the hot weather had already come on, and many of the Tear nobles had retreated from their New London manses to the country. Elyssa supposed she didn't blame them—well, no, she *did* blame them, for a whole host of other things, but not for decamping. New London stank in summer. Sewage, piss, rotten animal flesh . . . the city never smelled of roses, but in hot weather the stench could not be escaped. Even here, on the fourth floor of the Keep, some hundred and fifty feet above the rest of the city, Elyssa could smell it.

Or maybe what she smelled was right here in this room.

The man from the Blue Horizon had been beaten within an

inch of his life. His visible flesh was mottled with bruising: face and arms and even bare feet. His arm appeared to be broken; it hung limply at his side. When the two jailors released his arms, Elyssa saw that at least three of his fingernails had been ripped out. It wasn't her first look at Welwyn Culp's work, but she had never seen it so vicious before. Several ladies of the court had screamed at the man's appearance. Even Niya, Elyssa's own head maid, who reacted to all upset with a face of stone, had not been unmoved, hissing under her breath as Culp pulled the man's hood off.

But Elyssa's mother was not one to be moved by pity. A long time before, when Elyssa was only a child, a singer had composed an ironic song about the Queen, a ballad called "Arla the Just." The singer had died in the Queen's dungeons, but the nickname had stuck, and Elyssa's mother was no more merciful now than she had been then. Queen Arla the Just sat easily on the throne, drinking her tea, apparently unperturbed by the bruised and bleeding man before her. The entire court stood waiting, silent, while the Queen took small sip after small sip, the sapphire crown twinkling on her head. After several minutes she placed the mug back in its saucer, and then set both carefully on the table beside her.

"Who is he?"

"His contact gave us the name Gareth, Majesty. But that may be an alias."

"And where was he found?"

"Off the Cord Launch, Majesty," one of the soldiers below the dais replied. "Trying to escape in a skiff. We found more than a thousand pounds in the bottom of the boat."

"Indeed? And where did this thousand come from?"

"Bishop Laurence's manse. The bishop has confirmed that this is the fortune that was stolen from him several nights ago."

Low murmuring passed through the court. News of the robbery of Bishop Laurence had traveled the city like wildfire, despite the Church's attempts to keep it quiet; the bishop's servants were not discreet, and it was too good a tale. The bishop had invited a pro into his chambers, a woman dressed as a priest. The costume was clearly the most scandalous part of the tale, though Elyssa had hardly been surprised to hear it; God's Church was a collection of fetishists if she had ever seen one. When the servants came the next morning, they found Bishop Laurence unconscious, badly beaten, and his private store of gold cleaned out.

"Well, we all know that tale," Queen Arla remarked. Elyssa sensed private glee beneath her mother's words; the Queen loathed the Church. She might claim that her objections were philosophical, but Elyssa knew that the matter was jealousy. Her mother hated the priests' hold over the kingdom, hated the fact that there was widespread fear not inspired by herself. The Queen had to play sweet with the Arvath in public, to keep the Holy Father happy, but she loved to see the Church humiliated as much as anyone else.

"But this is no woman," the Queen said after a moment. "Where is his accomplice, the prostitute who dressed up as a frock?"

There was a long silence, and then Welwyn Culp replied stiffly. "I have been unable to compel that information, Majesty."

This time, the murmuring was louder. Culp was a virtuoso among interrogators; he never failed to produce answers. The Queen often declared Culp one of her most valued assets, but Lady Glynn, Elyssa's old tutor, had been a staunch opponent of torture, and Elyssa had taken her beliefs to heart. She hated Welwyn Culp, hated everything his lower dungeons represented, so much so that she had once presented her mother with a passage, carefully copied in her own hand from one of Lady Glynn's books, a historical analysis on the inefficacy of torture in interrogation. Elyssa had been only eleven or twelve then, still young enough to believe that her mother would be swayed by the passage's logic, its faultless combination of numbers and reason. Instead, the Queen had ordered her locked in Culp's dungeons for the night. It was Culp himself who had dragged Elyssa downstairs, past the regular dungeons and into the sunken chambers beneath: mold-encrusted rooms where the smell of blood hung in the air like rotten incense and the paving stones still bore traces of decades-old gore. Culp had locked Elyssa into an empty cell ... empty save for a long, raised wooden board, set with manacles at hand and foot, which stood in the center of the room.

Elyssa had stared at that board all night, her eyes wide, unsleeping. She sensed ghosts in the room, not spectral beings but something much worse: an echo of endless suffering, as much a part of the place as the foundation stones beneath her feet. In the morning, when Culp had come to let her out, Elyssa had gone as docilely as a lamb, and she had taken the lesson to heart. She never raised the issue of Welwyn Culp with her mother again ... but she should have, she realized now, staring at the bruised panoply of colors on the prisoner's skin.

"Well, Gareth, or whatever your name is," Queen Arla remarked, "you have a choice before you. You can either give me the name of your accomplice, or I can hand you back to Culp for another go. Depend upon it, he will make you talk in the end."

Elyssa shook her head in silent disagreement. This was not the first member of the Blue Horizon the army had captured, and others *had* talked ... but they had merely been middlemen: fencers of stolen goods or dealers who had provided the Blue Horizon with weapons. Gareth seemed different. Despite his injuries, he stood straight, with no hint of begging or obeisance, and his light eyes did not flinch from the anger in her mother's face. The Blue Horizon had incurred Queen Arla's wrath in a variety of ways, but Elyssa often thought that their real crime was this: they would not kneel. Her mother could threaten all she wanted; this man would never talk.

"Well?" her mother demanded. "Where is the woman? Your accomplice?"

"Picture a world where there are no rich and poor," Gareth said flatly. "A world where all are equally valuable. This is the better world. I see it all the time."

Elyssa could almost see her mother's ears begin smoking. The Queen probably didn't know the origin of the words, but Elyssa did; they were the litany of William Tear, who had founded the Tearling nearly three hundred years before. Lady Glynn had also been a great admirer of William Tear, though that was nothing that Elyssa's mother needed to know about. The Queen had brought Lady Glynn to the Keep to teach Elyssa about power politics, and while Lady Glynn certainly knew about such things, she was also a devout believer in William Tear's better world. When Elyssa was sixteen, Lady Glynn had taken an unthinkable step for a noble, dissolving her family seat and redistributing her acres to the nearly three hundred tenants who worked on her land. The Queen had been furious, the kingdom in uproar, when Lady Glynn disappeared.

Did you kill her? Elyssa wondered, staring at her mother. She asked this question often in her head, though she had never been able to bring herself to ask it aloud. But the entire Queen's Guard stood ready to kill at the Queen's command, and no one had seen or heard from Lady Glynn in nearly five years. She was dead, all right. The Queen's anger had been too terrible.

"Your Majesty would compel me to speak," Gareth continued from the foot of the throne, bringing Elyssa back to herself. "But Your Majesty does not understand the Blue Horizon in the least."

The Queen muttered something inaudible, but it had the ring of profanity. Gareth was right; she did not understand them.

Elyssa herself had never spoken with any member of the Blue Horizon, but thanks to Lady Glynn, she knew what they wanted well enough. A world with no rich and poor was only the beginning; William Tear had wanted to eradicate narcotics, trafficking, bigotry, illiteracy, ignorance, organized religion, greed . . . in short, all the ills of society. For a brief time, he had even succeeded, before his new civilization sank back down into the old mire. Now the Blue Horizon meant to follow in his footsteps. The rebels were a relatively new development in the Tearling; they had first shown up when Elyssa was a child. But they clearly weren't going anywhere.

How is he still standing? Elyssa wondered, staring at the dark-haired man below her. His injuries should have had him on his back, but instead he stared up at the Queen, defiance in every muscle. And Elyssa suddenly wondered why her mother had brought him here, to her audience chamber, when such an outcome was inevitable. Did she mean to demonstrate publicly that the Blue Horizon were intractable? That seemed to be it, for now her mother gave a rueful sigh, and spoke in tones of ersatz regret.

"All of you Blue Horizon fools are alike. You will not be reasoned with. Very well, you leave us no choice. Culp!"

Culp came forward. He was a tall, hatchet-faced man, eternally devoid of expression. Technically, Culp was a member of the Queen's Guard, but he did not wear a grey cloak, and Elyssa knew that the other guards were glad of it. Culp didn't sleep in the guard quarters; he made his home in the dungeons, and though the reason was ostensibly one of efficiency, Elyssa was fairly sure that in the guard quarters, Culp would have had to sleep with one eye open.

"Majesty?" Culp asked.

"Take him back downstairs," the Queen said dismissively. "Let him find his better world in the dungeon."

"Yes, Majesty." Culp grabbed Gareth's shoulder roughly, clearly hoping to make him cry out. But Gareth didn't so much as wince, and this, too, made Elyssa think of William Tear ... William Tear, who had feared nothing, who had been strong enough to lead two thousand utopians across the ocean in search of a perfect society. There was strength in the man who stood before the throne, great strength, and in the face of that strength Elyssa felt suddenly ashamed that she had ever been cowed by a night in the dungeons, that she had ever feared her mother's glare.

I have never risked anything, she thought unhappily. *I have lived in a castle all of my life, and I have never put myself on the line. When I take the throne, how brave will I be?*

"We renew our condemnation of the rabble known as the Blue Horizon," Queen Arla announced. "Further, we raise the existing bounty. The Crown will now pay seventy-five pounds for any member brought in alive."

Foolish, Elyssa thought, and she heard confirmation a moment later, low muttering from several corners of the hall. Queen Arla's audience was dominated by nobles, but a handful of people from the lower classes—entrepreneurs, mostly, but even some of the poor—always managed to get in, and they would make up an even greater proportion now, when so many nobles had returned to their local seats. The poor had embraced the Blue Horizon without reservation, particularly in the two years since the drought began; hardly surprising, but they weren't the only ones. According to Givens, her mother's Captain of Guard, a surprising number of merchants were clearly covering for the movement: providing weapons, storing and moving stolen goods, even providing safe houses for fugitives. Raising the bounty would only further alienate such people from the throne.

Culp hauled Gareth away, jerking him up the aisle that divided the crowd in two. Now Gareth finally stumbled, falling to one knee, and Culp kicked him in the ribs. The man was not made of iron, after all; he groaned loudly, the sound echoing across the room. Several of Elyssa's guard muttered low curses behind her, and Niya drew a short, wounded breath. Elyssa's stomach took a slow roll. She decided that the very first thing she would do upon taking the throne would be to sack and then imprison Welwyn Culp . . . but a moment later she realized that wouldn't be good enough.

All of these people, she thought, watching the crowd . . . but the eye of her mind was looking much farther, beyond this room, out over the city below the Keep, the thousands of miles of tenanted farmland surrounding. More than three million people lived in the Tear, and one day they would all look to Elyssa, just as they now looked to her mother. Queen Arla was not popular, but she *was* feared, and the kingdom scurried under her gaze like ants . . . all except the Blue Horizon.

"The better world!" Gareth shouted now, heedless of Culp's attempts to clap a hand over his mouth. "I see it! Circumstances of birth don't matter! Kindness and humanity are everything!"

"Yes, yes," the Queen murmured. "And golden unicorns shall fly out of William Tear's ass."

Laughter echoed across the room. Culp finally succeeding in muffling Gareth's words, locking his head and dragging him forcibly up the aisle. But Gareth was still trying to speak, and he must have bitten Culp's hand, for Culp uttered a low curse, then hauled back and slapped him.

"Mother!"

Elyssa's mouth had spoken of its own accord. The eyes of the room were suddenly upon her, and she swallowed hard, feeling something thick and starchy blocking her throat.

"Yes, Elyssa?"

Her mother's voice was cold; she might not know what was

coming, but she knew she wouldn't like it. She did not turn toward Elyssa, but that was not surprising; Queen Arla did not turn her head in public for anyone. People were expected to present themselves before her, and after a moment's hesitation, Elyssa did so. The Queen's Guard parted before her, allowing her to move in front of her mother and drop to her knees.

"I would petition you, Mother, for this man's life."

"*What?*"

"His life, Mother. I ask you to grant the prisoner clemency and release him."

The Queen went white with anger. For a moment she seemed to have lost the ability to speak, and Elyssa had time to think that she might well be facing a worse punishment than a night in the dungeons, but then the room exploded with shouting, several voices echoing across the vast expanse.

"True Queen! True Queen!"

"The moon falls!"

"She comes!"

"Muzzle that!" Givens shouted angrily, snapping his fingers at several guards who stood at the bottom of the dais. Elyssa heard them go, but she couldn't see them. She didn't dare break her mother's gaze. The Queen stared down at her, furious, but beneath the anger Elyssa sensed impatience and deep frustration. Before the Queen banished her from court, Lady Glynn had often remarked that Queen Arla was like every parent of a teenager in history, and though Elyssa was twenty-one now, well out of her teens, the dynamic she shared with her mother had not matured. Out of the corner of her eye, Elyssa saw her younger brother, Thomas, smirking; he loved to see her in trouble.

Go ahead and smirk, you filthy little rapist. When I take the throne, I'll imprison you too.

"This man is a terrorist," the Queen said slowly, clearly

choosing her words. "A danger to the kingdom. Why should we release him?"

"Because he knows nothing. If he did, Culp would have gotten it out of him. Welwyn Culp is, after all, the most feared interrogator in the New World . . . after Benin Ducarte, of course," Elyssa added sweetly. The whole Keep knew that Culp hated being rated second against the Mort inquisitor.

The Queen's eyes narrowed. Elyssa could have made many humanitarian pleas on behalf of Gareth, but she hadn't bothered, for her mother only recognized and responded to coercion. The Queen couldn't very well admit in open court that Culp hadn't been able to flip a single real member of the Blue Horizon; such an admission would only add to the mystique around the movement, a mystique that was already causing Queen Arla considerable trouble. The Blue Horizon's leader, the man they called the Fetch, was rumored to be either a magician or a shade. The mask he wore was said to have magical powers, the ability to turn men to stone, but it was his skills as a tactician that gave the Queen headaches. Nobles constantly came to court to complain of being robbed. Blue Horizon agents liked to travel the Almont periodically, distributing food and goods like Father Christmas himself, before disappearing like smoke. The Blue Horizon had stolen more than thirty thousand pounds' worth of gold and arms in the past year alone.

Elyssa felt sure that her mother was considering all of these factors. Her brow was furrowed, and she tapped her nails on the arm of the throne, a sign of impatience. The Keep Priest, Father Timpany, standing just beside the throne, was not so restrained; he glared openly at Elyssa, who glared back. Six months before, God's Church had excommunicated all members of the Blue Horizon, and the movement had responded promptly by robbing a caravan carrying an entire quarter's tithe and hanging the escorting priest from a lamppost in the New London Circus. Atheism was the Blue Horizon's most striking feature, distinguishing it from all the tiny rebellions that had come before. Blue Horizon speakers routinely counseled their audiences not to fear Hell, for Hell was here. It was a movement designed to draw in the poor and the downtrodden, but for Queen Arla, the Blue Horizon presented a political problem, and the Queen was nothing if not a creature of politics. She could not afford to alienate the Church or the nobility by being soft on the revolutionaries, but even less could she afford to anger the poor . . . not now, not with a popular terrorist movement abroad, one that would take all recruits. Father Timpany could glare all he liked.

Power politics, Elyssa thought, staring up at the Queen. *You wanted me to learn, Mother, and I am learning.*

"Our daughter's tender heart is well known," the Queen announced. Her knuckles were white points against the gleaming silver arms of the Tear throne. "We have heard her plea for clemency and been moved. Our own medics will tend to this young man's wounds, and he will be released as soon as he is well. Culp, take him to the Queen's Wing, and see that no further harm befalls him."

Elyssa finally dared a glance behind her. Welwyn Culp nodded, his face expressionless, and signaled for two members of the army to help him support Gareth. As they took him up the aisle, Gareth's feet dragged; he had fainted. Elyssa thought she might faint herself; the moment her mother broke eye contact, she stood and moved quickly back to her corner of the dais. Her legs were trembling. Standing up to her mother in private was one thing; doing it in public was another matter entirely. Father Timpany had begun to mutter in the Queen's ear, but the Queen waved him to silence. The crowd murmured uncertainly, and Elyssa wondered if they could feel it as well, the odd power around these Blue Horizon people. William Tear was long dead, and yet—

"Majesty," Gullys, the chamberlain, announced. "Lord March."

"March," the Queen greeted him warmly; in a world of courtiers and panderers, Lord March was a rare genuine friend. The Queen's voice was so casual and pleased that only Elyssa knew what lay beneath.

I am in trouble, she thought. *Quite a bit of it.*

And what of that? a caustic voice spoke up in her mind. *This* kingdom *is in trouble, Elyssa. Grow up.*

"What can we do for you, Lord March?"

"Majesty, I come on behalf of the Almont Coalition."

The Queen's pleased smile melted away. Elyssa bit back a smile of her own. The Almont Coalition was a loose union of some three hundred nobles whose acres covered the Almont Plain. Lord March was a friend, yes, but first and foremost, he was a noble. This would be about the drought, for certain.

"And what would the Coalition have of us?" the Queen asked, her voice cold.

"The drought, Majesty. The situation in the Almont has become critical."

That was an understatement, Elyssa thought. She read the Crown harvest reports, probably more carefully than her mother did. After two straight dry years, there had been almost no snow over the past winter, not even in the mountains, and it had not rained once since February. The vast farming plain of the Almont was utterly dependent on the two rivers, Caddell and Crithe, but at last report, both rivers had been down several feet, and the tributaries were almost dry. The Tear's natural irrigation systems were crippled. If it didn't rain soon, there would be no harvest to speak of.

"There is no water, Majesty," Lord March continued. "The top of the Crithe is already drying up. There are barely any early crops."

"Surely you have hoarded water?" the Queen asked. "My intelligence says you have a cistern on your acreage."

"Your Majesty is well informed," Lord March replied, and Elyssa could hear the displeasure in his voice. "But the cistern is barely enough to carry me and mine through the winter. If the rivers run dry, we will need all of our stored water to drink."

"Well? Do you think I can compel the rain?"

"Perhaps, Majesty," Lord March replied, executing a polite bow. Chuckles echoed through the hall. "But our concern is food. What little crop has sprouted so far is wilted. I will not have enough to feed my household, let alone my tenants. I have given them license to hunt game on my lands, to ward off starvation through the harvest. But that will not last once winter comes. I have twelve hundred tenants on my acreage, Majesty. Even with a tight belt, my hoarded stores won't be enough to feed a tenth of them through the winter. Every landowner in the Almont faces the same problem."

"And again I ask, March: what do you want me to do about it?"

"The Crown storehouses, Majesty. We seek an assurance that if the drought continues and worse comes to worst, Your Majesty will open her stores to us, for distribution to our tenants."

"The weather will turn, March."

"Yes, Majesty, but if it doesn't—"

"It will," the Queen replied, in a tone that cut off all discussion. "This is the only assurance I give you."

Lord March clearly longed to argue, but after another moment he bowed again and said, "I have apprised you of our concerns. Thank you, Majesty."

"Dismissed."

Lord March retreated into the crowd. Elyssa stared after him, biting her lip. She rarely ventured out into the city; security concerns were too great. But she read her mother's intelligence reports. The city had already begun to feel the bite of the failing harvest; even now, in May, prices for produce were rocketing upward. If the drought went on, things would only grow worse. Water was not a concern in the city, at least not to drink; unlike the Almont, which was dependent on the two rivers, New London got its drinking water from a deep-buried aquifer that ran down from the Clayton Mountains to join the Caddell south of the city. But the aquifer would not provide food for the city, and nothing would help the million tenants in the Almont. Men could live for some time without food, but no one could survive for more than a few days without water.

"Majesty," someone said below her, interrupting Elyssa's thoughts. Lord Tennant stood at the base of the throne, a heavily cloaked figure on his arm.

"What can we do for you, Tennant?" the Queen asked. She had begun to drink her tea again, giving the impression that she had dismissed Lord March's dire warnings entirely from her mind, but Elyssa didn't know whether she truly had; her mother was an enigma when she chose to be.

"Why, nothing, Majesty," Lord Tennant replied smoothly. He was a fixture around the throne, one of the most unctuous of the Queen's courtiers, and today he was garbed in bright purple velvet from head to toe. Long, bell-like sleeves revealed the flicker of a tattoo on one hand. "On the contrary, I come to bring you a gift."

"What gift?"

Turning to the figure beside him, Lord Tennant reached up, slowly and gently, and pushed back the cloak's hood. Gasps filled the audience chamber; Elyssa jerked in surprise, and even Niya made a small involuntary movement beside her.

The woman was pure white. Her hair, her skin, her lips . . . all of her was white as milk, even her dress. Her eyes were blue, Elyssa was almost certain, but of a shade so icy that they might as well have been two pools frozen in winter. She was not old, but Elyssa could not say for sure that she was young either. When Lord Tennant pulled the cloak from her shoulders, Elyssa saw that the woman's hands, too, were white, no sign of blood even in the nails.

"God save us," one of the guards muttered.

"What is the nature of this gift, Tennant?" the Queen asked, and Elyssa saw that she, too, was unnerved, her jaw tight.

"This is Brenna, Majesty," Lord Tennant announced. "A tenant on my lands. I have brought her to serve Your Majesty. She is a seer."

Mutters echoed through the crowd . . . most of them skeptical, Elyssa thought. True seers were as rare as two-headed cats; the only one Elyssa had ever heard of lived at the Red Queen's court in Mortmesne, and it had long been a sore spot with her mother, that the Red Queen had a genuine seer while she did not. The Keep was always filled with palmists and tarot readers, but though her mother found them amusing, Elyssa was certain that she knew they were charlatans. A real seer would be a gift indeed . . . but despite the woman's extraordinary appearance, Elyssa found herself skeptical. Lord Tennant was a fop, but not an utter fool. He would never give away something so valuable without good reason. Her mother must have been thinking along the same lines, for after a few moments of studying the woman, the Queen repeated, "We ask again, Tennant: what can we do for you?"

"Nothing at all, Majesty. Consider this a simple sign of the continuing loyalty of House Tennant. If the seer does not please Your Majesty, by all means return her to me. I could always use a jump on next month's weather."

The audience laughed, but the Queen only gazed narrowly at Tennant. Elyssa felt a dart of unwilling admiration. Vain, her mother was, and autocratic, and often blind . . . but not stupid. Elyssa herself felt sorry for the albino, for she could well imagine the life the woman led, the treatment she must have endured. But deep in her mind, Lady Glynn's voice echoed in warning: a lesson from many centuries before, its message not faded with time.

Beware of Greeks bearing gifts.

"We accept your gracious gift, Lord Tennant," her mother finally replied. "Should the seer prove genuine, we shall not forget your generosity to us."

Tennant bowed, his velvet cape swirling around him.

"Gullys!" the Queen called. "Is there anything more?"

"No, Majesty!" the chamberlain called, after a last look around the room.

"Then we're done."

"This audience is concluded!" Gullys announced. "The Queen thanks you for your attendance! Please leave in as orderly fashion as you came in!"

The crowd began to break up. Many of them tried to linger, staring at the white woman who waited at the foot of the throne, but the soldiers stationed on the walls moved forward, shepherding them out. Elyssa was relieved to see that her mother's attention, too, was on the albino; she crooked her finger, signaling Brenna to come forward. As Brenna climbed the stairs, the Queen's Guard drew together without speaking, forming a block in front of the throne.

"Let her through," the Queen ordered.

"Majesty," Givens, the Captain, protested. "We haven't even searched her. The Mort—"

"The Mort are too devious to send such a conspicuous creature as an assassin."

"And Tennant is not a man to give gifts from the warmth of his heart, Lady." Givens was digging in now, a bulldog expression on his face. "He's ambitious, yes, but even a weasel doesn't give away a bag of gold. There is danger here."

The Queen considered him for a moment, then turned to the white woman.

"Are you a danger, seer?"

"Seers are always dangerous, Majesty," the albino announced in a low, warm voice, startling for its contrast with her icy appearance.

"Always dangerous? How so?"

"The term *seer* itself is misleading, Majesty. The sight is incidental to what we do. In reality, we are vessels of time, and nothing is more dangerous than time."

This answer clearly intrigued Elyssa's mother. Queen Arla was an easy mark for anything dealing with the unseen world.

"Let us at least search her for weapons," Givens pleaded hopelessly; he too had seen the gleam in the Queen's eye.

"I am unarmed," the albino replied. "But you may search if you wish."

"Not necessary," the Queen decreed, waving Givens away and beckoning Brenna closer. The Captain gave way, but reluctantly, his hand on his knife as the seer ascended the last few steps and knelt before the throne. She was not as old as Elyssa had first thought; her face was still unlined, and might even have been beautiful ... if only the rest of the package was not so grotesque.

"What can you offer us, Brenna?" the Queen asked.

"What do you wish, Majesty? Knowledge of infidelities, of pregnancies, of intended marriages?"

"I can get gossip from my servants," the Queen replied dryly. "What else do you sell?"

"The road to greatness, Majesty."

The Queen's eyes sharpened with interest. "Meaning what?"

Brenna reached out, heedless of the guards who drew swords

around her, and picked up the blue jewel that lay on the Queen's chest. Almost automatically, Elyssa grasped her own sapphire. They were identical, the Queen's Jewel and the Heir's Jewel, heirlooms that supposedly went all the way back to William Tear. Like all Tear relics, the sapphires were supposed to be magical, but Elyssa had worn the Heir's Jewel since her eighth birthday, when she was officially declared the heir to the throne, and she had never seen any magic in it. When she ascended the throne, she would remove the Heir's Jewel and put on the Queen's, and the second jewel would be put away for her firstborn; it had been so since the time of Matthew Raleigh. As far as Elyssa knew, no one had ever dared to touch her mother's sapphire, but the seer was now examining it closely. After a single stunned moment, the Queen snatched the jewel back.

"Men have died for less, palmist," Givens snarled. "Step away."

But the Queen checked him with a gesture. She was looking at Brenna oddly, and Elyssa sensed an unspoken conversation taking place.

"Leave us," the Queen said abruptly.

"Absolutely not," Givens replied. Elyssa waited for her mother's explosion, but the Queen turned a surprisingly benevolent eye upon Givens. She had a soft spot for him . . . for all the men who had fallen into her bed over the course of her reign, Elyssa thought sourly. Lady Glynn had often said that the basis of a good Crown was fairness, but her mother played a merciless game of favoritism.

"Givens, you may stay. Clear the rest of the room."

Givens frowned; he didn't like it, but the Queen's latitude only went so far. He signaled the rest of the Guard to leave, and Elyssa too tried to melt away . . . then froze, as her mother's voice rang out.

"Elyssa?"

"Yes, Mother?"

"Later, at a time of our leisure, we will discuss what happened here today."

"Yes, Mother," Elyssa replied, feeling her stomach drop. She waited, but her mother said nothing else, and after a moment Elyssa darted to the back of the dais and scrambled off, heading for the hidden door at the back of the throne room, guards re-forming around her as she went. Barty, the Captain of Elyssa's Guard, grunted in disapproval–he had remonstrated with her many times about simply running off without a word–but said nothing. Two of her guards, Elston and Coryn, opened the cleverly concealed door behind the throne, and Elyssa hurried out, toward the staircase that led up to the Queen's Wing.

"Well, you're in for it now, Highness," Niya remarked beside her. Elyssa hadn't even noticed the maid following, but she was rarely far away. That gift for unobtrusive closeness had promoted Niya to Elyssa's Dame of Chamber, though she was far newer to the Keep than any of Elyssa's other servants.

"I am in for it," Elyssa agreed bleakly, then turned to Barty. "Barty, send someone to look after that man from the Blue Horizon."

Barty frowned. "Your mother's medics will take care of him."

"I don't trust my mother's medics. For that matter, I don't trust my mother. I want you to keep an eye on him."

"If you insist, Highness. Coryn!" Barty barked.

"Sir?" Coryn asked from behind them.

"Your duty. Check on the boy when we get back, and then at least twice a day."

"Sir."

Barty turned back to Elyssa. "Satisfied?"

Elyssa nodded. Coryn was in training to be a medic himself; he would know whether Gareth was getting proper care.

"Niya is right, Highness," Barty remarked, after several more flights. "You shouldn't poke at your mother. She will jab back."

"I didn't do it to poke at her."

"Then why?" Barty asked, eying her suspiciously. "Because he's a handsome young man?"

"Was he handsome? I couldn't tell beneath all the bruises."

"Ah, this is about Culp, is it?" Barty shook his head. "I like that reptile no more than you do, child, but this is the world. You, too, will need an interrogator one day . . . Culp or some other."

"I will not," Elyssa replied, but she knew Barty didn't believe her. He had captained Elyssa's Guard since she was still in nappies, and Elyssa loved him like family, but sometimes he understood her well and sometimes not at all. Wishing to change the subject, Elyssa turned back to Niya.

"The seer. Do you think she's genuine?"

"Perhaps, Highness."

But Niya's voice was tight with disapproval.

"You think she's a fraud?"

"I don't know, Highness."

"Then what?"

"Let's just say I dislike gifts, and particularly from men who whip tenants when they come up short on their quotas."

Elyssa frowned at this news, but she did not doubt it, for Niya seemed to know everything. That was part of her value.

"When did this happen?" she asked Niya.

"On the last harvest. One of Lord Tennant's farmers came up short, and so Tennant offered him a choice: he could either take it out of his family's subsistence allowance, or take a whipping. The tenant had four children, so it wasn't truly a choice."

"Why whip the tenant? Wouldn't the injuries only decrease his output further?"

"Yes, Highness. But some men simply like to whip."

Elyssa grimaced. This was precisely the sort of victimization of the poor that her mother's Crown was content to tolerate.

Arla the Just, Elyssa thought bitterly, climbing stair after stair. *One day—*

"I didn't like the seer," Carroll remarked behind her. "She made me feel cold. Hopefully the Queen will tire of her quickly, like all the others."

"Ah, but the others were fakes," Coryn pointed out. "What if this one's the genuine article? She certainly looks the part."

"Enough about the seer," Barty growled. "What was that they were yelling out in the crowd? Something about the True Queen?"

The question was general, but Elyssa thought that Barty, too, was asking Niya. Niya understood much more of the world outside of the Keep than even the Guard did; she had been born on the streets of New London, and knew them as well as Elyssa knew the stones of the Queen's Wing. But this time Niya said nothing, and so it was Kibb, one of the younger guards, who finally answered.

"I heard about it, sir. Last week on leave. There's a rumor making the rounds in the city: some old woman has prophesied the coming of the True Queen." Kibb paused, almost shyly, then added, "They—the people—think it means the Princess."

"Christ," Barty muttered. "All we need."

"Perhaps it will help, sir," Coryn suggested. "If the common people think—"

"It's not the common people we have to worry about," Barty growled. "Saviors are only useful to people who need saving. People who are fat and happy don't want anyone meddling with the status quo."

"But, sir, don't you think—"

Elyssa listened to them bicker, only half hearing. *True Queen.* That was an old legend, much older than the Tearling; it went all the way back to pre-Crossing Anglia, to Arthur . . . the True King, the ruler who restored peace to the land and saved them all. No doubt someone had revived the old tale, to give people hope. They surely needed hope from somewhere; with a pulse of misgiving, Elyssa recalled what Lord March had said about the Crithe River, already drying up. Prolonged drought had brought down greater nations than the Tearling.

The True Queen, she thought again . . . the idea not detached now, but threaded with longing. *If only I could do that, be that for them! If only I really could save them all!*

Then she told herself to stop thinking like a child. She was well past nineteen, the Tear age of ascension, but her mother was not yet fifty, and healthy as a horse to boot. The Tear throne would be Elyssa's one day, yes, but that day was as distant as dreams.

At the door of her chamber Elyssa dismissed Niya and went inside, relieved to have a few minutes to herself. She fell on her bed, curling her hands beneath her pillow, meaning to nap, to gather her strength for the inevitable moment when her mother's summons came. But she found she could not rest. She kept seeing Gareth's mottled skin, the ragged red wounds where his fingernails had been. Elyssa admired the Blue Horizon, for they wanted the same things she had always wanted: everyone taken care of, and justice for the low as well as the great. William Tear's dream had failed, but it still lived, and Elyssa wanted it for her kingdom, wanted it with all her heart.

At times such as these, she missed Lady Glynn. Lady Glynn had a blessedly practical ability to get to the heart of the problem, and she had a knack for finding solutions in history books. Since her disappearance, there was no one for Elyssa to talk to about these things, about the broader vision she saw for her kingdom. Barty would listen, but his mind had too narrow a focus on Elyssa's safety; he tended to dismiss all ideas, all courses of action, that would open her to greater danger. Her other guards were too young and, with the possible exception of Carroll, not serious-minded enough. Niya would listen; she always did. But she would not engage. Whatever Niya's opinions of the future of the king-dom, she guarded them like a miser with his hoard. "I see it all the time," Gareth had said, and Elyssa envied him. She wanted a bet-ter world too, but she could not envision it. After a few fruitless minutes spent trying to sleep, she got up and opened the door.

Niya was still waiting in the hall, talking with Elyssa's Guard. Niya was not required to wait; technically, after being dismissed, she was free to go to her own room down the hall. But she always waited. As Elyssa emerged into the hallway, the maid and guards stopped gossiping and stood at attention.

"Highness?" Niya asked. "Did you need something?"

"Where have they put that man? Gareth?"

"In the infirmary, Highness."

"Come on."

The pack of guards followed them down the hall to the infir-mary, a large room near the guard quarters. Elyssa had been quar-tered in there when she broke her leg riding, and Thomas had once been quarantined for pneumonia when he was little, but most of the time the room catered exclusively to the Queen's Guard, and it showed. There was a pile of dirty laundry in the near corner. The far wall was clearly being used for overflow from the arms room; it was lined with fletches full of arrows, and sev-eral swords covered with nicks and scars leaned there, waiting for the armorer.

"Highness."

Beale, her mother's senior medic, bowed before her, and the other two followed. Coryn didn't bow, but that was only because Elyssa had ordered her own guards not to.

"How is he?"

Beale shook his head, his mouth pinching in disapproval. He might be her mother's man, but he was still a medic, and none of the medics cared much for Welwyn Culp's work.

"He has been badly beaten, Highness, and not just with fists. I have found two broken ribs. A broken arm. Three fingernails torn out. He has burn marks on his forearms, and both kneecaps are badly swollen. I have not yet determined whether any of his internal organs are seriously damaged. We will have to watch his digestion."

Elyssa moved up to the side of the bed, nudging in as Coryn made room for her. Seen up close, Gareth wasn't so old as Elyssa had first thought; he might even have been close to her own age. He appeared to be sweating, though his face was so swollen that it was difficult to tell. Thinking of the wooden board, the manacles, Elyssa felt anger well inside her, not only for what went on in the dungeons but for all of it: her mother's heavy-handed reign, her reliance on force. Elyssa placed a light hand on Gareth's brow, then jumped as his eyes opened. They were light grey, and they seemed overly bright, almost feverish, as he stared up at her.

"The True Queen," he said weakly. "Are you her?"

Elyssa stared down at his bruised face, thinking of her mother taking delicate sips of tea. Of Welwyn Culp's watery eyes. Of well-fed nobles laughing in the throne room. Of the tenants facing starvation in the Almont. Last and most of all, of Lady Glynn's histories: tales of good, but much more of evil, of humanity's vast suffering, a suffering that could have been averted at so many turns if only there had been someone of true heart, of good intent. . . . If only that person had stepped forward at the right moment. . . .

"Yes," she replied. "I am."

CHAPTER 3

TAPESTRY

To call the Creche merely a series of tunnels is to call the wide world a simple sphere.

—JAMES BENEDICT, LORD EVANS THE NINTH

Most visitors to Whore's Alley gained entry via a set of stairs that led directly down into the Creche from the center of the Gut. These stairs had been specially built more than twenty years before by a loose confederation of bookmakers and pimps who had been smart enough to recognize the mutual interdependence of their wares. Win or lose, the culls wanted to fuck afterward, and the staircase had been a good investment.

Christian had never needed to use the stairs. When he was seven, he had discovered a small opening at the east end of the Alley, a tunnel that ran steadily downhill all the way to the third level of the Creche. The tunnel was mercifully dry, but so low that now he was forced to crawl through on his hands and knees. An uncomfortable journey, but he was Lazarus, the best fighter in the Creche. He didn't like having his comings and goings observed, and he had a vague idea that the fewer people who knew he visited Maura, the better. This particular tunnel had the added benefit of emerging just outside Mrs. Evans's stables, close enough to provide him with some measure of privacy.

The Alley was a broad tunnel, perhaps fifteen feet across, which bisected the southern section of the Creche. The tunnel's walls were broken by many doorways, entrances to the various stables. As Christian passed the Sessions stable, he saw a jumble of letters painted in blue on the wall, and beneath them a crude drawing of a sun rising on the ocean. Like most denizens of the Creche, Christian had never learned to read, but he knew what the letters said: "The Better World." The drawing of the sun was the calling card of the Blue Horizon, the revolutionary group. They would post themselves in the tunnels, babbling about the better world to anyone who would listen. Preaching in the Creche was a good way to get killed, but the Blue Horizon were nothing like the frocks from the Arvath; they came armed and armored, and they knew how to fight. Even the enforcers were no match for them. But Christian still didn't understand what the fools were doing down *here*, preaching love, kindness, and, most laughably, an admonition to take care of each other. Whenever Christian saw the symbol of the Blue Horizon, or heard one of them blathering on about William Tear, he wanted to grab the whole bloody movement and shake them by the shoulders. Didn't they know where they were?

As he neared Mrs. Evans's stable, a whore leaned out of one of the doors, leering at him. Christian ignored her. Several of the pimps in the Alley had already offered him free use of their girls; the great Lazarus would be a high-profile customer, and on some nights, when he couldn't sleep and his cock stuck up like a steeple beneath his trousers, Christian could feel the great pull of such offers. But he distrusted sex almost as much as he did morphia, for he had already observed that both were dreadfully addictive. And as much as he didn't—couldn't—feel sorry for his opponents in the ring, he did have sympathy for the whores. They had all been shopped down here, none of them given a choice, and if the Creche was the lowest of vice districts, then it was also a tapestry, a vast weaving in which they were all joined by the tightest of threads. Christian fought because he must, but if he made use of the girls in the Alley, he would be no better than Wigan, or the dozens of hungry johns who swarmed the tunnels every night.

Crofter was on the door today. He was a big, misshapen man, but he seemed to have a genuine concern for the girls in his care. He never bothered Maura for a free run, as some of the other enforcers did, and Christian had never caught him asleep at his post. All of Mrs. Evans's enforcers knew about Christian's friendship with Maura, but only Crofter seemed to understand that Christian intended no mischief with his visits. The rest were less flexible.

"Go on, boy," Crofter rumbled, his voice deep with phlegm. "She's not engaged."

Christian darted past the front room and down the long hallway of private chambers. Not so private; the doorways here were covered only with flimsy sheets of brown wool, and Christian could hear the sounds of sex all around him, grunting and panting and an occasional high moan that made him shudder in revulsion.

May I never sound such a fool.

Maura's chamber was the seventh on the left. Christian knocked on the wooden panel outside, feeling suddenly and absurdly guilty, as though he were a john himself, waiting eager and slobbering outside the door. The sickly-sweet smell of morphia made him wrinkle his nose. Several of the whores in Mrs. Evans's stable were on the stuff, but Maura at least had the good sense to steer clear.

"Come in!" Maura called, her voice not the seductive lisp she used with the johns, but a clear and friendly chirp.

The bed was made, which was a mercy; Christian hated to come in and see the sheets disarranged. He turned to scan the rest of the room, and someone clapped a hand over his eyes.

Christian's reaction was both instantaneous and involuntary. He shoved backward, driving with his legs, and heard a crunch as something slammed into the set of shelves that held Maura's clothing. He turned and found Maura, sprawled in a pile of clothes and shelving.

"Ah God," she moaned. "My head."

Christian scrambled to help her up. She should have known better than to sneak up behind him; they had discussed such things before.

But you should learn to control yourself as well, his mind cautioned, and he felt suddenly ashamed. He had made his life in the fighting ring, but what good was that, if he could not leave his instincts behind when he needed to?

"I'm sorry," he said, pulling Maura to her feet. Only then did he see the tiny cake smashed on the floor beside her, a mess of sultanas and crumbs.

"And a happy birthday to you, too," Maura grumbled.

"Birthday?" Christian asked, startled. He had forgotten.

"If I'd known you planned to destroy your cake, I might have bought you a present instead." She picked up a chunk of cake, then tossed it into the tiny basket beside the bed. "No, on second thought, I wouldn't have."

"I'm sorry," he repeated. It wasn't his real birthday, of course—neither of them had the slightest idea of when they'd been born—but long before, Maura had picked two dates at random and deemed them birthdays. She insisted on celebrating, pretending that they were still family long after Wigan had sold her to the Alley. The year before she had made Christian a small raspberry scone, though God alone knew where she had gotten the raspberries; fresh fruit was as rare as sunlight down here.

Christian had never gotten Maura any presents. It was a sore spot, but he didn't have the money to buy her anything nice, and couldn't imagine bringing her something cheap. He visited her as often as he thought was prudent and tried to bring her extra food whenever he could. This was vast altruism, at least by Creche lights, but each "birthday" stood as a stark reminder that it wasn't enough.

"Ah well, I'm not sure it was any good anyway," Maura replied cheerfully, tossing the last of the cake into the basket. "Thing about birthday cake; you can't taste it first and make sure it's good."

"I'm sure it was good."

She straightened then, smiling, a tall girl of twenty-one who looked much younger. She was merely pretty, Christian supposed, but for her hair, long and blonde and ethereal, glowing almost white in the torchlight. He understood from Alley gossip—though he wished he did not—that Maura's hair made her a very popular buy. Mrs. Evans certainly thought so, for she took scrupulous care of Maura's hair, washing it often, buying the most expensive apothecary products to keep it straight and shining. Maura would have aged out of the Creche long ago, but for that hair and the fact that Mrs. Evans worked so hard to make her look young. Thank God Maura hadn't shouted as she fell; the fact that it had been an accident would not weigh with Mrs. Evans. She would only see damage to an investment.

"Well, then," Maura said, "no cake, no presents, have a kiss instead. You're twenty today."

She kissed him lightly on the cheek, and against his will, he smiled. The johns might have a lot more of Maura, but that kiss, small as it was, had been *real*. No one had paid her to do it.

Maura turned back to the shelves, fitting them back into their grooves and picking up her fallen belongings. Christian sat down on the floor and began to fold the pile of clothing. This task was more difficult than it should have been; he had won on Saturday night, as he always did, but the opponent had gotten in one good blow that nearly dislocated his shoulder, and Christian's arm hadn't felt right since.

"Is your head all right?" he asked her.

"I'll live. How's the ring?"

"Same as ever." He handed her a neatly folded dress.

"I heard you won again on Saturday."

"I always win," Christian replied flatly. He didn't want to talk about the fights, not here. But neither of them was eager to discuss Maura's work.

"Do you ever think about topside?" Maura asked abruptly.

"No," Christian replied, bewildered. "Why would I?"

"Well, there are always stories, you know. Girls and boys who escaped the cribs and made something of themselves in the upper world. Probably lies, but I always liked those stories as a baby. Old Marie used to know a few of them."

Christian didn't know who old Marie was, but he didn't ask. The tone of Maura's voice told him that the answer would only depress them both. The turn of the conversation was making Christian uneasy, giving him the feeling that something had jolted out of place. When he was young enough to daydream, he had thought often of topside, even hatching elaborate plans in which he and Maura would escape to the surface and live together, well fed and content. Those daydreams had been his original impetus to explore the vast labyrinth of the Creche, to map it in his head. But getting out of the tunnels was far more than a matter of geography. Maura was a crib baby. Last weekend, Christian had opened a man's carotid and watched him bleed to death.

He still believed in topside, yes . . . but what place could either of them have there?

"What's all this about topside?" he asked, more roughly than he meant to. "What's happened?"

"Nothing," Maura said, with a casual air that did not quite deceive him.

"Not nothing. Tell me."

"Well, I've been requested."

Christian absorbed this information quietly. *Requested* . . . it meant that Maura had been summoned for delivery, to service a client not down here in the Creche but topside, in the city. Every pigeon in the Creche aspired to be requested, for it meant not only a paid journey to the upper world but also the possibility of an arrangement with a client, one rich enough to import from the Creche. If Maura caught herself a rich client, she could expect all manner of better treatment from everyone in the stable, Mrs. Evans on down. Christian knew that being requested was a good thing for her, an important thing . . . and yet his stomach felt like lead.

"Congratulations," he said dully. "When?"

"Tonight. I'll have to start getting ready in a few minutes, so you'd better help me clean up this mess."

Christian could think of nothing further to say. He bent to grab another dress, then hissed as something deep in the pile of clothing jabbed his palm.

"Christ!"

"Are you all right?" But Maura's question was perfunctory. She was already grabbing the clothing away from him, her blonde hair falling in a sheaf to hide her face.

"I'm fine. What was that?"

Maura did not answer, only turned away from him to dump the pile of clothing on the bed, and so Christian, who had always been one to know things without being told, understood that he had grabbed a syringe.

"You're on the poppy," he said flatly.

"Only a bit."

This reply did not ease Christian's mind in the least. Career fighters in the Creche accumulated so many wounds that they needed an almost constant supply of narcotics, and though morphia was reserved for only the worst injuries, Christian had still seen enough of it to know that that particular habit could dig its claws deep in no time at all. And although he had just been pondering the foolishness of his child's daydreams of topside, he found himself suddenly furious with Maura, as though she had dug up those old daydreams, soaked them with oil, and lit a match.

"I suppose it was only a matter of time until you went on the needle."

"Tend to your own business!" Maura snapped. "Unless you've suddenly grown a cunt and it's open for sale, then you've no idea how to tend to mine."

Christian felt his cheeks grow scarlet. She had never spoken so openly about what went on in here, and some small part of him—a tiny corner that somehow pretended, against all odds, that Maura and her men had tea and traded gossip—hated her for it. And yet the greater part of him was ashamed. Hadn't he just been thinking, bare minutes ago, that all of them—Christian, Maura, the pigeons, the whores—were in the same boat? But of course they weren't, not at all. The promoters sold Christian out, yes, but it wasn't the same. He suddenly remembered the two of them, him and Maura, standing on the auction block in the vast room, holding hands, shivering; the room had been cold, and both of them naked. How old could they have been? Four, five? Too young, that was certain; too young to understand what was in store. He thought of the bracelet she had given him one night in the ring, a bracelet woven with the symbol of the Blue Horizon. It had disappeared long since, grown far too small for his wrist, but now Christian found himself wishing that he had kept it.

"Listen," he said suddenly, impulsively. "We'll get you off the poppy. I'll help—"

The curtain over the door was suddenly yanked back, and Christian snapped his mouth shut at the sight of Mrs. Evans.

"I'm sorry to interrupt you," Mrs. Evans said kindly, with great solicitude. She had likely been an excellent whore; every word reeked of sincerity. Only by watching her eyes did one see the truth.

"Maura, it's time. We need to get you bathed and dressed."

Maura nodded. She clasped Christian's shoulder in farewell, but he barely noticed, for now he had caught sight of the figure behind Mrs. Evans: a young man, several years older than Christian, tall, awkward as a gantry, his bright blue eyes taking in every detail of the room. By now, Christian knew most of the pimps by sight, if not by acquaintance, and this one, Arlen Thorne, was rumored to be one of the worst flesh peddlers in the Creche. All manner of rumors surrounded him; some said he was a bastard-born child of the nobility, others that he was a crib baby who had murdered his handler when he was little more than a boy and taken over the entire operation. Thorne's stable wasn't even in the Alley proper, but two floors below, in the Deep Patch, where stranger things than children were sold. Some said that Thorne's menagerie included a witch, a white woman who could kill a man with a glance. Christian didn't believe in witches, or anything else he couldn't see with his own eyes; still, he would sooner have trusted Maura with a Reddick wolf than the likes of Arlen Thorne.

"Lazarus, you should leave now."

Mrs. Evans spoke with regret, but only a fool would miss the note of steel that had entered her voice. Behind that steel stood not just six enforcers but enough contacts and knowledge to bring down the Creche and half the city behind it. Christian turned to Maura, but the beseeching look on her face said everything. Suddenly Christian hated the lot of them: Mrs. Evans, Thorne, even Maura herself.

Tend to your own business.

He would have liked to ignore Maura's words, but he could not, for she was right. Unless he was prepared right now, at this instant, to take her away, to remove her utterly from this life—

But even then, you wouldn't have the right to take the syringe out of her hand.

After another long moment's hesitation, Christian turned and walked away. Many times he had dreamed of simply wringing Mrs. Evans's neck, but that was just as much a fantasy as topside itself, and it wouldn't have changed anything anyway. Customers paid, tricks turned . . . the players changed, but the game never ended. Only the suffering was real. As Christian ducked through the grating of his shortcut, he suddenly saw Maura as he had first seen her: the tiny girl who had taken his hand when they were both in the pens, waiting to go on the block. For those few days, they had stayed together, keeping each other from panic, as sale drew closer and the darkness closed in. Even after Wigan bought them both, Maura had done her best to create an invisible circle around the two of them, making birthdays, singing songs, tending his wounds after fights. They had protected each other.

But I can't protect her now, Christian thought bitterly. *Not even from herself.*

CHAPTER 4

NIYA

*The second iteration of the Blue Horizon was a strange ani-
mal: utterly committed, yet innately contradictory. William
Tear had condemned the use of arms, but the Blue Horizon
carried steel and used it well. They longed for a peaceful
world, but did not flinch from violence in pursuit of that goal.
William Tear had despised organized religion, and so the
Blue Horizon naturally railed against God's Church, yet its
members worshipped William Tear like a god, speaking of
him as though he were alive. No Christian sect ever had such
a powerful Holy Ghost.*

     –The Early History of the Tearling, AS TOLD BY MERWINIAN

She was in the lowest part of the Hollow when they caught her.
The first man stepped out of the mouth of an alley just as his
two companions came up behind. Both grabbed a bicep, whipping her arms behind her, and as she tried to wrench free, the first
man slipped a hood over her head. They brought her arms together, manacling her hands at the waist.

With the appearance of the manacles, Niya dismissed her initial assumption that they were simple villains, bent on assault.
Women who spent any amount of time in the Gut had to know

how to defend themselves; Niya had even heard that one brothel held weekly hand-to-hand combat classes for its pros, classes taught by an army lieutenant who liked his free tumble now and then. Rape occurred all the time in the Gut, but the men leading Niya remained coolly professional. As they led her up the steps out of the Hollow, one of them even tucked a hand beneath her elbow, an almost courtly gesture, designed to keep her from stumbling.

Do they know who I am? she wondered. The Fetch had forbidden her to attend any more meetings once he had placed her in the Keep, but it was always possible that someone had recognized her from the early days, for in a kingdom where redheads grew scarcer all the time, Niya sported a head of bright, coppery hair.

Has someone betrayed us?

At first her three captors remained on their guard. Niya was no easy piece of business, and if they knew who she was, they would know that too. But three on one was three on one, and the captive was hooded, and somewhere between Clewes Alley and the Great Boulevard, Niya sensed all three of them beginning to relax. That was their mistake. Niya's parents had both died in a pub fire when she was eight, and she had grown up a pickpocket on the streets of New London, earning and eating only what she stole. She did not need eyes to see her way. She knew the Gut the way she knew her own heart.

I am Blue Horizon, Niya thought, as the men tugged her along. This was the most important fact about her, the first thought she had in the morning and the last at night. If someone had asked Niya who she was, she would have replied with the same single phrase. She was Blue Horizon, and her other life, her *old* life, mattered not at all. The other Niya had been burned away.

They dragged her around a corner, into a roar of humanity and the overwhelming smell of food and horses: the New London

Circus. Niya had been heading for the Circus when the men grabbed her, meaning to check the makeshift apothecary stalls there. Elyssa sent her down every few months to replenish her syrup supply, and Niya always went alone, for the errand was a difficult business. Buying birth control was a gamble in the Tearling; legitimate apothecaries couldn't carry it, and the illegal ones who dared were just as likely to be on the grift as they were to have any real knowledge of botany. Elyssa trusted only Niya with this errand, and Niya took a strange pride in her own success. Every month that the Princess did not conceive was almost a personal victory. But now it looked as though Elyssa would have to go without syrup for a while.

"Is she really that ugly, boys?" a man's voice catcalled drunkenly from Niya's left. "Give her to me! I'll even keep the bag on!"

"Keep clear!" one of Niya's captors snapped. "And for the love of heaven, sober up! It's nine o'clock in the morning!"

Niya raised her eyebrows. Very prudish they were, for mercenaries. Not Caden assassins, certainly, and probably not Queen Arla's people either. Niya jumped as another voice shouted close by, this time to her right.

"The True Queen comes! I see a revelation, a rebirth! I see her, as clear as through a glass!"

"Oh, leave off!" another of her captors moaned. "If I have to hear any more of their—"

"Shut up," the first man cut in again. The leader, Niya decided. The street preacher's words faded from hearing, but almost immediately another one sprang up, this one a woman, her voice elevated, straight ahead.

"Elyssa Regina! We have waited, we have prayed, and now she comes to save us! Elyssa, the True Queen!"

The prophecy. One could not escape it anywhere in the city. Niya hated the prophecy, but not because she was tired of hearing about it, like the man at her shoulder. No, Niya hated the prophecy for one simple reason: it placed Elyssa in greater danger.

She had not felt this way at the start. When the girl's story—a room full of men, an ancient seer with white eyes—had first begun to circulate several weeks before, Niya's initial reaction had been ridicule. The Blue Horizon was not interested in prophecies or magic. They wanted real things for real people: food and shelter and clothing and education. The Fetch derided prophecy as the work of simple minds, of people not willing to put any actual effort into bringing the better world to pass, and Niya had agreed with him. But when Gareth spoke up, even the Fetch listened.

"We have to test it, that's all," Gareth told them one night. "We have to see what she'll do. If she's made of the same stuff as the mother, then no prophecy will mean anything. But if she's not..."

She's not, Niya thought now. After more than a year in the Keep, Niya knew, better than any of them, that Elyssa was as different from her mother as a child could be. The True Queen prophecy had proven extremely useful to the Blue Horizon in the past weeks, for it had been the easiest thing in the world to direct it onto Elyssa, thus weakening both Arla and the Arvath. Propaganda was the Fetch's specialty, but Gareth dealt in deeper truths, and he had insisted on seeing Elyssa for himself. If Niya and the Fetch had known that Gareth planned to land himself in the Keep dungeons—and in the hands of Welwyn Culp, of all people!—they would have fought harder... but done was done.

"Please!" a man begged nearby. "Some bread, for my wife!"

"I have bread," another man answered. "A full loaf, if you'll give me three pounds."

The words burned in Niya's brain, but it was not the first time she had heard such an offer. With the drought worsening, even flour was becoming a luxury, and speculators of all kinds had jumped into the market. A few more months without rain, and three pounds for a loaf of bread would look like a bargain.

"This way, girl," said one of her captors, nudging her gently to the left. "Stop dawdling."

The Church, Niya realized. *It must be.* If the Queen's people had identified her as Blue Horizon, they could simply have taken her on any given day in the Keep. But the Holy Father had offered one hundred pounds on the head of any proven ringleader, and her captors were moving her steadily east, toward the Arvath. Under the guise of discomfort, Niya flexed her arms lightly within the limited parameters of the manacles, stretching her back.

William Tear, guide my hand.

They came around Hell's Bend—Niya recognized it because of the crying of old Maeve, who always set up her stall on the same southeastern corner and shouted, "Chickens! Chickens! Roasted chickens!" from sunup to sundown—and as they rounded the corner, Niya launched herself sideways at the man holding her arm, driving with her legs and crushing him into one of the sharp-edged brick moorings that kept most of the houses in the Gut from falling down. The man grunted in surprise, but the grunt cut off almost immediately, and Niya felt warm wetness splatter her arm and shoulder.

The other two were on her immediately, but not quickly enough to keep her from pulling off the hood, and once sighted, she was able to back away from them, giving herself a two-meter clearing to work with. The man she had sidelined was sprawled on the ground, blood streaming from his left arm, which had torn open at the bicep. From the way he curled on the pavement, Niya felt certain that she had sprung one of his ribs as well. In a quick blink, she identified her surroundings: the long, claustrophobic alley that backed between Hell's Bend and Murderer's Row. This early in the morning, the alley itself was empty; the pubs were closed, and even the cutthroats and independent pros had long ago found a bed. The Blue Horizon had no presence in the Row, nowhere to run to. Niya was on her own. Two on one was still poor odds, but—

But numbers don't matter, the Fetch whispered in her head. Niya grinned at the memory, feeling the old glee slip over her now, stretching her muscles, giving her strength. Men always thought her merely a pretty bit of fluff, and Niya never tired of giving them an education.

"You're up past your bedtime, lads. Run along now."

Their eyes widened, and they shared an uncertain look. Each of them outweighed Niya by at least four stone, and both had knives . . . a fact they seemed to remember in that instant, for each drew. But Niya merely smiled, and the sight of that smile made them both pause again.

"If you kill me, there's no bounty. Be careful."

"Maleficos non patieris vivere," one of them muttered, and both men crossed themselves.

"Thou shalt not suffer a sorceress to live," Niya translated. Spotless Latin, and now she noticed a second fact as well: all three men were clean-shaven, without so much as a shadow of beard. Not simple mercenaries, seeking to collect a bounty; these were Holy Guards, of the Arvath itself. Despite the manacles on her hands, Niya felt her defensive instincts expand, twisting into something that was almost predatory. She hated God's Church, hated it with every muscle, for beneath every injustice in the kingdom, every degradation of the powerless, one could always find a priest. When a parishioner emerged from the stables in the Creche, there was always a priest waiting, happy to take his coin and offer absolution. Frocks littered the Almont, holding Hell over the tenants' heads, counseling obedience and patience. Without the bolster of the Arvath, the tenancy system would have collapsed long before. The Church might have snowed the rest of the kingdom, but the Blue Horizon was not deceived. God's Church was anathema to all they fought for.

"Well?" Niya asked pleasantly. "Come on, then."

They moved in warily, knives held too far out in front. The Fetch had always said that the Arvath Guard was just for show; the Caden, or even the Queen's Guard, could have taken them easily. These two were frightened, Niya knew, and there was no greater liability in a fight. It was a lesson she had learned from her earliest years, fending off sots in the Gut. She had been afraid then, for she had only been a child, and starving. But she was not afraid now.

One of them leapt forward, swinging his knife sidearm. Niya dropped low, moving with the fluid dancer's grace that had first caught the Fetch's eye. Clutching her manacled hands together, she knocked the man's knife hand aside, popped to her feet in front of him, and battered his nose with her locked fists. There was a satisfying crunch as the nose fragmented, and the man fell backward, his hands clapped to his face, blood gushing between his fingers.

The other one had moved behind her; Niya felt his breath on the nape of her neck. She ducked to her left, spun, and straightened to find him overbalanced, his knife now sweeping in a downward arc toward his knees. Niya tackled him, driving him backward into the soot-covered wall of the pub. His head thudded against the stone, and while he tottered there, dazed, Niya drove her booted foot into his groin. He went down without a sound.

Panting, Niya backed away. She was sweating, though it was a chilly morning. A fine shroud of mist had begun to collect at either end of the alley. Niya wondered whether she should question one of these God-monkeys, find out how they had identified her and, more importantly, whether they knew about her identity in the Keep. But she quickly abandoned the idea. The sun was well up. Soon the early-morning pros would be stirring, and publicans slept all around her. Screaming would awaken someone.

After another moment's thought, Niya reached for the man who lay on the ground. She yanked his shirt open at the neck and saw without surprise the gold cross, inlaid with diamonds: the mark of the Arvath Guard. Niya jerked the cross from his neck–the chain snapped easily–drew his head back, and cut his throat. Then she dug into his pockets, looking for the keys to her manacles.

They were all wearing the crosses, which pleased Niya; the diamonds alone would fetch enough to feed an Almont village for a month. The second guard was unconscious when she sliced him, but the third, the leader, woke up as she pulled his head backward. The man looked up at her with a gaze that Niya fancied imploring, but she was not moved. If these three had managed to get her to the Arvath, His Holiness would have handed Niya over to the Queen–and thus to Welwyn Culp–without a thought. The man on the cobbles gasped, struggling to cry out, and Niya sliced him, as neatly as old Maeve would slice up one of her chickens, smiling kindly at the children who gathered around every morning to watch. Then she took his cross as well, slipping it into her pocket with the others.

"Diamonds for God," she murmured to the three corpses at her feet. "Diamonds and gold, while the rest of the kingdom starves. But we are the Blue Horizon, and we don't fear your God. In fact, we're coming for his head."

CHAPTER 5

CUTTING TIES

Seen in the light of our times, the tenancy system of the early Tear centuries was a horror. Nobles set the quota for each harvest, independent of conditions or circumstance, doled out a subsistence portion to the tenants, and took the rest to sell for profit. Nobles' bailiffs—and now that history has progressed, we can call these bailiffs what they actually were: overseers—had the power of life and death over the tenant farmer, his house, and his family; a tenant's output was what the bailiff said it was, and rape was a routine perquisite of the job. There was no court of appeal, no independent arbiter to whom the tenant could complain, save the monarch, or the noble himself. Needless to say, complaints were few.

—Out of Famine: The Almont Uprising, ALLA BENEDICT

Aislinn was tired, so tired that she felt her arms would fall off if she tried to lift the basket of strawberries. But lift it she did, hoisting it carefully onto one shoulder as though it were filled with precious stones. In a normal June, they would be buried in strawberries as far as the eye could see, but this year most of the plants lay limp and wilted, crushed into the ground. There had been no rain for months, and what berries had grown in the patch had a wrinkled, desiccated look. But they were berries, all the same. It had taken Aislinn the better part of an hour to find enough to fill the basket, and she was determined that her family should get every ounce of credit for the haul.

She lugged the basket around the edge of the plot in which her brothers and sisters remained scattered, picking. The Martin family's share of Lady Andrews's acreage covered three enormous plots: one of strawberries, one of corn, and one of potatoes. As soon as strawberry season ended, they would turn their attention to the corn, though that looked none too healthy either, lopsided and ungainly. The husks themselves looked fine, but when you stripped the green away, the kernels were invariably sickly and shriveled, not yellow but a dyspeptic-looking ochre. Aislinn's mother was deep in the cornfield, working on one of the stalks. Picking off locusts, most likely. Aislinn waved, but her mother did not wave back, too intent on her task.

They are so tired, Aislinn thought. She knew that Mum and Da had been skipping dinner lately, quietly portioning out their shares to each child. The sight of them, forking pieces over to the plate of whichever child was talking, made Aislinn burn inside. Lady Andrews, the noblewoman who owned their plots, lived on the eastern end of the acreage, in a castle so high that its shadow fell over the strawberries in the morning. Lady Andrews was never hungry, nor were any of her bailiffs. The lady wore velvet dresses sewn with jewels. Sometimes, when she came down to inspect the tenants, a servant came with her, a man whose sole job appeared to be holding a sun cover over Lady Andrews's head. Aislinn might be only fifteen, but she knew right from wrong, and when she looked out over the vast Andrews acreage and saw all of them, hundreds of tenants, hunched over in the fields—sometimes by lamplight, long after dusk had fallen—she burned.

This cannot be all of our lives, she thought. *This cannot be everything we have to aspire to. There must be something else. Something better.* The Blue Horizon always said so, whenever they visited the acreage. They always came disguised, as performers or traveling merchants, in order to slip past the bailiffs, but Aislinn recognized their message in all of its guises. They were sincere, the Blue Horizon people, and even Aislinn had been charmed by the picture they painted: a world without the distinctions of wealth or class, a world where everyone was equal. Aislinn liked the idea well enough in theory, but she was not gullible enough to believe that the Blue Horizon knew how to get there. They brought food and clothing, sometimes even medicine, but a few brief questions easily elicited the fact that their better world was as distant as the moon.

Father Moran called the Blue Horizon heretics and terrorists; a good part of his Sunday sermon was always devoted to the topic, carefully sandwiched in between the constant lectures on industry and godliness and knowing one's place. The sermons were dull as dirt, but Aislinn didn't mind Sunday mornings; it was the only time she got to take a nap. Father Moran would have called her a sinner, but Father Moran was not above bedding the wives of the acreage in exchange for absolution. The Church was no better than any of them; in fact, it was worse, precisely because it claimed to be better. Aislinn didn't know why the Church and the Blue Horizon fought so bitterly; both were selling dreams in bottles, after all. The last time the Blue Horizon came through, they had brought new stories as well as food, tales of a magical queen who would lift the drought and redistribute the land. The better world was at hand, the young man had claimed, and Queen Elyssa would be the gate. Aislinn's younger siblings listened to these stories with open mouths, but Aislinn had outgrown fairy tales. There would be no better world, no magical ending. This was all life was: endless, backbreaking work, for which one collected a reward of slow starvation. Aislinn had no quarrel with the Blue Horizon, but as far as she was concerned, they could take their True Queen and stuff her out back.

She had reached the large, rickety wagon at the far end of the cornfield. This wagon was shared, placed every day in the rough center of four families' acres: the Pearces, the Martins, the Vines, and the Grahams. As soon as it filled up, one of the fathers—they rotated the duty—would hitch up the horse and drive the wagon over to the storehouse for delivery to the bailiffs. This required some trust, as there was nothing to stop any one man from claiming another family's output as his own. But so far as Aislinn could tell, there had been no thievery, and in their small group of families, she saw an interdependency born of desperation. Starvation hung in the air over all of them, a constant shadow. No one dared to fuck anyone else over, for once that door was opened, it could never be closed again. Whatever small amount of honor they retained would be gone.

With a grunt, Aislinn hoisted the basket of berries into the wagon, then walked over to say hello to Bertie, the mule. The drought had hit Bertie as hard as it had the rest of them; what grass grew in his tiny paddock was sparse and dry, and Aislinn could see each rib in the poor animal's wasted sides. She clicked her tongue, hoping to lure him to the fence so that she could scratch his ears.

"What are you doing here, girlie?"

She whirled to find Fallon, one of the bailiffs, standing just behind her. He was a big man, as all bailiffs were, and he carried a knife at his belt. He grinned, revealing several missing teeth.

"Slacking off, are we? You'll never meet the quota that way."

"It's not your business how we meet the quota."

"You think you'll meet it, do you?" Fallon asked. "Sure, and pigs will fly."

"You'd know pigs," Aislinn replied dismissively, turning back to Bertie. But the mule apparently liked Fallon no more than she did, for he turned, went back to the center of his paddock, and began to munch despondently at the sparse grass.

"Lady Andrews don't like slackers."

"How would you know?" Aislinn demanded. "Lady Andrews wouldn't even let a filthy creature like you through the kitchen door."

Fallon flushed, his eyes squinting down into ugly slits. It was not the first time he had bothered her; twice now, he had even come sniffing around the cottage, saying terrible things, things that made Aislinn ashamed . . . not for herself, but for her mother and father, who could do nothing but stand beside the old, patched stove, pretending they hadn't heard.

"You should be nicer to me, girlie," he growled. "Ain't been no rain for months. The Crithe is drying up. A few more weeks of this, and my share of Her Ladyship's cistern will be all that stands between your people and the salt death."

"Maybe so. But I'd sooner fuck a goat."

Fallon grabbed her by the shoulders, and Aislinn was readying a kick when a horn sounded across the fields. Fallon looked up, his eyes suddenly anxious, and released Aislinn, giving her a shove that knocked her to the ground.

"Get yourself into line, girlie. Put up a good show when Her Ladyship comes by, and I might forget about this."

Aislinn scrambled up and trotted away. Fury gnawed at her brain, but there was nothing to do about it. Lady Andrews was coming to inspect, and they were all expected to put on an industrious front and look happy, as though toiling in the fields fourteen hours a day were all a man could want. Aislinn kept a wary eye over her shoulder for Fallon, but he had disappeared into the cornfields to gather up the Vines and their children.

"Where have you been, girl?" her mother demanded as Aislinn came around the corn and into sight of the strawberry patch. "Her Ladyship is coming. Straighten your dress and get that corn silk out of your hair."

Aislinn did so, but only to please her mother. The tenants could have been naked, for all Lady Andrews cared; all that mattered was how much produce they were able to mine from the ground. Aislinn's mother went to each of her younger siblings in turn, straightening and tidying, and her father was busily combing his hair with his fingers. At moments like this, Aislinn felt utterly distant from her parents, as though they were unknown to her. She did love them, she supposed, but it was a love that seemed to wither each year, like the corn plants in the heat. This life, the work of the tenant, seemed almost designed to cut ties. Aislinn and her parents might have been no more than business associates, partners in an enterprise that was constantly failing.

The Vines, Grahams, and Pearces had joined them now, all of them standing at attention on the side of the path. Fallon stood beside them, removing his hat. Liam Graham crossed his eyes at Aislinn, but she ignored him; he was a pest. Little Willie Pearce still leaned on the crutch he had sported for the past week. Willie was six, and he had taken a bad cut to his leg with a scythe as they harvested the last of the winter wheat. The Pearces had washed the wound, but the leg had begun to plump almost immediately, and now it looked like a sausage above his socks. As Willie shifted impatiently, Aislinn spotted the streaks of green running up his calf.

That leg will have to come off, she thought grimly.

The horns grew louder, then louder still, and Lady Andrews and her retinue appeared. All of them were horsed on stallions, save the lady herself, who rode a fine mare, its mane strung with tinkling bells. Aislinn had admired those bells when she was younger, too young to understand that she would never have a horse of her own.

Lady Andrews slowed to a trot as she rode past all of them, her eyes seeming to note and mark each tenant in turn. But when she got to Aislinn, she stopped, drawing her horse back.

"This one," Lady Andrews remarked. "This one has a very insolent look, which I do not like at all. Who is she?"

"Aislinn Martin, Lady," Pryse, the bursar, replied, checking his book. "Fifteen years old."

"I see," Lady Andrews replied, staring at Aislinn. It was the first time she had ever singled out any member of their family for attention, but it was the wrong kind; Aislinn could almost feel her parents quaking beside her. She lifted her chin and gazed back at Lady Andrews, meeting her stare for stare.

"Check this family's output very carefully, Pryse," Lady Andrews finally said. "I wouldn't think this little one above stealing."

"That's rich, coming from you."

Aislinn did not know she had said it aloud until her mother gasped in horror. The rest of the assembled families gaped at her, even little Willie Pearce, who had been fidgeting steadily on his crutches.

"Shut your mouth, you bitch!" Fallon roared from the end of the line. But Lady Andrews raised a hand.

"Hold my reins."

One of her retainers took hold of them, and Lady Andrews swung herself to the ground. She was a pretty woman, just leaving youth. Aislinn had never seen her so closely before. There was a Lord Andrews, supposedly stashed somewhere in the castle, but Aislinn had never seen him either. There was a running joke among the tenants that Lord Andrews was actually made of straw.

Across the path, Liam Graham was subtly shaking his head at

Aislinn, telling her to keep her mouth shut. As the lady approached her, Aislinn took a deep breath but held her chin up.

"You need a lesson in manners, child," Lady Andrews remarked softly. She was smiling, but her eyes were cold. "I could give it to you myself, certainly . . . but I don't fancy the lice. Fallon!"

"Yes, Lady?"

"Take the girl back to her hovel. You have the night. The rest of her family will remain out here until morning; just reward for raising a brat with a smart mouth."

These words had not even penetrated when Fallon seized her by the hair and yanked her backward. As they passed her family, Aislinn saw that her mother and father wore identical looks of horror, but neither of them said anything. They had six younger children to think about, and in their silence, Aislinn understood, then and forever, that she was alone. Fallon gave her hair another sharp jerk, and she squealed, resisting him, digging her heels in, but the soil was too dry to provide any stopping power. Slowly, inexorably, he was pulling her toward the cottage.

"Let this be a reminder to all of you," Lady Andrews's voice rang out behind her. "You are tenants. It's of no concern to me how aggrieved you feel, only whether you produce my quota. Think on this little bitch the next time any of you wants to open his mouth."

Aislinn tried to dart sideways, to tug free, and then winced as strands of hair pulled from her head. Behind her, she could see Mr. and Mrs. Vine looking carefully away. Had Aislinn just been thinking, a few minutes before, that they all trusted each other? But the Vines had children of their own. They could not afford to get involved.

They cut our ties, Aislinn thought again. *Threat; exhaustion; violence; they cut our ties deliberately, but if only we could all come together, just once, all of us at the same time. . . .*

But even this thought faded as Fallon threw her through the doorway. Aislinn landed, sprawling, on the hard-packed dirt floor of the cottage, and a sizable puff of dust rose into the air around her, causing her to cough. Fallon was advancing now through the open doorway, little more than a hulking silhouette against the sunlight. He outweighed her by at least five stone. The world was not a fair place; Aislinn had accepted that fact long before she could walk. But fair or no, this should not be the choice a woman faced: to give in and live, or fight and die. Fallon grasped her ankle, and it was then that Aislinn saw the poker, lying half out of the fireplace. Someone, probably her sister Lita, who was lame and could not work in the fields for long, had been stoking the fire in preparation for dinner, and there was a good blaze going. The poker's tip glowed a bright and cheerful red; Aislinn stared at it as though hypnotized.

"Come here, girlie," Fallon whispered, tugging her leg, pulling her toward him. "You be nice, now—"

But he got no further, for Aislinn had already grabbed the poker and swung it around, bashing him in the face.

The screaming was terrible, so terrible that it brought Aislinn's parents and the rest of the tenants running across the field. But by the time they got there, the deed was already done: Fallon lying on the floor, covered with burn marks and large, round wounds where Aislinn had stabbed him with the poker. Eventually word was sent to Lady Andrews's castle, and the search was begun. But Aislinn had already disappeared, fled into the open Almont, knowing that there was no other option, that they would kill her if they found her.

She spent that first night in a cornfield, picking locusts from her hair, shivering though the night was hot, and when she rose the next morning, hungry and thirsty, she knew that the best course of action was to flee farther. She had no water, but she could follow the remaining trickle of the Crithe, work her way toward the central Almont, and perhaps find a new village, distant enough from Lady Andrews's acreage that she would not be known. This seemed a decent enough plan . . . until Aislinn thought of Fallon's stupid grin, his grasping hands, of Lady Andrews tapping her chest with the crop.

That was when she knew that she wasn't going anywhere.

CHAPTER 6

THE EMPRESS

For a supposedly Christian nation, the Tearling has evinced a stunning ability to accept the presence of magic. Seers, ghosts, even street magicians coexist happily alongside God and the Devil, and people who cross themselves will also live by prophecy. This is a contradiction of confounding proportions, but this historian believes that it can be explained by a single defining event: the Crossing.

No one but William Tear has ever understood how the Crossing itself was accomplished, how two thousand men and women departed America that was and ended up on a shore that existed on no map. The little information available to us suggests that the mechanism of the journey was a closely guarded secret, even among Tear's inner circle. But explanation is not necessary for belief. More than three centuries on, that single voyage continues to hold the popular imagination, far more tightly than the Bible ever will.

—The Glynn Queen and the Rise of Atheism in the Tearling: *A Treatise,* FATHER TYLER

Highness, we shouldn't be here," Barty said. He spoke in a low, urgent voice, as though he had not already made this remark some ten or twelve times. "Your mother will surely hear of it."

"Of course she will," Elyssa replied. "But it doesn't follow that we shouldn't be here."

She crept closer to Gareth's bed, moving quietly . . . but not too quietly. She wanted him to wake up. She had spent the past week going over her mother's various security reports on the Blue Horizon, finding them almost entirely worthless. Oh, they covered the Blue Horizon's nefarious deeds well enough: acquisition of arms, robbery of nobles, raids on Arvath storehouses. But they did not include, to Elyssa's mind, the important information. They did not report who had founded the Blue Horizon, or when, or why they had suddenly appeared in such force in the past few years. They did not report why the Blue Horizon had targeted the Arvath for their fury. They did not report who the Blue Horizon blamed for the slow and steady decline of the Tearling, or what the movement was really after when they named Elyssa the True Queen. These omissions were hardly surprising; Queen Arla was an autocrat, and autocrats were not interested in why. Her mother's agents knew that as well as Elyssa did, and they tailored their reports accordingly. But Elyssa was not her mother, and she was determined to know the Blue Horizon, to understand them.

"He's awake," Barty remarked suddenly. A hint of humor crept into his voice. "A good spy, this one, listening for information."

Elyssa pulled a chair up to Gareth's bed. She had waited until the senior medic left for lunch; the junior medics she could handle, but Beale was another matter, for he had her mother's ear. Elyssa had sent the two junior medics away, and so there was no one here but the three of them.

"Why not open your eyes?" she asked, and Gareth smiled.

"Because, as your captain has surmised, one hears much more useful things by keeping them closed."

He opened his eyes, and they were just as Elyssa remembered them: a bright and piercing grey.

"Your Highness. What can I do for you?"

"I've come to ask you some questions."

Gareth raised his eyebrows. "Welwyn Culp couldn't compel answers with his knives and pokers, and you think I will break down before your pretty face?"

Elyssa winced, stung both by the implication of vanity and by the reminder of what went on in her mother's dungeons. In her mind's eye, she saw again the wooden board, the manacles. The bloodstains on the floor.

"I am a creature of the Keep," she told Gareth. "I rarely leave, save to accompany my mother at hunt or to ride along in one of her processions. For intelligence, I have to rely on my mother's agents, and they are biased. My maid, Niya, has a wealth of information on the city, but she knows little of the Blue Horizon."

"And what would you know of the Blue Horizon?"

"I only want to understand. I want to build a better throne than my mother's. I want to listen. What is your movement's grievance with the Crown, with the Church? Why do you think a better world is possible now, when even William Tear could not make it work the last time around? I want to know what you believe."

"What we believe? It's very simple, really."

"Nothing is simple about belief."

"Good." Gareth nodded approvingly. "Lady Glynn taught you that much."

"What do you know of Lady Glynn?"

"Only that she was your tutor. The city says she's dead, murdered by Arla the Just."

Something tightened in Elyssa's stomach. "She was a good tutor. I miss her. She was . . ."

"What?"

Elyssa shook her head. *Like a mother to me,* she had been about to say . . . but that was wrong. A better comparison was old Vincent, the swordmaster. Lady Glynn was not there for mothering. She had come with a purpose and a will.

"She was a friend," Elyssa finished lamely. "I don't know what happened to her."

"Of course you do. She redistributed her acres and shattered the universe open. Such people rarely survive the fallout."

"I don't want to talk of Lady Glynn. Return to my question. Pretend I'm an ordinary person, someone you're trying to convert. Explain it to me, from the very beginning. Please. What do you want?"

"Kelsea."

"Kelsea?" Elyssa frowned. "Who is that?"

"Not a person, an idea. Kelsea comes from an old word, bastardized Anglican of the pre-Crossing. Loosely translated, it means 'the victory of ships.' William Tear crossed the ocean seeking a better world, a world where all were fed, clothed, housed, educated, doctored. When we achieve the better world, the perfect summation of William Tear's dream, then we will have Kelsea."

Fed, clothed, housed, educated, doctored, Elyssa thought wistfully, taken despite herself by the vision he presented. But under Barty's watchful eye, she was forced to remain skeptical.

"William Tear might have reviled weapons, but I've read the reports on your Blue Horizon," she countered. "You rob, you kidnap, you kill. Last winter, the Fetch hung one of Lord Winter's bailiffs from a tree in the near Almont. You hardly practice what you preach."

"True," Gareth acknowledged, tilting his head. "The road to the better world is a complex one."

"'Complex,'" Elyssa repeated dryly. "Damascus had fewer approaches than your better world."

"But we will have it in the end, all the same."

"In a drought year?" Elyssa asked, thinking of the new reports from her mother's agents in the Almont. "Crops are dying everywhere. If rain doesn't fall soon, people will be killing each other over a head of lettuce. How important will your better world be then?"

"More important still."

"I don't understand."

"Join the Blue Horizon. In time, perhaps, you'll know all of our secrets."

"You'd never take me."

"Why not?"

"My mother had you beaten within an inch of your life."

"Bruises heal. So do fractured ribs."

Elyssa glared at him, trying to decide whether he was joking. The corners of his mouth were tucked in, and his silver-grey eyes twinkled at her. . . . Yet beneath these signs of humor, she detected seriousness, sensed him watching her closely.

"How did they capture you?" she asked.

"What makes you think I was captured? Perhaps I'm here by choice."

"For what possible purpose?"

"To have a look at you."

"At me? Why?"

"The Blue Horizon, as a whole, does not believe in sorcery, or prophecies," Gareth replied. "But we know as well as any opportunistic seer that this kingdom needs a ruler, and certainly a better ruler than Arla the Just. So when we hear that the Eye of the Crithe has prophesied the coming of the True Queen, we pay attention."

"What makes you think she was talking about me?"

"Who else would she be talking about? Not your mother, that's certain . . . though I hear even your mother seeks the comfort of prophecy these days."

"The albino's no prophet," Barty growled. "She's just a cheap palmist, like the rest of the Queen's menagerie."

"Be careful in that assessment, Captain," Gareth replied, his face suddenly grave. "Arla is a despot, and despots are always most desperate to know the future."

Alarmed, Elyssa glanced toward the open doorway. She saw no one, but it seemed best to move the discussion away from both her mother and the seer. This was the Queen's Wing; someone was always listening.

"Your movement has done a good job of painting me as the True Queen," she told Gareth. "And I assume a tidy profit went with it. More converts, more donations, more volunteers. So don't play with me and pretend that the Blue Horizon believes in prophecies or saviors. You have too much to gain."

"The Blue Horizon doesn't believe in the prophecy. But I do."

"Why?"

"Because I see far. Further than any of them."

Elyssa blinked, unable to make sense of this statement. At her chest, the sapphire gave a slight shudder, reverberating with her own jagged heartbeat.

"Are you the True Queen?" Gareth asked, and Elyssa realized that he had no memory of that delirious moment after he had woken. Perhaps it was better so, for she had answered him then with her heart, not her head. But by now, she had had days to consider his question, to answer it for herself.

"I'm not the True Queen. But it hardly matters."

His eyes brightened with interest. "How so?"

"As you say, this kingdom needs a ruler. A good ruler, one who will take care of the weak as well as the strong. I don't believe in prophecy, or destiny either, and so I don't claim to be the True Queen. But that doesn't mean I can't be. The True Queen is only the shape of the vessel this kingdom requires, but I will fill it, because those people out there need a leader. And because there's no one else."

Barty grunted in approval. Gareth considered her for a long moment, then remarked, "Your mother would have answered very differently."

"She would have," Elyssa agreed, for her mother would happily seize any scrap of mystique that would augment her power. Elyssa was surprised that she had not already laid claim to the prophecy for herself.

"Speaking of your mother," Gareth remarked, "has she come up with a solution for the situation in the Almont yet?"

Barty stirred uneasily, and even Elyssa shifted in her seat, thinking of dinner last night. Her mother had consumed a fair amount of wine, and the words struggled out of her mouth like slippery olives. "Naught to worry about. It's a dry year, but we've had them before. The nobles will open their storehouses and cisterns; they'll have to."

Elyssa had not said anything; her mother was too drunk to take advice, and wine in particular always made her belligerent. But the blithe assurance in her words had chilled Elyssa. Nobles did indeed warehouse large stores on their land, and in a normal year, a given noble's stores would be sufficient to see several villages through the winter and planting. But this was the third straight dry year. Few of the nobles had realized profit from last year's harvest, and most had taken an outright loss. They would be hoarding their stores for themselves. Her mother could order the nobles to open their warehouses and cisterns, but if shortages of food and water got bad enough, they might refuse. Her mother only ever saw the nobility smiling and openhanded, but Elyssa knew what they really were.

"No, then," Gareth replied softly, answering his own question. "I thought not."

Someone knocked on the door, making Elyssa jump.

"Come!" Barty called.

Elston leaned his head in. "A message from the Queen. She demands that the Princess attend her."

"Where?"

"Private court."

Elyssa and Barty turned to each other, and she saw an expression of consternation in his eyes to match her own. The time of reckoning was here.

"I must go," she told Gareth, rising from the bed. "I'll come back tomorrow, if you permit it."

"I permit it. I enjoy trying to convert you."

"You will not convert me," she replied tartly, turning to face him. "Your movement's ideology is a bit too flexible for my taste."

"Is it?" Gareth smiled, tipping his head. "We'll see."

Elyssa wanted to smile back, but instead she turned and went out the door, into the waiting circle of her Guard. Niya, too, had appeared from nowhere, walking beside Elyssa as she swept up the hall.

"That criminal is too impertinent with you, Highness," Barty remarked. "You should not encourage him."

"I didn't encourage him!"

Barty snorted.

"We were only talking!"

"'Talking,'" Barty repeated. "Yes, I know that sort of talk."

Elyssa frowned, wanting to say something cutting, but she could think of no remark that served her purpose. Several of her guards—Carroll, Dyer, Mhurn—were grinning broadly, and Elyssa had a moment to reflect that Queen's Guards were truly a mixed blessing. They defended her life, certainly, but they also crawled around inside it. Niya, Elyssa was pleased to see, was looking straight ahead, her expression disinterested.

"Were you never young, Barty?" she demanded. "Were you never tempted by someone you couldn't have?"

This was a shot in the dim, but not entirely in the dark. For years, Elyssa had suspected that Barty was in love, or at least in admiration, with Lady Glynn. The two of them fought like cats and dogs, and Lady Glynn invariably saved the roughest side of her tongue for Barty, particularly when she caught him drinking in the Queen's Wing. But when the old tutor disappeared, Barty too had vanished for more than a week, reappearing drunk as a plowman's bitch. Givens had nearly kicked him off the Guard, but even after he was allowed to remain, Barty had been in a bad mood for months.

"We're not speaking of me," Barty replied stiffly. "I am not the heir to a crown."

"My mother has spent the past twenty years bedding half the kingdom," Elyssa shot back. "I can't see that it's done her any harm."

"Bedding is one thing, Highness. The fate of a throne is another. Your mother had already produced a legitimate heir and spare before she went her merry way."

"And she's had no children since . . . or at least, none legitimate," Elyssa amended, for there had always been talk about her mother. Elyssa's father had died when she was still in nappies, and her mother was hardly one to practice celibacy; rumor said that Queen Arla had borne at least one child on the wrong side of the sheets. "My mother is very careful; don't you think I might be at least as clever as she is when I drop my knickers?"

That, at least, silenced Barty; he turned red and remained

mercifully mute until they reached the set of broad green doors that opened onto her mother's private throne room. At the sight of them, Elyssa began to tremble.

I am the Crown Princess of the Tearling, she told herself firmly. *I am not afraid.*

But she was afraid, and all the brave pronouncements in the world would not convince her muscles otherwise. The ornate scrollwork on the green doors before her seemed to ripple and writhe, like some sinister animal. Elyssa had challenged her mother, challenged her in open court, and Queen Arla believed in punishment.

A gentle hand clasped her shoulder. Elyssa looked up and found Barty looking down at her, his gaze sympathetic.

"It will be all right, child," he murmured. "Don't let her frighten you."

The other guards nodded. Carroll offered Elyssa his flask of water, and she took a grateful drink, then wiped her mouth.

"I will go with you, Highness," Niya offered, "if you wish it."

Elyssa did wish it. She would have liked to have all of them in there, around her. But then her mother would know she was afraid.

"Thank you, Niya," she said. "But I must go myself." Her mother's guards began to open the green doors, and Elyssa moved forward, her head held high, not flinching even when the doors banged shut behind her.

Her mother sat on her private throne, a smaller version of the great silver chair that sat in the throne room. But at first Elyssa didn't even notice the Queen, for all of her attention was taken by the white woman, Brenna, who sat at the low table before the throne, dealing cards. Brenna did not look up as Elyssa entered, and after a moment Elyssa realized that the cards she dealt were of the tarot variety. Brenna flipped them up, and Elyssa saw three of them in rapid succession: the Hanged Man, the Empress, the Seven of Swords.

"Leave us alone," her mother commanded.

Brenna gathered her cards and scrambled to her feet. Her mother's guards also left the room—though, Elyssa noted, they waited until Brenna had left as well. None of the Queen's close guards liked the seer, and Barty had told Elyssa that several of her mother's men were convinced that Brenna was a witch. Elyssa would have chalked up their animosity to Brenna's appearance, but she herself wondered. There was something unsettling about the seer; even Elyssa, who fancied herself relatively hardheaded, could feel it. Givens and Barty both wanted Brenna gone from the Keep, but the Queen had decreed that she should stay. Servants' gossip said the Queen and Brenna were closeted together several times a week, and Elyssa wondered what her mother could possibly be getting out of the relationship to justify the odd air around the woman. Carroll was right; she left one feeling cold.

"Elyssa Anne."

Elyssa flushed. She was twenty-one years old now, but that tone never failed to make her a child again. Once, when she was five, she had wet herself in the face of her mother's anger, fear and shame simply rolling into a ball until her bladder let go.

I am not five years old, Elyssa told herself. *And no True Queen would ever flinch, so long as she was in the right.*

"Mother."

"How is your little friend? I trust you found him well."

Already? Elyssa thought, dismayed. Her mother's spies were everywhere in the Keep!

"Beale tells me he will heal," her mother went on. "And then I will have to make good on my promise and release him. You dealt me a pretty blow that day, I can tell you. Do you know how many missives I've received from His Holiness in the past week on this issue alone?"

"I assume that after the first, the number becomes redundant."

"Be careful, Elyssa." Her mother's voice had chilled, lost even the false note of playfulness. "Your little game has brought the wrath of the Church down on us."

"And what of that? Didn't the Holy Father once call you Arla the Godless?"

"Yes, and I call him a filthy old hypocrite whenever his name arises. But there's all the difference in the world between what we believe of others and what we need from them, Elyssa."

"Lady Glynn would have called that hypocrisy indeed."

"Carlin Glynn is no longer your tutor." Her mother's voice turned to ice, as it always did at the mention of her former friend. "I curse the day I ever brought that bitch in here. She filled your head full of socialist drivel, and now it begins to wear holes in your sense."

"Is that why she disappeared, Mother?"

"Do not think to distract me with Lady Glynn. We were speaking of you."

"All right," Elyssa replied, and sat down in one of the sumptuous armchairs scattered before the throne, tipping her head back as though she were bored. Her fright was as great as ever, but it seemed important, so important, that her mother not see. "What about me?"

"This little flirtation of yours with the Blue Horizon has gone far enough. It's time for you to repudiate them, once and for all."

"And how am I to do that?"

"Next weekend, we are invited to the Arvath for the thirtieth anniversary of the Holy Father's assumption. I was going to skip it; it will be a dull affair, and I would rather play hearts. But now, thanks to your foolishness, I must go and mend my fences. You will go with me."

An alarm bell went off in Elyssa's head. She had only entered the Arvath once in her life, on the day of her christening in the Great Cathedral.

"Go to the Arvath? For what purpose?"

"To control the damage. I cannot have conflict with the Holy Father now. Food is becoming scarce. If the drought continues, civil unrest comes next, and we want no fighting in the streets."

So she does fear the drought, Elyssa thought. *What has changed her mind?*

"Don't you see, Elyssa?" her mother asked, leaning forward. "This is the great use of the Arvath. People who worry about their everlasting souls don't have time to take up arms."

"How very godly of you, Mother."

"I never claimed to be godly, child. I am hardly such a fool. But the Church has a function in this kingdom. God is morphia, and he anesthetizes most effectively when Crown and Arvath work in lockstep."

"And what has that to do with me?"

"Don't play stupid, Elyssa." Her mother's voice had chilled again. "You are the next ruler of this kingdom, and the Arvath demands your public support, just as it demands mine. So on Saturday night, in front of the Holy Father, the nobles, the priests, you will denounce the Blue Horizon and swear allegiance to the Church."

"I will not."

"Really?" the Queen asked, smiling, and suddenly the fear was back, gripping Elyssa more tightly than ever. She knew that smile.

"They're calling you the True Queen in the city, my girl. Elyssa Regina, the one who saves us all. Did you know that?"

"I have heard of it," Elyssa replied cautiously, not understanding the tangent, but not liking it . . . nor her mother's tone.

"They say you will right wrongs, heal all the wounds of the kingdom," her mother continued. "And I know you, Elyssa. Carlin went to work on you before you were even out of nappies, and her cursed campaign was effective. You *want* to be the True Queen. You want to save them all, and you want it badly, at any cost . . . even that of my throne. My legacy."

Elyssa blinked, bewildered. Who cared for what the Arvath historians wrote down in a hundred years? People were starving now.

"Your *legacy*," she repeated bitterly. "Not everything is about you, Mother."

But again, her mother refused to rise to the bait.

"The time has come for you to grow up and assume your responsibilities, Elyssa. You *will* heal this breach with the Arvath, and you will do it on Saturday, in full view of every noble in the kingdom."

"And why is that?"

Her mother leaned forward, smiling again. "Because if you do not, I will strip you of your designation as heir."

"You would not."

"I would."

"And give it to *Thomas*?" Elyssa demanded. Her disbelief was genuine, for a worse ruler than her younger brother could hardly be imagined. Thomas had raped two girls that she knew of, likely more, and had run up gambling debts with half the bookmakers in the city. At first, Lady Glynn had taught both Thomas and Elyssa, but only until Thomas was eight, after which she delivered the damning judgment that Thomas was not worth teaching. Thomas's ability to do mathematics ended with subtraction, and historical analysis had proven an impenetrable mystery. He disdained reading, appeared to care only for gambling and whoring and raising hell in the Gut. As a prince, he was a liability. As king, he would be disastrous.

"You would not do this, Mother. You loathe Thomas. You hate him even more than I do."

"I do hate him," the Queen replied. "A fool on the throne would be a blow indeed, but fools, at least, can be guided by others. If I asked Thomas to make such an announcement at the Holy Father's party, he would do it without a thought."

"Because he has no conscience! How many girls have there been, Mother? I know you're paying at least two families for their silence, but I assume that's the tip of the iceberg. How many have there been?"

"More than two, that's certain," her mother replied, with another of those false sighs meant to approximate regret. "He's an expensive piece of baggage, your brother. I blame his father. That man was an angel in the bedroom, but a devil everywhere else . . . and Thomas clearly doesn't even have the bedroom skills to boast of."

"It's not a joke!" Elyssa shouted. "There's an entire kingdom at hazard here!"

"I know that, Elyssa. Better than you, apparently. You want to be the True Queen, yes? So why don't you do me, yourself, and the kingdom a favor? Come to the Holy Father's party, pledge allegiance to the Church, denounce the Blue Horizon, and then help me to calm the populace."

Elyssa stared at her mother for a long moment, her anger slowly fading. "I see. You need the True Queen, just as much as those people out there . . . not to feed them, but to bend them over."

"Put it however you like. The kingdom is running out of food. We will have panic soon, and we cannot afford it."

"I thought you weren't worried about the drought!"

"I wasn't. But Brenna has convinced me otherwise."

"Brenna? The palmist?"

"Oh, she's much more than a palmist, child. If you only knew—"

"Knew what?"

Her mother's face seemed to fold in upon itself then, becoming tight and secretive. "Nothing. Suffice it to say, the drought will continue, and it will be worse than anything we can imagine. Farming will come to a standstill, and thousands will die."

Elyssa stared at her, feeling sick. "This is what Brenna has told you?"

"Not Brenna," the Queen replied. Her hand crept up to grasp her sapphire, an involuntary gesture. "I did not need Brenna to see it."

Elyssa blinked, unsure how to interpret that. "What about the Crown stores? The food—"

"There isn't enough food to help the farmers. Only to help ourselves."

"What? Mother, there's enough in our warehouses to feed everyone for months!"

"And what if the drought should continue beyond that time?" the Queen asked. "What if this isn't the last dry year? We must plan for these contingencies."

"What do you mean to do?"

"What any sane man does in a meager time: hoard."

"And what happens to the Almont?" Elyssa demanded. "I read the harvest reports just like you! The Caddell is already down three feet in the central plain. There are a million people out there, Mother! What will the tenants do, when the food runs out?"

The Queen put down her mug of tea, smiling gently. That smile chilled Elyssa, for in it she suddenly saw the void inside her mother, the black and faceless gulf that existed where empathy should be. The Queen tipped her head, and silver gleamed in the light: the crown, that tiny circlet that weighed so little and yet meant everything.

"If those tenants are smart, they'll pray for rain."

CHAPTER 7

POPPY DREAMS

In pre-Glynn New London, the morphia trade boomed. Under pressure from God's Church, the Beautiful Queen had outlawed the production of narcotics; predictably, in the wake of this decision, planting of poppy fields exploded. New London's morphia trade was controlled by a handful of syndicates and individual operators, all of them at each other's throats constantly; the gangland warfare of the pre-Crossing could hardly have been more brutal. Their customers came from all walks of life, but competition was fiercest in the Creche, where, for obvious reasons, demand was most severe.

—A History of Drug Trafficking in the New World,

PROFESSOR ELLEN MARQUAND, NEW LONDON COLLEGE OF HISTORY

My name is Christian.
He rolled over, repeating the phrase to himself in the dark, as though his name were a thing he could grab and hold. These days, he found the boy Christian increasingly overshadowed, overtaken even in his own mind by the myth he had become: Lazarus. He didn't want to lose sight of who he truly was.

He rolled over again, shifting his weight carefully. The week before, his opponent had kicked him in his left hip; it was one of the few good shots the boy got, but it had stung like a bastard, and the bone remained bruised. Christian had a soft mattress these days, rather than the hard pallet of his earlier days with Wigan, but no mattress could ever be soft enough to quiet old wounds.

My name is Christian.

He didn't know his family name. Wigan had claimed to know it; he used to hold that information over Christian's head when he wouldn't obey. But Christian didn't care who his parents were. In fact, he preferred not to know. He felt nothing but contempt for them all: his parents, Wigan, the anonymous broker who had overseen the sale of a newborn. They all scrambled for themselves alone . . . all except Maura.

But Christian found that it hurt to turn his thoughts to Maura. The last time he had journeyed over to Whore's Alley to see her, she had been nearly unconscious, the head of a syringe buried in her arm. Gwyn, one of the other girls, had whispered to him that Maura's topside client had ordered her for a repeat engagement.

"He likes her hair," Gwyn whispered, as though relating a secret. Gwyn herself had mousy brown hair, and she had never been requested and never would be. Her only value lay in her youth; she was nine.

Lazarus. Christian. Christian. Lazarus.

He rolled back the other way, wishing the vicious circle in his head would stop. Falling asleep had always come particularly hard for him; he could not make his mind be still. Some nights he thought he would give anything to be able to simply go under as others did, easily and without struggle. Sleep was a lost darkness, an oblivion, but the more Christian longed for it, the further it receded.

Someone knocked at the outer door.

Christian sat up in the darkness, listening. There were no real doors in the Creche, only apertures in the tunnel walls, but denizens of the tunnels practiced a strange, unspoken courtesy; you never walked right into someone's rooms without announcing your presence. The knock repeated, then, a minute later, repeated again. Whoever it was, they weren't going away. Christian lit the candle that lay beside his mattress, pushed himself to his feet, and went into the other room.

The man in the doorway was unknown but familiar. Though not old, his face was wizened, one of the many leering circles that Christian had seen beyond the bright lights of the ring. Gambler, most likely. The cunning in those ancient eyes was enough to put Christian on his guard.

"What do you want?"

"To talk to you, boy."

Christian considered the visitor, registering many things: the strangeness of his accent, broad and flat; the thick cloak and boots, made of an unfamiliar material that nevertheless looked expensive to Christian's eyes; the knife that flashed at his waist. After another moment's thought, Christian beckoned the stranger inside.

He had never thought before to be ashamed of these small rooms; they were a world of improvement after the old cramped hole in Whore's Alley that he had shared with Wigan. But as the stranger ducked through the doorway, Christian caught him looking around the living area with distaste. When he sat down in one of the beaten chairs, a puff of dust rose into the air.

"Who are you?"

"My name is Arliss," the man replied, and Christian stiffened. He had heard the name; everyone had. Arliss was indeed a gambler, but he was also much more: one of the biggest poppy dealers in the Creche. Christian thought of Maura, her eyes dull and distant. Had Arliss sold her the poppy?

"You know who I am?"

94

"Yes," Christian grunted, but this man was not at all what he would have expected. Before he came to the city looking for easy money, Arliss had supposedly been a farm boy from the Almont. A genius for numbers had vaulted him into bookmaking, and rumor said he owned vast acres of poppy fields on the edge of the Dry Lands. Arliss was a farm boy turned gangster turned dealer . . . yet the man sitting before Christian looked like none of these things.

"You're judging me, boy," Arliss remarked.

"So?"

"So I think it takes a hell of a nerve. Only a fool blames the dealer."

Christian felt anger trying to kindle, but he crushed the impulse. Anger was a liability in this situation, and a pointless one, for very little was personal in the Creche. Keeping his face neutral, he sat down across from Arliss and locked his hands on his lap.

"What do you want?"

The bookie's face cleared, as though he, too, were relieved to get down to business.

"I've a proposal for you. How much do you know about gambling odds?"

"Not much."

Arliss leaned forward, steepling his fingers beneath his chin. His face became suddenly animated, as though a switch had been flipped, and Christian understood that though Arliss might deal in poppy, his real passion was plainly in numbers, in gambling.

"Every time you win a fight, boy, the odds on you go up. That means my bettors have to lay more money with me in order to get the same amount back. I've seen some impressive fighters down here over the years, but never anyone like you, boy. You're becoming a figure of some legend. They say you can't lose."

"Not can't," Christian said, lifting his chin. "Won't."

"I believe you. That's why I'm here. A fighter like you presents a unique opportunity for people in my business."

"What opportunity?"

"Do you like living down here?"

The question was so unexpected that it made Christian look around, seeing the place as though with new eyes: the furniture, worn down to the wood in some places; the old bloodstains on the stone floor; the piles of filthy clothing in the corners.

"Of course you don't," Arliss continued, answering his own question. "No one likes living down here. Tell me, boy, have you ever been topside?"

Christian shook his head, repressing a scowl, for the word itself irritated him, made him think of Maura and her damnable *client*.

"It's better up there," Arliss continued. "Cleaner, and the air reeks less. People smile more. When you look up, you see bright blue sky instead of slime-covered stone."

Christian nodded. He had heard such stories all his life, and he supposed he believed them, but he didn't trust them. Smiling people? Bright blue sky? What place was there for him in a world like that?

"If topside is so wonderful, why don't you go and live there?"

"I am, boy," Arliss replied. "Poppy and numbers, I'm slowly selling all of my interest in the tunnels. Within six months, I'll be gone for good."

Christian stilled. Arliss out of the Creche . . . it would rock the place almost to its foundations, leaving the poppy trade controlled by a handful of lesser dealers.

Don't let him distract you.

"What are you selling?" he demanded.

Arliss smiled, though Christian noted, again, that the smile never touched his eyes. "A man could make a good life topside. Even a killer like you."

"You need money to live topside. Food is expensive up there. Dwellings cost rent."

"Indeed they do. That's why you would need to leave here with a great hoard of money, enough to last your lifetime."

Christian looked up sharply, and Arliss leaned forward, his eyes bright.

"What would you say if I told you that we could fix a fight, boy? One fight, only one, but on that one fight we could make enough money for us both to retire."

Christian blinked. "You want me to throw a fight?"

"Would that be so hard, boy? Surely you've won enough."

"I'm not a boy. I'm twenty."

"Listen to me," Arliss growled. "The odds on your fights are now astronomical. Up in the Gut, they're talking about closing out bets on you altogether. We go long, and both of us make a killing. We could wipe out half the books in the city."

Christian frowned. Arliss was right. He had won so many fights that no one doubted his gifts anymore. So why did he feel as though losing a single bout would mean that he had lost everything?

Because you have nothing else.

Ah, that voice. Lazarus or Christian, it didn't matter . . . that voice knew him well. He had never lost a fight, not even in the early days, when he was a child pitted against older children. On the worst days of his life, when all else was up in the air, he had always known that he would never lose, and he clung to that knowledge as moss clung to stone . . . or, perhaps, as a hanged man clung to the rope.

"Why do you need to fix a fight?" he demanded. "Don't you make a fine living already, stringing out girls in the Alley?"

"Ahhh." Arliss leaned forward, and the keenness of his gaze made Christian uncomfortable. "Someone special over there, boy? Mother? Sister? Friend?"

"No!"

"We could get her out too, you know. An ordinary whore? We could make enough to buy her clear as well. Use a blind broker, and the price stays good and reasonable. You and your special girl, out of this cesspool."

Christian remained silent for a long moment. He did not trust this poppy dealer, with his thick boots and world-sized promises. But a deeper part of his mind was already working over the man's words. If he could get Maura out as well . . .

This is what the dealers do, the voice in his mind spoke up suddenly. *Sell dreams, but at the end they're only nightmares.*

And yet this admonition, too, seemed the voice of cowardice, of the boy who still clung to the Creche as the only world he knew. Arliss was right; he could not go on winning forever. The money would not allow it. Things must change, whether he wanted them to or not.

"Why are you leaving the tunnels?" he demanded.

"Christ, boy, do you think I enjoy peddling the needle to people who trade in children? I don't, no more than you enjoy the slaughter. I am not a good man, but I am not a bad man either, not by a long shot."

Christian stared at him, wide-eyed. The words might be new, but the idea was utterly familiar, the same idea that haunted him on these nights when he tossed and turned on his small mattress. Killer or not, he had never thought of himself as bad.

"There's plenty of misery topside, too," Arliss remarked. "Whole goddamn world's drying up this summer, and people are starving. They'll need my wares just as much as the girls in the Alley. More, maybe."

Arliss stood, the expensive cloak dropping to cover him, and in that moment, Christian realized that the gangster was actually quite small. The aura of the successful dealer had made him seem much taller, even seated.

"I'm easy to find, boy, if you ever decide you want to take up my offer." Arliss paused, then, unexpectedly, put a light hand on his shoulder. "There's a better world, you know. So close we can almost touch it."

Christian didn't respond, only stood motionless as Arliss left. Several shadows detached themselves from the doorway to follow him: bodyguards. Arliss had left them outside.

Christian returned to his mattress in the far room, but no sleep waited there. His mind was too full of the picture, the damnable picture that Arliss had painted for him. Topside . . . he would not dare wish it for himself, perhaps, but if he could truly buy Maura's freedom and take her with him—

Christian realized then that he had been seduced, just as Arliss had intended, by the mere possibility of freedom. A seduced man was a fool, a mark; hadn't he seen as much in the stables, in the wet and rolling eyes of the johns? But Christian couldn't help himself. The better world, Arliss had said, and that was a laugh, this worst of dealers taking the Blue Horizon's words and turning them to his ends. But now Christian wondered whether there wasn't a better world out there after all, one just for him and Maura. Blue sky, dry air, a small house that would be their very own . . . and suddenly he was up and out of his den, heading toward the Alley.

The enforcer on Mrs. Evans's door was new, but he seemed to know who Christian was; his mouth dropped open as the fighter approached, and even though the enforcer was half a head taller, he let him by without a murmur.

Mrs. Evans was nowhere in sight, which seemed a mercy. Christian waved to several of the girls who sat in the common area, waiting for clients, then headed down the hallway toward Maura's room. When he knocked, however, it was not Maura who answered, but a childish, lisping voice.

"Come in."

He ducked through the curtains and found the little girl, Gwyn, kneeling by the side of the bed, dabbing Maura's face with a dry rag. Maura's eyes were closed; she looked to be unconscious. A single candle burned weakly on the bedside table, but it was quite enough to illuminate Maura's pulped cheek, and a split lip that had swollen to twice its normal size.

"What happened?" Christian whispered hoarsely. He leaned back, moving out of the light, for in that instant it seemed important that no one should see his rage, not even the nine-year-old girl who knelt on the floor.

"Her special client," Gwyn answered, with all the naive candor of the child who does not know which things are meant to be secret. "He hit her last time, too, but Mrs. Evans said it was nothing, and she gave Maura some poppy. She looks much worse this time, though."

"Who is this client?"

"Nobody knows," Gwyn replied pertly. "It's always Arlen Thorne comes and takes her away, and brings her back too. Maura told Jilly the john has a tattoo—"

"What kind of tattoo?" Christian asked, trying to keep his voice casual.

"A clown," Maura said. "On his hand. Do you have any poppy?"

"No," Christian replied slowly. "No poppy."

"That's too bad." Gwyn turned back to Maura, dabbing at her swollen lip. "It made her all better last time."

Under Gwyn's ministrations, Maura moaned softly. Christian

longed to go to her, but he also knew that Maura wouldn't want him to witness this ... any of it. She always tried so hard to pretend on his visits, to make believe that they both lived pleasant lives. She would be mortified if she knew that Christian had seen her this way. He could go and find Arlen Thorne, get the client's name, and beat the life from his body ... but Maura wouldn't want that either. *Tend to your own business*, she had told him, and he had listened, and now look where they were.

You don't own her, Christian reminded himself, breathing deeply. *Any more than Mrs. Evans does, or anyone else. What happens next is her decision.*

But this was the Alley; no one had choices. Looked at broadly, even the decision to take the first hit of morphia had been determined long before Maura had picked up the syringe ... determined by statistics, if nothing else. After another moment spent mastering himself, he moved toward the doorway.

"Are you going?" Gwyn asked, confused. "Don't you want to stay until she wakes up?"

"No. I have to go. Do me a favor and don't tell her I was here."

"All right," Gwyn replied guilelessly, but Christian didn't know whether she could be trusted; she was, after all, only nine.

And what of that? his mind demanded nastily. *When you were nine, you crushed Alja Mueller's windpipe and ate a good dinner afterward.*

He ducked through Maura's hangings, heading back up the hallway, ignoring greetings from Benia, who had clearly just finished with a john and was heading toward the bathroom. He barely saw the common room, the enforcers who glimpsed his face and automatically drew back. He was thinking of the auction block again, of the way that Maura had shivered in the dankly cavernous room as they took off her clothes. Christian had wanted to stop them, but he had been even smaller than she, and seeing her naked had hurt his heart. Somehow he understood, even then, the power of that forced disrobing, the debasement that came with it. Wigan had bought the two of them as a package, but Christian had gone into the ring right away, while Maura had been a buy-and-hold; Wigan had spotted her long white-blonde hair and seen the potential for a good investment. He held her until she was eight, when he brokered her sale to Mrs. Evans and made a tidy profit.

I begged him to keep her, Christian remembered now. *I begged him. Maura begged him. But he only laughed and said the thing that made me furious, about the bubbles in the ale. What was it?*

Christian couldn't remember. All he remembered were Maura's giant eyes, staring into his, when Mrs. Evans's enforcers came to take her away. He supposed it could have been worse; she could have been sold to the Deep Patch, and at least when she was in the Alley he could keep an eye on her.

And what a fabulous job you've done.

Christian winced. Maura had been in no state to hear about Arliss's offer, but the very instant she was better he would tell her about it, about topside. Perhaps he could convince her. Perhaps she would even come of her own free will. Perhaps he should have broached the subject, despite her weakened state. One way or another, he would have to get her off the poppy, and from what Christian knew of most addicts, that was probably going to mean locking her up.

Are you sure even that will work? his mind whispered. *That girl who made the bracelet, who held your hand until they put you on the block, how much of her is left?*

Christian wished he knew the answer.

CHAPTER 8

MEN OF GOODWILL

In hindsight, it seems clear that Queen's Guards were no better than other men. They drank; they gambled and whored. From time to time they murdered civilians, or even each other. But this is not the popular image of the Guard, which was supposed to embody an almost courtly ideal: men who were not only the best with a sword but the purest of heart. This pretty fiction took a curious hold, persisting long after it had become patently obvious that the average Queen's Guard was neither. A man whose heart was as fine as his sword would be an extraordinary find indeed, but if such a Queen's Guard ever existed, then history has forgotten him.

—The Tearling as a Military Nation, CALLOW THE MARTYR

Carroll had thought that it would be a simple matter to track the seer. Her appearance, after all, made it almost impossible for her to blend into a crowd, and she did not hurry on her way, merely sailed serenely down the streets of the Hollow. Following her should have been an easy business, but it had gone wrong right from the start.

The albino kept her hood on, for one thing. Brown hooded cloaks were everywhere you looked in the city. Once Carroll thought he had lost her entirely, only to find her behind him, standing on a corner, nothing visible but the grinning white flash of her jawline. She had doubled back, he thought, flanked him deliberately. Elston said the white woman was a witch, and though Elston saw demons in every shadow, his distrust of the seer resonated throughout the Guard. Arla's close guards whispered that the witch was teaching the Queen to read the future. Even Captain Givens was certain that Brenna was more than she seemed; he thought she might even be a Mort spy. Several times a week she left the Keep, and Givens wanted to know where she went, whom she answered to. He had passed the task down to Barty, reasoning that a member of Elyssa's Guard would be less familiar to the seer, and Barty had given Carroll the assignment, selecting him even over the older, more experienced guards like Elston and Coryn. Carroll knew that this was no confidence in his own abilities; rather, Barty knew he was the only guard who would not be tempted from his mission by the variety of entertainments outside the Keep. But the rest of them would never let Carroll forget it if he came back empty-handed. He was determined not to fail.

But the seer seemed to know the Gut well, much better than Carroll did. He had been down here only twice, on the Queen's business, and twice was enough. He understood that such areas served a purpose; every city needed its pubs, its gaming hells, perhaps even its brothels—though that idea sickened Carroll, who was a devout Christian and thus hated the very idea of prostitution. Father Timpany said that it was best that such establishments were quarantined in one area, kept far from the innocent. But Father Timpany, like most Arvath priests, had a rich man's view of Christianity—utterly divorced from Christ—as well as a truly appalling command of scripture. Carroll himself made a better Christian, and he certainly would have made a better priest. Long before, he had actually thought of joining the Arvath novitiate; he was a Keep child, and so that path had been open to him, along with so many others. But the hypocrisy of the Arvath sickened him, and if Father Timpany was the best the Church had to offer, then Carroll had likely made the right choice. He loathed the Gut, and as a result he did not know it well. If Brenna wanted to slip him, she probably could.

He followed the seer down a winding street that he believed led to the Circus . . . but here, again, he was deceived. The street came out in a narrow alley, so dark and claustrophobic that Carroll paused before entering. Corruption seemed to infect the alley, shrinking it, making it dark. On either side people leaned against the walls, their expressions dazed, their faces covered in soot, or perhaps it was filth. The alley reeked of shit, but beneath that stench was another, so sweet that it cloyed. Carroll thought it might be morphia. Despite the retreating figure of the seer, for a moment he could not bring himself to take another step.

Come on, he told himself. *You're a Queen's Guard!*

After a moment he began walking again, his eyes on the seer's back. Someone tried to pick his pocket, and Carroll slapped the offending thief away, then saw that it was a child, a girl no more than four or five years old, with the sunken eyes and brittle-looking skin of starvation. Carroll had not thought much of the reported famine, for there was always plenty of food in the Keep, and the state of the kingdom as a whole was not the business of the Guard. The sight of the child shocked him.

What else has been softened for us? he wondered suddenly. *What else do we not hear about?*

Without thinking, he tore the pouch of dried fruit from his belt and gave it to the child. She took it, with a smile of gratitude that made Carroll feel sick . . . but almost immediately another child snatched it from her and sprinted away, diving into a broad culvert that led beneath a building. The little girl was left behind, screaming, and Carroll could take no more. He fled, breathing a sigh of relief when he emerged from the alley and found himself in a wider boulevard.

But the relief did not last long, for here loitered all the denizens of the Gut: prostitutes and pimps, bookmakers and marks, foot-pads with knife handles sticking from their socks. As Carroll passed the food stalls, he saw that the prices for both food and wine had gone through the roof since the last time he had been down here. Six pounds for half a chicken! Four pounds for a loaf of bread! This last made sense, for grain was now so scarce that the price of beer had more than doubled as well; all of the Guard had been complaining about it after furlough. Carroll wondered whether fruits and vegetables were similarly exorbitant, but as he went down the boulevard, he could not see any produce available at all. They had fresh fruit every day in the Keep . . . and now Carroll felt new shame wash over him. Arla's people would never want for food, or for anything else, and as much as Carroll would have liked to tell himself that he was in the Queen's Guard on his own merit, he knew better. His father had been a Gate Guard, and Carroll had spent mornings in the Keep from his earliest childhood. Elyssa had known his name when he was only twelve years old, and when he was fifteen Carroll had begged to join her Guard. He saw fairness in Elyssa, a fairness that was entirely absent in the Queen. Arla was hard, not fair, and as a result, the Tearling was hard as well. It was luck, simple luck, that had put Carroll into the Queen's Guard; it was luck that kept them all in apples and meat. If Carroll thought otherwise, he had only to look at the sea of grim faces on this street, their deep-pouched eyes and bone-stabbed cheeks. He had known there was misery without the Keep; of course he had. But the Keep was insular, narcotic. It allowed a man to forget the world outside.

Focus! his mind snapped. *The seer!*

Carroll did his best. It was easier if he didn't look to either side but simply kept his eyes on Brenna's back. He was just beginning to overtake her again when she turned and darted down a staircase. The stairs, jammed between a pub and a brothel, were even darker than the alley had been ... or perhaps it only seemed that way because the sun had now disappeared behind the buildings. There could be any number of thieves and cutthroats waiting just below the level of the street. But Carroll had been given an assignment, and he was only twenty years old, young enough to feel the sting of ego in failure. If he came back and told them that he had lost the albino—a woman, and an utterly distinctive one, at that—what would they say? Barty would be disappointed, and Dyer would be merciless. But if Carroll came back with something useful, some vital piece of information linking the seer to the Caden, or even to Mortmesne, that would quiet them all ... even Carroll's own mind, which sometimes liked to whisper that he was no Queen's Guard, only a rich man's son.

Protect me, Lord, Carroll thought, then turned left, following the white woman down the stairs.

The tunnels were not what Carroll had expected. He thought that they would be dark, and several steps down he had already realized, chagrined, that he should have grabbed a torch. He expected mold and damp as well, perhaps mud. But when he reached the bottom of the staircase—more than a hundred steps—he found himself at the end of a bright stone tunnel, its floor professionally cobbled. The light was so good—torches stood in holders every five feet or so—that Carroll could even see, far down the tunnel, the hooded, retreating back of the seer, just before she disappeared around a corner. The floor was so clean that Carroll was sure someone swept it regularly.

What on earth was I worried about? he wondered. *This place is cleaner than the Keep!*

He hurried down the tunnel, trying to walk light on his feet as Vincent had taught him. Vincent was old—he would undoubtedly retire soon, leaving the arms room in the hands of the much younger Venner—but he knew more about footwork than any man alive, and Carroll had been taking lessons from him since he was fifteen. More than swordcraft, Vincent had also taught him the art of dancing light on his feet, and Carroll used it now, nearly skipping down the passage. There were no intersections, only a series of turnings. Carroll went around several large curves before he began to hear the roar.

For a moment he thought that he must have gone the wrong way and ended up near the sluice gates that fed into the Caddell, for the roar was loud and angry, like the river when it reached its full flow in springtime. But after another moment he realized that this sound was human, many voices yelling at once. He turned a final corner and blinked.

Every inch of the room seemed bathed in light. Fire was everywhere, torches and candles and chandeliers suspended from the ceiling. But Carroll barely marked them; he was too busy scanning the enormous crowd of backs. There were at least two hundred people here, mostly men, and Brenna had disappeared neatly into the throng.

Feeling more than ever that he had made a mistake, Carroll nevertheless pushed his way into the crowd. It was easier than he had expected; the smells of whiskey and ale permeated the place, and most of the men he shoved past barely had their own balance. In a short time, Carroll had made his way near the front. Some sort of fight was going on; Carroll could just glimpse the flickering, heaving outlines of two figures. Boxing, most likely; Dyer and Fell liked to gamble on their off days, and Carroll had heard them talk about the boxing in the Gut. Though they were both younger than Carroll, neither Dyer nor Fell had grown up in the Keep, and he liked to hear them talk about the wider world.

I should have listened better. I should have asked some questions.

Now Carroll heard a sound he recognized: the snap of a breaking bone. It echoed even over the din of the crowd, and the man behind Carroll roared his approval.

"Bring all the ringers you want from the country, Miller! He'll crush them all!"

"Put him away!"

A bone broken, Carroll thought. *The round should stop now.*

But it didn't. It kept going, and a few seconds later there was another high snap, followed by a scream. Dread fell over Carroll, seeming to squeeze his heart. What sort of fight was this?

You don't want to know. Walk away.

But he could not. He needed to see. As though someone else guided his steps, he ducked and angled through the crowd. Carroll was agile, and his slim build allowed him to quickly push his way through to the front.

What he saw would be with him until the end of his days.

The ring was not large, only some twenty feet square. The floor was stained with blood, some of it fresh. On one side lay a man, his arm twisted at a grotesque angle, shrieking. His left leg had nearly been severed; it hung by only a few strips of sinew, and blood jetted from the ravaged flesh. While Carroll watched, the injured man collapsed into unconsciousness, and only then did Carroll turn to look at his opponent: a young man, even younger than Carroll perhaps, his eyes deep and dark, trained on his fallen antagonist in the manner of a hunting dog. The boy was tall, much taller than Carroll, and his arms and hands were covered with their own myriad of wounds. But these wounds were well scarred, and a distant part of Carroll's mind noted that many of them were shiny and stretched, as childhood wounds when the limbs grew and lengthened.

"Finish him, boy! Don't toy with him!"

It was the same man who had spoken before, his voice hoarse with drink, and suddenly they were all shouting, demanding finality, demanding death. Gradually all of the voices merged and blended into a single chant, and this, too, Carroll would never forget: the sound of the mob, unsatisfied and hungry.

"Kill! Kill! Kill! Kill!"

What more do they want? Carroll wondered wildly. *That poor bastard will bleed to death inside of a minute. What more must he do?*

But the boy seemed to know, for as Carroll watched, he lunged forward and kicked the bleeding, unconscious man in the face, knocking him backward. In a series of movements almost too fast for even Carroll's quick eyes to follow, the boy had straddled the man, grabbed his neck, and twisted it in a single expert movement. The corpse collapsed to the ground. The crowd howled its approval, and Carroll, who had seen wounded men before—even a dead man once, when a drunken Keep servant had stumbled and fallen to his death off the parapet—felt his gorge rise. He had had nightmares about the Keep servant's dead body, his arms and legs lying bonelessly in a pool of blood on the drawbridge. But the violence of that death was eclipsed by what he saw here. The crowd parted, and Carroll suddenly glimpsed the albino, across the fighting ring, near the back of the crowd: just a flash of white grin beneath the hood. Then she was gone, darting into the black tunnel at the far end of the room.

Carroll pushed past several men, who shoved him backward, cursing blearily. Spit landed on his face. He kept going until he found himself in the tunnel the witch had taken, his running footfalls echoing around him. He passed by a long wall that had been painted with Blue Horizon graffiti–*THE BETTER WORLD*, the letters blared, some five feet high, and Carroll thought wildly that the rebels, well-meaning though they were, were wasting their time down here–but then the light disappeared and so did the letters, fading into darkness behind him. He thought he might be gaining on the seer, but after rounding several turns, Carroll was forced to dive against the wall, crouching on all fours, and let it all come up: eggs and toast, the breakfast he had eaten this morning, bathed in the warm, safe light of the Keep.

I will tell the Queen, he thought wildly as his guts heaved. *I will tell her, and she will make it stop.*

But here again he found himself uncertain. Queen Arla had plenty of courage, yes. She frightened Carroll, and she frightened others too; he saw it when petitioners came to court. She was a tough woman, not shy of the fight. But would she ever come down here and fight for *these* people? For the child pickpocket in the alley? For the man in the ring? Carroll didn't think so. Only Elyssa would do that. Only Elyssa had *moral* courage.

Finally, after a span of time that seemed endless, the agonized clenching of his guts eased, and he was able to totter a few feet farther down the tunnel, away from his own sickness, and collapse against the wall, breathing deeply. Acid welled in his throat; Carroll cleared it and spat, and only then did he realize where he was: alone in the dark.

Fifteen minutes later, he was forced to admit that he was lost. He had thought it would be a simple matter to backtrack to the well-lit room–though that was no reprisal he was looking forward to, for certain–but he had clearly run farther down the tunnel than he thought. There were several splits, and he must have chosen wrong. Every staircase he encountered went down. Even this tunnel led steadily downward, and once Carroll realized how lost he truly was, he halted and stood panting in the dark.

Every Queen's Guard, from the Captain down to Kibb, carried a simple kit of survival gear, compact enough to tuck inside a belt. Carroll opened his and found the flint and a small vial of oil, carefully wrapped in a piece of cloth. The cloth would be enough to light a torch, but it wouldn't burn for long, and after a moment's thought Carroll pulled off his shirt. The floor was littered with something he took for sticks; only when he had grabbed one, wrapped it with cloth, and lit it did Carroll realize that he was holding a long, splintered human bone. After a brief shiver, he did not examine his makeshift torch again.

These tunnels were not the clean affair he had first encountered at the bottom of the staircase. The walls dripped endlessly, their stones stained nearly black with centuries of mold. There were no torches in holders; indeed, there were no holders at all. *Someone* clearly used this tunnel regularly, for boot prints tracked through the muck, but whoever they were, they must bring their own light. Beyond the small circle of illumination provided by his torch, Carroll sensed limitless miles of tunneled darkness, the vast bulk of the earth weighing down on his shoulders. Claustrophobia wrapped him like a moist blanket.

Don't panic, he told himself. *You're a Queen's Guard of the Tearling.*

But these words carried little weight. Carroll had not proven himself, like Mhurn or Coryn, Almont farm boys who had come from nothing and won their places on brains and swordcraft. Carroll had never drawn his sword outside the practice floor, had never even been in a fistfight. Yes, he was a Queen's Guard, but in this moment, he felt that he would have traded his grey cloak in an instant, no bargaining, in return for a staircase that led straight up to daylight. Even the steady drip of water, a sound that Carroll enjoyed on rainy nights in his room, now began to seem oppressive, as though it were the voice of the darkness speaking steadily in his ear.

He began walking upward again—if for no other reason than that up was surely better than down—moving as quietly as he could, trying not to think of the seer or of the fight he had seen. Getting out of here, that was the problem at hand, and Carroll hurried faster up the tunnel, keeping an eye on his torch, which was beginning to burn out. Well, if need be, he could light his trousers as well.

But there was no need. He had backtracked perhaps half a mile when he heard men's voices, the scuffling of footsteps ahead of him.

"Hello?" Carroll called.

The footsteps stopped, and so did the voices. Now Carroll could see several pricks of torchlight in the distance. He hurried forward, continuing to cry out joyfully, but when he was perhaps fifty meters away, something made him stop.

There were four of them, he could see now, though they were only dim shadows in cloaks and hoods. Two were tall, two short, and each held a torch. But they did not come forward, and they said nothing. Carroll had the impression that they were studying him.

"Hello?" he asked again, hesitant now. Belatedly, perhaps, he had remembered where he was, what he had seen of this place. Carroll had always believed, deeply and fundamentally, that the world was full of men of goodwill. He believed it still. But he did not think he would find many of them down here.

The shortest of the men suddenly began to howl with laughter, nearly doubling over. His hood fell back, and Carroll saw that he was a round, ruddy man, with several days' worth of stubble on his jaw.

"Ask and you shall receive, Ellens!" he guffawed. The slur of consonants told Carroll that the man was very drunk. "Not even your birthday!"

"Great God, you're right!" the tall man on the left–Ellens, presumably–boomed back. He too was drunk, though not quite so sloppy as his friend. "A good night at the tables, and then God sends me a pigeon as well!"

Pigeon. Carroll took an involuntary step backward. He had never heard that word applied to anything but birds, but there was no mistaking the threat in the men's tones. Pigeons were for plucking. They would rob him, perhaps take his sword.

"I am a Queen's Guard of the Tearling," Carroll announced clearly. "Let me pass."

All four of them collapsed in laughter, holding each other's shoulders for balance. Four drunks at the end of a long night were no danger to anyone . . . but Carroll's nerve endings said differently. There was an undercurrent here that he did not understand, and he felt anew his own lack of preparedness for this mission, how little he knew of this world. Realizing that he was half naked, dressed only in trousers, Carroll drew the sword from the scabbard at his back.

"Stand by and let me pass."

Three of them continued to chortle, but the tallest, who had not spoken yet, straightened up, staring at the sword.

"Where did a little cagey bird like you get a piece like that?"

Carroll hesitated. He had heard the man's voice before, though for the life of him he couldn't remember where. At court? It seemed unlikely. He knew all of the Queen's courtiers, even their voices.

"I am a Queen's Guard of the Tearling," Carroll repeated steadily, holding the sword in front of him as though it were a cross. "Let me pass, or the wrath of the Guard will find you."

The tall figure drew his hood down over his brow, and Carroll, who had been a perceptive boy all his life, suddenly understood that here was a highborn, a man with something to lose. Oh, Carroll knew that nobles went down into the Creche, just as he knew that they abused their tenants and withheld food from the starving. But knowledge was easier to ignore in the Keep.

"You take this seriously, lad?" Ellens demanded. But he was not speaking to Carroll.

"Not sure," replied the hooded man. "But that's good steel the boy is carrying. Where would a pigeon get such a thing?"

"Stop calling me that!" Carroll snapped, hating how childish his own voice sounded.

"Fuck it," one of the short men said. "Let's just rush him. He's too small to use that sword."

But the hooded man grabbed two of them as they started forward. "I can't afford to be identified."

"By who?" the shortest demanded. "Your wife?"

The hooded man ignored him. "What's your name, boy?"

Carroll hesitated, but there seemed no value in concealment. Perhaps the man would know him, know that he was telling the truth.

"I'm Carroll, of Princess Elyssa's Guard."

The hooded noble sat back on his heels, nodding, but the mutinous muttering from the other three had intensified, and Carroll understood that if the hooded man *was* the leader, it was a nominal business only. Rogue dogs sometimes formed packs, but that didn't stop them from eating each other when the time came. The gruesome quality of this image, the way it had come so naturally to his mind, said more than anything to Carroll about what this place had already done to him. A burning drop of sweat trickled into his left eye.

I must get out of here.

Abruptly Ellens shoved the hooded man out of the way, and the three of them came for him, flinging away their torches. Carroll swung his sword, and the short man in front crumpled, shrieking, a high, womanish sound. But this tunnel was too close; at the end of its swing, the tip of the sword buried in the porous stone of the wall and lodged there. The hilt was jerked from Carroll's hands as the other two hit him and took him down to the floor. His head rapped hard against the flagstones, and his vision went as dark as the night sky, full of bright, eye-bursting constellations. He struggled, kicking and scratching, trying to remember what old Vincent had taught him . . . but most of Vincent's lessons had dealt with swordcraft, not close combat.

"Christ, help us hold him, Latimer!" Ellens shouted. "Boy's like a damned fish!"

"My name, you fucking piker. You used my name."

Ellens offered no apology. And now Carroll knew where he had heard that voice before: Lord Latimer, who had once been Prince Thomas's guardian. He had fallen from favor several years before, though no one would tell Carroll why . . . but he thought he knew now. Latimer had moved into the fray, his hood thrown back now to reveal the narrow face that Carroll remembered seeing around the throne from time to time, and Carroll found his own legs suddenly and securely pinned. After that it was an easy matter to pin his arms. They might be drunk, these three, but they were strong.

And still Carroll did not understand, not until he felt a hand yank down his trousers and touch his privates. He screamed, fighting harder, but the hand pinning his legs held him fast, the breathing above him roughened.

This place, Carroll thought, despairing, not even knowing

what place he meant—the tunnels? the Gut? the Tear?—and shut his eyes as a second hand slid between his legs. *This place breeds monsters. I am going to die down here, and worse, and no one will hear, no one will ever know—*

Torchlight flared above his head.

Carroll looked up, but tears were swimming in his eyes and he couldn't focus. The figure above them was no more than a dark blur.

"What goes on here?"

The brief flare of hope that had been born with the light died in Carroll's mind. The voice belonged to a young man, and there was only one. Another "pigeon," probably, and Carroll's sense of fair play, which had been with him since his earliest memory, suddenly came to the fore.

"Run!" he screamed at the vague blur in front of him. "Run for your life!"

But the silhouette did not move. And now a miracle happened: the hands holding Carroll's arms and legs were suddenly gone. He could move again, and he rolled over in a quick convulsive movement, yanking up his trousers, weeping. Above his own harsh sobs, he heard Lord Latimer speaking quickly.

"We want no quarrel with you, Lazarus. If you want the pigeon, take him with our apologies."

Carroll wiped his eyes. In torchlight, it took him a moment to recognize the figure before him: the surviving fighter from the ring, not a warrior now but only a young man, with wild hair and a deep black bruise on his cheekbone.

"I don't know this boy from Adam," Lazarus replied, and that dead gaze swept all of them, Carroll included, before focusing on Lord Latimer. "But I do remember *you*, my friend."

Latimer turned pale. "I have never met you."

"That's true. We have not been formally introduced, and it *was* years ago. But from what I see here, you have not changed a bit. The Prince's handler, is it not?"

"Yes, I am," replied Latimer, drawing himself up.

"No, he's not!" Carroll cried, not sure why except that he did not like lies, and certainly would not support them from this piece of human sickness. "He's fallen from favor, banned from court!"

"That so?" The fighter's dead eyes seemed to come to life, glowing from within, like twin sparks in a slowly kindling fire. It was not a good sight; Carroll felt as though some beast had woken before him, not sleepy but maddened, already hungry for the kill.

"Fallen from favor, have we?" Lazarus repeated. "Lost our cozy royal post?"

One of the men—Ellens, it was—grabbed the sword stuck in the wall and began to yank on it with all his might. He managed to pull it free, but his hands shook so badly that the sword clattered to the ground.

"We want no quarrel with you, no quarrel at all!" another of them babbled. "Take Latimer, the boy if you like, but let us go free!"

Moving casually—but oh, what a deceptive casualness that was; even Carroll could see that it hid a wealth of purpose—Lazarus set his torch on the ground, where it continued to burn lopsidedly, illuminating the short man whom Carroll had gutted. The crimson sparkle of innards made him feel sick . . . but not regretful.

"I suppose you paid this pigeon for his services, too," Lazarus continued. "I suppose he was agreeable to have the four of you gang up on him in the middle of a filthy tunnel?"

Ellens and his short companion suddenly broke forward, trying to dodge. Lazarus grabbed Ellens and swung him around, bashing him against the wall. Latimer had broken toward the upper level as well, but Lazarus caught him easily, wrapping an arm around his throat. Their shorter companion fled, screaming, and Lazarus watched him go for a moment, then shrugged. His eyes flicked to Carroll, then to the sword, which lay on the ground.

"You. Take your steel and leave."

Carroll picked up his sword. Latimer, his neck still locked beneath Lazarus's arm, had begun to wheeze and choke. Every nerve in Carroll's body told him to go, flee, but he held his ground. He could not flee, for he owed a debt now . . . and though the boy in front of him might be no more than an animal, even animals deserved to have their debts paid.

"I am Carroll, of the Queen's Guard. I owe you, sir."

"Sir!" The boy lifted his eyebrows, and again Carroll had the sense that he stood before a beast, held from him by the most flimsy of cages. "Well, Carroll of the Queen's Guard, you're a polite boy. Far too polite for this place. Get out of here. I have business with this man."

"What business?" Latimer demanded, wheezing. "I have never met you!"

"You have a tattoo on your hand that interests me. We will discuss that first, and then go on to lessons."

Latimer's eyes had gone wide and glassy with fright. But it was Lazarus's eyes that held Carroll transfixed, for he could *see* the murder there, flat and lifeless and not choosy in the least.

"Go now, Queen's Guard," Lazarus repeated. "Run, and don't look back."

Carroll's store of bravery was all used up. He fled past Lazarus, mindless of the darkness now, only wanting to get as far from that deep stretch of tunnel as he could. He ran faster when Lord Latimer began to scream, terrible screams that echoed in Carroll's ears long after the true sound had ceased. He felt sick and dirty, infected . . . but this was an infection he did not suffer alone.

They know. The thought pounded wildly through his head

with each step. *They know. The Queen, the nobles, all of them. They know what's down here, and they do nothing.* He felt himself tottering right on the edge of madness, knowing that these tunnels would be in his head, always, even if he lived to be a hundred. He would not escape, not now and not ever, but still he ran, not even trying to navigate, only caring that he went upward, out of this lightless hell that lay beneath the earth of the quiet home he had always known.

An unknowable length of time later—minutes or lifetimes, they were all one in the dark—Carroll climbed a ladder and, as though for the first time in his life, saw stars.

CHAPTER 9

THE TABLEAU

All hurricanes begin in exactly the same way:
As a breath of calm air on a bright, pleasant day.
    —*Songs from the Almont Rebellion,* as compiled by Merwinian

The cottage was dark as Aislinn came up out of the fields, keeping her head down, crawling through the grass. It was past two in the morning, an hour at which even the ultra-industrious Grahams would be home in bed, and Aislinn felt safe enough. She knew the topography of their acres well, and no matter which bailiff Lady Andrews had picked to replace Fallon, he could not be up to speed yet. Only the barest sliver of moon lit the path, but Aislinn had been living without torchlight for two weeks now, and she had grown used to finding her way.

But her family's cottage was dark.

Aislinn crawled out of a tiny tussock, all that remained of the Vines' winter wheat, and pushed herself up. After a quick glance around to see nothing stirring, she hurried down the lane, past the Vines' cottage and her family's cornfield. As she went, she said a silent apology to both the Vines and the Grahams. She had been living on their food for the past two weeks, and though she might comfort herself with the notion that the food really belonged to

Lady Andrews, there was not enough to begin with. Soon there would be even less, for more than thirty feet of the Crithe had already dried up. Aislinn might call herself desperate, but the fact remained that she was a thief.

The door of the cottage stood ajar, a black rectangle against the deeper grey stone. Aislinn considered it for a long moment, then moved forward, slipping the knife from its sheath at her waist. She had stolen the knife from Fallon's own equipment shed six days before, and it had allowed her to gut two rabbits and a fox . . . almost certainly the same fox that had been stealing chickens from the Wilings in the next acreage. All of the animals she caught had been tough and water-starved, but Aislinn was getting better and better at hunting, and that was the first thing she meant to tell her parents. No one on the acreage had had meat for months.

Look, she would tell them, *we can stay here, living on the edge of starvation, or we can go elsewhere. Anywhere. All the way to New London, or even New Dover. I can get us meat. Not much, maybe, but more of a mouthful than we were getting here.*

But when she stepped through the doorway, she knew immediately that they were gone. No snoring from her father or her brother Jensen, no embers glowing in the grate, and most of all, none of that particular sense of habitation that the cottage always gave off, an inevitable residue of the nine people living there.

After another quick look up and down the footpath, Aislinn pulled a candle from her pocket. This, too, she had liberated from Fallon's shed, along with a flint and two empty canteens. Out in the open Almont, water was even harder to find than food, but Aislinn, while tracking the fox, had come upon a tiny pond hidden under thatches of blackberry brambles, their thorns so vicious that no one in his right mind would even touch the berries. After a day's work and scratches innumerable, her dress torn to ribbons, Aislinn had cleared a path to the pond. It was nearly dry, but there had been enough to fill her two canteens, and now they were hidden back in her tiny camp, along with the rest of the cooked meat. She had not wanted to bring even a single canteen with her on this expedition, for the latches were shifty, not to be trusted. Losing the water would be bad; giving herself away would be worse.

When she struck the match, she saw them: all eight of them, lined up against the far wall. Their throats had been cut, but that was not even the worst of it; the worst had been visited upon Mum and Lita and Eve and Bailey. Bailey's scrawny thighs were sticky with blood. Bailey, who was only eleven years old.

For me, Aislinn thought sickly, watching the way the pooled blood on the floor seemed to change and move in the candlelight. *Because they couldn't find me.* Lady Andrews's face popped into her mind, and Aislinn amended her thought.

Because she *couldn't.*

Suddenly she realized what she was doing: standing here in front of eight corpses, somehow deluding herself that this wasn't a trap. There was no smell, not a whiff of decay; the bodies had been fixed and preserved, then posed on the wall for Aislinn to see. They had simply been waiting, waiting for Aislinn to do something stupid like come back. She whirled to look behind her, already knowing that it was too late, that they were standing there, the group of bailiffs, and all of them ready—

But it was not the bailiffs. It was only Liam Graham. He was not even looking at Aislinn, but at the bodies, his face all eyes and his jaw hanging to his chest. He was seventeen, two years older than Aislinn . . . but in that moment he seemed only a few years old.

"Liam," she whispered, and he jerked.

"You're not a ghost," he said.

"No."

"Lady Andrews told us they caught you, took you to the manse.

But I knew they were lying." With some effort, Liam pulled his eyes from the corpses and turned back to Aislinn. "If they'd caught you, they would have hung you out for everyone to see."

"They would have," she agreed absently, for now she had noticed the pale, rounded discs that sat between the lips of each member of her family. Holy wafer. Father Moran had been here, had seen it all, and laid them to rest afterward.

"I saw your light," Liam went on. "I came to see if it was you."

"I'm going to put the candle out now. I should never have lit it in the first place."

Liam glanced toward the bodies on the wall, then swallowed and nodded. Aislinn doused the candle, but she could still see them in the dark, a tableau of corpses lined against the blue flare in her vision.

"What of the other families?" she asked.

"They're fine. 'Twas only yours got hit. I suppose she doesn't dare kill off the entire workforce."

Aislinn raised her eyebrows. She had always considered Liam Graham to be a bit thick, and when they were young, he had been something of a bully as well. But the bitterness in his voice made her pause. Aislinn's mother and father had never been angry—or at least had never been able to show it—and so she had assumed that she was the only one. Were there others?

"Little Willie Pearce is dead, though," Liam muttered.

"Dead? How?"

"His leg. Him being so young and all, his family went to Lady Andrews, asking her to hire a proper surgeon from the city. But she wouldn't; wouldn't even give them her horse doctor for a day. So they had to take the leg off themselves. We all heard it. It was—" Liam broke off, then said simply, "Willie bled to death."

Aislinn's throat closed. Little Willie Pearce, who used to toddle around the acreage pulling a tiny cart full of carrots. The violence

visited upon her family was terrible, but it had at least been delib-
erate, done with a twisted sense of purpose. Willie's death seemed
almost worse in that moment, because it was so pointless, so easily
avoided.

"What will you do now?" Liam asked.

Against her will, Aislinn turned back toward the wall, the unseen tableau that waited there. She could go anywhere, yes, but
where could she really go, that she would not see the eight of them,
heads crooked and legs spread, wafer drying forever in each
mouth?

"I don't know," she said. "I–"

"Shhh," Liam said suddenly. "Listen."

For a few seconds there was nothing but the unending buzz of
locusts in the surrounding fields, and then they both heard it: the
crackle of stealthy footsteps coming through dry grass, more than
one pair.

The light, Aislinn realized, cursing herself. *They* were *waiting
for me, and they saw the light.*

Liam took her arm, pulling her toward the back of the house.
Toward the corpses.

"The window's open," he whispered. "Can you feel the draft?"

Aislinn could. Lady Andrews's bailiffs had not even bothered
to close the windows before they did their work. Aislinn wondered whether the screaming of her family had been very bad as
well, whether the Vines and the rest of their neighbors had heard
it all.

"Here," Liam said, and offered her a hand, meaning to boost
her up.

If they find him here with me, they will kill him, Aislinn
thought, and grabbed his arm.

"When you get to the ground," she murmured, "crawl after me,
out toward your wheat patch."

"Where will you go?" he asked.

I don't know, Aislinn meant to reply, and then Lady Andrews's face popped suddenly into her mind: high cheekbones, cold eyes, cruel mouth.

Something undone.

"Nowhere," she replied. "I'm staying right here."

"You'll need water. Food."

"I have both. Help me up."

He pushed her up and out, and Aislinn wriggled through the window, dropping as soundlessly as she could to the ground. The bailiffs were coming for the front door; now Aislinn could hear them, muttered voices and the low clinking of metal. Lady Andrews had claimed to already have her in the manse, Aislinn remembered. They would have to keep this little party quiet. Liam boosted himself out the window, and she caught his hands, helping him to the ground. But as they turned, a dark figure emerged around the corner of house.

Aislinn pressed herself back against the wall, pulling Liam with her. The stone of the cottage was dark enough that the bailiff might not spot them. He ambled along, some five feet from the wall, not hurrying, and Aislinn decided that they had told him to watch the back. She should be afraid, she realized, and yet strangely, she was not. The sight of her family in the cottage had done that much for her, shown her the worst that could happen. She pulled Fallon's knife from its place in her sleeve and remained as still as stone, trying not to breathe.

When the man came past, Aislinn reached out and clapped her hand to his mouth. He uttered a muffled sound of astonishment—"Hawp!"—but that was all, for Liam was there as well, clapping his larger hand atop Aislinn's, adding his leverage to hers as she bore the bailiff to the ground. He struggled, but he was nowhere near Liam's size, and Liam held him down as Aislinn shoved her knife into his belly. A dim, distant part of her was astonished at this turn of events, all of it—that she should do these things, that Liam should help her—but the astonishment did not penetrate into her muscles, which performed the actions of killing and silencing as though they were the most natural things in the world. The bailiff's shudders ceased, and Aislinn jerked her knife from him, leaving him to bleed in the grass.

"Come on," she whispered. "Into the wheat."

They went on their bellies. Dry grass and rocks scratched Aislinn through her thin shirt. Light flared behind her just as she and Liam slipped into the last uncut patch of winter wheat. Belatedly, it occurred to Aislinn that the men in the cottage were almost certainly the ones who had come for her family, who had raped her mother and sisters. She considered going back, but a cold voice spoke up in her mind.

Today you can only get yourself killed.

She and Liam huddled in the cover of the wheat, watching the silhouettes of men move back and forth against the windows of the cottage. They had torches, and the light shone out brightly, illuminating the strawberry patch and the cornfield beyond. Voices rose; they were arguing with each other. One shadow exited the building, then another, and they finally congregated at the back of the cottage, staring down at the dead body of their companion.

"The Blue Horizon came again while you were gone," Liam murmured. "Talking of the True Queen."

Aislinn rolled her eyes.

"They said that the True Queen will end such things, give justice to all of us, to your family, to Willie Pearce. They brought a little food, and blankets for winter. They were kind. But they don't understand how it is out here. They can't."

Aislinn turned to him, surprised, but his eyes were fixed not on her but on the cottage. Liam's mother was dead, Aislinn knew; she had died bringing him into the world. He was his father's only son.

He has little to lose, Aislinn realized, and the thought was not sympathetic but calculating. *He has little . . . and now I have nothing.*

Without thinking, she turned toward the eastern horizon, where the bulky outline of Lady Andrews's castle reared over the fields, blocking the starlight.

"Are you brave, Liam?" she asked.

"Brave? How would I know?" he replied frankly.

"By finding out. Follow me."

CHAPTER 10

BLAMING THE DEALER

Strange, how often a turn in the wrong direction eventually leads us right. In a universe as perverse as ours, only a fool would believe that he charts his own course.

—GREIVE THE MADMAN

When Christian emerged from the culvert outside Mrs. Evans's stable, he was pleased to see Crofter on the door again. But as Christian approached, Crofter held up his hand.

"You can't come in, lad."

"Why not?"

"It's not a good day."

Christian stretched to peer around Crofter's shoulder. Some sort of tumult was going on in the stable; he could hear a woman's voice raised in anger.

"Is Maura . . . engaged?"

"She's not fucking, no," Crofter replied, and despite the roughness of the word, Christian sensed a degree of care being taken. He tried to duck beneath Crofter's arm, found himself pushed back.

"Don't go in there, lad. It's a mess."

This time Christian put all his weight behind it, lowering his head and driving Crofter out of the way. The big enforcer fell backward, crashing into a low table that rested beside the doorway, and Christian darted toward the source of the noise, a clear stream of cursing and threats that could only be coming from Mrs. Evans. Compared to her competitors, she was a young woman, only forty or so, but she stood nearly six feet tall, and all Whore's Alley trembled at the thought of incurring her wrath.

"I don't care about fucking misuse! What about the damage to my merchandise, you bastard! Where is my compensation?"

"She took too much," the man's voice replied, utterly cool, in a broad, flat accent that made Christian stiffen. "Almost twice the recommended dosage."

"How was she supposed to know about dosage? Little twit couldn't read her own name, let alone the label on a vial of poppy!"

Christian pushed through the crowd of onlookers that had gathered in the common room, shoving several girls out of the way. The room was lit with torches, and their bright light showed everything in horribly stark relief.

A girl lay on one of the sofas, her eyes open but unseeing, limbs flung out every which way. For a terrible moment, Christian thought it was Maura, but it wasn't; this girl had hair the color of honey, not the bright white-gold of Maura's locks. The long strands were matted with whitish matter streaked with brown: vomit. Christian didn't know the dead girl, but she too showed some signs of rough handling: bruises in the shape of fingers on her throat, and a cut on her cheek. One of her outflung arms still sported a syringe.

Above the body, Mrs. Evans and Arliss stood nearly toe-to-toe. One was backed by enforcers, the other by bodyguards, but their respective muscle seemed to shrink before the two of them . . . two gods at war, except that instead of straddling the world, these two stood astride the Creche.

"The girl's ability to read, or not, is not my problem," Arliss stated blandly. "She asked me for poppy, and I sold it to her. From the look of her, she needed it."

Mrs. Evans's eyes narrowed. "Are you questioning my management of my own product?"

Arliss looked at her with distaste. "I'm saying that this tragedy could perhaps have been averted. Regardless, I am not responsible for misuse of my poppy. Your 'product,' as you put it, damaged herself."

Mrs. Evans turned nearly purple but did not speak; for the moment, at least, she had no response. Christian, who had been looking around the room for Maura, spotted little Gwyn standing at the edge of the crowd, her wide eyes fixed on the corpse. He waved a hand to get her attention, then beckoned her over.

"Lazarus!" she whispered, smiling happily. Christian guided her away, a bit down the hallway, noting almost absently the sharp angles of her elbow beneath his hand. As the topside drought progressed, the price of food was climbing sharply, and Alley girls were fed poorly to begin with. Gwyn seemed nothing but bones.

"Where's Maura?"

"Gone."

"What?" Christian asked blankly.

"She's gone. Mrs. Evans says for good."

"Gone where?" he demanded, feeling something black uncoil inside him.

"No one knows."

Christian restrained an urge to shake the girl. She was only a child, after all . . . a crib child, just as Maura had once been, so he patted her shoulder and thanked her. But Gwyn seemed to sense his anger, for she tugged at his sleeve and whispered, "Bella told me her special client took her away to live in a big, pretty castle. Like a fairy tale."

Christian straightened. Rage was coming, only simmering now, but not for long. Bella's tale was all very well for Gwyn, but Christian didn't believe in fairy-tale endings, especially not when the prince liked to beat the maid bloody. Beneath his anger lay hurt; how could Maura have left so abruptly, without even leaving him word?

"Lazarus?" Gwyn asked anxiously. "Are you angry with me?"

He looked down at her and felt his rage melt away. Gwyn would spend all her days down here, living on her back. For a moment Christian wished he could help her too, just as he had always longed to help Maura, take the child topside and find her a better life. But what was the point in saving one child if he could not save them all?

"I'm not angry with you," he told Gwyn, patting her shoulder. "No one should ever be angry with you."

The girl smiled brightly, but Christian didn't notice, for he had already moved onward in his head. The titled lord he had finished on the third level had given him some information, but not enough. Christian had made his life by violence, but he did not have the cruelty to be a good torturer, and in the end he had been able to do little more than threaten. Offering to spare the man's life had been more effective. The clown tattoo, Latimer had said, was a sign, almost a password, among a club of noble nonces who operated throughout New London. But Latimer was not Maura's special client; he liked adolescent boys. The man relayed this information matter-of-factly, without a hint of shame, and Christian had suddenly understood the great danger of this so-called club: it gave the nonces normalcy. Latimer saw nothing wrong in his behavior; he was only worried that others would find out. Once the man had told all he knew, Christian had killed him without hesitation.

He turned back to the common room, where Mrs. Evans and

Arliss were still battling it out. Maura's client was a noble, had to be. But there were hundreds of nobles in the Tearling; even Christian knew that. In a better world, there would be a prince indeed, some man on a white horse to find Maura and take her away from all this. But Christian was the closest thing Maura had to a hero, and all he had to work with was the tattoo.

"You'll never deal in the Alley again," Mrs. Evans spat. "When I'm done with you, you won't be able to move so much as a single ounce."

"You may be right," Arliss replied wearily. "But we're done here."

He signaled his two bodyguards. Numbly, Christian observed that the bodyguards wore heavy leather belts beneath their cloaks, that each belt seemed to be nothing but weapons: knives and swords and other handles that were difficult to identify. Theirs was a world of weapons, and Christian had never been meant for such things. And now, as Arliss turned to leave, Christian found himself looking speculatively at the dealer . . . not a cold speculation, but one fueled by rage. *Her special client took her away*, Gwyn had said, but that wasn't really true, was it? *Morphia* had taken Maura away. Morphia had made her so eager to get topside, and when the fairy-tale prince had blacked her eye and swollen her jaw, morphia had soothed her injuries, made her willing to go back again. And now the man who dealt the morphia stood right in front of Christian, less than ten feet away. Arliss's gaze met his, and in the second before the older man's eyes widened in alarm, Christian saw something terrible: Arliss was truly sorry for the damage he had done, for the dead girl behind him.

"That won't save you," Christian whispered. "Not from me."

Arliss drew breath to shout, but it was too late; Christian had already moved, lightning-quick, and grabbed a handle from the belt of the nearest bodyguard. The weapon, whatever it was, did not come easily; Christian gave a mighty yank and heard the rip of leather stitching, and then it was in his hand, unrestrained. He wondered if fighting dogs felt this way, when they finally slipped a muzzle and sank a mouthful of dripping fangs into the handler's leg.

Something I can wield.

He felt the bodyguards coming for him and ducked away, bending and diving around them to come up on the far side with a clear shot at their backs. He went in low, swinging with all his force at the blue-clad man in the center, and as the head of the weapon whickered past, Christian saw that it was not a knife, as he'd thought, or even a hand axe, but a strange clublike thing, its round head covered with metal spikes that tore through Arliss's side.

Arliss screamed, a deafening sound in the small room, and the bodyguards came for Christian. Ducking beneath the first man's swing, he buried his new club in the man's belly, where it lodged with a splintering crack of ribs. The man dropped without a sound.

The second bodyguard paused now, and Christian knew that the man had recognized him. Arliss lay on the floor, badly wounded, his right hip a flayed mass of raw tissue. Such wounds usually incentivized Christian, sent him in for the kill ... but now he halted, astonished to find that sometime in the last few seconds, the beast inside him had vanished, simply tucked tail and retreated to its dark den. Arliss was powerful, yes, but he was only a cog in a much larger machine, and as Arliss had said himself, only a fool blamed the dealer. What Christian really wanted was the life of the one who had built this place. The one who allowed it.

"Take him," he told the remaining bodyguard. "Take him topside and find a doctor."

His words only seemed to alarm the bodyguard further, for the man stared at Christian with deep suspicion, adjusting his grip on his sword.

"I mean it. Take him out of here." Christian lowered the dripping red club, feeling suddenly exhausted. "I have no more quarrel with him. Maybe I never did."

Still holding his sword, the bodyguard reached down to grasp Arliss's arm, hauling him to his feet.

"Can't walk," Arliss groaned, and the bodyguard hesitated, looking from his master to Christian; he could not carry Arliss and hold a sword at the same time. Recognizing the man's dilemma, Christian carefully placed the club on the ground and backed slowly away.

"This is a mistake, boy!"

The words were a hiss in his ear: Mrs. Evans, who had made her way around the melee to stand at his side.

"Better to finish him off now. You're signing your own death warrant if you let him go."

She clutched his shoulder, purple-painted nails gripping like claws. Mrs. Evans had a grudge to settle, and she was a good trafficker; like a good blacksmith or stonecutter, she would use the best tool that lay to hand.

"She's right, lad," Crofter told him. Crofter's lip was bleeding from where Christian had knocked him down, but he did not seem angry, only sad. Christian wondered how many girls' corpses Crofter had hauled to the sluice gates that fed the Caddell.

"You shouldn't allow him to live," Crofter rumbled. "He won't forget it."

Maybe I shouldn't be allowed to live, Christian nearly replied, but he did not. Such a statement would be lost on Crofter, on Mrs. Evans, both of them so steeped in the Creche's culture of basic survival that they would not understand his meaning, not even if he explained it to them, step by step.

The bodyguard hoisted Arliss's slight frame over one shoulder. This operation was completed in silence, for Arliss had passed out. Crofter was right; the dealer would not forget this, not even if he healed, and one day Christian would be walking down a tunnel and not hear the scrape of boot on stone, nor sense the blade coming until it slipped between his ribs. He watched the bodyguard disappear through the doorway, Arliss's limp form dangling over his shoulder, leaving a trail of blood behind. The club still lay on the floor, dripping red from its spikes, and at the sight of it, Christian felt perversely elated. This was not the ring, but the real world. He had made a choice, perhaps the first of his life.

"Go, boy," Mrs. Evans muttered, disappointed. "Run and hide, down in the Deep Patch. You'd be a fool to linger here."

She was right, but Christian did not go. He dug in his pockets and pulled out his only coin, a five-pound silver. Holding it up, he saw Mrs. Evans's eyes flash, lit with that sparkle that never came but from the sight of money.

"Where is Maura?"

"I don't know."

"What *do* you know?"

Mrs. Evans's eyes narrowed, and Christian saw the quick calculation as she debated her next move. After another moment, she muttered, "I don't know where she is, truth. Arlen Thorne brokered the deal, four days ago, paid me good gold. He didn't take any of Maura's things, but he said we wouldn't be seeing her again."

Christian nodded, then handed her the silver, which vanished in a quick, practiced movement from hand to pocket. Almost without thinking, Christian retrieved the spiked club from the floor. He didn't know what good it would do—he sensed there was an art to wielding it, one that eluded him—but all the same, he liked the feel of the weapon in his hand.

"Go, boy," said Mrs. Evans. The urgency in her voice told Christian that she was expecting someone important soon: a churchman, perhaps, or even a royal. She was anxious to have the gruesome scene cleared away. Christian took a last look at the dead girl, then ducked through the doorway and left the stable.

Mrs. Evans was right; he should disappear into the Deep Patch, the lowest levels, and hide there while Arliss's people raged for him across the Upper Creche. That was the way to survive, yes, but Christian had never cared less about survival. He saw Maura as she had lain in her sickbed: her split lip, her pulped cheek. Then he blinked and saw Arlen Thorne, the scarecrow man of the Creche, smiling his nasty, knowing smile.

I am coming for you, Christian thought, striding up the tunnel with the club clutched in his hand. *You'll beg for death, believe me, and I will give it to you . . . as soon as you give me a name.*

CHAPTER 11

THE BETTER WORLD

The better world is no easy undertaking, but difficulty does not frighten us. We are not discouraged by setbacks, for setbacks are only discrete steps on the road to victory. No amount of darkness can extinguish hope.

—*The Book of the Blue Horizon,* AS PRESERVED IN THE GLYNN LIBRARY

I don't understand this," Elyssa said testily. "You want a better world, fine. Wonderful. But William Tear's better world had no weapons. Every man in the Tear carries a knife, at the very least, so how on earth are we to get rid of weapons at this late date? Confiscate them?"

Gareth smiled. It was a smile that annoyed Elyssa, because it would have belonged better on a much older man. Whenever she sat at Gareth's bedside, she felt very young. He was only twenty-three, if he was to be believed, but there was all the difference in the world between mental and physical age. It hadn't been so bad when he was still laid up on his back, but now that his ribs were healing, he was able to sit up while they conversed. For Elyssa, it was like being in Lady Glynn's schoolroom all over again.

"Confiscation of weapons wouldn't work," Gareth agreed. "But force isn't the goal. The aim is to create a society where weapons would become superfluous. No one has to force a man to discard something he doesn't need."

Elyssa tried to picture such a society, and failed. Steel was wound into the very fabric of the Tearling. Rights in the Almont were essentially held at the point of a sword, and even in New London, where simple laws were at least nominally enforced by city constables and the army, no man dared to travel without a blade. And yet Lady Glynn, too, had talked this way ... as though logic would have to win out someday, as though reason had ever been any part of why men carried weapons.

"What about robbery?" she asked. "Even a utopian society wouldn't wipe out humanity's tendency to covet. Surely people have the right to defend their own possessions from thieves."

Gareth shrugged. "Thievery only thrives because it's tolerated. In William Tear's town, if someone stole something, he would never be able to keep it. There are no secrets in a connected society. Everyone would know, and someone would turn him in. There was no thievery ... not in the beginning, at least."

"How do you know so much about William Tear's town?" Elyssa demanded. It was another sore point with her: Gareth's impossible familiarity with the fledgling settlement of the Landing period. Even Lady Glynn, who had admired William Tear enormously, hadn't had anywhere near as much detail. But then the Blue Horizon were fabulous propagandists; look how they had co-opted the True Queen prophecy, wrapped it so tightly around Elyssa that the city was singing ballads about her now. But all the same, Elyssa didn't think that Gareth was lying about the past. He seemed to understand Tear's world as one who had lived there.

"Not everything from the Landing period was lost," Gareth replied. "There were records kept."

"What records? I never heard of any, and Lady Glynn said—"

"Records don't have to be written down. And as clever a woman as Carlin Glynn was, she didn't know everything."

Elyssa frowned. Of course Lady Glynn hadn't known *everything*, she knew that . . . yet her heart disputed it.

"Was Lady Glynn one of you?" she demanded. "Blue Horizon?"

"Yes."

Elyssa nodded. Somewhere deep inside herself, she had known. Lady Glynn's long diatribes on the vast gap between rich and poor; her disgust with the Queen's tolerance of the traffic in the Creche; her deep and enduring hatred of Welwyn Culp . . . but most of all, the hope in Lady Glynn's voice, the way she had been able to make the solutions to all of the kingdom's problems seem very near, perhaps even within reach, if they could only put aside all their meaningless conflicts, their greed, their hatred—

We take care of each other, Elyssa thought now. That was all Lady Glynn had really been saying to her, every day, and Elyssa had been comforted by the vision Lady Glynn presented, bewitched by the better world. How could she stand in judgment on the Blue Horizon, when Lady Glynn had believed as hard as they did, when they wanted the same things for the Tearling that Elyssa wanted herself?

"Why did she come here?" she asked Gareth. "Why come and work for the Crown, for my mother?"

"Because we needed you to be different. Lady Glynn had been friends with Arla since childhood; it was a unique opportunity to plant one of our own at court."

"Have you planted others?"

Gareth smiled but said nothing.

"Is Lady Glynn dead?"

"We don't know, and believe me, we have looked. If she's alive, she's not to be found."

Elyssa drew a deep breath. Once upon a time, Lady Glynn's eye of disapproval had been so fierce that Elyssa had been reluctant to hand in a substandard historical analysis. Now she had spent the week imagining her tutor's reaction, wondering what Lady Glynn would think when she heard that Elyssa Anne Raleigh, noted atheist and sympathizer with the poor, had embraced the Church and denounced the Blue Horizon. Elyssa shrank from the very idea, and the child in her felt a sneaking relief at Gareth's words, that Lady Glynn was indeed gone, that she would never have to stand before her old tutor and account for her deeds.

Gareth took a sip of the water by his bedside. Elyssa winced, but then reminded herself that Coryn himself had already tasted the water; he checked it every time the glass was refilled. Elyssa did not have a single guard in this room, not even Barty, who had made a veiled threat to tell her mother when she ordered him to stay outside. But Barty wouldn't tell her mother. None of them would. Her Guard knew about the speech she was expected to give tonight in the Arvath, and they were furious at her mother's tactics. Barty in particular had been almost livid on Elyssa's behalf. Close guards could be a misery . . . but they could also be kind. Tears gathered in Elyssa's eyes, and she could not will them away. She looked down at the coverlet, rubbing at her eyes as though to rid herself of a speck of dust.

"What is it?" Gareth asked.

"Nothing."

"Tears of a princess? It's not nothing."

"I must do something terrible tonight. Something I don't wish to do." She swallowed, then looked squarely at him, unsure why she told him these things, except that she trusted him instinctively to understand. "My mother demands that I denounce the Blue Horizon."

"Is that all?"

"All?" She stared at him, astonished. "That's everything!"

Gareth shrugged. "We've been denounced by every ruler since Matthew Raleigh. We will surely survive."

"That's not the point!" Elyssa protested. "How will I look myself in the mirror tomorrow?"

"I assume the leverage over you is great."

Elyssa nodded, wiping more tears away. "My mother, she—"

"No need to tell me. I know Queen Arla well."

"You do?"

"Well, not personally, but as they say in the Almont, you needn't know a pig to know it will grunt. Your mother is a ruthless creature."

"She says she'll take it from me," Elyssa whispered. "Take my heirship and put Thomas on the throne. Thomas! He—"

"Oh, you don't need to tell me about your brother either. Your mother must be desperate indeed."

Elyssa smiled through her tears. Gareth grinned back, then he began to cough. Elyssa handed him the glass of water, and he took another sip. The cough pained him, Elyssa could tell, probably because of his ribs. His bruises had faded to an ugly yellow. His fingers would never be pretty, not now, but they had first scabbed over and then begun to heal beneath their bandages. The burn wounds on his arms had crusted. His fractured ribs would take longer, but not forever. Soon Beale would release him, and after that, Elyssa did not deceive herself that she would see him again. If he had truly come to the Keep of his own free will, then he would not return . . . and even if not, Elyssa didn't think her mother's people would capture him a second time. She had been involved with several young men in the Keep over the years—two servants and a groom—and none of them had cut her deep. But the thought of Gareth's departure made her feel hollow and hopeless.

There was a knock on the door, and Beale poked his head in.

Elyssa sensed that the senior medic had only been circling, waiting for an opportunity to kick her out. Barty, too, peered around the doorway, his expression similarly disapproving.

"My patient is tired, Highness," Beale told her, sweeping into the room. "He must rest."

"And you need to get ready for the party, Highness," Barty chimed in. "Your mother sent word to remind you that her carriage will leave promptly at seven. She expects you on time."

"Of course she does!" Elyssa snarled. "When one means to sell out, one can't be late."

A hand clasped hers: Gareth's. She looked sharply down at him—if Barty saw the touch, he would be outraged—but Gareth was not looking at the men in the doorway, only at Elyssa. His hand seemed to burn her.

"Have courage," he told her. "They call you the True Queen for a reason. I believe in you."

Elyssa gaped at him, but a moment later he had let go of her hand and turned over in the bed, as though he meant to go to sleep. Mercifully, Barty had missed everything. Elyssa walked toward the doorway, feeling very little, as though her body had gone numb . . . all except her hand, which burned with cold fire.

Have courage.

It sounded so good in theory. But in reality, it would mean leaving her kingdom to the mercy of Thomas.

Do you really believe your mother would do that?

Elyssa didn't know. Unlike her brother, she was not a gambler. Given certain outcomes, she could make a decision and feel confident. But this . . . her mother seemed ready to cast the kingdom into the wind. As they passed Thomas's chambers, Elyssa glared at the slightly open door, then jerked to a halt as a low squealing echoed from within.

"Don't! Please don't!"

Elyssa had a moment to reflect that her brother was now so brazen that he didn't even bother to close the door for his predations, but that cool assessment was swept away as she slammed the door aside.

Thomas had the girl pinned to the bed. She was young, ridiculously so; Elyssa would have guessed her age at no more than fifteen. She had long brown hair, so light that it was almost red. She was not crying, not yet, but her eyes were full of unshed tears, and at the sight of their sparkle, Elyssa forgot about Gareth, the Arvath, Lady Glynn, all of it. Darting forward, she grabbed her brother, hauled him from the bed, and flung him across the room. Thomas bounced off the wall with a satisfying thud, then landed on the floor, and Elyssa was on him in the next moment, pummeling him with both fists.

"Leave off!" Thomas shouted, covering his face. "Leave off, you bitch!"

But Elyssa did not. Dimly, she was aware of her Guard, ranging themselves around the room, keeping a respectful distance. They would not interfere, for they absolutely loathed Thomas. "Tommy the Spare," they called him, when they were not calling him something worse. Elyssa wished this were the first time she had come upon her brother this way, but it was not. She gave him a final square punch in the face, then hauled herself up, panting, her knuckles red with his blood. Dyer and Kibb were helping the girl up from the bed, and Elyssa observed that her dress was ripped, her mouth swollen. She turned back to Thomas, who was pulling himself from the floor now, his eyes narrowed in rage.

"At it again, are we?" Elyssa demanded. "Didn't Mother threaten to put you in prison the last time?"

The Guard chuckled, and Thomas turned red. Once upon a time, that helpless flush on her brother's face had made Elyssa feel sorry for him, for if her mother was hard on Elyssa, she was merciless with Thomas, parading his failures for all to see. He did not even have a full guard, for the Queen had decreed that a spare did not need guards. Thomas's life was full of such small cuts, but by now Elyssa could not help sharing her mother's contempt. The rapes, the endless gambling debts, Thomas's predatory manner with the Keep servants . . . her brother was a mess that required constant cleaning up.

"Give her back," Thomas told Kibb, who was supporting the girl in his arms. "She belongs to me."

"Fuck off, you little spare," Elston growled; he was on guard at the door. "In my village, you would have been gelded long ago."

Thomas colored further, then turned back to Elyssa. His nose was bleeding freely, but there was a triumphant gleam in his eye that she did not like at all.

"Mother said that I should go ahead and pick one woman," he announced. "She said that if it would keep me out of trouble, it was worth it to her. So she gave me the money. I bought the girl yesterday, and she belongs to me. I can do whatever I want with her."

Elyssa felt her stomach lurch. She had a momentary hope that Thomas was lying, but hope died quick. Thomas was a terrible liar, and this was exactly what her mother *would* do, for Queen Arla was a pragmatist, first and foremost. She could not stop her son's depredations, no, but nor could she imprison or hang him. So she would make sure that the rape was kept quiet, troubling no one important, causing no scandal. Elyssa wondered what Lady Glynn would say about this turn of events.

"Give her back!" Thomas told Kibb, more forcefully this time.

After a questioning look at Elyssa, Kibb released the girl. Thomas beckoned her, but the girl retreated, scurrying away from him, around the bed.

"Kibb, you stay right here," Elyssa told him. "Someone will

bring you dinner. Thomas, the girl will have a guard at all times until I have discussed this with the Queen."

"You can't do that!" Thomas snarled.

"You think not?" Elyssa moved forward again, and had the pleasure of watching Thomas back up against the wall. "Don't test me, little brother, or the very instant I take the throne, I'll see you in a dungeon. Maybe even at the end of a rope."

Turning, she stormed out of the room and down the corridor. She had been dreading the carriage ride to the Arvath with her mother, but now it seemed like the perfect opportunity to bring up this little arrangement. Elyssa could not stand by . . . not here, in the Keep, in this kingdom that would be hers someday. She sped up, almost running now, as she emerged in the great chamber . . . and then came to a sudden halt.

The seer, Brenna, was seated at the enormous oakwood table that sat in the center of the room. She was alone but busy. She appeared to be casting bones. As Elyssa approached the broad table, Brenna's low mutters became audible.

"Six, twelve, fifteen. Crows murder, and stars fall." She threw another handful of bones across the table, stared at them for a moment, then murmured, "Children lost and children gained. Blood spilled on silk."

Behind Elyssa, one of the guards muttered in disgust.

"The hidden child. The lost child. Flames in a black sky. Six, twelve, fifteen. Charred bones and flesh—"

Barty cleared his throat rudely. Brenna looked up, and Elyssa noted with interest that her nearly colorless pupils were dilated, clear grey pools floating on a sea of pale blue ice.

"Surely you have a private chamber where you can do that," Barty remarked coldly.

Slowly, almost insolently, Brenna began to gather her bones.

She *did* have a private chamber; it was only three doors down from Elyssa's own rooms, a matter about which Barty had complained to Captain Givens more than once. But Givens, who was even less superstitious than Barty, had dismissed his concerns . . . or at least ignored them. Givens knew which way the wind was blowing. The Queen had raised the seer to the level of a high councilor; now, even in a time of drought, she spent more time alone with Brenna than she did with her treasurer or her minister of agriculture. As Brenna stuffed a handful of bones into a small pouch tied to her belt, Elyssa noted, disturbed, that the pouch was the exact color of blood.

"Witchery," someone muttered behind Elyssa. Elston, it had to be; she always knew him by the height of his voice. Elston was no Christian, but he had been raised in the country, and he evinced a deep-rooted distrust of anything that smacked of magic.

"Fuck witchery, it's disgusting," Dyer replied. "Don't we have to eat on that table?"

But the resulting chuckles quickly died, for Brenna had suddenly frozen in place, staring down at the scatter of tiny bones still on the table, seeming to eat them with her gaze. She touched one small bone, then a second, and after a moment she looked up, straight into Elyssa's eyes.

"Wishing makes you weak, Highness. Only in action is there strength."

"Here, now!" Barty barked. "How dare you speak to the Princess? Clear up your filth and get gone!"

Brenna smiled . . . a strange smile, smug yet somehow pitying at the same time. She rose from the table but continued to talk directly to Elyssa, ignoring Barty and the rest of them, as though they were not even in the room.

"You wish for so many things, Highness. I see them all. You may have them, but only if you are brave enough to act."

Elyssa stared at her, alarmed, for a bizarre, paranoid certainty had suddenly taken hold of her: Brenna knew about Gareth. She knew that Elyssa thought of him almost all the time. She knew that Elyssa had begun to visit Gareth in the night, that she sometimes sat there for hours, simply watching him sleep. She knew that Elyssa found herself pitiable, even loathsome, in her own growing obsession.

"I can help you, Highness," Brenna told her, gathering the last of her bones into the bag. "Believe me, I specialize in dreams."

"Get out of here, witch!" Barty snarled. "And take your carnival tricks with you!"

Brenna gave Elyssa another odd, sympathetic smile, then moved toward the hallway.

"I apologize, Highness," Barty said stiffly. "I will lodge a complaint with the Queen."

But Elyssa was still staring at Brenna's departing back. Her mother was forgotten; even her disgust over Thomas and his so-called purchase seemed to fade in that moment, for something dark had uncoiled in her mind. She saw the future, not bright and shining but dim and shifting, as though glimpsed through smoke: the True Queen, Elyssa, with the crown on her head and her mother gone, all restraint removed, nothing to hold her back, to keep her from ordering the world just as she wished it. . . .

I specialize in dreams. Have the courage to act.

"Highness?"

"It's time for me to get dressed." Her own voice sounded strange.

"Should we get you a tray, Highness? For dinner?" Carroll asked. He was the sweetest of her guards, and certainly the only one who would think of dinner on a night like this. Digging up a tired smile, Elyssa shook her head, then turned to Barty.

"Barty, do me a favor and send someone else to help Kibb look after that poor child. She should not be left alone with my brother, not for one instant."

Elyssa retreated to her chamber, giving a cursory glance to the blue silk dress that had been laid out on the bed. Niya should be here, to help her dress . . . but no, Niya was gone, on her monthly holiday.

I should give her more holidays, Elyssa thought blankly, almost disconnectedly. *One weekend a month is not enough.* And yet she wished that Niya were not gone now, for she could have used the maid's advice. Niya was always helpful, always practical, a distant echo of Lady Glynn.

If she's alive, she's not to be found.

Reluctantly, Elyssa found herself accepting the truth: her mother had murdered Lady Glynn. She would not have done it herself, no; most likely the order had gone to Givens, who was both discreet and competent. But whoever had done the deed, Lady Glynn was surely dead, her bones buried in the deepest basements of the Keep, or out in the small forest that made up the Queen's hawking preserve. Elyssa would never have Lady Glynn's eye of judgment upon her again, but in that moment, she would have braved it, if only to have her tutor's advice once more. She sat down in front of her vanity glass, staring at her own reflection. It pleased her, as it always did; fine blonde hair, bright green eyes, high cheekbones, a pointed chin. She looked like what she was: a girl in the very prime of her youth.

Then why do I feel so wretched?

That question answered itself. She felt sick at her own lack of control. She might argue with her mother, yes, and she might even make some headway. But Thomas's purchase was only one girl. Elyssa did not have the power to help all women; she could not even choose her own life. Tonight her mother would force her to repudiate Gareth and his better world. Elyssa had never been in love before, and now she understood why so many people referred to it as a sickness. She felt as though she had a fever.

Wishing makes you weak.

She got up and went to the window. Below, the Keep Lawn stretched out toward the Great Boulevard, the vast stretch of rooftops descending toward the Caddell. The city was hazy, twinkling in the early dusk. Across the distance, a bell began to ring: the Arvath, tolling out six o'clock.

I love this kingdom, Elyssa thought, but even love was tempered, strengthened by responsibility. There was no room for the personal; obligation crowded all the rest. The twilight deepened, darkening the room until it was only a chamber of shadows, barely seen, and now Elyssa realized that she had only been waiting for the darkness, for the strange sort of permission that came when light slipped away. She reached out to the wall beside the window, where a tiny catch protruded, three stones over and seven stones up, invisible to the naked eye. Elyssa put her finger on this catch, lightly, almost testing it with her finger.

She had been using the tunnels since she was six years old, mostly to hide: from her mother's wrath, from her nursemaid, even from Thomas when he used to torment her. The tunnels beehived the Queen's Wing and traveled downward into the Keep proper . . . even farther than that, though Elyssa had never dared to venture beyond the moat. When her mother sent her to bed without supper, Elyssa would sneak down to the fourth floor and steal food from the kitchens. When she wanted to go somewhere without the company of her Guard, she took the tunnels as well.

Even Niya used them, whenever she snuck down to the Circus to find Elyssa's syrup. The tunnel behind Elyssa's chamber gave access onto the arms room, the infirmary, and several of the family rooms, including the chamber three doors down where, even now, the white woman waited. Elyssa *knew* she was waiting, that she would sit up all night if she had to. Perhaps she did not even sleep at all.

Beware of Greeks bearing gifts.

Lady Glynn's voice again, deep inside her head. Because fate had allotted Elyssa a throne, she had to take care of her people, all of them, before she looked to herself. Desire would always be secondary. At her chest, her sapphire gave a sudden shiver, as though it were capable of feeling her chill.

Kelsea. The victory of ships.

The better world.

I specialize in dreams.

"No," Elyssa whispered, turning away from the wall and moving back to the window to stare out across her kingdom, this damnable, maddening kingdom that had once had such potential to be great. Everyone seemed content to accept the fall . . . everyone except the Blue Horizon, with their better world.

It doesn't matter that they don't know how to get there, Elyssa realized suddenly. *It doesn't even matter if we never do. The important thing is to die trying.*

"Barty!"

A moment later, Barty poked his head around the door. "Highness?"

"Saddle my horse, and all of yours."

"Highness?" Barty asked. "Your mother expects you to ride with her in the carriage."

"I know she does," Elyssa replied, tossing the blue dress aside.

"But we're not going to the Arvath. Say nothing to my mother or her people. Just saddle the horses."

"And where are we going?" Barty demanded, bewildered.

"Where I should have gone all along, Barty. To the people. To the Circus."

CHAPTER 12

ON THE PLATFORM

In examining the Blue Horizon's motives and ideals, it is perhaps easy to overlook the group's practical impact, which was hardly admirable. The Blue Horizon was one of the biggest movers of stolen goods in the Tearling, keeping any number of fencers and middlemen in business. Their armorers bought weapons in proportions almost as great as those of the Tear army, and they were not above kidnapping and ransom when the price or the information was right. Those who informed on the movement often disappeared, never to be seen again.

Seen in this light, the popular image of the Blue Horizon— that of starry-eyed idealists offering food with one hand and freedom with the other—is risible. In fact, William Tear's disciples were highly-trained terrorists, led by one of the most violent criminals in the history of the Tear. Do not be misled by the fact that he often gave his ill-gotten gains away, for he was quite happy to murder to get them....

—The Fetch: An Unpopular History, MARTIN BANNAKER

This won't do," the Fetch remarked, looking over the sheet of figures in front of him. "We need fifty, not twenty-five."

"This is the best I can do, sir," Glover replied, lifting his hands. "I have two boys out sick and one lamed in a forging accident. It will take two weeks to fill the order as it is."

The Fetch stared at the smith, unblinking, until Glover began to turn pale. Niya felt a brief pity for the man, for she knew the sting of that look. The Fetch's mask was bad, but the eyes behind were worse: dark and cold, with no pity for interruptions or unexpected events.

"Ten days," Glover amended. "And we will provide thirty."

"Fine," the Fetch replied, handing back the sheet of paper. "My associate here will collect, and don't be surprised if she comes at the darkest hour of night."

"No . . . no, sir, of course not," Glover quavered. "We will be ready at any time."

The Fetch nodded, signaling Niya. They left through the back door of the smith's shop, and emerged into the wide expanse of the Harrowgate. Dusk had fallen while they were in the smithy, and as always, darkness seemed to confer a strange license on the Gut, an invitation to open its doors. Everywhere Niya looked, she saw pickpockets and pros, shifty men with even shiftier wares to sell. Behind the cheap brick facades of the pubs rang laughter and screams, the occasional clash of steel. Above their heads, half-clad pros leaned from the second stories of brothels, hawking for customers, their breasts bouncing like ripe moons, cheerful cries echoing along the street.

"This place," the Fetch remarked, with a sour chuckle. "So much life . . . and so much waste."

Niya nodded. The Fetch often said such things, and even if she could not always understand them, they seemed right in feeling. All around them, people drew back as the Fetch passed, as they caught sight of his dreadful mask. The expressions on their faces were identical, not pure fear but a sort of terrified awe, as though the Fetch were a pagan god.

"Are you sure Glover can be trusted to deliver on time?"

"Yes," the Fetch replied, waving away her question. "He was lowballing, giving himself a cushion. He's a good businessman. Will thirty swords be enough, do you think?"

"For certain. But the casualties will be dreadful."

"Casualties always are."

The Fetch fell silent then, and Niya watched him with some curiosity. He was a dark-haired man, neither large nor small, with a handsome precision in his features. It was a kind face, trusting and trustworthy . . . or so a thirteen-year-old Niya had thought, just before she slipped her hand into his pocket. She had managed to reach the coins, but not to take them out, and now, ten years after she had mistaken the Fetch for a soft mark, she trailed him through the Gut, her hand on her knife. A drunken lout stumbled into Niya, groping, and she shoved him out of her way. He landed in the mud, cursing as they left him behind, and the altercation seemed to shake the Fetch awake, pull him back from whatever dark void he had been traveling.

"What of the Princess?"

Niya jerked as though stung, for she had just been wondering the same thing, whether Elyssa had reached the Arvath yet. Niya got only two days of holiday per month, and they belonged to the Fetch, but yesterday was the first time she had been reluctant to leave the Keep, reluctant to leave Elyssa alone. She didn't know why Elyssa had decided to go to the Holy Father's party—Elyssa had never expressed any interest in visiting the Arvath before— but Niya didn't like it, just as she didn't like the white witch who had now taken up residence in the Keep. Barty had sent Carroll to find out where the witch had come from and who she was really working for, but Carroll had come back not only empty-handed but scared to death. He would not speak of what had happened, not even to the Guard.

We must find out who the witch really is, Niya thought. *And until then, Barty had better be as vigilant as I believe him to be.*

She thought of saying as much to the Fetch, then didn't. The Fetch already knew about Brenna; he had put Lila and Martin on to the matter. The witch certainly hadn't come from Lord Tennant's acreage. Lila had already determined that much, but little else.

One of the street vendors of the Gut, braver than the rest, suddenly ran up to the Fetch. Niya grabbed her knife, but the vendor merely reached out a hand, entreating the Fetch to shake. The Fetch did so absently, and the man retreated to his stall.

"The witch continues to meet with the Queen in private," Niya said. "The guards say she seems fixated on the sapphire ... always watching it, touching it whenever she can."

"That tracks."

"Why? I thought they were only heirlooms, those jewels."

"To most people, they are. Certainly to the Raleighs."

"Then what does the witch want with them?"

"Hard to say. Those jewels belong to William Tear, even now. No one else can use them, only Tear ... Tear, and those of his blood."

"William Tear had no living descendants."

The Fetch nodded, but his eyes remained troubled. He was concealing something, Niya thought, but she didn't take offense. She was an important foot soldier in the Blue Horizon, certainly, but a foot soldier nonetheless, and the Fetch had done her a great honor by choosing to place her in the Keep. Niya had long ago accepted the fact that she didn't need to know everything, but she wondered what secret could bring that look to the Fetch's eyes. He seemed to sense her scrutiny, for he changed the subject in a clumsy manner that was not really like him.

"How's Gareth?"

"He heals quickly. Most of his bruises have faded, and the medics claim that even his ribs will be healed after another two or three weeks. His arm will continue to trouble him for a while; the fracture was severe."

"We must have been mad to let him go in there."

Niya did not reply. No one ever let Gareth do anything. He had wanted his own look at Elyssa, and so, despite all objections, he had allowed himself to be taken. Gareth was guided entirely by his own stars.

"But we must be doubly careful now," the Fetch continued. "The closer he gets to freedom, the more Arla will be looking for any excuse to keep him."

"Elyssa will protect him."

"You have more faith in the Princess than I do. She may have taken a liking to Gareth—"

"More than a liking, unless I miss my guess."

"Well, Gareth's no fool."

"Neither is Elyssa."

"You like her too much, Niya. It impairs your judgment."

"Maybe," she replied, flushing. "But until Gareth comes back, my judgment is what we have. I see goodness in Elyssa. She wants what we want."

"You want her to be good, certainly. But history is full of fools who allowed want to undermine was."

Niya accepted the rebuke in silence, though she longed to argue further. But it was not the Fetch's opinion that would matter. He was the nominal head of the Blue Horizon, and his dreadful mask was the face the world knew. But that was only smoke and mirrors, designed to cloak the true nature of things. By keeping the eye of the world on the Blue Horizon's face, they successfully camouflaged the movement's beating heart. Niya wondered what Gareth made of Elyssa. The two of them had had several private conversations now, conversations in which neither guards nor medics were present, which had scandalized the entire Keep. Elyssa sympathized with the Blue Horizon; Niya knew it already, but if Gareth pronounced Elyssa true, no one in the Blue Horizon would say otherwise. What they couldn't do with a true believer on the throne—

"Please!" a man begged to her right. "For my little ones!"

Turning, Niya saw a family of four huddled just between the doors of two pubs on Hell's Corner, begging for the scraps that publicans usually fed to stray dogs. A farm family; they had the poor country mouse air of those who find themselves lost in the big city. They were trickling in steadily from the Almont; only a few now, but as the Caddell continued to dry up and the harvest failed, more would surely come. It didn't matter that they were leaving their homes behind, for it was better to be homeless in the city than starving in the plains. And yet even scraps were becoming a luxury; most people were hoarding their refuse for another meal. As Niya watched, the publican shooed the father away from the pub door, banging it angrily shut behind him. The family huddled in miserable disappointment, and for a rogue moment Niya longed to go to them, tell them that they should not despair, that there was a better world out there, so close they could almost touch it. But what good would words do these people? Men could not eat belief.

"What is that?"

The Fetch had stopped behind her, tipping his head. Listening for a moment, Niya heard a roar of voices, muffled by the buildings on their left.

"West," she told him. "The Circus."

"Come on."

Niya followed him through the crowd, keeping her eyes on the back of his neck, which was tanned dark from his recent trip to the Almont. The Fetch went out there personally at least once every few months, even though it might slow down operations in New London. Niya didn't know why he made such a point of it; even now, after ten years under the Fetch's tutelage, she understood him little better than she had on that long-ago day when he grabbed her arm and yanked her hand from his pocket. No one knew where the Fetch had come from; he claimed to have been born a street rat, but Niya had her doubts. The Fetch sought the better world as doggedly as any of them, but he was no bright-eyed optimist like Gareth, or even a cautious optimist, like Niya herself. The Fetch did not dream freely, as the rest of them did. Rather, he seemed compelled, driven independently of his will to take on the evils of the kingdom as he found them. "Repairing the gap," the Fetch called it, and the grim tone of his voice seemed to suggest regret. Culpability.

That was nonsense, of course; the Tearling had fallen into decline centuries before the Fetch was even born. If any single person was to blame, it was Matthew Raleigh, the first king of the line, who had dismantled William Tear's system of collectivized land ownership and dispensed most of the kingdom's acres in private grants to his friends and followers, progenitors of the modern-day nobility. There was no blame anymore, except for the ubiquitous guilt that lay across the breadth of the Tearling, the vast multitude too busy scrabbling for scraps to look up and act.

He takes too much upon himself, Niya thought now, watching the set of the Fetch's shoulders, the tension of muscles in the back of his neck. She loved him, not in the silly way of men and women, but something much more important. She loved the Fetch the way she loved Gareth, Amelia, Lila, Dylan, all of them. They saw the better world, and they saw it together; hope had welded them tighter than blood. But the Fetch felt every new setback deeply, as though a boulder had landed upon him. Niya only wished that she could pull him free, take some of the weight.

At this late hour, the New London Circus should have been clearing out, for most of the food vendors usually closed down shop after dark, and street preachers ran a real danger of being beaten once drunks began to stumble from the pubs. But tonight some sort of mob had gathered in the vast open-air market, a mob of so many people that they overflowed down the side streets. Apollon Road was so crowded that the Fetch was forced to literally shoulder people aside, Niya worming her way through behind him.

"What—" she began to ask, and then the words were cut from her in a harsh gasp as the Fetch pointed, directing her gaze upward.

Elyssa was walking up the steep staircase that wound around Preacher's Seat, the tall, rickety platform that sat in the center of the Circus. The Seat was some twenty feet tall, and it overlooked the entire expanse of the marketplace. Every morning the street preachers would get together, draw straws or deal cards to decide who got to have the Seat that day; the rest of them would be relegated to stumps or chairs or tabletops.

How can Elyssa be here? Niya thought frantically. *She's supposed to be at the Arvath! Where are the guards?*

"Steady, Niya," the Fetch murmured. He had found a box to stand on, craning his neck over the crowd, and now he rested a hand on her shoulder. "I mark four Queen's Guards at the foot of the staircase, and four more spread around the Seat. Calm yourself."

Niya relaxed, but only slightly. Elyssa was of the Keep, not the city; she didn't know how rowdy the Circus could become. Her guards, too, would be out of their depth. An odd, disconnected part of Niya's mind noted that Elyssa was wearing not the blue gown they had selected together two days before for the Holy Father's party but a plain, unadorned dress of pale green wool.

Her riding dress, Niya thought. *She rode down here.*

Elyssa had reached the high platform now. For a long moment she stood looking out over them all: a pretty young woman, serious of face, her blonde hair pinned back in a simple coil at the nape of her neck. And now an extraordinary thing happened: the roar of the crowd quieted. No one said a word; no one hushed the others or called for silence. The multitude of voices around Niya simply lessened, dying away until there was nothing, a silence so complete that Niya could hear everything: the warm whine of the night wind blowing through the nooks and crannies of the surrounding rooftops, a woman coughing on the far side of the Circus, even the deep breath that Elyssa took, just before she started to speak.

"I am Elyssa Raleigh! I have come here to speak, and I ask you to listen!"

The crowd did not respond, only remained silent, staring up at the slight figure atop the platform. Elyssa's face was pale, her jaw set, and Niya, who knew the Princess from long observation, saw that she was frightened. But her voice came out without so much as a tremor.

"My mother has commanded me to speak tonight!" Elyssa cried. "She demands that I publicly denounce the Blue Horizon and make my peace with God's Church!"

Of course, Niya thought sourly. *I should have known.*

"But I will not do these things!" Elyssa shouted hoarsely. "I do not share my mother's beliefs, nor her allegiances! God's Church is a blight on this land, and the Blue Horizon seeks a better world!"

"Great God," Niya whispered. Elyssa paused now, taking a

heavy breath, almost a sob, and in the sudden silence Niya heard the Fetch murmur, "Great God indeed. Her mother will murder her for this."

"And what of the drought?" a man shouted. "Can William Tear's ghost give us food?"

Niya frowned, though she had been thinking the same thing only minutes before. For a moment, she thought that Elyssa would give up and retreat, but Elyssa took a deep breath and spoke firmly, her hands gripping the wooden railings that encircled the Seat.

"William Tear can no longer help us, sir. And neither can I, for I am not Queen yet. My mother should open the Crown hoards, commandeer the nobility's storehouses. She should offer food to all, but she will not."

"Fuck the Queen!" a woman shouted, and the crowd roared agreement. Niya felt the moment trembling on the edge of violence, her own pulse pounding toward panic. The crowd was vast, and Elyssa looked so helpless, all alone up there. She was Arla's daughter, and a mob might not make distinctions. Elyssa must have sensed the mood as well, for her face fell paler still, but when she spoke, her voice was strong with anger, an anger that even Niya could feel, twenty feet below.

"I do not sit the throne! I may never sit the throne! But if I do, I swear here and now that my rule will be guided by the principles of the Blue Horizon! I will govern fairly! I will gut the tenancy system and redistribute the land! I will close down the Creche and end the traffic! I will eradicate the spiritual tyranny of the Arvath! I will work toward a kingdom in which everyone is fed, clothed, housed, educated, doctored! I will protect the low as well as the great! This is my promise to you!"

"True Queen! True Queen!"

The crowd erupted, so loudly that Niya almost clapped her

hands to her ears. She winced, for hands were upon her, slapping her on the back and pummeling her arms, a communal sort of violence, the people around her gone wild. She fought to stay near the Fetch, but he was suddenly gone, carried away from her in the whirls and eddies as the crowd surged toward the base of the platform. Niya too was carried forward, so close that she could see Barty and Galen, swords drawn, standing at the foot of the Seat's steps, and Niya ducked her head, not wanting them to see her. The air felt cold on her face; only then did Niya realize that she was weeping.

Elyssa had clearly said what she meant to say; she was descending the platform. All eight of her guards had surrounded the staircase now, but they were not going to be nearly enough to fight off the crowd, and Niya wondered that Barty did not know it. A great judge of assassins, Barty, but perhaps not of people, for he clearly thought this crowd intended violence. The guards raised their swords, but the horde was determined to get to Elyssa, and after a moment Barty and the rest were hauled away, pulled free of their places and raised in the air . . . not violently, but in places of honor, on people's shoulders. They struggled mightily, but they were no match for the wave that enveloped them. Barty went into the air just beside Niya, two men holding him high as he flailed, his legs kicking.

"Put me down!" he shouted, raising his sword, and without thinking Niya reached up and grabbed his leg.

"No, Barty!" she shouted. "Do not!"

Barty gaped down at her, but at that moment the crowd reached Elyssa, pulling her from the steps and hoisting her high in the air. Niya took a trembling, relieved breath . . . but not too relieved. There was no danger in the mob, but the Fetch had placed his finger on the heart of the matter: when Arla found out about this little excursion, the world itself might shudder open.

"True Queen! True Queen!"

All around Niya people screamed the words, transported, and despite her misgivings, Niya too was borne along. She didn't know whether Elyssa was the True Queen or not, but in that moment it hardly mattered, for she was swept along with them, tears rolling down her face, screaming in jubilation as the people carried them off: the eight guards and the True Queen, borne out of the Circus and into the heart of the city.

BOOK II

CHAPTER 13

THE DEEP PATCH

And now we must turn our attention to Arlen Thorne, who presents a unique puzzle for a historian. Who was this man, who started as a simple Creche sale and went on to a career of such infamy that, each year on William Tear's Day, men would dig up his grave and literally piss on the bones? We could call Thorne many things: pimp, villain, traitor, butcher, criminal . . . even war criminal, as the later Glynn archives reveal. All of these names fit, yes, but their use remains an empty exercise in vocabulary, for history has shown us that the Arlen Thornes of this world are far too complex for a single term. His kind defies description.

—Famous Traitors of the Tear: A Compendium, Evan Crawford

Christian thought that finding Arlen Thorne would be an easy matter, for rumors about the young pimp flew around the Creche like moths. They said that he was a noble's bastard, sold into the Creche shortly after birth. That he had had some sort of wasting disease as a baby, so that his body would not take nourishment, keeping him thin as a rail. They said he owned a seer, a woman of fabulous ghost-white skin whose eyes could dissect a man. All of the rumors combined to create a figure who was positively glamorous by Creche lights, and so Christian had assumed that the voices of the Creche would direct him straight to Thorne, like signposts in the dark.

But Thorne's stable was not easy to find. He denned in the Deep Patch, and Christian tried never to go there, for even in the twisted moral hierarchy of the Creche, the Deep Patch had an unpleasant reputation. Dogfighting ran on the fourth level, and if one had a stranger fetish than children, he was likely to find it on the fifth. Few men down there would talk about Thorne at all, and they were particularly reluctant to talk about Thorne's stable. But Christian finally found a man he knew, a longtime ring promoter who now handled dogs, and this man directed Christian to a stifling recess on the fifth level.

The enforcer on the arched doorway was an easy piece of business, half asleep. Christian covered his mouth with one hand and wrapped the other around his neck, cracking it easily. Killing a man outside the ring, he had found, was no different from inside, not when the death was necessary. After laying the slumping figure against the outer wall, Christian pulled the spiked club—*the mace*, he reminded himself; one of the men he had questioned had told him its name—from his belt and crept through the archway.

He found himself in a squalid little cave that made Mrs. Evans's common room look the height of luxury. Then, as he saw them scattered around the room, Christian finally understood the secrecy surrounding Thorne's stable, the reason no one would talk about this place, not even in the Deep Patch.

In the far corner were two dwarves, a boy and a girl. They sat together on a low sofa, clearly built for their height, but even standing, Christian thought that they would not reach his thighs.

One of them held a thin boy, perhaps five years old, whose right arm was a withered stalk.

Nearer to the fire, sitting on a small stool, were two little girls, twins. At the sight of them, Christian instinctively lowered his mace. The twins turned to look at him, and he saw that they were joined, their hips fused. All of these children were filthy, their faces and arms and legs smeared with soot.

"Good morning," the boy with the withered arm said, smiling shyly. "How can we help you? What sort of diversion do you seek?"

For a long moment, Christian could not reply. He thought he had seen every terrible thing the tunnels could conjure, but that was the nature of the Creche, wasn't it? There was always something worse, waiting just around the corner of the world he knew.

"Where is Thorne?" he asked, in a voice that stuck in his throat.

For a moment, none of them answered him. The boy's bright smile disappeared, like a candle snuffing out, and then he pointed down a corridor to Christian's right. Feeling as though something enormous had lodged in his airway, Christian turned and stalked softly down the corridor, which ended in a door that stood slightly ajar. Bright torchlight leaked around the edges. Christian paused, blinking, trying to clear the obstacle in his chest.

"You said she would be easy to control," said a man behind the door.

"She will be, master," a woman replied, her voice cool and pleasant. "But we must have the sapphire first, and it must come of her own free will. Try to take it by force, and we will both suffer."

There were at least two of them in there. The fact that one was a woman made no mind; in the Creche, women were often as dangerous as men. Christian crouched down, placing his ear beside the edge of the door, trying to decide where each stood in the room.

"Have it your way," Thorne replied, his voice betraying impatience. "But it's taking too long."

"Do not rush me, master." The woman's voice had lowered into a snarl. Christian was almost certain she was on the far side of the room. "You have made that mistake before."

"I am not trying to rush you, dearest, but that cunt has upset everything with her damned sermon. The prophecy was already causing problems, and now this? It's an earthquake."

"Trust me, master. Youth is vulnerable, and the girl has many cracks to be used against the mother. I have already begun."

"And what of the Blue Horizon? The Fetch?"

"He is a difficult mark, but I am tracking him. They have a spy in the Queen's Wing; I am sure of it."

Christian had heard enough. He was certain that they were both standing on the far side of the room, opposite the door. Taking a good grip on his mace, he batted the door aside and charged into the room.

Thorne sat behind a large oak desk. Later, Christian would remember nothing of this desk except that it was perfectly clean; only Thorne's clasped hands rested on top.

"Welcome, Lazarus."

Christian leapt forward, raising the mace, his other hand reaching for Thorne's neck. But the leap ended abortively; he felt his muscles seize, his brain unable to command, to give even the simplest orders. He crashed to the floor, landing painfully on one elbow, and lay there, staring wide-eyed at his mace, which had landed two feet away.

"I expected you to be along, as soon as you heard about your whore. And here you are, as predictable as time!"

Christian tried to get up, but he could not move. He couldn't even see clearly. All of his senses were off; Thorne's voice sounded first in front of him, then off to the side. Christian sensed another presence standing behind him, but he couldn't make himself roll over to see.

"Let him speak," Thorne said, and Christian felt the tightness that locked his throat suddenly ease, allowing him to groan.

"I am curious, Lazarus, as to what you intended in coming here. I'm not the one who harmed your whore."

"You pimped her out," Christian snarled. He tried to push himself up again, but his arms would hold no weight.

"So I did," Thorne replied. "But what of that? She was pimped out long before I came on the scene."

"Where is she?"

"Topside, and you should be thanking me for that. You know the survival rate for whores down here."

Christian wrenched himself from the ground, his breath shrieking through his teeth with the effort. He made it two inches, then collapsed, all the strength running out of him.

"I told you to hold him!" Thorne snapped.

"I am," the woman's cool voice answered behind Christian. "But he's a fighter."

Of course I'm a fighter, Christian began to say, then stopped, for she had not been talking about the ring. And now Christian realized who the unseen speaker must be: Thorne's witch, the fabled white woman of the Creche, who killed men with a single glance. Christian had never believed the stories, but now he was fast reconsidering. Each of his muscles seemed to be clamped in its own vise.

"I'm going to bind you now," Thorne told him. "You may struggle if you wish, but it will avail you little. Brenna saw you coming. She always does. She would end you if I allowed it."

"Well, what are you waiting for?"

"Oh, you're much too valuable to kill, Lazarus. Arliss has put two hundred pounds on your head, and he'll be along presently to collect you. That's why I don't mind you listening behind doors."

"Arliss?" Christian asked stupidly. He had forgotten all about the dealer.

"Brenna says you're clever, but I think not. Attacking the biggest poppy man in the Creche? What could you possibly hope to gain?"

"It wasn't about gain."

"No? Then you *are* a fool." Thorne began to bind his ankles. Christian could not even move a muscle to try to fight him.

Blindsided. This is what it feels like. At last I know.

"Who was Maura's client?" he asked Thorne. "Who marked her up?"

"And why should I tell you that?"

"Because whoever he is, he damaged the merchandise. Bad for business."

Thorne paused, his arms braced on his knees, and gave Christian an odd, speculative look.

"That's true, you know. I don't like the beaters. Don't understand them. I don't know why they can't simply take the fuck they paid for and be done. Transaction is efficient. Violence is waste."

"So give me the beater's name. I'll rid the earth of him."

Thorne chuckled. "Bold words, Lazarus. But once Arliss gets here, you'll be in no position to storm the Keep. It'll be all you can do to pray for a swift death."

The Keep. Christian seized on the words, making no murmur as Thorne began binding his wrists. Christian knew little of the Keep, only that it was where the royals lived, a giant pile of stone somewhere in the city. But if Maura was there, then there Christian would have to go.

I have to live, he thought grimly. *I have to live somehow, if only to find her and kill the client. And if I run upon any more members of that fucking club, I'll kill them too.*

"Benny!" Thorne called, and after a moment one of the dwarves wandered through the door.

"Sir?"

"Send a runner to Arliss. Tell him we have Lazarus."

The dwarf disappeared.

"Lovely stable you have out there, Thorne," Christian muttered. "I thought I'd seen every fucked-up thing the Creche had to offer, but you—"

"Why be dramatic?" Thorne asked. "I'm a businessman, no different from any other. I judge no man, merely offer wares that people want to buy. Grotesquerie raises value."

"I hope it's me who ends you."

"Unlikely." Thorne looked up at the witch. "Arliss will bring drugs, but even bound, I don't trust this one not to make a fuss. Put him out, will you?"

He turned back to Christian.

"Well, Lazarus, it's been a pleasure doing business with you. I don't expect we'll meet again."

Christian tried to answer him but could not, for his mind seemed suddenly as ineffectual as his body. He was exhausted, too tired to string words together. His thoughts seemed to crawl through mud. He wondered if this was how most people went to sleep, drifting off easily, while he tossed and turned in the darkness.

"This is a curious piece of work," Thorne murmured. He had picked up the mace now, and begun examining it. "Should I sell it, do you think?"

"No," the woman's low voice answered. "Give it to the bookmaker. A favor, to cement future dealings. Arliss is about to move topside. When you move into the Keep, we'll need friends in the Gut."

The Keep, Christian thought muzzily. Thorne was going to the Keep. But what business could a Creche pimp possibly have there?

Christian's eyes sank closed.

CHAPTER 14

IN THE MOMENT

Youth is a time of great wonder, and more of foolishness. But the wages of even the most extreme foolishness cannot entirely eclipse the wonder. Some moments are never forgotten.

–The Words of the Glynn Queen, AS RECORDED BY FATHER TYLER

When Elyssa woke, she was standing just outside the witch's door.

She didn't know how she had gotten there. Barty was nowhere in sight, nor were any of her other guards. It was late, and the corridor was deserted. But that couldn't be. Even in the dead of night, there were always two guards on her mother's door, at least.

How did I get here?

She had gone to bed early. In the past few days, she always found herself sleepy in the early evening. The weather, undoubtedly; as June moved into July, the heat had climbed, and now it was almost unbearable. It had been eleven days since the night in the Circus; her mother had not summoned her yet, and Elyssa, in no hurry to hasten that process, had been taking dinner in her room. It seemed only natural to go to sleep afterward. And–

And how did I get here?

Elyssa looked around again, seeing no movement beyond the

torches, flickering in their holders. The corridor stretched away from her on either side, seeming much longer than it did in the daytime. And now she was beset by an uncomfortable certainty: she was all alone in the Queen's Wing. The entire Keep was deserted. When she closed her eyes, she could visualize the city of New London below her, eerily silent, not a soul in sight. She was the only one left in the entire Tearling, and the silence of her kingdom pressed in upon her, as though the world were a tomb.

Get hold of yourself! her mind snapped. *You've been sleepwalking, that's all, and tonight you had the bad fortune to do it while Barty snuck off to the john.*

But there were always two guards on Elyssa's chamber, always. And where was Niya? Elyssa could not remember a single night when she had been wakeful that Niya did not present herself within seconds. For a moment Elyssa debated going to Niya's room and waking her up, but then something crawled over her skin, tickling, like fingers, making her gasp. There was nothing there, but she ran her hands up her arms all the same, trying to rid herself of the sensation. She couldn't stay out here in the hallway forever; she was wearing only her shift, and she was freezing.

Go on, her mind whispered. *Go into her room. You've been wanting to for days.*

Elyssa frowned at the certainty in that voice. Ever since the heat had climbed, she had been having terrible dreams, but their substance faded far too fast for Elyssa to remember upon waking. Only one image stuck with her, and it was so fleeting that she could not describe it without sounding foolish: a pair of blind eyes, hovering over her in the dark. The vision seemed so real that Elyssa had sat up, clutching her sapphire, and for a moment, she could have sworn that the jewel had been glowing bright blue.

Without knowing it, Elyssa had put a hand on the door handle. Voices echoed in her mind. The sapphire cushioned between her breasts seemed to throb, as though it were alive.

She's in there, waiting. Casting her bones and waiting for you.

Beware of Greeks bearing gifts.

You can have everything you want. But you must have the courage to act.

Abruptly Elyssa turned and fled down the corridor. It seemed to lengthen before her, the end retreating from her flying feet, but at last she reached the door she wanted. For a long, terrible moment she thought that she would find it locked, but the handle moved easily under her fingers.

The infirmary was dark, save for a single candle burning at Gareth's bedside. The flame illuminated the tiny bell that Beale had given him to ring for aid. Beale was gone; as the senior medic, he did not work nights. But his two assistants sat snoring in the corner, not awakening even when Elyssa closed the door loudly behind her.

My God, she thought wildly. *She has put them all to sleep! The entire castle!* It was like something from a fairy tale, but not the pretty kind that Elyssa had enjoyed as a child. She felt as though she had stumbled into Lady Glynn's old book of Grimm, where fair faces hid cold intentions and queens were always demanding someone's cut-out heart. When Elyssa's mother had banished Lady Glynn from court, Lady Glynn had taken her enormous library of books with her, but Elyssa had already read most of them, and the Grimm had always stuck in her mind. The fairest of face could not be trusted, but did that make a grotesque-looking creature like Brenna any more trustworthy? Elyssa didn't think so.

"Highness?"

Elyssa jerked with fright. Then, with unutterable relief, she realized that Gareth had spoken. He was awake, sitting up in bed, his now-healed torso barely visible in the candle's thin glow, his head in shadow. His arm was still encased in plaster.

"I am sorry," she said feebly. "I didn't know where to—"

"What are you running from?"

"From her. The witch." Fear had loosened her tongue. "She knows what I want. She knows everything."

"What witch?" Gareth asked sharply.

"The white woman. Brenna."

Gareth was silent for a long moment. Then he said, "I have seen her."

"She's been in here?" Elyssa was suddenly outraged, for it seemed, somehow, a direct intrusion on her own life, a shot aimed at her.

"No," Gareth replied. "But I have seen her, all the same. Don't be frightened; she will not dare come in here. She knows I see her, as clearly as she sees me."

Elyssa didn't know what to make of this statement. In the corner the two medics slept on and on, gentle smiles on their faces, as though they dreamed the pleasantest of dreams.

"I heard about what you did," Gareth murmured. "In the Circus."

"What else was I going to do? Sell my soul to the Arvath?" Elyssa kept her tone light, but it was difficult, for the memory of that night still had the power to move her deeply, more than any other single moment in her life. They had carried her away on their shoulders, and it had gone on all night: visits to pubs and restaurants, drinks offered to her on the streets, people leaning in close to touch her hand or the hem of her dress. She had spoken to so many people, heard so many stories . . . shopkeepers, merchants, pros, the idle. But it had finally come to an end, and as she had snuck back into the Keep with her Guard through the tunnels, she felt much as she imagined a young girl of the city would feel after being out all night with a boy: both furtive and proud, terrified of the sound of her mother's voice. She did not regret what she had done, but she did not deceive herself that the price would not come due in blood.

"Still, you have declared for us," Gareth told her, his light eyes clear, almost brilliant. "And we do not forget."

I love him, Elyssa thought. It was when she talked to Gareth that she came closest to seeing the better world, not as a vague dream but a reality, a place that they could reach together . . . and that *was* love, Elyssa suddenly understood, much more than any of the feelings she had ever had for men before.

"What will you do?" Gareth asked. "When your mother calls you on the carpet?"

"Try to be brave, I suppose." Elyssa wished it were as easy as she made it sound. "Pray she doesn't give Thomas the throne."

"She will not. Don't worry about Thomas. We will deal with him shortly."

The statement carried such quiet assurance that Elyssa could only nod. She wondered whether the Blue Horizon meant to kill Thomas, and found that she didn't care, not in the slightest.

"You will be a good queen, Elyssa," Gareth told her gently. "I am certain of it."

Elyssa nodded, smiling . . . but her eyes were full of tears. She would be a good queen, and that should have been enough, but she couldn't help wanting other things.

"You can have them, Elyssa," he told her, taking her wrist. "Everything you want."

At that point, Elyssa became certain that she was dreaming. And that was a blessing, because everything was acceptable in dreams. Dreams were no one's fault, and no one could be held accountable for them later. When Gareth slid off her shift, using his good arm, she did not feel even the slightest twinge of shame, for she understood now that the moment was everything. When she got old, when she reached her mother's age, she knew that youth would have faded, lost its brilliance and turned dark and muted, like a pre-Crossing photograph. All she would have were flashes of memory, single moments . . . and she wanted this to be one of them. Gareth grabbed her hair, yanking her head back, and the feeling was so unbearably exquisite that Elyssa shuddered, forgetting all about her missing Guard, the two medics sleeping in the corner, even about the white witch down the hall.

It was only when they were nearing the end—Elyssa could sense that end, approaching for both of them, was working toward it with all her heart—that she turned her head and saw the witch, just beside the bed, less than a foot away. The albino's face was twisted in a grin, lascivious and predatory at the same time, and her colorless eyes gleamed, a bright and burning white. She had loosened her dress, and her hands cupped her own breasts, which were firm and young, a terrible contrast to her ageless face. At that moment Elyssa began to climax, a dreadful, crowning spasm that seemed only partly hers. She moaned, and the witch moaned with her. Elyssa began to scream, and in that moment, the witch vanished.

"What is it?" Gareth asked roughly. His voice was drifting, almost lost, as though he too had been dreaming.

Maybe we both were, Elyssa thought wildly, feeling a desperate hope. *Maybe none of it was real.*

But the hope vanished in an instant, for she could still feel Gareth between her legs, warm wetness beginning to drip down her left thigh. And now her mother's medics were sitting up, staring at the two of them: Elyssa astride Gareth, neither of them wearing a stitch.

"Great God," Elyssa breathed.

The medics ran for the door, shouting for the Guard, and Elyssa leapt off Gareth and sprinted toward the far wall, not bothering with her clothing. All around her, she could feel the Queen's Wing stirring, all of them waking from a deep dream. She heard the pounding footsteps of Queen's Guards in the corridor. They were coming, swords in hand.

"Over here!" she cried to Gareth. "Now, if you don't wish to die!"

Gareth followed her, grabbing his trousers as he went. Elyssa fumbled against the stones until she found the invisible crevice that triggered the door. It opened into darkness, and Elyssa nearly shoved him through. His bad arm hit the wall, but he did not cry out.

"Go left," she ordered him. "Go left, find the staircase, and keep going down, under the moat. Run. The Guard know the tunnels. They will come for you."

He looked at her for a moment, and Elyssa thought perhaps he would say something; some ultimate summation that would crown her memory when long years were gone. But he said nothing; in fact, he looked as horrified as she did, and now Elyssa began to wonder whether he actually had been dreaming, whether the entire night had been his doing at all, or even hers. But it was too late to ask. Gareth disappeared into the darkness, and Elyssa yanked the hidden door closed.

Gone, she thought. *Gone, but we had our moment first.*

Her shift still lay on the floor by the bed; she darted that way, but the door burst open before she even came close, and the entire Guard seemed to pour into the room in small, tight groups: Givens and Barty, Elston and Coryn and Dyer, Bowler and Kibb and Wallace. Elyssa stood before them as though paralyzed, her thighs sticky, her entire body red with shame. When Givens charged off toward the hidden door, she tried to stop him, but he shoved her aside, and Elyssa could do nothing but huddle on the bed, wrapping her arms around her legs to cover her nakedness . . . and waiting for her mother.

CHAPTER 15

SONG OF THE SCYTHE

The Almont Uprising was unique in the history of the Tear, in that it had no clear catalyst. Conditions were certainly ripe for discontent; that summer remains the driest in Tear history, and there was little food and even less patience. But we must ask: what caused a nucleus of downtrodden tenants to coalesce around the figure of Aislinn Martin, a fifteen-year-old girl who could not even wield a sword? Comprehensive history is often a matter of simple word of mouth . . . but in this matter, no one has ever talked.

—*The Early History of the Tearling,* AS TOLD BY MERWINIAN

"Push!" Aislinn shouted. "Push, for your lives!"

They drove the wagon forward down the rutted dirt road, gaining speed and power with each step. As they neared the bottom, Aislinn felt her muscles singing, not with exhaustion but with exhilaration, oncoming and inexorable victory. More than ten tenants lined each side of the wagon, pushing with all their strength. They had been at work on the doors for more than an hour, and reward was at hand. The ram slammed into the double doors of the storehouse, breaking them open. The bolt on the far side snapped, and pieces of wood flew in all directions; Aislinn heard grunts and screams as the wood connected. At least five bailiffs had holed themselves up in the storehouse; Aislinn hoped they were not all dead, for she meant to end at least one or two herself. Liam had helped her to set her family's cottage on fire, but before they lit the match, Aislinn had gone in to have one more look at the line of corpses on the wall: eight, far too many to have been the work of one man.

They were all in on it, she thought now, baring her teeth. *They're all the same.*

"There they are!" someone shouted behind her. "Get the bastards!"

In the next instant, Aislinn's companions had begun to leap over the remains of the doors, heading toward the corner of the storehouse, where a group of bailiffs were huddled: Parnell, Wyndham, and several others Aislinn did not know. Most held pitchforks; two had knives, but even these two were white-faced and frightened, ringed as they now were by more than thirty tenants.

"What do we do with them?" Liam asked. His own father stood behind him, but the question was meant for Aislinn, and she considered the seven men for a long moment. Bailiffs were convenient villains, but they were only what their nobles demanded they be. Did that excuse them? Aislinn thought of Bailey, the bloody legs that sprawled from her tiny emaciated frame, and the issue was decided.

"Bring them outside."

The tenants moved forward, roaring happily, seemingly oblivious to the pitchforks and knives in the bailiffs' shaking hands. Aislinn heard several cries of pain as tenants were wounded, then howls of glee as the bailiffs went down, subsumed under a human wave.

"What do you mean to do?" Liam asked her.

Aislinn paused. More than a month had passed since she had returned to the acreage, and the entire period felt like a fever dream, an ongoing panoply of anger and violence. They had killed the priest, and that might have been the end of it, for Aislinn had been looking no further than revenge. But then, just as she was trying to decide what to do next, some thirty tenant families had missed their quotas for June, and Lady Andrews had sent word that she would be adding the shortfall to their aggregate debt. This was standard practice during the normal harvest, but unheard of in a dry year, let alone a drought. When Aislinn and Liam had set fire to the cottage, they had emerged to find more than fifty tenants waiting outside, holding pitchforks and spades. Aislinn had never led anything in her life, but her single act of defiance in killing Fallon seemed to have inflamed the other tenants, emboldened them somehow, and she was at least old enough to recognize the duty implicit in that situation.

Word had traveled fast; as Aislinn emerged from the storehouse, she saw that some hundred new tenants had arrived from the far corners of the acreage, and now they stood outside, just beneath the high scaffold used for drying produce, waiting.

"Aislinn?" Liam asked again. "What should we do with them?"

"String them up."

She expected some argument; few of the tenants had needed to be talked into anything, but Liam's was the voice of caution. He said nothing, however, and as the eager tenants hauled the bailiffs forward, he turned and pointed them toward the scaffold.

It was done quickly. The storehouse was full of rope, and old Guinness and John Pearce were both good hands with knots. They tied seven nooses, threw them over the scaffold, and then stood, waiting, for the screaming group of men who were being dragged from the storehouse. One by one, the bailiffs went gagging into the air. They strangled slowly, and Aislinn, who had been worried that she would be unable to watch, found herself not only able but pleased. Seven Fallons hung above her, and beside them dangled the white-clad figure of Father Moran. Liam and Aislinn had strung him up three days before, just after they burned down the church, and though the priest's corpse was rotting quickly and horribly in the July heat, no one had suggested taking him down.

"What should we do now?" Liam asked.

For a long moment, Aislinn did not answer. The bailiffs swung back and forth, some of them kicking, and the swinging ropes reminded her of something.

It's clever puppetry, she thought, staring at the eight men who dangled from the beam. *Three-card monte, a shadow show. But I saw her face, and I do not forget.*

"I'm going to the manse."

"You can't do that," Liam's father said, breaking from the crowd. "You're brave, girl, for sure. But Lady Andrews has more than fifty retainers up there, and twice that many servants. You'll never even get through the doors."

"Not alone, no." Aislinn turned to face the crowd, a sea of faces in the lamplight. "Who will come with me?"

Except perhaps for Liam, she truly did not expect any of them to come. Stealing food, and even killing bailiffs, was one thing. Attacking a noble was another. But several tenants came forward immediately–Willie Pearce's parents, their faces grim and hungry, were the first–and soon another ten or twelve followed.

"We have the food!" someone cried. "Why don't we just take the food in the storehouse and run?"

"Run where?" Althea Pearce demanded. Her face was pale with grief, but her mouth was set. "Food won't last forever, and there's barely any water out there! Over the hill is just another noble's castle! We're all dead already ... but I'll have that bitch before I go."

"Aye!" someone else shouted; Aislinn thought it was Anna Liles, who had no husband and four children, who had been forced to expose her newborn during the winter just past. The acreage didn't speak of such things, but they were there, all the same. Aislinn turned back to the remaining tenants, most of whom stood staring at the swinging bodies overhead, their expressions horrified. If she could not hold them, they would soon panic and bolt, and then they would be easy meat.

"We have done this thing," she announced firmly. "We have done it already. Lady Andrews is not forgiving, nor will she hear pleas for mercy."

"She can't kill us all!" someone shouted. "Who would farm the land?"

"Whoever she hires to do it!" Liam snapped, moving up to stand beside Aislinn. "The Tear is full of poor farmers, and she will replace us and think nothing of it. If need be, she'll borrow tenants from some of her noble friends . . . or steal children perhaps, as we've heard they do in the lower Almont."

Several people nodded, murmuring agreement. Aislinn shot Liam a grateful look.

"What of the Crown?" a man demanded. "We could go to New London, send someone to plead our case!"

"To *Arla*?" a woman replied, disbelieving. "You're out of your mind."

"Not to Arla. To the True Queen."

"You've always been feeble-minded, Mills!" the woman snapped back. "There is no True Queen; that's just a fairy story the Blue Horizon cooked up for the city folk. The Martin girl has the right of it. There's no way out of this, not unless we break through, like we did with them doors!"

This time the roar of agreement was louder.

"Fine!" Mills cried. "But what happens if we move on Her

Ladyship? Even if we could do it, the Crown will come right down on us, hammer to anvil! Arla will send the army! Won't none of us live through it!"

"Maybe not," Aislinn cut in evenly. "Mills is right, and Liam too. Tenants are expendable, and if we raise hell, even way out here, the Crown will have to come and make an example of us."

"You think we should run?" Althea demanded.

"No," Aislinn replied. "I think we should fight."

The crowd remained silent for a moment, turning this over.

"We've raised hands against a noble," Aislinn went on, feeling her voice grow stronger. "We're all dead men walking, and there are too few of us to accomplish much. But that doesn't mean we shouldn't try. Lady Andrews has profited from us for far too long. She has food hoarded up there, and water too, an entire cistern. It's wrong, and no matter what we might lose, someone has to make the fight. I'm going, and anyone who wants to can come with me."

In the end, some thirty people followed her up the hill. Many of them held torches, a few knives, but all of them looked grimly determined. Aislinn would never know who began to sing, but she recognized the tune: a reaping song, a song of the scythe. Gradually Aislinn became aware of more voices raised, and then more still, and when she looked back, the flat field at the bottom of the slope was empty. They had all followed her now: more than five hundred farmers, the tenancy of the entire acreage, all of them moving steadily up the rise toward Lady Andrews's manse.

CHAPTER 16

A BUBBLE IN THE ALE

Expecting nothing, one may gain everything.

—CADARESE PROVERB

"Wake up, boy. Wake up."

But he didn't want to. His head felt as though it were full of boulders.

"Wake up, Lazarus. Lazarus."

My name isn't Lazarus, he wanted to say. But he couldn't seem to find the energy to open his mouth. He was no longer bound; he sat slumped in a soft chair, softer than any piece of furniture he had ever encountered. His arms and legs were free, but he could barely move them.

"Christ, he's turned to mush. What did you dose him with?"

"Nothing, boss," another man's voice answered, high above him. "We didn't need to. The witch had already put him out."

"Ah, the witch," the first voice replied. Christian knew that voice: high and tinny, its accent broad and flat. "And did you pay Thorne?"

"Yes, sir. But he demanded assurances too, that we meant to kill the prisoner."

"And did you give such assurances?"

" 'Course I did, sir."

"Good. Leave."

Footsteps shuffled away, then: "Almost forgot, boss: Thorne said to give you this. He says it's yours."

"Leave it on the table."

The man dropped something with a heavy clunk, then closed the door behind him. Light bloomed behind Christian's closed eyelids, then he felt heat. A flame had just been placed close to his cheek.

"Your eyes are wiggling around beneath their lids, boy. You're just playing possum now. Come on, wake up."

After another long moment—for Christian did not want the dealer to think he did anything by his orders—he cracked his eyelids and found himself in a low-ceilinged room. There was something wrong about this room, though Christian could not have said what. It was no different from any other room in the Creche, tiny and cramped and dark . . . but something was not the same.

Arliss sat across from him in a high armchair, so big that it made the dealer's frame seem childlike in proportion. The armchair was upholstered in a thick, rich material that Christian thought might be velvet. He had never seen such a luxurious piece of furniture in his life. Arliss's legs and torso were swaddled in a thick blanket, hiding his injured hip. Behind the chair, two lamps sat on either end of an enormous oak desk, dangerously close to the unwieldy piles of paper that covered the surface. In fact, as he sat up, Christian saw that paper was strewn all over the office as well, covering the surfaces of chairs, the spread of the floor.

"I would think a morphia kingpin could afford a tidier life."

Arliss shrugged. "This is my private office. I have a system. It works for me."

Christian sat up, clutching his head. Whatever Thorne's witch had done to him, it wasn't finished yet; the ache was terrible. His chest throbbed, and his legs felt loose and wobbly.

"I'd hoped that the bounty would bring you in, but I didn't expect it to happen so fast," Arliss remarked. "Going after Thorne on your own? Are you mad, boy, or just stupid?"

"Stupid," Christian replied, massaging the nape of his neck. "How's your hip, old man?"

"Shattered. The doctor said I'll never walk right again."

If Arliss was waiting for an apology, he wasn't getting one; Christian sat in truculent silence. But now Arliss looked at him with a strange expression, one so foreign to life in the Creche that it took a moment for Christian to identify it as sympathy.

"Was she your special girl? The one who overdosed?"

"No," Christian replied slowly. "But she could have been. That entire stable is hooked on the poppy."

"Aye, and they have to be," Arliss replied grimly. "An entire life spent fucking on demand? At least my morphia lets them sleep."

"Right. You're a real prince."

Christian tried to stand as he said this, but it was just as he'd feared: his legs were jelly. There would be no daring escape, but at least he would not beg, the way his lesser opponents had sometimes done in the ring.

"Sit down, boy, and stop being a fool. It will take you time to recover, hours perhaps. You're lucky Thorne's witch didn't kill you."

"How do you know she's a witch?"

"She's got a particular skill set, that's certain. None of us can compete. They say the witch is better than any poppy. I've heard she can even alter memory."

"Alter memory? Who would pay for that?"

"Queen Arla, for starters. Don't you listen to any gossip, boy? The witch is moving up in the world. Thorne's installed her in the Keep, right at the Queen's very ear."

"Why?"

"Who knows? I've heard Thorne's noble-born, but talk is cheap in the tunnels. Memory as well."

Christian nodded automatically, though he didn't agree. The Creche had a very long memory. Arliss might not hold a grudge himself, but he would still kill Christian; he would have to. Even the slightest hint of weakness and Arliss would be finished, torn apart by any one of the other dozen aspiring tinpot dictators who battled constantly over rule of the narcotics trade. Arliss would kill him, and Christian did not begrudge it. He himself had spent his own life killing . . . not because he wanted to, but because it was expected of him. And now he suddenly remembered what Wigan had said on that long-ago day when he had sold Maura to Mrs. Evans, the words that had made Christian so angry that he had tried to strike Wigan, and received a beating in return.

Most of the culls down here, even if they weren't born to the life, as you were, they've accepted it. They root and scramble and scratch, never looking upward. But I know you, Lazarus. I've watched you fight since you could barely walk. You may keep your head down, like the rest of us, but some part of you is staring topside, all the time. You think you're better. You think you deserve better, and pigeons like you, exceptional pigeons, are dangerous. They make others start looking upward.

What does that have to do with Maura? Christian had demanded, near tears. He had only been seven, still young enough to burn with the unfairness of specific moments. But even at seven, he knew what went on in the Alley. What Maura was in for.

Think of Maura as dead weight, boy, Wigan had replied. *A rock around your ankle. I don't like bubbles in my ale, and I don't like you looking topside. I will sell your little friend, and I will do it to keep your head down here, where it belongs.*

And so Christian had tried to hit him, but Wigan was taller and heavier, and when they were done, Christian had sported two black eyes. But the shiners had been nothing. In selling Maura, Wigan had delivered an injury much worse than any Christian would ever receive in the ring. Maura had gone to the Alley, and Christian had kept his head down. *Lazarus* had kept his head down.

"I have cleared myself from the Creche," Arliss told him, breaking Christian's thoughts from the past. "What you saw in Mrs. Evans's stable was the last bit of business I intend to conduct down there. From now on, I will deal and book topside."

"Why tell *me*?"

"Because I bear you no ill will, boy. You should bear me none either."

"Just kill me and have done with it."

Arliss sighed in exasperation. "I'm not going to kill you, you tiresome little shit. I'm going to let you go. And when I do, I would rather not spend my life looking over my shoulder."

Christian stared at him. "You're letting me go."

"Yes."

"In exchange for what?"

"For nothing."

"That's a kind repayment for crushing your hip."

"Topside is a different world, boy. I'm dealing with a better class of people now. Not heroes, but better. I've no need to save face among them by flaying your skin from your bones. You're free of me."

"And what about the bounty?"

"I will call off the bounty," Arliss replied evenly. "I'll tell the world that I've forgiven you . . . which I have."

This statement so alarmed Christian that his legs twitched, almost in spasm. He grasped the arms of the chair and wobbled his way to his feet, staring down at Arliss. The dealer was undoubtedly a career liar, but Christian saw no lie in his face.

"You're a poppy dealer," he said slowly. "Why would you need to forgive anyone? Why not kill me just for spite? Or even sport?"

"Because I wish to be better. All of us can be better."

"Better than what?"

"Better than the man I was before. The past is powerful, but it need not control the future."

The words rang a faint bell in Christian's mind. Listening to Arliss was like listening to the frocks from the Arvath who came down to try to win converts in the Creche . . . except that Arvath forgiveness always required coin. Arliss's words had a different ring, a ring that Christian had heard before, if he could only remember—

"Holy hell," he blurted out. "You're one of them. The Blue Horizon."

Arliss said nothing, merely looked at him. And now, out of nowhere, Christian suddenly identified what had struck him strange about the room: it had slabbed stone walls, like any room in the Creche, but there was no mold sliming the stone. Not even a trickle of moisture marred the smooth surface.

"Where are we?"

"Haven't you guessed, boy? We're topside. Out of the dark and into the light."

Arliss reached over to the table that sat beside the sofa. For the first time, Christian noticed that his mace sat there, still crusted with the bodyguard's blood. Arliss offered the mace, but Christian only looked at it, thinking: *Topside. Blue sky and white clouds.*

But Maura was supposed to be here with him. Everything had gone wrong.

"Keep it, boy," Arliss insisted, offering the mace again. "The man who owned it is dead, and clearly you have some aptitude for it. Maybe it will even keep you safe, though if Arlen Thorne wants you dead, you're on a dangerous path."

"He said he was moving into the Keep," Christian murmured, trying to remember. The effort made his head hurt. "Or no, the witch said that. What could Arlen Thorne possibly want in the Keep?"

"I don't know. Last I saw, he was busy expanding his business. He's been buying children like there's no tomorrow."

Christian nodded, grimacing. "I saw his stable."

"Not for his wretched stable. He's buying pretty children, from all corners of the Creche. My man says Thorne's paying top dollar for straight teeth and unblemished skin."

Christian felt a sick tremor ripple through his stomach. He clutched his temples, trying to stop the pounding inside his head.

"Look at you," Arliss muttered. "About to get sick all over my nice carpet. Webb!"

The door opened, and a man a few years older than Christian came in, his hand on his knife. He presented himself before Arliss, but his narrowed eyes never left Christian.

"Give him ten pounds," Arliss ordered. "Then show him out. He might need help walking to the door."

I don't need help from anyone, Christian almost said. But that wasn't true, because now, for the first time in his life, he owed a debt. For a moment he considered telling Arliss that he still held a grudge . . . would always hold a grudge. It was easier to murder the past than learn to live with it, and Christian wanted to be in no one's debt. Then Arliss held out the mace again—his arm shaking the slightest bit—and before Christian knew what he was doing, he had taken it, grasping its solid weight in his hand.

"There's a better world out there," Arliss told him. "So close we can almost touch it. The Blue Horizon has given you your life. Do not waste it."

Christian said nothing, not even when the bodyguard, Webb, placed a hand under his elbow and guided him toward the door, holding him up as though he were an invalid. He took Christian down a long hallway, toward a door that seemed to have about fifty deadbolts on it. At Webb's nod, the two men on the door drew multiple bolts and pulled the door inward. Then Webb led Christian through, out the door and down a step, where he let go of Christian's arm. The air smelled so crisp and sweet that Christian wondered how he had ever breathed down below. Water misted against his face, and he looked up, seeing the entire world through a curtain of tiny droplets that fell from the darkness above.

"What is that?" he asked Webb, and Webb looked at him as though he were an idiot.

"Rain. First fall in months."

It's real, Christian thought, looking around him, seeing more new sights: the long straight street, not lined with cobbles but simply a vat of mud. Several beasts were hitched in front of a nearby structure, their long tails swishing, and Christian realized that these must be horses. The structure was lit with bright lights, but above it stretched a dark canvas: the sky. In all of Christian's imaginings, the sky had been blue, but now it was a swirling black.

"Here," Webb said, and offered him a tiny purse. "Take it."

Unable to think of a reason not to, Christian took the purse and shoved it into his pocket.

"The boss said to get you gone from here," Webb said. "Go on."

"Where do I go?"

"How the fuck should I know? Just get gone."

Christian stepped down from the stoop, wandering forward. After a few steps, he stopped, his legs shaking beneath him. He meant to turn around, to ask again where he should go, but Webb must have sensed it coming, because Christian found the door slammed in his face.

He turned and began wandering, unsure of his direction, his eyes drinking in the wide world as though it were water. The rain sprinkled lightly on Christian's face, and he thought that nothing had ever felt so good. So clean.

But all the buildings had strange, oblong openings that allowed him to see through the walls, and as he walked he saw men drinking, women with tight bodices showing off their wares, brutes fighting each other. For a few minutes Christian wondered whether topside had anything new to show him at all. Then he rounded a corner and emerged onto a street wider than anything he could ever have imagined, even in his dreams. Every inch seemed to be lined with banners and awnings and windows, and an ocean of movement lay before him: people and horses, dogs and wagons, all of it gleaming with glass and color and torchlight. In that moment it became too much, and Christian was forced to close his eyes, seeking the cool dark.

Where do I go? he thought helplessly. Arlen Thorne wanted him dead, and Arlen Thorne's witch was in the Keep . . . in the Keep, where Christian had to go, if he meant to find Maura. He closed his eyes and saw her lying on the bed, her bright smile dulled with poppy; saw Mrs. Evans, her eyes gleaming with coin; saw boys without number, their mouths wide in agony as they died in the ring. All of them, none of them, swept away into the past. What happened next would depend entirely upon Christian. He would have to make a choice, and then live with the consequences.

Do not waste it.

The rain abruptly ceased, leaving the air damp and clear. Looking upward, Christian saw tiny pinpricks of light above his head. Stars . . . he had heard of them, but had not pictured them this way at all: bright but limited, their brilliance trapped in black night.

That was me, Christian thought, staring up at the twinkling points. *But what will I be now, in the light?*

The stars did not answer.

CHAPTER 17

THE EDGE ON THE BLADE

When we speak of Queen Elyssa, we never talk about Queen Arla. The relationship with the mother undoubtedly lies at the heart of the Shipper Queen's destiny, yet no one wishes to examine that relationship. Are we lazy? No, we are unwilling ... for Queen Arla had her own mother, and that mother her own as well. If the Raleigh Dynasty was a pyramid, building toward the Glynn Queen, then there was plenty of rotten stone as the ziggurat ascended.

—The Raleighs: A Comprehensive Analysis,
Sofie Hawkins and Violet Fisher

Elyssa was terrified.

She sat on the low sofa outside her mother's chamber, crossing and uncrossing her feet. It had taken more than a week for her mother to summon her, and in that time Elyssa had felt like nothing so much as a hermit hiding in her room, avoiding even her guards. They had all seen her naked, but that was only part of it. They had seen her in a moment of weakness, one that would never be forgotten. Each day that her mother's summons did not come only served to underline Elyssa's own powerlessness, but this was all part of her mother's punishment: to make her dangle and dance.

"Why does she do this?" Elyssa had once wailed to Lady Glynn, after she had tripped and ripped a tapestry from the wall. Her mother had not spoken to her for days; Elyssa had only been eight or nine, but it was the first time she could remember thinking that her mother's style of punishment was conscious, almost vicious.

Lady Glynn, who had known the Queen since childhood, had answered immediately. "Because it was just as her mother did, and her grandmother before."

"I will be different," Elyssa had vowed bravely. "I will change."

She had meant it, but even now, Elyssa had to admit that her mother's wrath was effective. She was twenty-one, not eight, but she felt no braver than she had on that long-ago day of the tapestry. Gareth, the speech in the Circus . . . Elyssa's latest infractions had been so great, so unconscionable, that she could not begin to imagine what lay in store.

"Princess," Bowler murmured. He had opened the door of her mother's chamber, and Elyssa had not even noticed. "She's ready for you."

Elyssa stood. Her legs wanted to wobble, but she would not let them. Taking a deep breath, she passed Bowler and went into her mother's chamber. The stocky guard remained outside, closing the door behind her—her mother wanted no witnesses to this conversation, apparently—and at the click of the latch, Elyssa's anxiety seemed to ratchet upward even further. She had meant to take this opportunity to raise the issue of Thomas and the girl he had purchased, a scandal that had now spread beyond the Keep and out into the city. But now she didn't know whether she would have the courage.

Gareth is safe.

Elyssa held to this fact as though to a lifeline. Rain had fallen several days before . . . only a night's shower, not enough to put a dent in the drought, but the city had gone mad, taken to the streets, and their joy had reminded her of Gareth. . . . Gareth, who had spoken with such certainty of the better world. Whatever was in store for her, she had traded it for Gareth's life. The Guard had been unable to track him in the tunnels, and in the days since, Elyssa had begun to think that they were even angrier with her than they were with him. When Givens spoke to her, it was with cold politeness only. Her own Guard—Kibb and Carroll in particular—seemed more sympathetic, but they would not show that sympathy, not where Givens could see. Fear threatened to overwhelm her again, and Elyssa closed her eyes and thought of that night with Gareth on the bed. It was not an entirely comfortable memory, for deep within lay the knowledge that the witch had seen it all, and the more alarming idea that the witch might have orchestrated the entire thing for reasons of her own. But Elyssa shied away from the latter thought. It was a *good* memory, that night with Gareth, and it had gotten her through all of these long nights of fear and doubt, the certainty with each dawning day that her mother would summon her, strip her of her birthright, and set Thomas in her place.

And what if she does? her mind asked. *If she truly means to strip you, what will you do?*

The last time Elyssa had asked this question of herself, she had found no answer. But now she saw the solution, saw it clearly in the memory of the screaming mass of humanity beneath her in the New London Circus. They had been wild, mad even, but their madness was born not of violence but of trust. They trusted Elyssa to protect them, and once upon a time Elyssa had wondered how far she would go for her kingdom. But now she knew. If her mother installed Thomas as heir, then he could not be allowed to ascend the throne.

"Elyssa."

She bit her lip, all resolve muting as her mother's form emerged from the enormous dressing room at the far end of the chamber. For a long moment the Queen remained in shadow, and Elyssa had time to think how imposing her mother was, how frightening in her own right. When she came into the light, still clad in her long morning robe, the impression was lessened . . . but only a little.

"Elyssa. What am I to do with you?"

Elyssa remained silent, for she knew her mother. Part of the Queen wanted an apology, and part of her did not. On some deep level, her mother was proud of Elyssa's insolence. She wanted, even expected, Elyssa to rebel. But she took equal enjoyment in crushing rebellion flat.

The Queen sighed, crossing the room to her vanity table, where an enormous gold-framed looking glass held pride of place. She sat down and began to brush her hair, seeming to ignore her daughter entirely for the moment. This was all of a piece. The sorrowful sighs, the rhetorical questions . . . all of them were only the rise of the curtain, the entr'acte on a murderous play. Soon or late, the knife would present itself; the question was only how sharp it would be.

"How many times have I told you?" her mother asked. "You are the heir to a kingdom. Your womb does not belong to yourself."

"I was careful!" Elyssa snapped. "I have my syrup!"

But, she realized suddenly, she did *not* have her syrup. Niya had been unable to find any on her last trip into the city, and Elyssa had taken her last spoonful a month before, or perhaps longer. She hadn't thought of it, for it had been more than a year since she had shared her bed with anyone. But now—

Only one night, Elyssa thought, fighting to keep the dismay from her face, for she could not afford for her mother to be right about anything, not now.

"Syrup is not the issue. You cannot simply bed with anyone you please."

"You do!" Elyssa shot back, unable to keep the venom from her voice. She hoped to provoke her mother's temper, but the Queen's face remained neutral, and Elyssa's fright deepened. Her mother had already chosen a course of action. This was not a conversation; it was a dance, carefully choreographed by her mother, a prelude to—what?

"Your little dalliance is not my primary problem," Arla continued. "Your defiance has opened a deep breach with the Holy Father."

"My heart bleeds."

The blow came so quickly that Elyssa barely even felt it, only the fall, the sharp rap of her head against the floor. She tried to sit up and could not.

"Why do you make me do this?" her mother asked. "Why do you always force my hand?"

"I force you to do nothing," Elyssa replied through gritted teeth, pulling herself up with the help of her mother's desk. "You are what you are, Mother. You cannot dodge responsibility."

"And neither can you, child," the Queen replied, smiling a little ... but the smile was predatory. "You are twenty-one years old now, old enough to make choices and live with the damage."

"Tell that to Thomas. I see how you've punished him for his transgressions."

To her mother's credit, she looked almost embarrassed for a moment. Then she shrugged.

"The situation with Thomas is unfortunate. I have chosen the best way to manage it."

"That girl is barely more than a child."

"I did not select the girl."

"No; you sent Thomas on a shopping expedition in the city." Thinking of the weeping girl Kibb had pulled from the bed, Elyssa clenched her fists. "I won't stand for it, Mother."

"You *will* stand for it, Elyssa, and keep your mouth shut. If it makes it easier, think of it as part of your punishment . . . but only part. Culp!"

At the name, Elyssa's stomach clenched. She wondered whether her mother's anger was so great that they had finally crossed some final line. But then, as Welwyn Culp emerged from the dressing room, Elyssa gasped, the sound harsh and cold on her own ears, like the drawing of a blade.

He can't be here! He got away!

Gareth was bound and gagged, a rope looped around his neck so that Culp could lead him, jerking him forward as one would a wayward steer. Culp's dead-eyed face was as impassive as ever, but Elyssa sensed a certain amount of pleasure in the interrogator's movements, silent satisfaction in each little jerk. Gareth would not look at her; his eyes seemed distant, almost lost.

No, Elyssa thought dully. *He got away.*

"He did not get away," said her mother, and Elyssa realized that she had spoken aloud. "Brenna warned me, long before the act, and Culp was waiting down in the tunnels when your little friend came through."

"Brenna?" Elyssa asked stupidly. "How did she know?"

"She knows everything, Elyssa." Her mother's face suddenly lost its cold reserve, became animated, her cheeks flushed. She grasped at the bodice of her dress . . . reaching, Elyssa knew, for the sapphire that lay beneath. "It's a pity you fight me so hard, for if you would only fall in line, Brenna could show you wonders. So many wonders."

"Do you honestly believe that creature acts for your benefit, Mother? Are you so foolish?"

"Magic is magic. Who cares about motive? These jewels, Elyssa!" She brought out the sapphire, and Elyssa noted that her eyes were wide, the pupils dilated, as though she had just taken a hit of morphia. "One could rule the world with these jewels!"

"And you call me naive."

Her mother's face tightened, and Elyssa realized that she had misread her mother slightly. Though the rest of this scene might have been contrived, the subject of the jewels had been spontaneous. Her mother had been sincere, had tried to share something with her. Elyssa felt a momentary regret, but it was too late.

"You *are* naive, Elyssa . . . which brings us back to your little friend here. Culp's been itching for another go. He would have begun interrogation immediately, but I told him no, we must wait."

The Queen smiled wide, and now Elyssa saw the blade before her, naked and shining.

Great God, they will torture him right here before my eyes, they will make me watch—

"I would have let him go, you know," the Queen remarked. "You played a nice hand when you put me on the spot in front of them all, and I would have had no choice. I would have nursed him and let him go. But life is about choices, Elyssa. Making choices and living with them. If you're to sit the throne after me, you must learn that. You may know it academically, but academics mean fuck-all with a crown on your head. Better, I think, to teach you a practical lesson . . . one you will never forget."

The Queen rose from her vanity table, and Elyssa saw, almost numbly, that she held a knife in her hand.

"I am going to give you a choice now, my little rabble-rouser. At the moment, your friend here is drugged to the gills, probably doesn't even know where he is. You may kill him quickly, here and now, and retain your claim on the throne. Or, if you refuse, Culp can take him down to the dungeons, wait for the drugs to wear off, and do with him as he pleases, while I strip you of your title and invest Thomas. The choice will be yours."

She cannot be serious, Elyssa thought, numb with horror. *It's a trick, a test. She just wants to know that I'm willing to do it, but she won't really make me, she wouldn't—*

But then Elyssa abandoned even that last, desperate hope, because her mother *would*. It was plain in her face, which wore the same blank, implacable expression that Elyssa recognized from so many punishments before.

"He may have information—" she began, but her mother cut her off.

"Not enough. As you were so kind to point out in front of the crowd, dear daughter, even Culp cannot wring a confession from these Blue Horizon lunatics. The man is of no further use to me."

Elyssa's mind ran back and forth, seeking a way out. The entire city knew that Gareth had escaped; according to Niya, the tale of his daring flight was being told in every pub and market. Culp had taken Gareth in secret, and the guards' pique had been too real; no one else knew about this. There was nothing to stop her mother from murdering Gareth in any way she liked, not even the wrath of the Blue Horizon. They would never find out, not unless Elyssa told the world.

But I can't do that either, she realized, suddenly seeing the true nature of her mother's move here. They thought Elyssa the True Queen; they believed in her. What would happen to that belief if they found out that she had murdered a member of the Blue Horizon in cold blood?

"Make a decision, Elyssa," her mother commanded. "You will

be queen someday, and the kingdom will not wait while you vacillate between your cunt and your better judgment."

For a long moment, Elyssa meant to tell her mother no. She even opened her mouth to do it. But the memory of that night was upon her—Gareth smiling lazily up at her—and she couldn't do it, couldn't say the words that would see him handed over to Culp, sent down to face the manacles. The board.

"Here, Elyssa," her mother said, holding out the dagger, a hint of pity in her voice. That, too, was part of the dance; her mother was always sorry, but only after the damage was done. "Take it."

Elyssa lurched forward and took the dagger. The hilt was smooth and cold, inset with rubies. The dagger had been a gift to her mother from the Cadarese king, and like all Cadarese weapons, it had a slightly curving blade. Staring at the gleaming surface, Elyssa could see her own eyes reflected: bright green eyes, wide and hunted, full of tears.

In that moment, she came within an ace of killing her mother.

She could see herself doing it, burying the dagger in her mother's stomach and jerking sharply upward, gutting the Queen as a kitchen boy would do a trout. Elyssa could even see the way the blood would flow: gouting from the wound, soaking her mother's dressing gown, spilling onto her feet. The Guard would come, the medics . . . but it would be too late. Arla the Just would bleed to death.

Do it, and you'll never take the throne.

Elyssa started, brought back suddenly by the steel in that voice—Lady Glynn's—and even more by the memory of the crowd in the Circus, their wild jubilation. The True Queen, they called her, but no regicide would ever mount the throne, and when Elyssa went to the axe, the kingdom would go to Thomas. Besides, Gareth was behind her, still chained, and if Elyssa killed her mother now, one way or another, Culp would have him. She blocked out that murderous vision—though it did not go willingly—and turned to confront Gareth.

He was not looking at her. His eyes rolled without direction, gazing toward the ceiling and then the far wall. The Queen had said he was drugged, and Elyssa believed it. Spittle bubbled between his lips and ran in a thin line from the side of his mouth. The drugs had dulled his wits, certainly, but would they dull his pain?

"Morphia," her mother said, sensing Elyssa's hesitation. "High-grade, the best in the city, from our own infirmary. He will feel nothing."

Elyssa stared at Gareth's slack face. Her knife hand was shaking slightly; she waited for a moment, willing it to be still, and then stepped forward. Culp backed away—was it mild disappointment she sensed in his dead eyes, or only a trick of the light?—giving her clearance.

Elyssa did not know how to kill a man. Thomas had been given lessons in arms when he was younger—though the gossip of the Queen's Wing said that Thomas was so terrible a fighter that the lessons might have served Elyssa better—but as a princess, she was not supposed to carry steel, or even know how to use it. She could try to cut Gareth's throat, but what if she botched it?

You caused all of this, her mind whispered. *You couldn't leave well enough alone.*

Elyssa drew a long, shaking breath. She closed her eyes and found Gareth there, standing before her mother's throne, bruised and bleeding, staring up at the Queen with blazing eyes . . . but even Gareth was overborne by the other images. The Circus. The starving children she had seen in the Gut, all swollen bellies and wide eyes. The broad sweep of the Almont beyond the city walls. She loved Gareth, yes, but that did not outweigh the fate of the kingdom, the millions of people outside this room. It did not even come close.

"I'm sorry," she whispered, and in a single sharp movement she jerked her hand sinister, burying the point of the blade in Gareth's neck. The drugs were strong, but not strong enough; Gareth's eyes opened wide, and for a long, nearly endless moment, Elyssa saw a terrible awareness there. She cried out, reaching for the knife as though to take it back . . . but it was too late. A hideous rattling sound emitted from Gareth's throat, and a moment later he fell to the floor. Elyssa wanted to turn away, to flee, but she knew that if she did, she would never forgive herself that cowardice. Too many unforgivable things had already happened in this room, and so she remained where she was, watching Gareth die. Only when the light had faded from his eyes did she kneel down beside him, placing her hand on his.

"What of the body?" she asked her mother. "Can I bury him?"

"No. The corpse will go to the Holy Father. We have made an arrangement."

Elyssa nodded numbly, realizing that she should have known. Culp was coming to clear away the body, but Elyssa remained where she was, holding Gareth's hand, staring at the stream of blood that had pooled on the stone floor. She needed something to look at. She needed to keep her eyes from her mother's face.

One day, she thought, *you will have no hold, no leverage over anyone I love. On that day, I will kill you . . . and believe me, Mother, there will be no morphia to ease your passage. I will watch you die, and I will smile when you scream.*

These thoughts came quite naturally; they were not theoretical but practical, her mother's life merely a problem to be solved. All emotion seemed to have drained from Elyssa, like the life from Gareth's corpse. Behind her, Culp began to drag the corpse away; Gareth's bare feet rasped against the stone, a sound that

Elyssa knew would haunt her later. Only when the corpse was gone did her mother signal that she should go.

Outside the door, Barty and Galen waited, Niya beside them. Barty's brow furrowed in concern as he saw Elyssa's dishevelment, the tear tracks on her face.

"Highness?" Niya asked. "Are you all right?"

"Fine," Elyssa returned mechanically. Niya put her arms around her, but Elyssa stood unmoving, unable to take comfort, and at length Niya let her go and simply offered a cloth. Elyssa took it and wiped her face. Galen looked away, uncomfortable; he was one of those men who didn't know what to do with tears, and he clearly thought that it was only a matter of seconds until the next storm of weeping descended.

But Elyssa's tears were done. Now she could think only of murder. Murder sent her walking steadily back to her chamber, murder allowed her to eat a hearty dinner . . . and later that night, when the entire Queen's Wing was asleep, murder lightened Elyssa's feet as she danced down the hidden tunnel behind her chambers, heading for the witch's room.

CHAPTER 18

TOPSIDE

In the often tumultuous history of the Queen's Guard, no fig-
ure has been so misunderstood or overly interpreted as that of
the Mace. Despite the determined effort to make the Mace into
a complicated man, shadowy and enigmatic, there is no basis
for such convolution of simple facts. The Mace's background
was well known and unremarkable: he was a farm boy out of
the northern Almont, brought to the attention of the Guard
for his skill at boxing. His rise in the Guard was exceptional,
almost meteoric, but that is not surprising, considering his
singular skills. He went on to be a superlative guard, one of
the finest in Tear history, yet that same history has decreed
that there must be something odd, almost sinister, about this
particular character. My esteemed colleagues have even gone
so far as to suggest that the Mace may have been a victim of
childhood abuse, but this is laughable. Abuse does not vanish
with the onset of adulthood; it follows the victim, creating
fault lines—alienation and violence—that grow deeper over
the years. But from his earliest appearance in the Queen's
Guard, the Mace showed none of these faults. He projected
nothing but strength and an almost steely resolve.

—Lecture by Dr. Thomas Kerwin, Professor of History,

University of New London (later condemned and sacked)

211

_6∂_

Y ou want what?" Carroll asked.

You heard me, Christian thought of saying, but did not. He was guarding his tongue carefully in this conversation, for everything was different now. He was no longer in his domain, and the boy he had saved in the Creche was no longer a tiny, naked pigeon but a member of the Queen's Guard. Carroll was still shorter than Christian by at least half a foot, but height didn't come into it, for the power differential had shifted. Carroll belonged here, while Christian was an interloper, a Creche baby trying to climb . . . not merely topside, but higher than any Creche baby ever dared to dream.

They were seated in a pub on the Broadwater Road, some ten blocks from Arliss's office. Despite all of the dealer's Blue Horizon talk about forgiveness, Christian had thought it best to put some distance between himself and Arliss's territory. He had not known whether Carroll would come to meet him here, or even whether the skeptical Gate Guard he had shadowed and then accosted would carry his message into the Keep. But the man had, and here Carroll was, clad in a grey cloak that clearly meant something on the streets of this city. Already several men had fallen all over themselves trying to buy Carroll a drink, and no fewer than four whores had cruised the table, displaying their wares with an eagerness that made Christian feel queasy.

"I am a good fighter," Christian said, trying to sound humble. "Even in the Creche, they say that your Queen's Guard has weakened in hand-to-hand combat. You rely too much on swords, on steel."

"Do we?" Carroll asked stiffly. "What else do they say?"

"That you're no longer a match for the Caden. Not man to man."

Carroll colored slightly; there must be some truth to the

rumors after all. As a guild of assassins, the Caden were the main concern of the Queen's Guard, an enemy that the Guard must be able to repel. But the Guard's skills were on the wane, while the Caden were as sharp as ever. Christian had heard such talk from time to time, mostly around the ring. But he had never expected to care about idle report, and even less to use it to beg for a job.

"We could use you," Carroll admitted slowly, though Christian could tell the admission pained him. "Elyssa has ten guards at present, but that will not be enough. She made a speech—"

"I heard about it." And Christian had; even now, weeks after the event, it was all they talked of in the Gut. Even the starving peasants who slept near Christian in Bull Alley wouldn't shut up about her. True Queen this and True Queen that . . . it was enough to drive a man mad. These topside people didn't seem to understand how easy it was to mouth words, how little they mattered. A real True Queen would have gotten these people some food.

"She's picked a fight," Carroll said flatly. "With the nobility, the Church . . . in short, everyone with enough money to hire the Caden and pay for assassination. My captain says we're in for a dangerous time, and I think he's right."

Dangerous, Christian thought, restraining a snort. He had been living rough on the streets of New London for only four days, but he already knew that its dangers paled in comparison to those of the tunnels. As if to prove his point, a mob of people moved past the windows of the pub, packed so thick that their skin flattened as they pressed against the windows. But their faces were bright and hopeful, almost transported. Their voices thundered down the street.

"The True Queen! Elyssa Raleigh! The True Queen! Elyssa Raleigh!"

"Is she?" Christian asked, for despite his skepticism, the crowd had aroused his curiosity. They seemed so damned certain of the Princess, all of them, even the beggars. "Is she the True Queen?"

Carroll took a moment before answering, and Christian was intrigued at the change that came over the guard's face, the softening of eyes and mouth. Carroll looked like a man in love, or like the Blue Horizon fools when they raved about their better world.

"I don't know whether she is or not," Carroll finally replied. "But I know she wants to be. She wants to save us all; she has the will, and that's more important than any prophecy. She will be a great queen . . . if we can only keep her alive until she takes the throne."

"So bring me on. If times are so dire, I can certainly be an asset."

"The Princess will need all the guards she can get, no doubt about that. But the Queen's Guard . . . it's not all about fighting, you know. There are other things. Honor, and loyalty, and—"

"Come off it," Christian snorted. "I've seen the grey-cloaks in the tunnels. Not so often as the priests, mind you, but they come down, all the same. Don't try to sell me on the honorable Guard. That's not what it is."

"It's what it's supposed to be!" Carroll snapped. "What good to improve in combat, if we let the rest fall to pieces? I owe you a debt, yes, and I mean to pay it. But bringing you into the Guard, it's . . . it's not . . ."

He trailed off, as though realizing that nothing he could say would improve matters. Christian said nothing, merely watched him. Food was expensive, and the remainder of the ten pounds Arliss had given him would only last another three days at most. Christian supposed he could have caught on with a labor crew of some sort; he certainly had the strength, and he had heard the foremen crying for volunteers in the streets. *They* would not care where he had come from or what he was, only how much he could lift and tote. But laying brick or cutting stone would not get him into the Keep, where Maura's client was ... perhaps Maura herself. Each rung on this ladder required precise steps, but Christian had already observed that topside, like the Creche, operated on favors and debt. The Queen's Guard was clearly a coveted position in this society, but even the Queen's Guard could not operate wholly on merit. He believed what he wanted could be bought.

Floundering, Carroll took another pull of his ale. Christian had bought pints for them both, though the cost had been atrocious, an entire pound. The drought—another popular topic of conversation in the streets—had now killed off the grain supply; soon beer would be nearly as precious as gold. Christian had not touched his own pint, and he was worried that Carroll might take offense, but he did not even seem to notice. In the Creche, it was considered an insult to refuse to share food or drink, but an entirely different code operated up here.

Wigan used to tell me the sky would make me sick, Christian remembered suddenly. Two days before, the clouds had finally cleared, and he had seen the daytime sky for the first time, its blue so bright that it was almost hard to accept. The brief spate of rain had been important in the city; Christian had picked up that much from talk in the cramped alley where he spent his nights, wrapped in a blanket he had stolen from the back of an unguarded wagon. The entire city had hoped that the rain would last for weeks, and when it stopped, when the sky cleared, there had been an almost collective groan of disappointment over the expanse of the Gut. But Christian could not share in their misery, for what was a drought to him? He could only stare at the sky above, thinking, *What would it mean?* What might every child in the Creche be, if instead of torchlit stone over his head, he could look up and see that blue expanse?

This place is changing me, he realized, slightly alarmed. *Changing me already. But into what?*

But the novelty of this new world could not last forever. Already Christian found himself looking around, picking out the rot: the starving families who begged in the streets, waiting outside pub doors and holding up cups before the passing carriages of the wealthy. When he walked through the Gut, he could see the brothels, with their complements of girls leaning out the windows and dangling their breasts in the air, and smell the poppy dens burning all night long. Topside might not be another Creche, but it certainly wasn't the gates of heaven. Even the royals were not impressive, for Christian had heard that the Prince himself had bought a girl and enslaved her in the castle. He was becoming disenchanted with this place, and if he did not get about finding Maura, finding Thorne, he sensed that his diminishing wonder would lead him right back down to the tunnels, the life he knew.

"You have admitted that you owe me a debt," he told Carroll. "This is the way you can repay it. There will not be a second opportunity."

"They won't take you!" Carroll protested. "Captain Givens, the Queen, once they find out who you are—"

"And how are they going to find out? I'm certainly not advertising."

"I would be honor bound to tell them," Carroll replied, clenching his jaw.

"Your honor is quite the movable banquet, Queen's Guard."

Carroll looked down, clearly unhappy, and Christian felt a sudden contempt for him, this well-fed topsider who could be twisted by such an amorphous concept as guilt. In the Creche, a man took what he wanted and simply tried to get away clean. Then again, this boy was ready to spend his entire life guarding another person, so he was clearly a fool to begin with. What could he possibly get out of it?

"How do I know I can trust you?" Carroll asked suddenly.

"With the Queen, the Princess? The Queen's Guard take an oath to lay down their very lives. How do I know you can keep your word?"

The question startled Christian. Keep his word? He had never *given* his word to anyone before. He supposed he had known that the Queen's Guard took some vow or other, but in his eagerness to get into the Keep, he had forgotten.

"What reason would I have to harm the Queen?" he asked Carroll. "Or the Princess? I have spent my life killing men."

"And children," Carroll said softly.

Christian felt his temper flare. It was not like the Creche, this place. In the Creche, no one judged a man for what he did to survive. Here, Christian could be called to account at any time, even by a smug little bastard half his size. The idea of having to explain himself, to *justify* himself, was so repugnant that for a moment Christian considered simply clouting Carroll across the face and storming out. But caution ruled. Christian was trying to pass through the eye of a needle, and he needed every millimeter.

"I will not apologize for my past," he said, gritting out each word. "Had you been born into the tunnels, you would know that there is no choice down there. But these are not the tunnels."

Carroll absorbed this message quietly, studying Christian with an odd, unreadable gaze. His hands came together on the table: topsider's hands, tanned and without scars. Christian wondered whether Carroll had ever been in a real fight, anything more than two boys playing silly with toy swords. It was not an empty offer Christian had made; he *could* teach the Queen's Guard, teach them how to grapple and close, how to gouge and rend, how to squeeze the life from a man. If Carroll was any indication, they could certainly use the lesson. But now he wondered whether any of them would be capable of learning what he had to teach.

"My father, God rest his soul, used to say that you do not judge a man by what he does in the breach, with all eyes upon him," Carroll remarked. "You judge him by what he does in the quiet, when no one is looking."

Christian didn't know what "in the breach" meant, but he was annoyed to find the rest of Carroll's meaning coming through clear as day, and even more annoyed to find himself in total agreement. He thought of the priests he had seen creeping through Whore's Alley, of the furred and jeweled nobles outside the ring, screaming for blood. The Creche, after all, was only one big quiet. Nothing a man might do topside, no matter how good or right, could erase the foulness done down there.

But Christian did not mean to erase it.

"You have a hidden purpose here," Carroll continued, holding Christian's gaze. "I am young for the Guard, and inexperienced; Dyer calls me Little Wide-Eyes, and there's enough truth in that to make me hate it. But I'm no fool. You did not wake up yesterday with a burning desire to become a Queen's Guard. You're playing a long game."

Carroll paused, but it was not a demanding pause; he did not expect a response. He turned away, looking out the window, and Christian saw that he had cut himself shaving. His jaw was nicked in several places, and there was not even a hint of beard growth to hide the cuts.

He told me to run, Christian remembered suddenly. *He told me to save myself.*

"You have made a brave show here today," Carroll continued. "And you would be a glittering addition to the Guard, I have no doubt . . . at least to those who care only for brawn and steel. But make no mistake, this is how you will be judged: on what you do in the quiet."

Judged by who? Christian wanted to ask, but did not, for he found himself strangely mute. The boy's words reminded him of a story Maura had told him once, something of knights and a magic sword. Dignity seemed to enfold Carroll, clothing him even more tightly than his grey cloak, and in the face of that dignity, Christian found himself compelled to speak.

"I mean no harm to you, or the Princess, or the Queen. My word may be worth shit, but I give it, all the same."

Carroll stared at him for another minute, and then extended a hand. The gesture made Christian recoil, and it was not until several seconds had passed that he realized that he had been accepted, that Carroll's hand was offered in friendship, that taking it signified some sort of accord.

He shook, and became a Queen's Guard.

CHAPTER 19

THE SEVEN OF SWORDS

Truth is always easier than a lie. In fact, truth sells a lie,
much better than the lie sells itself. Simple self-interest man-
dates at least a pinch of honesty in all of our dealings.

–*The Words of the Glynn Queen*, AS RECORDED BY FATHER TYLER

N iya."
Niya put down her needle and thread, clearing her throat.
She was meant to be sewing up a rip in one of Elyssa's shifts, but
in truth she had been miles away, thinking hard.

"Highness? What can I do for you?"

Elyssa didn't look well. Ever since the heat of August had come,
no one in the Keep had been sleeping particularly soundly, but
the Princess was pale and wan, as though she were ill as well as
tired.

"I want to talk to you," Elyssa told her, beckoning from the
doorway. "They're trying a new guard on; will you come?"

Niya glanced at her watch; only twenty minutes past four.
Plenty of time. With some relief, she dropped the ripped shift and
got to her feet. She didn't know what she was doing sewing, anyway; one of the undermaids would surely attend to it. But mun-
danity often paid dividends in clear thinking, and there was a

puzzle to be solved. The last coded message Niya had received from the Fetch had been brief but to the point.

The witch belongs to Arlen Thorne.

"My mother's birthday is coming, the first week in October," Elyssa told her, as they walked down the corridor toward the arms room, Barty and Cae trailing behind them. "I want to give her a dress for her birthday. Something special."

"A nice idea, Highness," Niya replied. "What sort of dress?"

"Red. It should be red. She will have a party, an enormous one. The dress should be magnificent, something she can wear that night and astound the world. I could use Mrs. Loys, but I don't think she would keep a secret from my mother. So I need you to find a new dressmaker for me, one who's willing to work quickly."

"Of course, Highness," Niya said absently, while her mind reviewed everything the Blue Horizon knew about Arlen Thorne. He was a pimp, one of the most notorious in the Creche. The Blue Horizon was still laying groundwork in the tunnels, but when they were finally ready to move, Arlen Thorne's infamous stable was one of the first that they meant to close down. Thorne's origins were hazy; there was some rumor of noble blood, but such romantic rumors floated around the Creche all the time, with rarely any substance.

Of course, Thorne had been branching beyond the Creche in recent years: delivering specialized whores topside, forging ties with the brothels in the Gut. But that was all par for the course; every Creche pimp aspired to move topside. More disturbing was a recent rumor that they'd picked up from Arliss's people: Thorne was buying up children, the most physically perfect specimens the Creche had to offer. According to Webb, Arliss's man, Thorne was paying a particularly steep premium for straight, even teeth. The witch belonged to Arlen Thorne, but Thorne had not brought her to court; he had no entrée there. Lord Tennant had brought her, and while Niya could well believe that a man like Tennant owed Thorne a favor, she could not understand what Thorne meant to gain. Brenna had been in the Keep for months, and though the Guard was uneasy about many things—her witch's tools, her otherworldly manner, her clear fascination with the Queen's sapphire—nothing dreadful had happened. But all the same, Niya could not escape a sense of urgency, the feeling that something huge and unseen was closing upon them all.

"What in God's name is that?" Elyssa asked, as several shouts echoed from the arms room. Barty and Cae drew in closer, slipping in front of her, but they relaxed as the roar came again: men's voices raised in enthusiasm, not violence.

"Dyer and Mhurn must be matching for drinks again," Niya remarked dryly.

"I wish everyone would forget about that," Barty muttered. "I censured them both. No, it'll be the new guard, the one Carroll brought in."

Entering the arms room, they found two figures struggling on the practice floor. Niya recognized Elston's broad shoulders easily, but she didn't know his opponent: another giant, only slightly less monstrous in frame than Elston himself. As Niya and Elyssa watched, the other man knocked Elston flying, and Elston landed in a heap of armor and curses, rapping his head on the floor. The other man jumped on his back, pinning him, then jammed an arm under Elston's neck and hauled his head upward, so that his forearm could pressure Elston's windpipe. The guards circling the ring hooted and catcalled again, but as Elston's face turned red, and then redder, they fell silent. As Elston's opponent increased the pressure, Elston began to gag.

"Hold!" old Vincent, the Queen's swordmaster, called, limping out onto the practice floor. "Let him go."

With some reluctance—Niya could see that reluctance, though

she wasn't sure anyone else in the room would have been able to—the dark-haired man released Elston. He held his hands up, a gesture of harmlessness, then retreated across the practice floor and waited.

"Bloody hell," Mhurn muttered at the far edge of the floor.

"Carroll!" Givens called; he had moved up to stand beside old Vincent. "Over here now! And you, the new lad—Mace, is it?—you come too!"

Mace went, following Carroll. Several of the other guards moved in to help Elston up; Elston shot Mace a look of pure venom that would have petrified another man, but Mace seemed not even to mark it.

"Nerves of steel," Elyssa remarked quietly, and Barty grunted agreement.

"I am Captain Givens," Givens told Mace. "Head of the Queen's Guard. Who are you? Where are you from?"

"My name is Mace Wyler, sir. I'm of the Almont."

"No shame in that, lad," old Vincent muttered, inspecting Mace with a gleam in his eye. "Plenty of farm boys here; Kibby and Mhurn—"

"Where are you from?" Givens demanded again.

"The northern plain, sir," Mace replied. "A village called Grey's Close."

"Barty?" Givens called.

"Aye, I know Grey's Close," Barty replied, stepping forward. "Who's your lord?"

"Lord Wells, sir."

"And what do you grow?"

"Cattle, sir. Forty-two head on my family's acreage."

Barty nodded to Givens, but the Captain clearly wasn't convinced.

"Carroll! Where did you find this man?"

Carroll began to answer, but Mace cut him off.

"I came to New London to try my hand at boxing, sir. Carroll saw me in an amateur bout in the Gut."

He's lying, Niya thought, and for the first time all day, the problem of Arlen Thorne retreated a bit from her mind. He was a very good liar, this Mace, and Niya wasn't sure that anyone not trained by the Fetch would be able to see it, but she knew instinctively.

"Is this true, Carroll?" Givens demanded.

"Yes, sir."

"You've no taste for blood sports, boy. What were you doing in the Gut?"

"I went there on my last day off. I've—" Carroll's voice faltered, and he looked a little shamefaced. "I've met a girl."

Barty snorted. The rest of the guards snickered, and Dyer rubbed Carroll's head gleefully before Carroll batted him away. But Niya didn't laugh. She was watching Mace, trying to push past the layers of deception she sensed here . . . not only from Mace himself but from Carroll as well. They were telling a lie, and telling it together.

Is he a spy? she wondered. *An assassin?*

She turned to Elyssa, to see what the Princess made of the new man, but Elyssa was looking at the ceiling, her eyes glazed, as though she were bored.

"I want him," old Vincent announced abruptly.

"What for?" Givens demanded. "He may be a decent enough boxer . . . though what we've seen here was closer to wrestling. But his swordcraft is atrocious."

"Swordcraft is easy. Footwork isn't," old Vincent replied. "You can't teach reflex. I've spent my life training fighters, and believe me, this is good material. I can teach him to wield a sword."

"Well, I don't want him on the Queen's detail. Barty would have to be willing to take him."

They both turned and looked at Barty, who stood silent for a minute.

"Why are you here, lad?" he finally asked Mace. "Why do you want to be a Queen's Guard?"

Niya turned to the newcomer and saw an interesting thing: he was warring with himself. There was something he was meant to say, but he did not want to say it. After a long moment, he shrugged and replied, with an odd dignity, "I'm not sure I do, sir. But I'm tired of fighting for no reason. If I raise my hand to another man again, I would like to have some purpose behind it."

Some truth there, Niya thought. Barty considered Mace for another long moment, then said, "I'll take him. But he's your responsibility, Carroll. You teach him the ropes and rules."

Carroll nodded, flashing a brief smile at Mace. Mace didn't smile back.

"But he'd damned well better learn quick with that sword," Barty muttered. "You, Mace! Come on over here!"

The hulking man approached, and as he did so, Niya finally got a good look at his eyes: deep and dark, without warmth, the eyes of a wounded animal. As he moved to stand before Elyssa, Niya tensed, her fingertips resting lightly on the handle of the dagger in her pocket.

"Your Highness," Mace said, without inflection. At Elyssa's nod, he knelt before her, though he was clearly uncomfortable in doing so. No courtier, this one. Elyssa smiled, but again Niya was struck by how ill she looked, her skin pale and clammy, her eyes circled dark. She wondered whether the Princess had caught something, whether she should drop a word to the medics, have them look Elyssa over. But Elyssa's smile, though tired, was genuine enough.

"Are you true, Mace Wyler?" she asked the kneeling man.

"I am, Your Highness."

"And do you swear to guard me against all danger, though it may cost you your own life?"

"I do, Your Highness."

"Then kneel no longer. Welcome to my Guard."

Elyssa extended a hand, and Niya, who had seen this ceremony four times already since coming to the Keep, found herself inexplicably moved by the bewilderment on Mace's face. He eyed Elyssa's hand as one would a new and possibly dangerous creature. After a long moment, he allowed Elyssa to pull him to his feet, and the rest of the Guard gave a cheer . . . even Elston, whose neck had already broken out in deep purple bruising.

"Come, boy," Barty said. "Carroll will get you to the armorer. Highness? Your orders?"

"Where is my mother today?" Elyssa asked.

"Downstairs, Highness. In the private throne room."

"We'll go down there."

Elyssa preceded them all to the door, Niya following a step behind. She kept her eyes on Elyssa's back, but she was acutely conscious of the tall man behind her. He had the size and strength for farming, certainly, but the muscles were all wrong, concentrated not in his arms and hands but in his shoulders and chest. And although his hands were covered with scars, as most tenants' were by the time they reached adulthood, the scars were wrong too, stretched and distended. Farmers took their wounds from harrows and scythes, tools only wielded in early adolescence or later. Mace's scars had been inflicted in childhood.

Not a farmer, Niya thought. *But what?*

They emerged into the great chamber to an unpleasant sight: the white witch, Brenna, dealing her damnable tarot cards at the dining table. The entire Guard gave a collective shiver of dislike, and the puzzle that had briefly left Niya's mind now returned with a vengeance. What was the witch doing here?

Elyssa passed the seer without a glance, but the new man, Mace, came to an abrupt halt just past the threshold, breath hissing inward as he saw her. At the sound, Brenna looked up, her mouth stretching in a ghastly smile . . . but the smile went jagged as she saw Mace. She shot up from the table, snarling, and the tarot deck convulsed in her fingers, spraying cards all over the table and floor.

"The Seven of Swords," she snarled, never taking her eyes from Mace. "The reaper of death. But I have never seen—"

"Don't let her bother you, lad," Barty broke in, and the forced jocularity in his tone made Niya wince. "I know she looks like the ass end of hell, but she's just one of the Queen's frauds."

"I see," Mace replied, his eyes never leaving the witch. Niya sensed something curious passing between the two of them . . . recognition? Memory? The guards feared Brenna—were right to fear her, Niya thought—but Mace didn't. The witch clearly knew it and wanted no part of him, for she gathered her tarot cards into an untidy stack and hurried down the hallway, muttering to herself.

"Well, Brenna doesn't like you," Dyer remarked, clapping Mace on the shoulder. "That's good enough for me."

The Guard chuckled, but Niya saw Mace withdraw, almost flinching away from Dyer's hand on his shoulder. Dyer must have sensed it as well, for he left off, his friendly face puzzled. Niya checked her watch again and found that it was nearly five.

"Highness," she whispered to Elyssa, as though in sudden distress. "I feel unwell. May I return to my room?"

"Of course!" Elyssa said, looking concerned. Well she might be; Niya was never ill. "Do you need a medic, or—"

"No; just to lie down. A brief nap, and I'm sure I'll feel fine. I will begin work on the matter of your mother's dress."

"All right," Elyssa replied, her face still troubled. "Let Fina know if you need anything."

"I should be fine to dress you for dinner."

"Fina can dress me. You're relieved. Go and sleep."

Niya smiled. Elyssa always behaved so to servants, with a kindness unheard of in the noble class, and no matter how many times Niya saw it, she was always moved. She bowed, then retreated, heading back down the corridor, checking her watch again. Five minutes to five, all the time they needed. She only regretted that Gareth could not be with them—but this thought, too, brought up a thread of disquiet. Where was Gareth? The story of his flight from the Keep was now a favorite; the singers were even making ballads of it down in the Gut. Gareth went where he would, and often disappeared for long periods of time. But six full weeks had now passed since he had left the Keep. He had never been away so long before. Even the Fetch was worried.

Never mind, Niya thought. *He'll show up.*

She darted into her chamber, changing into a red dress utterly unlike her usual wardrobe, and donned a long cloak she had chosen specially, one with a hood so full that it draped low over her face. She pinned her hair up, then tucked a rag in her pocket. At two minutes to five, she stood before the Prince's door. With a quick glance up and down the empty hallway, she put on her mask, tucked a few rebellious strands of hair inside the nape, and knocked.

"Come!" Thomas called.

Niya entered the room. She had mentally prepared herself for whatever she might find there—had been preparing for days, in truth—but still she had to restrain a gasp when she saw the girl, Mary, lying naked on the bed, her hands and feet bound to the four posters. The servants said that the Prince had simply purchased the girl, like a calf at market, from a family with too little income and too many mouths, and that the Queen herself had countenanced the arrangement. But it was one thing to hear tell, another to see.

She's so young, Niya thought, staring at the child. The girl did not even twitch under her scrutiny, only stared at the ceiling, her eyes dull and lost. Niya wondered whether she was drugged.

"Ah, just on time!" Thomas announced, turning away from his desk. He had been reading, Niya saw with some surprise . . . and then she realized that the document spread out before him was hand-printed foolscrap; one of the scandal sheets that circulated New London like a plague. As he approached, Thomas gave her figure an appreciative once-over, and Niya fought to keep still. Glancing at her watch again, she saw that it was one minute to five. She pulled the door closed behind her, her thumb softly sliding the deadbolt home.

"Well, pretty, take off the cloak. Show us the goods."

Niya nodded, curtsying, and opened her cloak. Behind Thomas, a crack appeared in the stone wall. Niya glanced again at the girl on the bed, willing her to keep quiet. But Mary didn't even seem to notice the widening crack, the door that was slowly opening beside the hearth.

"Oh, don't worry about her," Thomas said, misreading Niya's glance. "She's only a girl I bought in the filthiest part of the Gut . . . not quality at all. But you—"

He reached out, clearly meaning to put a hand on her shoulder, but Niya could not allow it. She grabbed the hand before it reached its destination, twisting it mercilessly, whipping Thomas around and shoving his elbow up his back. At the same time she pulled the rag from her pocket and jammed it into the Prince's mouth. A gasping, heaving sound came from him . . . but no real noise.

The Fetch came through the hidden door. He surveyed the bed in one glance, shook his head, and then turned to Amelia, who stood behind him. Amelia was the only one of them not wearing a mask; Niya kept a hard pressure on the Prince's elbow, so that he could not turn around and see her face.

"Cut her loose and get her dressed," the Fetch told Amelia.

Amelia bent over the bed, murmuring to the girl in a soothing voice. She pulled a knife and began cutting her bonds, and the Fetch turned his attention to Thomas.

"Well, well, Highness, this *is* a treat. I've heard so much about you."

Thomas hauled in another deep, gasping breath through the cloth, his eyes huge with fright. Niya had seen the Fetch's mask so often that she had grown inured, but it never failed to frighten the new marks.

"I'm sure you can explain yourself," the Fetch went on, pulling off his leather gloves. "I'm sure you can tell us how Mummy never loved you, how abandoned you felt, how the grief was so great that all women everywhere owe you recompense. Did I leave anything out?"

Thomas shook his head frantically ... not in agreement but in panic. Behind him, Amelia had cut Mary free and was helping her totter to the wardrobe. Even from here, Niya could see the marks on Mary's wrists, the deep red welts on her ankles. The Blue Horizon had always meant to deal with Thomas at some point, but the purchase of the girl had forced their hand. At a signal from the Fetch, Niya shoved the Prince into a chair, with far more force than was necessary.

"Thing is," the Fetch continued, perching himself on Thomas's desk, "I don't really care about why. There is no excuse for men like you, Thomas. There never will be."

"No!" Mary wept in the corner. "Don't touch me!"

"I won't touch you," Amelia returned calmly. She was the best of them for situations like this, a former pro who had seen it all before. It was Amelia's contacts in the Gut that had allowed them to intercept the girl Thomas had requested. "You can dress yourself, child. Here."

"Now, I could kill you," the Fetch continued quietly, just as mindful as Niya of the dicey situation in the corner. "I would enjoy it enormously."

Thomas murmured inarticulately against the rag. Tears had begun to leak from the corners of his eyes.

"But we are Blue Horizon. We mean to do better, and your death would serve nothing, for there are thousands more of you out there. I think it far more useful to let you live, to serve as a warning. What do you think?"

Thomas nodded frantically.

"Is she ready?" the Fetch asked.

"Just about," Amelia said, fastening the last of Mary's buttons. That done, Amelia selected a wool cloak from several that hung in the wardrobe and draped it around the girl's shoulders. The cloak was far too hot for this weather, but the tunnels were never warm, not at any time of year.

"Ready," Amelia said.

"Go," the Fetch replied, never taking his eyes from Thomas. "Take care of her."

Amelia nodded, then ushered Mary through the open door, murmuring in her ear. Mary did not look back. As the latch clicked, Niya moved up to stand beside the Fetch, both of them staring down at the gagged prince who sat in the chair.

"And now, Highness," the Fetch remarked, "you have our full attention."

CHAPTER 20

LOST GIRL

Second Witch: By the pricking of my thumbs,
   Something wicked this way comes.
   Open, locks,
   Whoever knocks!
Macbeth: How now, you secret, black and midnight hags?
   What is't you do?
All: A deed without a name.

              —*Macbeth*, WILLIAM SHAKESPEARE (PRE-CROSSING ANGL.)

The sapphire was hurting her. It burned the skin between her breasts like a brand.

Elyssa took the jewel in her hand, but that was no good; it burned her palm as well. She was forced to drop it. Her legs were tangled in the bedsheets; she kicked them off and rolled over, revealing a wet patch on the sheets. She had not slept in four days. Nothing seemed real anymore. Her limbs felt heavy and helpless. Moving through court was like swimming in sand, and the nights were even worse.

Take it off.

"No," she whispered.

The sapphire throbbed hotter, demanding it.

"Leave me alone!" Elyssa begged, close to weeping. But the sapphire seared her flesh.

Take it off. It belongs to me.

"Fuck you!" Elyssa hissed. "I won't!"

She rolled again, leaving a new patch of sweat on the silken sheets. She tried pushing herself up, letting the chain dangle away from her breasts, the sapphire resting on the pillow. But that was no help. The burning was not physical.

A rasping noise came from the corner, and now Elyssa did weep, not bothering to muffle the sounds. Two guards stood outside the door, she knew, but they might as well have been on the far side of the Dry Lands. No one could help her inside this room.

What did she do to me? Elyssa wondered, for perhaps the thousandth time. *What in God's name did she* do?

She could not remember. She remembered entering the witch's chamber, sitting down on the low chair that the witch had offered in silence. The witch had sat down as well, and then—

Then, nothing, only the dreamlike blend of the last days: wandering the Queen's Wing as though compelled, though she did not know what she was searching for, the sapphire growing heavier and heavier against her heart.

What is happening to me?

That sibilant, rasping sound again. Movement flickered in the corner of Elyssa's eye, and she buried her face in the pillow, not wanting to see.

"Elyssa," the voice whispered ... *his* voice, muffled and sibilant with the larynx rotted away, but still unmistakably his.

"Go away," she sobbed into the pillow. "Please, just go away."

But the rasping noise continued, coming closer and closer, dead feet dragging on stone. Elyssa clenched her fists in the pillow for a moment, then flung it across the room and sat up.

Gareth was tottering across the room toward her, his hands

outstretched. One leg was badly twisted, as though it had been broken, and the foot dragged behind him, rasping across the floor. His face was puffed, the flesh of his cheeks turning black with decay, his eyes wide and staring.

"You're not real," Elyssa whispered.

Gareth grinned vacantly, a mindless yet dreadful parody of the drugged expression she had last seen on his face. His blackened hands searched for her, the fingers reaching, as though testing the air. His head turned this way and that, his blind eyes scanning the room, seeking her out.

"They're starving," he whispered. "Millions of people, starving to death. Neighbor feeding on neighbor, parents dining on children . . ."

No, Elyssa thought. *That can't be happening.*

"Water," Gareth whispered. "The end of water." And suddenly he seemed to decay before her eyes, features melting and withering. The tip of his blackened tongue disintegrated, and a writhe of maggots boiled out, spilling to the floor. Elyssa screamed, pulling her nails down her cheeks, furrowing them, trying to rend herself, to finally wake herself up.

"God, God, God!"

She was vaguely aware of the Guard around her then: Barty and Carroll, Dyer and Elston. Niya as well, all of them leaning over her bed, holding her arms. But beyond them, past them, Gareth remained, featureless but hideously real.

"Coryn!" Barty panted. "Get a shot ready!"

They were holding her down. Elyssa tried to point, but she could not move her arms. She tried to tell them, but her mouth could do nothing but wail. One black hand snaked between Barty and Carroll, and Elyssa had time to see that three of the nails were missing before Gareth's fingers grasped her nipple and pinched. Elyssa screamed then, long and endless screams, and she did not care whether they gave her a shot, or even whether they strangled her, just so long as she would not see him any longer.

"Elyssa."

The voice was low, almost melodious. Elyssa turned her head and saw the witch, standing on the other side of the bed, just beyond the circle of guards who ringed the canopy. Her white face was regretful, almost sorrowful. She looked so tall, so regal, standing there that Elyssa's mind dug up an immediate parallel: her mother, standing before the throne.

They are alike! Elyssa realized, horrified. *They are so alike!*

"Take it off, Elyssa," the witch said. "Take it off, and all of this will end."

She's not really there. If she was there, the Guard would see her, hear her. They would throw her out.

Would they? her mind rejoined. *Would they really?*

"Take it off, Elyssa," Brenna coaxed, her voice almost honey-sweet. Above the ring of guards bent over the bed, Gareth's decayed head nodded in dreadful counterpoint.

"Give it to me."

Why not? Elyssa asked herself, finding relief in the simplicity of the question. *Why not?*

Her abrupt calm seemed to have eased her guards' concern; they backed off, straightening, allowing her to sit up. Gareth, too, was suddenly gone, and that seemed so much a mercy that Elyssa reached for the clasp of her sapphire necklace without thinking, her fingers fumbling for the tiny catch. It was only an heirloom, after all.

You know better.

Lady Glynn's voice was sharp, the words as loud and clear as though they had been spoken in her ear, and they acted on Elyssa like a slap. Across the room, Brenna suddenly hissed in anger, the corners of her mouth rising to bare her sharp white teeth. Elyssa could almost see Lady Glynn's face before her: the rigid jawline, the hawk's eyes. She was dead, long dead, murdered by Queen Arla the Just . . . but it made perfect sense that she should be here now, for the room was already full of ghosts.

You know better, Elyssa Raleigh. If it were only an heirloom, the witch would not be going to such lengths. Don't you dare take that sapphire off. Not until—

Lady Glynn's voice cut off sharply. Brenna was striding toward the bed now, her white face twisted in fury . . . just as the Queen always looked during Elyssa's little rebellions. The similarity between the two women struck Elyssa again.

Until what? she demanded. Lady Glynn remained silent, but even so, there came an answer, soft and diffuse, like a distant echo inside Elyssa's mind.

Kelsea.

Brenna had closed the distance between them now. She reached down and grabbed Elyssa by the hair, jerking her up off the bed. Around Elyssa, the guards recoiled, and Carroll crossed himself, murmuring a prayer. They saw, yes . . . but they could not *see*.

"Listen to me, my girl," Brenna snarled. "Give me the jewel, or you will suffer the worst I have to offer. No nightmare you've ever had will begin to compare."

Elyssa believed her, for she suddenly saw many things, with a merciless clarity that cut through her mind like a blade. The witch was powerful, more powerful than anyone in the Queen's Wing suspected. Famine was here; Elyssa saw it, as clearly as though the Almont were spread out before her like a vast chessboard. Even those who managed to find water would still die, and Elyssa saw it all: abandoned fields, starving children, corpses rotting in their hovels while the nobles feasted behind locked gates. She saw her mother, sitting on the silver throne, hoarding the kingdom's meager food in the city while thousands died outside the walls. Her mother would not prevent this famine. Elyssa might have prevented it, had she been less a fool, but that opportunity was gone. The witch's threat was real, and Elyssa would not be given time.

I will never be the True Queen.

Something deep inside her seemed to wail, but Elyssa did not listen ... could not. She was transfixed by the image in her mind: a vast black cloud on the horizon, moving swiftly toward the Tearling, growing in power and strength. Her sapphire pulsed at her chest, but it was not painful now ... only warning.

Magic, Elyssa thought. *Real magic, and oh, what I could have done with it, if I had known—*

But it was too late for *if.*

I can't take it off, Elyssa realized ... and then, more firmly, clutching the sapphire in her right hand: *I won't.*

"You won't have it," she told the witch. "Not now, not ever."

Brenna screamed with rage, and this time even the guards heard it; dimly, Elyssa saw both Dyer and Carroll jump, all of them looking around, as though at a distant alarm. Then the witch bent over her, and Elyssa began to scream, for the face above hers was no longer that of a woman, or anything human at all, only a glaring whiteness from which eyes as blue and cold as death itself spiraled downward, twisting into a hell so deep that it could not be charted, and Elyssa saw the end of everything there: of Gareth, of Tear's better world, of Elyssa's dreams for her kingdom, of her own future. There was no future, Brenna's eyes promised, and no past either, only the unspeakable present ... and the present was infinite.

CHAPTER 21

PEACOCKS

The divide between wealthy and poor in the early Tearling was nothing short of an abyss, but the gap was made even worse by the total absence of that concept the ancients called noblesse oblige: *the notion that power and privilege convey responsibilities as well as rights. However misguided this principle in application during the pre-Crossing, that aristocratic sense of obligation at least allowed for the possibility of shame. But for nobles of the Raleigh era, privilege came with no strings at all.*

—*Socialism in the Greater Tear,* Michael Klunder

Twenty minutes into his first royal audience, Christian had already discovered that he did not like the nobility. He didn't like their clothes, which were elaborate to the point of ridiculous, or their hair, which was more ridiculous still. One of the first things Carroll had done after they came to an accord was to take Christian to a barber, who shaved him and sheared his head down to a thin layer of dark brown. The tortured tresses of the horde of rich beggars in front of the throne offended him in some way he could not quite articulate, except to say to himself: *These people have money, more coin in a week than a Creche child will likely ever hold. This is how they choose to spend it.*

But his contempt went unnoticed, for the nobles who approached the throne ignored the Guard entirely, as though Christian and the rest of them were merely pieces of furniture. They would treat their servants the same way, Christian thought, and the woman who knelt before the throne was no exception. She wore a cloak of material so fabulously mottled and spotted with bright color that Christian could barely credit it as real. Only when he heard Elston and Kibb muttering to each other did he realize that the material was peacock feathers: hundreds of them, sewn together in layers. Peacocks, Christian knew, came from the distant land of Cadare; in the Tear, they were an imported luxury. The cloak told its own story, but as the woman rose from her knees and pulled back her veil, revealing her face, Christian read more; in her cool eyes and ungenerous mouth he saw pure indifference, a lack of charity so great that it became cruelty by default.

"Lady Andrews," the Queen greeted the noblewoman. "What can we do for you?"

"Majesty, I come to ask for Crown assistance. A tenant uprising has overtaken my acres."

The room stirred, nobles muttering to each other in low tones. Christian watched them, ostensibly looking for trouble, but always his attention returned to the same man, who stood slightly below and to his left: short and round, dressed in an outfit of tan silk. He had a greasy smile and dark hair that had been combed straight back from his widow's peak. As he covered his mouth with one hand to whisper to the woman beside him, the tattoo of a clown flickered in and out of sight beneath the edge of his sleeve. He could have been Maura's client, but Christian didn't think so. Over time in the Creche, one got to recognize the look of degeneracy, its textures and gradations. Something about the sunken eyes and overly mobile mouth told Christian that Maura would be too innocuous a vice for this particular noble, and if he needed confirmation, there it stood beside the tattooed man, in the tall and angular figure of Arlen Thorne.

Carroll nudged Christian gently in the back, and Christian realized that he had been caught wandering. He was supposed to be guarding the Princess Elyssa, who stood on the Queen's left side, turned out in a dress of lustrous green material, her blonde hair pinned neatly on her head. Carroll had said that the Princess was both intelligent and engaged, but her expression was blank, almost bored. There had been an uproar in her bedchamber several nights ago, though Christian had only heard about it secondhand; he would not be allowed on chamber duty until his swordcraft improved. But the Princess had had some sort of fit, and there had been whispers among the Guard that the witch was involved . . . the witch, who now stood just to the right of the Queen's throne. From time to time Christian sensed Brenna's eyes upon him, but he was determined not to meet her gaze. He glanced down at the audience again, where Thorne and the nonce stood together in the front row. Thorne was staring at the witch, blinking continuously, like a lizard; after a moment, Christian realized that it must be some sort of code. But it was too fast for him to break.

Pretty children, he thought uneasily. *What do you need with pretty children, Thorne?*

On the far side of the Princess stood the Prince, Thomas, his thin face glowering at everything and everyone. Every few minutes he would reach up, almost unconsciously, to scrub his palm against his forehead, where the word RAPIST still stood out clearly, the blue letters only slightly faded. Whatever dye the Blue Horizon had used, it was intractable; the Queen's medics had been trying every trick they knew to get rid of the ink, but the process was slow and painful. The skin of the Prince's forehead was a blistered red patch. Christian often found himself puzzled by the undercurrents in the Queen's court, but there was no mystery surrounding Thomas. No one liked the Prince, not even his own mother, who had expressly forbidden her son from wearing any sort of covering on his head. Dyer and Fell were taking bets on how long the dye would hold, and all of the guards made a point of asking Thomas whether there was any word on the girl, Mary, who had so far vanished without trace. The public story, the one Christian had heard, said that the girl had been taken while she and the Prince were out shopping in the city. But this story did not explain the word on the Prince's forehead.

"What sort of uprising?" the Queen asked calmly, taking a sip of her tea. Carroll had explained to Christian that the Queen was allowed to eat and drink as she pleased during audiences—was, in fact, expected to—while the rest of the world might go hungry and thirsty for hours, waiting on her pleasure.

"Two months ago, some twenty tenants in Grace Bend missed their quotas on the harvest," Lady Andrews replied. "I added the aggregate to their debt."

Christian blinked. He had paid only the barest attention to news of the drought in the Almont, for it did not concern him. But now, as he watched many of the nobles around the room nod in approval, he realized that this was considered an acceptable solution: to burden poor tenants—and they *were* poor, as poor as any inhabitant of the Creche; Christian had at least picked up that much—with additional debt, debt they could never possibly hope to repay.

"What happened then?" the Queen asked.

"The tenants broke open one of my storehouses. My bailiffs tried to stop them, but they were overrun. The tenants hanged the bailiffs, stole the stores, and then marched on my manse."

This news stirred the crowd even more; low mutterings came from all corners of the audience chamber. Christian had to restrain a chuckle, for these nobles were fools. He suddenly remembered a moment from his own childhood: crouched in a corner, gnawing a scrap of bone that some noble had tossed away. Christian was a fighter, so Wigan had fed him better than most... certainly more food than the girls in the Alley got. But there had been long periods, particularly when he was taking on his adolescent growth, when Christian was always hungry, when he would lie on his mattress at night dreaming not of Maura, or even of topside, but of feasts, banquets, an end to the gnawing in his stomach. He had stolen his share of food over the years, and never regretted it. Next to unceasing, relentless hunger, it had not even felt like theft.

"Marched on your manse, you say?" the Queen asked. There was no hint of emotion on her face, but Christian sensed her enjoying herself; unless he missed his guess, the Queen liked Lady Andrews no more than he did. "But your manse is well fortified, Lady Andrews, and made of good stone. What danger could a bunch of tenants pose?"

Lady Andrews's face colored as Arla spoke; she knew she was being played with.

"My servants proved . . . less than trustworthy, Majesty. When they saw the sheer number of tenants, they threw open the doors and joined the mob."

"Terrible," Queen Arla remarked. "Terrible. Who could have foreseen that treating servants as abominably as you do would result in such an outcome?"

"I manage my own household as I see fit," Lady Andrews snarled. "Incidentally, the tenants also burned down my acreage church and hanged the priest. I have lodged a complaint with the Arvath as well."

This news did disturb the Queen; Christian saw her frown. "Well, that's neither here nor there, Katherine. I ask again: if the tenants succeeded in gaining entry to your manse, what are you doing here?"

"I . . . fled."

Christian bit back a smile, and he was not alone. The entire throne room suddenly seemed full of snickers and whispering. Lady Andrews heard it too, for her color deepened, but she pulled herself up and spoke loudly, overriding the chatter.

"I have been living at my New London residence, hoping to deal with the problem myself. My retainers have made several attempts to retake the acreage, but failed. Last night a note was delivered to my footman. I have it here."

Lady Andrews opened the note and read, her voice triumphant.

"'We are tenants no longer. We are free farmers, and we claim our acres by right.'"

This statement caused an uproar, so immediate and furious that no individual voice could be heard. The tattooed lord was shouting something, his gaping mouth almost comical against the background of sound. The crowd was a hotbed of activity now, and all of the guards were suddenly on edge; most of them were balanced on their toes, and Galen had nearly drawn his sword. Christian, too, readied himself, but he saw no real threat here, only a bunch of peacocks. Only one person in the room was contemplating violence, and she was not in the crowd at all, but standing right beside Elyssa, watching the heaving audience without reaction. She was a pretty woman, Niya, with red hair that was much admired among the Guard, but rumor said that she was cold, not to be approached. Niya's face remained impassive, as a good servant's was supposed to be, but her eyes were as open to Christian as her face was closed, and he saw clearly that she would like to tear Lady Andrews limb from limb. Did the rest of the Guard see it? No, the Guard knew violence, but not murder. Christian was only one who recognized that cold speculation in the maid's eyes.

"Settle yourselves!" Gullys, the chamberlain, called. "Please, ladies and gentlemen, calm yourselves! Let the Queen speak!"

"This is all quite disturbing," the Queen announced, when the crowd had settled. But her voice was supremely undisturbed. "What can the Crown do for you, Lady Andrews?"

"My retainers have been unable to deal with the problem," Lady Andrews continued. Her tone suggested that the retainers might be in even worse trouble than the tenants. "I ask Your Majesty to call out the Tear army to help me retake my manse and punish the tenants responsible."

"Aye!" several men shouted from the crowd. Gullys entreated them to be silent, this time to no avail. Glancing at the Princess, Christian found her expression the same as before, utterly pleasant, as though she had been listening to the Queen and Lady Andrews discussing the weather. And now Christian sensed another pair of eyes upon him, neither hostile nor friendly, only curious. Looking out over the crowd, he spotted Arliss at the end of the third row: a gnomelike figure, hopelessly crooked, his body bent over a jeweled cane.

"Mace," Carroll whispered beside him. "Remember yourself."

Christian nodded, returning his attention to Elyssa. On the far side of the Queen, the witch emitted a sudden chuckle, and at the sound, the temperature of Christian's blood seemed to drop ten degrees.

Brenna saw you coming.

"Shut the fuck up!"

The Queen's voice echoed over the room, and silence fell with it. Christian felt a moment of reluctant admiration for the woman who hunched on the throne like a vulture, glowering at them all. The crowd had been silenced not by the volume in her voice but by the steel. The Queen glared down at them all for another few seconds, then said, "Refused, Lady Andrews."

"Majesty!" one of the nobles barked from the crowd. Another well-dressed fop, this one; no tattoo, but just as dislikable as the rest. "A crime has been committed! Lady Andrews has been robbed and displaced!"

"We regret that Lady Andrews is experiencing a problem on her lands, March," the Queen returned smoothly. "But the Tear army is not a police force, and private squabbles among nobles and tenants are not our purview. If you need additional security to deal with starving tenants, Lady Andrews, we suggest that you hire the Caden."

The Queen must truly dislike the Andrews woman, Christian thought, for even the dullest observer could feel the undercurrent of panic among the nobility in the room. If one group of tenants claimed the land for their own, it was only a matter of time before more followed suit. The uprising would have to be put down; rather than choosing to become involved, the Queen would be forced to, and thus weakened. It was a mistake, but still Christian felt his quiet admiration for the woman ratchet up a notch. She was no pushover, that was certain.

"Mother."

The Princess had spoken up, for the first time that day.

"A word, Mother?"

The Queen looked annoyed, but her frown faded as the Princess bent to whisper in her ear. The crowd continued to bubble, nobles muttering and whispering among themselves, and Christian snuck another glance at Arliss. He had never been in the Almont, but he understood the dynamics of tenancy well enough: many living in misery in order to support a comfortable few. It was a system that any Creche child could recognize and respond to, and Christian longed to ask Arliss what his precious Blue Horizon was going to do about *that*.

"Our daughter has interceded on your behalf, Lady Andrews," the Queen announced, as the Princess straightened at her side. "We have changed our minds. We shall send the army to deal with your little domestic problem."

Christian heard a wounded gasp behind him: Niya, the maid. Turning to look at her, Christian nearly flinched at the expression on her face: shocked betrayal . . . but only for a moment, before her face settled into its former placid expression. Barty and Carroll, too, looked stunned, and Lady Andrews was simply flabbergasted. The crowd, equally bewildered, had fallen silent, and the Queen took advantage of the moment to beckon her chamberlain.

"We will hear no more petitions today!" she announced. "Gullys, if you please."

"Clear this court!" Gullys called. "The Queen thanks you for your attendance."

The crowd of nobles began moving toward the rear of the room, muttering among themselves, shooting distrustful glances at Elyssa. As they went, Christian nudged Carroll. But it took two nudges to get his attention, for Carroll was still staring at the Princess, his eyes dark with doubt.

"Who is that noble down there?" Christian asked. "The dark-haired one with the red shirt?"

"Lord Tennant," Carroll replied in an undertone. "You'll not find a more wretched climber anywhere in this court."

Christian watched the man retreat, the scarecrow figure of Thorne beside him . . . and then, almost automatically, he turned to seek the witch. Finding her pale, staring eyes upon him, he looked quickly away.

"Well, here's trouble," the Queen muttered as the last nobles cleared the doors. "A murdered priest? The Holy Father will be onto us, sure enough. We will have to find those responsible."

"Then why refuse Lady Andrews, Majesty?" Givens asked.

"I enjoy few things in the world so much as telling that bitch no. But it was never meant as a real refusal, only a chance for my daughter to publicly convince me otherwise." The Queen smiled at the Princess. "Her idea, and a good one."

"Majesty?"

"My girl has finally seen the light. No more rabble-rousing, no more playing at rebellion. Her first proclamation is being distributed as we speak. Elyssa wrote the documents herself, in secret, so that there should be no chance for the Blue Horizon to throw a wrench in the works."

"And what is the substance of this proclamation?" Barty asked.

"A public declaration," the Queen replied, with an approving nod at Elyssa. "Denouncing the Blue Horizon and declaring allegiance to God's Church."

Several of the guards around Christian stopped breathing; he heard it clearly.

"Also, it seems a good time to announce another bit of good news," the Queen said, beckoning Elyssa forward. The Princess took her mother's offered hand . . . but Christian sensed artifice in the gesture, and even more so in the Princess's smile. For a brief second, the corner of Elyssa's mouth twitched, as though in spasm. Barty, standing behind Elyssa, had turned pale, and Niya . . . even Christian, who had seen every possible expression of horror that a man's face could hold, found himself shrinking away from the look in the maid's eyes.

"Congratulations are due," the Queen announced. "In April, or perhaps May, I will be a grandmother."

For a moment they all stood still, as though the Queen had spoken in a foreign language. Givens recovered first.

"Congratulations, Majesty! And to you, Your Highness," he added, turning to Elyssa. And then, more delicately: "And who is the father?"

"Mhurn," Elyssa replied.

Several of the guards gasped, and even Christian raised his eyebrows. Mhurn was another of Elyssa's guards; Christian had spoken with him once or twice, and they had shared a shift in the arms room. Mhurn was a farm boy from the Almont—a true farm boy, not an actor like Christian. Christian wouldn't have thought that Queen's Guards were allowed to bed down with royals . . . but now he realized that, once again, something was going on here, some dynamic that he did not understand. Elyssa's guards were sneaking glances at each other, and Barty looked as though he had taken a bite of something rotten. Prince Thomas had gone so pale that the blue letters on his forehead seemed almost black.

"Come," the Queen said. "Let's go back upstairs."

The Guard formed up. Christian took his place on the outskirts of Elyssa's retinue, just beside Barty. Carroll had told him that he would not be allowed on the inner ring until he had been with the Guard for at least a year. It was a reasonable precaution, and Christian did not take offense, but the rule struck him as silly, all the same. He had taken the measure of these guards now, and if he so wished, the Princess's neck would be in his hands in less than five seconds. He was sure that Carroll knew this as well, but Carroll was in no position to break Guard tradition. He was too young.

"Incidentally," the Queen remarked as they walked, "we will need to eject Mhurn from the Guard. Barty, I trust you will take care of it. Give him a small severance and send him back where he came from."

Barty nodded, but Christian noted that his face was frozen; looking down, he found the old guard's hands trembling. Barty glanced at Elyssa, as though in mute appeal, but the Princess was not looking at any of them, only staring dreamily at the walls as they began to climb the stairs.

"Get General Cleary in here," the Queen told Givens. "We need to stamp out this nonsense in the Almont immediately, before it infects the city. God knows the last thing I need is a bunch of radical farmers linking up with those lunatics from the Blue Horizon. I want at least two battalions mobilized and ready to leave in a week."

"Yes, Majesty. Cleary's in the city. I'll summon him today, but there may be a bit of a delay."

"What sort of delay?"

Givens swallowed; he did not want to bear bad news to the Queen, and Christian could not blame him.

"There was an incident early this morning, Majesty. The Blue Horizon broke into Lord Welland's storehouses on the outskirts of the Hollow. Six dead and more than twenty injured. I believe Cleary is still clearing up the wreckage."

The Queen's face tightened. "And the food?"

"Gone, Majesty."

"What of the Fetch?"

"He was there, Majesty. Several soldiers saw him . . . or his mask, at any rate."

The Queen cursed under her breath. "Up the bounty on the Fetch again. A thousand pounds."

"It's no use, Majesty. No one will give him up."

"Then we must be cleverer than he is!" the Queen exploded, turning on the landing to face them all. "Is my entire army incompetent?"

Givens said nothing—wisely, Christian thought. The maid, Niya, was looking up the next stairwell, as though the conversation bored her, but Christian sensed a vast well of upset beneath that serene exterior. By contrast, the Princess herself seemed genuinely uninterested, examining her fingernails as though they were fascinating.

"Is there more we have not been apprised of?" the Queen asked coldly. "Any further catastrophes that you were not planning to share?"

Givens flushed, but replied, "No catastrophe, Majesty, only a small problem. Lord Latimer has disappeared."

"Says who?" the Queen asked, turning to begin climbing again.

"His family, Majesty. Apparently, Latimer disappeared in the Gut. The family sent a messenger last night, reminding you that he was once the Prince's caregiver and demanding a full investigation."

"No body?"

"None yet, Majesty."

"Send them our regrets," the Queen replied blandly. "Or do one better: tell them we hope he's dead and burning. We do not grieve when stoats meet their end, regardless of how much cattle they own."

"I will perhaps change the phrasing, Majesty."

The guards chuckled, but Christian did not. *Stoat,* the Queen had called Latimer; she had known about him, then. Christian snuck a glance at Carroll, but the other guard's face might have been made of wood for all it revealed.

"I must see Brenna," the Queen announced as they entered the Queen's Wing. "Have her come to my chambers."

"Majesty—"

"Don't start with me, Givens. Do as I say."

Givens's face darkened, but he nodded to Bowler, one of the Queen's other close guards. The Queen continued down the hall toward her chambers, several guards in tow, and Elyssa followed her, with Galen and Cae trailing close behind.

The rest of the guards gathered around the table, awaiting

dinner. Christian sat beside Carroll without asking; he wasn't sure any of the rest wanted to sit next to him, and he didn't want to sit next to them. Barty was on his other side, but he was deep in muttered conversation with Givens. Christian did not need to eavesdrop; he would have heard the conversation whether he wished to or not.

"We must do something."

"What am I to do?" Givens demanded. "The Queen thinks she can make her immortal, help her see the future, God knows what else. And the things the witch carries around! Chicken scraps, blood in vials ... I found what looked like a child's arm bone last time I tossed her chambers! I want that creature here no more than you do. But what am I to do?"

Barty's reply was so low that Christian almost missed it.

"You were there; you saw. She has already begun to work on Elyssa, and I will not have it. I will kill the witch, if it comes to that."

"And how will you do that, Barty? Have you been studying sorcery on the side?"

Barty didn't answer, for the servants brought their dinner then, a simmering tureen of stew that smelled like heaven to Christian. He looked forward to meals more than a guard likely should, but he could not get over the food ... the variety, the quality. Yet even as he dipped his spoon into the rich dish, Christian found himself glancing sideways at Barty, considering him. A common goal ... it was the last thing he had expected to find in this place, but it was there. They must get the witch out. The Guard did not like her, but only Christian knew her real purpose in the Keep: to pave the way for Arlen Thorne. In a sharp blink, Christian saw Thorne, as clearly as though the pimp stood before him, his bright blue eyes veiling a wealth of purpose, merciless depth of plan.

"You are not eating, Mace," Coryn remarked from the far side of the table, cutting through the myriad conversations taking place around them. "Lamb not to your liking?"

"The lamb is fine," Christian replied easily, taking a bite of his stew. It was more than fine; it was delicious. "But where there are sheep, there are also wolves."

"Is that what we are?" Dyer asked, digging into his own bowl with relish. "Wolves?"

Christian shook his head, smiling. He did not dislike Coryn and Dyer; they were good men of their kind. But like all Queen's Guards, they had no way of knowing that *they* were the sheep: bound by honor and decency and rules, hamstrung in the belief that these things would make a difference. But Christian, not so bound, knew what the rest could not: that the wolf was coming.

CHAPTER 22

THE LADDER IS DOWN

At the outset, the Almont rebellion was badly overmatched. It was a desolate winter in the farming plains, and the rebels had neither food nor warm clothing. They were able to provision themselves from the castle they had taken, but there was not enough food to last the winter. The rebels had precious little skill with steel or military strategy, no real idea of where to go or what to do next. Defeat seemed both imminent and inevitable.

—*Out of Famine: The Almont Uprising*, ALLA BENEDICT

"Aislinn!" Eamon called from the doorway. "More coming in!" Aislinn looked up from the dough she was beating with her fists. They had found several massive canisters of flour in the cellars of Lady Andrews's castle, and every day Aislinn made fresh bread, enjoying the solitude of the task. But now Eamon was leaning through the doorway, his face worried.

"How many?" Aislinn asked.

"An entire village, from the looks of it."

"Will they never stop coming?" she murmured to Liam, who sat silent at the end of the table.

"You could always bar the doors."

She glared at him, then realized that he was joking. But the joke wasn't funny, for she had received just this advice, in earnest, from several of the men who had come in from other acreages. She understood their reasoning: the food and water in Lady Andrews's cellars would not last forever. Eamon had made a conservative estimate that they had no more than three months' worth to feed everyone, and more refugees poured in all the time. The castle now held nearly seven hundred people. Clapping the flour from her hands, Aislinn rose from the table and left the kitchen, Liam at her heels.

Lady Andrews's castle was dominated by a high, hollow central hall, flanked by two massive, curving staircases. These staircases traveled from base to battlement, breaking briefly to create landings for each floor. With Eamon and Liam behind her, Aislinn began the long climb toward the roof. She kept her hand on the balustrade, knowing that once she reached the third or fourth floor, the height would begin to make her dizzy.

"More people will strain our rations," Eamon muttered. "Perhaps we should—"

"No," Aislinn said firmly, closing the discussion. Eamon scowled but remained silent. He had come in with a tiny band, only seven people, but his knowledge was invaluable. He had once been a soldier, and he could wield a sword, but more than that, he knew about castles, their defense and bolster. Yet his cowardice still shocked her. In the hundreds of square miles surrounding, people were now starving in earnest, and each new set of refugees brought their own stories of misery: tenants eating dogs, tenants eating mud, tenants eating the clay walls of their dwellings. One village had even dug up its own churchyard in desperation. Aislinn and her people had taken Lady Andrews's castle easily, for the servants had let them in, and now Eamon and the others would counsel her to bar the doors, to climb to safety and pull the ladder up behind them. But Aislinn couldn't do that, not even if they all suffered for it. None of them were any better or braver than those who arrived on foot, starving and desperate; they had simply been lucky. They had no right to close the gates.

The three of them reached the top of the tall staircase and climbed through the open trapdoor to the roof. Eight men were spread across the western battlement, staring outward, spyglasses in their hands.

"Here, girl," Morton said, offering Aislinn a spyglass. "Look and despair."

Aislinn took the spyglass from him and stared outward, over the parapet and across the bleak, barren fields of Lady Andrews's former acreage. It was late afternoon, almost dusk, and the autumn sun hung low on the western horizon. A haze of dust covered the ground out there, but Aislinn could see them clear enough: a wide line of men on horse, moving neither quickly nor cautiously, and behind them a broad, dark shadow, spread out over perhaps half an acre of the plains.

"Some two hundred men on horse," Jonathan Charlton muttered, looking through his own spyglass. "And at least twice as many on foot."

Coming for us, Aislinn thought. A pang of fear went through her chest, but she hid it as she put down the spyglass.

"What can we do?" asked Eamon. "My kinsmen have swords and bows, yes, and even know how to use them. But they are not soldiers. We will be easy pickings."

"I can fight!" Baylor, the young hothead from Guy's Creek, shot back. "And I will! We have seven hundred people here!"

"But how many women and children? Sword and horse make one man the equal of ten unarmed!"

"There is no help for it," Charlton said. He was a stout old man, one of the few among them who had actually been in the army once. "An entire battalion, perhaps even two, and all of them bearing steel."

They all turned to look at Aislinn then . . . some hopefully, some with badly concealed impatience. These eight men represented the leaders of their respective acreages, and most of them had been appalled to find, upon arrival, that the uprising they burned to join was being led by a woman, and a young woman at that. They would have liked to ignore her, Aislinn knew, or even oust her. But they dared not do that. Downstairs were four hundred and seventy-eight men and women who had been with her from the beginning, who would listen to no one else.

Our idyll is at an end, Aislinn thought. For more than two months now they had been holed up in Lady Andrews's castle, comfortable and safe, with warm beds and all the food and water they needed. Even the onset of cooler weather had not been any cause for alarm, for they had raided the castle's clothing chests as well, and found warm clothes, enough to outfit them all. Aislinn was wearing her first pair of real boots.

Perhaps it was the boots that lulled me, she thought now, staring down at their soft brown leather. She had deluded herself, and badly. She had truly thought that nothing would change, that they would be able to stay here forever, well sheltered and well fed.

"I'm going to go down and tell my people," she announced. "Maybe they'll have some ideas."

"Ideas!" Charlton snorted. "They'll only have panic, girl. You cannot conduct a rebellion by democratic vote!"

"How many rebellions have you conducted, Charlton?"

The old man's face turned red. "You would do well to heed my advice, girl. The Tear army is not the Mort, but they are not tourists, either. If we don't make peace, they will kill us all."

"And even if we do!" Aislinn snapped back. "You heard Colin's tales from the city! Lady Andrews has made her complaint, and this is the Queen's answer!"

"But Colin delivered our message to the Blue Horizon. They may yet–"

"The Blue Horizon will not help us," Eamon said, shaking his head. "Why would they? The Crown has marked us for death."

"Elyssa is the True Queen!" Tyre Duncan protested. "She would not betray us!"

Elyssa has betrayed us, you fool. But Aislinn did not say it, for Duncan was not the only person in the castle infected with prophecy. The Blue Horizon nonsense was like church; there was no arguing with it. But Aislinn was not a fool. All hands were turning against the Blue Horizon now; hadn't Colin told them as much when he returned from New London? With the withdrawal of Elyssa's support, the revolutionaries were suddenly hunted; Colin had had to range wide to find so much as a middleman to carry his message, and though he had remained in the city for two weeks, he had received no answer.

"You can run if you want," Aislinn told the group of men around her. "But I'm staying here. We won this castle fairly, and we were certainly owed it for our work, our families' work. Our families' lives. I won't leave."

"Well, I'll be taking my people with me," Charlton announced. "I'd advise the rest of you to do the same."

Aislinn turned away, drawing a deep breath. One would think that Charlton had never known any nobles at all . . . but then again, he came from Lord Gillon's acreage, and Gillon was supposed to be the best of the lot. The others–Duncan, who came from Lord Tare's lands, and Baylor, who had spent his life serving Lord Williams–knew better. She could see it in their eyes. Peace or no peace, they would hang, along with all the other tenants who had deserted their nobles' fields. But nothing had changed since that long-ago day when they had strung up the bailiffs. They needed to be here.

"Go, then, Charlton," Aislinn replied wearily. "We could use you, but it's your decision. Anyone who wants to stay, come downstairs with me. Heavy horse won't help them against thick walls. There must be a way to defend this heap of stone."

But it did not take her more than a few hours to realize that Charlton had been right: there was little to be done. The castle was not built for defense. There was no moat, no drawbridge, only the solid stone wall rising from the crown of the hillside. The main gate was made of thick steel; it should stand up well for some time. But the postern gates at the sides and rear were weak, Eamon opined: sheets of iron, each with a single deadbolt, not so much as a portcullis in sight. They would have to be defended by men . . . men with swords, a thing they did not have.

How did we come so far? Aislinn wondered, following Eamon down the hallway, only half listening as he remarked on the finer points of defensive strategy. How had they come from that single moment, Lady Andrews tapping Aislinn's chest with a riding crop, to here? She nodded as Eamon suggested putting six men apiece on the postern gates. Charlton had vanished, which was unfortunate; they could have used his expertise. But they did not need his dour predictions either.

"We will need oil too, lots of it," Eamon told her. "We should set up as many braziers as we can on the battlements."

"Oil?" Aislinn asked. "For what?"

Eamon gave a sigh of clear impatience, but his response was kind enough. "Hot oil, girl. We have several good archers, but there are too many of them, and they'll surely bring climbers to scale the walls. Oil will be our best bet."

Aislinn nodded sagely, as though she had known this all along.

"We should move the children to the high floors," she told

Liam. "Find parents who don't want to fight and send them up there too."

They emerged onto the battlements, and Eamon began throwing instructions at her: where to put braziers, where to place archers. Aislinn prayed that Liam was listening too, for it was too much for her to process. A rogue part of her wanted to go downstairs, take her people out and charge at the enemy, make it a clean fight . . . except when had any of them ever known nobles to fight clean?

"We might have a few days," Liam said thoughtfully. "The moon's still on the wane, and they'll want to come at us in the full dark. Gives them the advantage."

"They already have the advantage," Aislinn said shortly. But Liam didn't take offense; he never did, only waited silently at her shoulder while she peeped over the battlements at the steadily approaching force below. Liam's silences were the most valuable thing about him. He did not offer himself as a lover, or even as a friend, and that was good, for Aislinn did not need either. What she needed was a lieutenant, and Liam performed the job well. If he had doubts, he kept them to himself.

"It's not too late to flee," Eamon ventured behind her. "We could still leave, take what we have, and—"

"And what?" Aislinn demanded. "They have armed men on horse. We would be run down before we'd made it a mile, and the children not even so far."

"Still, it's suicide to stay."

"And all are free to leave!" Aislinn snapped. "If they want to steal away like cowards in the night, let them! You as well! But we earned this castle, some of us with blood. I'm going nowhere."

Eamon stared at her for a long moment, and Aislinn was struck by the difference in his face. He was a dark-haired man in his forties, and he might even have been handsome, but for the creeping, craven expression that perpetually marred his good looks. But now that weasel's expression was entirely gone, replaced by a look of frank assessment.

"You are not false," he remarked finally. "You believe . . . truly believe."

"Believe? In what? God?" Aislinn laughed bitterly. "God never helped me and mine."

"Not in God. In the better world."

"Blue Horizon nonsense. I believe in what I can touch."

Eamon nodded and turned away, his cheek twitching. He was laughing at her, Aislinn thought, but then Liam cleared his throat, bringing her back to the matter at hand: the army below. She took a deep breath, trying to inject her voice with an optimism she didn't feel.

"They'll be here past nightfall, but not long past. Let's go downstairs and see about that oil."

CHAPTER 23

KINDLING

I come to caution, I come to warn,
Of the pale horse ridden by Arlen Thorne.

—Songs of the Shipment, COLLECTED BY MERWINIAN

Y ou said seven o'clock!" Thorne hissed.

"Fear nothing," Brenna replied, her voice serene. "They will be here."

Thorne grimaced but fell silent, not wanting to show his agitation to Lisk. The Caden commander had been sitting with them for more than half an hour, under a sheltered awning that overhung a rubbish cubicle. The smell was appalling, and Lisk was growing impatient . . . but not as impatient as Thorne. The Queen's birthday party would begin in less than two hours, and Thorne would be there; Father Timpany would introduce him, on the Holy Father's orders. Thorne and the Holy Father had a long association, for the Arvath did as much business in the Creche as everyone else, and had a greater need for discretion besides. But that long-standing business relationship only went so far. Thorne had used up all of his capital with the Holy Father to arrange this night, and if it was all for nothing, he would never be able to ask the Church for a favor again.

"Perhaps she knows about us," he whispered to Brenna. "Perhaps she deliberately misled you."

"She did not," Brenna replied, and at the supreme confidence in her voice, Thorne felt his own doubts recede. She had been tracking the Fetch and his people for months, with the unwitting help of the maid, who was indeed Blue Horizon–Thorne, who did not take chances, had confirmed this fact himself by following the girl into the Gut two weeks before. As always, he felt himself slightly in awe of Brenna, of the extraordinary power she wielded . . . and slightly concerned, as well. Only loyalty kept dogs on the leash, and Brenna's loyalty was almost as much a mystery to Thorne as her power, power so great that Brenna could have taken over the Creche herself, if she had been so inclined. But Brenna was born to serve. She had belonged to Thorne's second pimp, Maxwell, right up until the moment Thorne cut Maxwell's throat. Thorne was no fool; his first act upon taking control of the stable had been to offer Brenna her freedom. But she opted to stay. She had suffered dreadfully under Maxwell, who had purchased her specifically for her white skin, and that suffering surely explained part of her loyalty . . . but not all. Thorne trusted her, as much as he was capable of trusting anyone, but he did not discount the possibility that she was probing around in his own mind this very moment, and he would never know.

"Your information had better be good, Thorne," Lisk growled, clearly sensing the anxious tone of their whispered conversation. "If this is a fool's errand you've dragged us on—"

"It's not," Thorne replied, pleased to find his own voice just as certain as Brenna's. "Wait, and watch. It will not be long."

But still, he was antsy, for in the past few months nothing had gone according to plan. Despite all of Brenna's careful work, the Princess had refused to take off the sapphire. Arla, too, was proving recalcitrant, and Thorne, who had thought that obtaining the

Tear sapphires would be a simple matter of pulling them from two women's necks, now found himself balked.

"Why can we not just take them?" he had demanded of Brenna. "Why can't we simply rip the things free?"

But Brenna had said no, with the maddening certainty she always displayed in such matters. "The sapphires cannot be taken, only given," she had told him, as though that should answer all questions. But it only opened up another one: if Brenna had control of Elyssa, as she said she did, then why wouldn't the bitch simply take the sapphire off?

Why do you need her to? his mind returned. *Why do you need the jewels so badly?*

Thorne shook his head to clear the unwanted thought, but it would not go away. The Red Queen was now offering five thousand Mort marks for each sapphire. Ten thousand marks would be a fine war chest to build upon, but Thorne could not convince even himself that gold was the object, for he was already well on the way to becoming a wealthy man. To the kingdom, the sapphires were merely a symbol of royalty. But to Thorne, they represented something else entirely: vindication. The life he had been born to. The sapphires were earmarked for the Red Queen, yes, but all the same, Thorne meant to have both of them around his neck, at least once.

"It's all right," Brenna said, and he felt her trying to soothe him, almost massaging with the nimble fingers of her mind. But Thorne shook her off, for he did not want to be soothed. Everything stood at a crossroads, and complacency would get them both killed. Insurrection was spreading in the Almont, leaping from village to village like a disease, and now it had infected the city as well. Elyssa had dealt the Blue Horizon a crippling blow with her new proclamation, but now the Almont rebellion was giving them new life. Just this morning, Thorne had arrived at his own offices in the Gut to find them defaced, the windows painted with the Blue Horizon's damnable sunrise. They were growing bold again. Several of them had been spotted preaching in the Creche, but Thorne knew what they were really doing there: reconnaissance. He knew the Blue Horizon, had studied them as carefully as he had ever studied any opponent across the chessboard. The revolutionaries hated the Creche with every fiber. They meant to close the tunnels down, but Thorne did not understand how, not precisely, and neither did Brenna. The Blue Horizon were a maddening variable, too diffuse to be pinned down, and other variables abounded as well. Lazarus most of all . . . what in great godly fuck was *he* doing in the Keep? According to Brenna, they called him Mace, and the Queen's Guard was treating him like their favorite country cousin, but it was Lazarus, all right. And Lazarus was supposed to be dead.

Arliss, Thorne thought, gritting his teeth. Arliss had played him, offered an empty bounty. Thorne never would have let Lazarus go, not for any price, if he'd thought the man would show up alive. They had found enough children now, and Thorne should already have been in the Keep, consolidating his gains. But he had delayed the move, not wanting to place himself under that murderous gaze. Lazarus had heard things he shouldn't have . . . not much, and certainly not enough to understand, but enough to cause trouble. Lazarus was a problem for which there was no easy solution.

"There," Brenna said, pointing. "That's him. The Fetch."

Thorne peered through his own tiny peephole. Five men were approaching the building across the street, hoods pulled down over their faces.

"You can't even see them!" Lisk protested in a furious whisper. "How can you know?"

"I know!" Brenna hissed back. "I know your Christian name. I know how much you skim from the guild on each job. I know what kind of men you like to fuck."

Lisk gaped at her, and Thorne turned back to the peephole, biting a smile. Four of the men had gone inside the building now, leaving one outside.

"That's the Cadarese," Brenna told them, gesturing to the remaining man. And indeed, Thorne could see the dark skin of the man's hands. The rumors were true, apparently; the Blue Horizon would take anyone.

"Will he be a problem?"

"No," Brenna replied. "He'll go inside when they're all here."

"Then we wait."

Thorne expected some pushback from Lisk on this, as the assassin wasn't exactly a patient sort. But Lisk appeared to have temporarily lost his tongue. Thorne wrapped his cloak around his legs and tried to wait, but it was difficult. The Crown reward on the Fetch had risen to a thousand pounds, and now they finally had him. There was a quotation Thorne had once heard from the Holy Father, but it had been bothering him for days, for he could only remember the first half: *Behold, I am come upon you like a storm in the night....*

Now the storm was almost here. All his life, Thorne had been outcast, rejected even by the other pigeons in his stables. His extreme height, his scrawny frame . . . these things had always alienated others. But there was something more. He had been sold into the deepest level of the Creche when he was only a few hours old, but unlike the other pigeons, he had spent his life looking upward, seeking topside. Seeking revenge.

Not revenge, his mind insisted. *Justice.*

Yes, simple justice. That was all.

People had begun to approach the doors of the mead hall now, furtively, in twos and threes. They were all cloaked and hooded, but here and there, metal winked beneath the cloaks. Blue Horizon, all right; they armed themselves like bandits.

Go ahead, Thorne thought, with a flicker of alien emotion that was almost joy. *All the steel in the world won't help you.*

They sat there for interminable minutes, waiting while the trickle of latecomers dried up. Thorne, who had been keeping a careful count, calculated that fifty-one of William Tear's disciples were now inside the mead hall. Fifty Blue Horizon, plus the Fetch himself! The bounties would be a fortune, and though Thorne would have to split the rewards with Lisk, this single stroke would also cement Thorne's relationship with the Holy Father. If he brought it off, the Holy Father would pave his way to the Queen.

One, then two more Blue Horizon crept out of the dusk. The Cadarese must have been counting as well, because when the last one arrived, the Cadarese disappeared inside, leaving the other man on the door.

"One guard," Lisk whispered. His tone was marveling, almost awed, and for once, Thorne agreed with him. One guard, for so great a prize . . . it was madness. But then the Blue Horizon *were* mad, all of them, made lunatic by their ridiculous overconfidence in the ghost of William Tear, in his better world. It was a pity that Thorne had to deal with these fools topside, for a good stint in the Creche would have sorted them out nicely, taught them that there was no better world, no moment of revelation, only the black grasp of greed beneath every open and extended hand. The children of the tunnels knew that. They absorbed it before they even learned to walk.

"I'm going," Lisk told them. "We'll be back within ten minutes. Send the witch if anything goes wrong."

Thorne nodded, though he sensed Brenna's chilly displeasure

behind him. Lisk legged his way out of the rubbish cubicle and was gone down the adjoining alley.

"When the Caden tire of him, I will give him to you," Thorne told Brenna, and her dead chuckle echoed briefly in the tiny space.

"Should we not be going, master?" she asked, a few minutes later. "That fool has the operation well in hand, and if something goes wrong—"

"Will something go wrong?"

She hissed angrily. "No. But we did not come this far by throwing caution to the winds."

"A few minutes more. Lisk will do the job, yes. I just want to make sure of it. We need no surprises with the Holy Father now."

They did not have long to wait. In short order, the man on the mead-hall door fell soundlessly to the ground, a knife in his throat, and a group of ten Caden, dressed in unobtrusive grey, emerged into the road, pushing two wagons ahead of them. Unless Lisk was a complete incompetent—and, Thorne reluctantly had to admit, he probably wasn't—another ten Caden were now one street over, at the back door of the mead hall. The grey-clad assassins kicked the dead guard out of the way as they pushed the wagons up against the twin doors, and one of them went to work with a set of chains.

"We should go, master, now."

Brenna's voice was threaded with anxiety. Thorne ignored her, watching as the Caden finished chaining the doors and moved back. Now two more darted forward and tossed torches into the beds of the wagons, where piles of excelsior waited, like sleeping fireworks . . . like the revolution the Blue Horizon pursued so hopelessly. Thorne regretted the imminent death of the Fetch, who was undoubtedly a clever man, ruthless and efficient, not balking at the things that needed to be done. But he was foolish, so damnably foolish, infected with the fever dream of the better world.

"Master, please."

Thorne turned a bemused look on Brenna. All of her earlier serenity had melted away; now she looked as nervous as a cat on a grate.

"What is it?"

"Nothing, master. I just . . . I do not like uncertainties. If there is something I have not seen—"

"You see everything, dearest," he replied absently, watching the flames lick at the wagon.

"No. I do not."

"Is this about the baby again?" he asked, exasperated. "Of course you can't *see* it. It's the size of a fucking slug."

"Master, please, listen to me. I see nothing. Nothing at all. I should have it fixed by now. I should know the sex, the father, the *future—*"

"Calm yourself," he said shortly, for her voice was rising to a dangerous level, and her sudden loss of confidence was feeding Thorne's own anxiety. The damnable baby had been no part of the plan; news of Elyssa's pregnancy had literally shocked Brenna into silence. The child was hidden, Brenna said, as though that explained everything . . . as though it could explain how Thorne's seer, who had never once failed to come up with the goods, was suddenly blind. She could not say with certainty who the father was—though even an idiot would know that it wasn't the hapless guard Mhurn, who had been thrown from the Keep last week like a sacrificial lamb—or what the child would become, or even whether it would be male or female. What good was prophecy, Thorne wondered, if it ceased to function when he needed it most?

The Caden had vanished now, quickly and quietly. The fire had consumed the wagon and begun spreading, climbing the dry-rotted walls of the mead hall like snakes scaling a fort. Smoke drifted into the dusky sky. Several minutes later, the first cry came from inside the building: someone raising an alarm.

"Shout all you like," Thorne murmured. "It will not help you."

The chained doors began to rattle. Screams echoed inside: men or women, who could tell, for panic had robbed them of anything but fear.

"Master, please!" Brenna begged, and her voice had tears in it. "Master, please! I can feel them! Please!"

Thorne, sensing Brenna approaching a complete loss of control, nodded and helped her up. The screams had multiplied into an endless cacophony. The entire building was aflame now, fire eating into the walls, a bright and hungry animal against the deep blue of the early-evening sky. High above Thorne's head, a figure crashed through one of the upper windows, spraying a storm of glass that sparkled orange in the reflected light of the flames. The figure seemed to pause in midair for a moment, then plummeted some sixty feet to the ground. This body was followed by another, and still another; they hit the pavement with bloody impacts that could be heard even over the flames and the assembled crowd's shrieks of horror. They had chosen a quicker death, a *cleaner* death, and Thorne could understand that . . . could even admire it. Regret assailed him again, as it so often did over things that could not be changed. The Blue Horizon would be broken, and that was a good thing, an efficient thing, for now things could move forward. But even so, Thorne regretted the conflagration before him. As he and Brenna rounded the corner, leaving the sound of screams behind, it occurred to Thorne that fire was a fine metaphor for revolution itself . . . revolution, which took so much effort that could have been expended in something useful. Revolution, which was invariably snuffed out.

What a waste, Thorne thought. He did not look back, only tucked Brenna's arm through his as they strolled up the street toward the new offices. A troop of fire marshals ran past them, and Thorne almost laughed. There was no water anymore; the marshals' cistern, like all of those in the city, had been confiscated for drinking. In this new, dry world, one could not fight fire, any more than one could compel rain.

CHAPTER 24

THE RED DEATH

Even in a line riddled with weakness and mental instability, Elyssa Raleigh remains a puzzle. What happened to her, this brave child who regularly deviled her autocratic mother, who preached socialism, who stood in front of the masses and pledged her throne to the Blue Horizon? How did the strong-willed Princess Elyssa become the infamous Shipper Queen? This transformation, more than anything else, suggests that something monstrous was hidden in plain sight at the Raleigh court.

—Megalomania and Madness: A History of the Raleigh Line
in the Pre-Glynn Era, EMILY SKAFF

Niya was prepared to have a terrible time at the Queen's birthday party. She had bathed and dressed resentfully—her best gown, a green velvet—and done her hair in five auburn braids. She looked very well in the glass, but inside she was a bundle of misgiving, and once they reached the Queen's ballroom, she found that her misgiving was well justified.

The room had been decorated to the hilt. Bunting in bright colors hung between the pillars, and new tapestry lined the walls. Here and there, naked human statues adorned the room, and though Niya had little modesty to speak of, she still found her conscience offended. In the hour they had been here, she had already seen dancing girls covered in veils and not much else, several dogs that had been trained to behave in concert, even a troupe of mimes . . . wholly irritating, but then, Niya had never known mimes to be anything else. Two tame peacocks, birthday gifts to Arla from the King of Cadare, strutted around the room.

But the entertainment was nothing compared to the food. The edges of the huge ballroom were lined with an endless border of tables, their surfaces covered in so much meat that Niya's stomach turned at the sight of it. Venison, beef, fish, boar, chicken, lamb, pork, and an unidentifiable substance that Niya finally discovered to be rattlesnake. All of the cattle herds had died; Niya could only assume that Arla had been feeding a private herd from the Crown stores. Where she had gotten the rest of the meat, Niya wouldn't even hazard a guess. The alcohol was more excessive still, with twelve huge tables allotted to hold nothing but kegs and bottles, and on smaller tables lay a buffet of breads and even more varieties of pastry, ten tureens filled with various soups, and a seemingly limitless number of side dishes: rice, potatoes, corn, stewed apples, minced pie.

They haven't even brought out the desserts yet, Niya thought numbly. In the Almont, tenants were dying, even killing each other, for the reward of a few apples or a basket of pumpkin seeds. Children were being hanged for stealing, and several whole villages had already been put to the torch in retaliation. The sight of all this food—the callousness it represented—staggered Niya. The sickness in her stomach was nothing compared to the upset in her head.

Elyssa was eating heartily, and Niya supposed she might well; she would be some three months along now. She was drinking too, and heavily . . . a fact that only Niya seemed to note. But really, who would say anything? Who would question the heir to the throne? Only Arla could check Elyssa, and Arla would not. Arla was pleased as punch about Elyssa's pregnancy, the continuation of the line . . . though Niya often wondered whether she would have been half so pleased if Elyssa had not first denounced the Blue Horizon.

All of our plans, Niya thought, her still face giving no clue of the despair that lay behind. *All of our plans, our hopes . . . all of it, wrecked in a single instant. What am I still doing here? I should have left the Keep long ago.*

But those had not been her orders. She had not heard from the Fetch since Elyssa's proclamation had gone out. On the day he told her to leave the Keep, she would, and gladly, but until then she was stuck in this vast room, surrounded by these horrible people.

She consoled herself with the thought that Arliss would be here later. Arliss had already begun to find his own odd entrée into court, wangling invitations from longtime clients. Tonight it was Lady Milford. The court maintained the polite fiction that Lady Milford was slowly wasting away of old age, but the lady was only fifty-two, her pallor and ruined heart the result of a late-stage poppy habit. In the better world, the sale of narcotics would be anathema, but Niya could not bring herself to dislike Arliss, who had an endearingly filthy sense of humor as well as a seemingly endless source of informants in the Gut. But he hadn't arrived yet. A strong whiff of slow-cooked pork assaulted Niya's nostrils, nearly making her ill.

"Can I get you some more wine, lady?"

Niya turned, bemused, and found a servant standing before her: a young man, his eyes lit with admiration; he had taken her for a noblewoman. Niya waved him off, returning her attention to Elyssa, who stood laughing several feet away, in a conversational cluster that included Lady Bennis and Lord Tare. As Niya watched, Elyssa downed yet another shot of whiskey.

Does she wish to kill the baby in the womb?

A month before, such a question would have been unthinkable, but oh, how things had changed. Niya found herself suddenly terrified for the tiny clump of cells behind the wall of Elyssa's abdomen . . . a terror that had no clear shape. Despite Givens's careful instruction to the Guard and the staff of the Queen's Wing that Mhurn was the father of the baby, Niya knew better. In the clumsy ejection of Mhurn from the Keep, Niya sensed panic: Arla's desperation to convince the Holy Father that the future heir to the throne was not a child of the Blue Horizon. Something had happened to Gareth; the entire movement knew it now, though they didn't speak of it. Gareth was the only one who might have been capable of rallying them, even in the wake of Elyssa's terrible proclamation . . . but he was gone, and the heart of the Blue Horizon had gone with him.

Near the far wall was Queen Arla, easily visible because of the red dress she wore: Elyssa's present, a bright combination of silk and satin, hung with fine wisps of muslin. Even Niya had to admit that the dress was beautiful, but the sight of it angered her as well, for the dress had cost enough gold to give a solid meal to half the beggars in New London. Niya knew nothing of sorcery—would not even have believed, a few months before, that sorcery existed—but she could no longer deny that Elston and Barty and the rest were right: Elyssa had been witched. There was no other explanation for the utter reversal of personality, for what she had done. In Niya's last message to the Fetch, she had told him the plain truth: they must kill the seer.

But she had not yet heard back.

A popping noise distracted her: Mace, the farm boy who was

not a farm boy, stood only a few feet away, cracking his knuckles. He was big and broad, dark-haired, with long legs held constantly in the slightly bent-kneed posture of a man always at the ready for a fight. His face might have been handsome, were it not so truculent.

"You're studying me," Mace remarked, never taking his eyes from Elyssa.

"Indeed. Books with closed covers are the most interesting."

A roar came from the assembled company; someone had proposed a toast to Queen Arla's health. Prince Thomas had materialized from somewhere and now hung around the edge of the Queen's entourage, peeping hopefully at his mother. But the vague outline of RAPIST was still visible on his forehead, and the Queen did not deign to notice him. Elyssa was speaking to Lady Willis; a nice enough woman who would never win any prize for brains, and beside her–

Niya's breath caught. Sometime in the last few minutes, Arlen Thorne had joined Elyssa, and now his arm supported hers, while his other hand held a glass of champagne. Mace had noticed as well; his posture was tense, his eyes fixed on the pimp. But when Niya looked around wildly, seeking that broad tightening of the Guard that always occurred when dangerous people visited the Keep, she saw nothing.

My God, they don't know who he is! Niya realized, shocked. Not knowing Arlen Thorne . . . to a denizen of the Gut, it would be like not knowing Lucifer himself. Thorne listened politely as Elyssa spoke, and Niya wondered that no one could see the contempt in his eyes, the sneer that hid just beneath the curve of his mouth. Or did her own mind do that?

"Vermin in the Keep," Mace murmured beside her. "Just as I always heard."

She glanced sharply at him. "You know that man?"

"Yes, and so do you, because we grew up far, far from here. But the throne surrounds itself with like. It's a weakness in the Guard."

"You're no guard," Niya stated flatly.

"No, Mistress Niya. No more than you're a lady's maid."

A man's thick, bellowing laugh echoed over the gathering; Niya could feel its vibrations in the floor. Cardinal Bannon, his white robes billowing around him, seemed determined to drink the entire ocean of whiskey that Arla had laid in for the occasion. Niya watched the priest without expression, hiding the faceless, impersonal hate she always felt whenever she beheld a frock. Near Elyssa, one noble had set his plate on the ground, the crowd around him laughing as the trained dogs licked up the leavings, and Niya suddenly asked the Mace, "Do you know Poe?"

"Poe?" Mace repeated, sounding genuinely bewildered.

"The writer."

"No," Mace replied, after a long pause. "I don't know him."

Niya knew that she should shut up, as a girl of her supposed background would never have had access to books. But it was too late; she was already speaking, bitterness flowing through her voice. "He speaks of just such a scene as we see here: excess within, misery without. Look at those tables: a glut of food, in a time of famine. Thus does the Queen reassure herself, and all of these other pit vipers, that the misery will remain without."

"It will," Mace replied, seeming not at all perturbed by her outburst. "Surely the Queen has enough food to last her until the end times."

"And that makes it all right?"

"That's not what I said."

Niya waited for him to speak again, but he didn't. They stood for some moments in silence, a silence that was strangely peaceable, until Mace asked, "Do you know that man? The one with the widow's peak and the purple clothes?"

Following his gaze, Niya nodded. "Lord Tennant. What of him?"

"The tattoo on his hand. It interests me."

"Why?"

"Because it's such an unfortunate choice. Clowns are meant to delight children."

Niya blinked. The Blue Horizon knew about the clowns; they had already caught and slaughtered two of them in the Gut, and Tennant was next on the list. But how could Mace know that?

"Niya. You're not drinking."

Niya started; Elyssa had materialized beside her. Once upon a time they had been friends, but now Elyssa's smile was only that of a party acquaintance, making small talk. The sight wounded Niya, but she had spent her life dissembling, and she did not let it show.

"Highness. Your present to your mother is a roaring success."

Elyssa did not reply. Niya was aware of the guards subtly relocating, re-forming the circle around them, not coming too close in case Elyssa intended private conversation. But Elyssa merely stood there, clutching her champagne glass . . . too tightly, Niya thought. Elyssa's knuckles stood out, anguished, white as bone.

"Highness? Are you all right?"

"How did I get here, Niya?" Elyssa asked, her low voice suffused with fright. "I don't remember. I don't remember anything!"

Niya turned to stare at her, and found Elyssa's eyes wide and panicked, transparent as glass. Without thinking, Niya dropped her own champagne glass and took Elyssa's arm, steadying her. She was suddenly aware that the Princess was close to collapse, that she was literally holding her up.

"What is it?" Niya demanded, keeping her voice low. "What has happened to you? Tell me!"

"She won't let me," Elyssa replied dully. "She says I belong to her, and she's right."

Her face sharpened, a terrible sight, her cheekbones arching into cruelty, her eyes growing cold. In that moment, Niya felt that evil itself stood beside her, and she twitched as a shudder worked its way up her spine. Thinking of her own words to the Fetch, long ago—*One more palmist, more or less. What difference?*—Niya felt her heart rend inside her chest.

"Ignore me," Elyssa said, with a light laugh. "I've been talking nonsense, that's all. Too much champagne."

Niya glanced around, seeking the witch, sure that she must be nearby. She fought the instinctive urge to move away, perhaps flee the room. The Blue Horizon had taken the prophecy for its own, anointed Elyssa, made her into the True Queen. They had not anticipated Thorne or his witch, but ignorance did not shield them from responsibility. Their propaganda had helped to create the Princess who stood beside Niya, her contemptuous gaze sweeping the room. Impulsively Niya grasped her arm, turning the Princess to face her.

"Fight her, Highness. Cast her out."

Elyssa's face suddenly began to upheave. One side smiled while the other turned downward in a grimace of agony.

"Fight her!" Niya repeated. "You're Elyssa Raleigh, the True Queen. Send her away."

"I try!" Elyssa whispered, one eye filling with tears. "I try all the time!"

"Tell us how to fight her, then!" Niya demanded in an urgent undertone. "Tell us how to stop her."

Elyssa's face continued to work. One green eye dilated with rage, while the other wandered the room helplessly. Tears trickled down one cheek. Niya glanced around to make sure that no guard was privy to this conversation . . . and found all of them turned away in studied ignorance.

Bless you, Barty.

"No one can stop her," Elyssa whispered, weeping quietly. "I can hide behind the blue light, but I can't make her go, and one day–"

"Highness. You promised me a dance."

Niya looked up to find Arlen Thorne just outside the ring of guards. Barty stood before him, his sword drawn.

"Who are you, scarecrow?" Barty demanded.

"Only a businessman," Thorne replied, his bright blue eyes amused. "A friend of Her Highness."

Barty did not move. Next to Niya, Elyssa gave a low moan, her face twitching, as though her muscles had seized. For a nearly infinite moment, Niya thought that perhaps she had won, but then Elyssa blinked, and that cool, contemptuous expression descended again, as tangibly as though the Princess had donned a mask. With a flick of her hand, she wiped her tears away.

"Delighted, Mr. Thorne."

Elyssa motioned for Barty to move. The old guard stood there a moment longer, his defiant gaze fixed on Thorne. Then he moved aside, allowing Thorne to take Elyssa's hand.

A deep boom echoed across the room. The double doors of the ballroom had opened to admit a cadre of white-clad swordsmen: Arvath Guard, two columns of ten, bearing something enormous between them, a vaguely flat shape draped with a sheet.

"Greetings to Queen Arla!" the herald at their head called. "His Holiness wishes the best for Your Majesty's birthday!"

"Well, what's that, then?" the Queen demanded drunkenly, pointing to their burden. "If he offers me God's kingdom, why wrap it in a sheet?"

The crowd laughed appreciatively. Niya looked around for Elyssa, but she and Thorne had vanished into the crowd.

I must send a message tonight, Niya thought wildly. *The Fetch will know what to do.*

"Your Majesty will undoubtedly reach God's kingdom one day," the herald replied diplomatically. "But in the meantime, His Holiness sends you this gift, and many happy returns."

The guards pulled the sheet free. Gasps and murmurs traveled through the crowd, but for a moment, Niya could not see clearly what the gift was. Something of gold, which sparkled brilliantly in the torchlight. Then they raised it vertical, and a woman screamed . . . fortunately, for it covered Niya's own wounded cry of recognition.

Gareth hung above her, impaled on a vast wooden cross that towered some ten feet above the crowd. His mouth yawned, eyes wide and face contorted in agony. His entire body had been painted with gold. Around his neck, a blue-painted sign read "The Better World."

"Happy birthday, Majesty!" the herald announced. "The Holy Father hopes that this ornament will grace your walls for many years to come."

Queen Arla approached the gift, studying it. Gareth had not been tied to the cross, as Niya had first thought, but actually crucified; huge iron nails had been driven through his palms and bare feet. His head had been shaved, none too carefully, for tiny nicks marred his skull. But Niya could see no other wounds.

Dear God, did they do this while he was alive? she wondered, her stomach clenching into rivets. *Did they hang him up to die?*

"Place it against the far wall," Arla replied carelessly. "We'll find some way to hang him up tomorrow. It won't smell, will it?"

"No, Majesty," the herald replied. "The body has been embalmed and fixed."

Niya watched numbly as they carried the cross toward the far wall. As they turned it, she saw that tiny crosses had been carved at regular intervals down the length of Gareth's legs. Niya turned away, unable to look any longer at the horror of her friend's corpse, and found Elyssa staring at Gareth's crucified body with a blank, almost curious expression, the look of a woman deciding what to wear that day or how she might take her tea. When the Queen called to the musicians, ordering them to strike up again, Elyssa turned to Arlen Thorne and extended her arm, inviting him to resume the dance.

Christian did not mistake Niya's fixed expression for serenity. Her mouth was set so tightly that her jaw seemed like to shatter, and her eyes were deep wells of horror. Blue Horizon; Christian had suspected it, but now he was sure. Many of the Guard had tried their luck with Niya and gotten nowhere, but Christian had already perceived that what might be mistaken for ice was really steel, inflexible control that never broke. But it was breaking now. The woman looked as though she might collapse, and before he thought better of it, Christian had offered his arm, allowing her to steady herself.

"My thanks," Niya murmured sickly, her face pale as milk. Her eyes darted toward the crucified figure that leaned against the wall, then away. "Too much wine, I think."

Christian guided her to a nearby chair, barely taking note of Carroll's approving nod. Every day he learned more about what a Queen's Guard was supposed to be, all the tiny courtesies that made one into a gentleman. But this was the first time he had performed such an act without artifice. He knelt before Niya, taking her cold hand.

"Your friend?"

Niya's gaze snapped to his, and they shared a moment of re-markable simpatico. They had already agreed that he was no guard, and she no maid, but in that moment the two of them seemed to travel further, each seeing and accepting culpability, criminality, and all that went with it, a shared understanding that neither of them belonged here. When two tears blinked from beneath Niya's lashes, Christian immediately produced the tiny scrap of cloth that all Queen's Guards kept tucked in their sleeves, then stood, shielding her, as she wiped away the tears.

"She's witched," Niya whispered. "Witched beyond recovery. So what am I still doing here?"

Christian didn't need to ask who *she* was, for the Princess was now whirling around the room on the arm of Arlen Thorne. The weekend before, Christian had been granted his first furlough, and he had spent the time oozing around the pubs in the Gut, asking about Thorne. But no one had heard a word of the sale of pretty children to the pimp, neither topside nor below. Christian had run upon one man whose boss, a silk merchant, had sold Thorne several lengths of his best silk, but that was all. Whatever Thorne was up to, he was smart enough to remain a ghost. The Guard, even Barty, seemed remarkably unconcerned at Thorne's proximity to the Princess, by which Christian understood that none of them knew Thorne, what he was.

Great God, they do need me here, Christian thought sourly, *if only to bridge the gap in knowledge between Creche and Keep.*

The witch was here as well; Christian had spotted her earlier in the evening, trying to pass herself off as a palmist. But now she had disappeared. When he first arrived, Christian had searched the party for Maura, hoping against hope that she might be here as well; Lord Tennant was in attendance, and surely the other nonces would be too. It was not unheard of for nobles to bring their doxies to court, even for such an important event as the

Queen's birthday, but there was no sign of Maura, and now Christian was glad of it. He sensed disaster, hovering close.

"It's her," Niya continued brokenly. "The albino. The witch. And if Elyssa can't fight her off, what hope do we have?"

Mace had no answer. He hesitated on the point of telling Niya that he, too, had once tangled with Brenna, and then did not. To confess such a thing would be to tell her who he was, and to tell that would be to tell everything, the tale that would make any self-respecting member of the Blue Horizon run screaming into the night.

I want her good opinion, Christian realized, astonished. *Why?*

Movement drew his eye: two Gate Guards pushing through the crowd. Carroll had told him that the Gate Guard did not approach the Queen directly unless the matter was dire. They went to Givens first, who listened to them for a moment, a frown deepening on his seamed face, then went to the Queen. The party continued unabated, but the Gate Guards' entry had not been unnoticed; all eyes were now turned toward the Queen. Even Elyssa watched her mother as she danced, her eyes intent, almost waiting.

"Hold!" Queen Arla shouted to the musicians, waving a hand in the air, her voice hoarse with wine. "Hold, I say!"

The musicians stopped, and the Queen began to gabble orders at Givens, her voice too low and slurred for Christian to understand. The news, whatever it was, had begun to make its way through the crowd now; Christian listened intently but could only make out scattered words.

Fire.

Blue Horizon.

All dead.

"Then call out the army!" Arla suddenly shouted at Givens, her face red and furious. "Plenty of them left in the city! I want two legions in the Hollow before midnight!"

"Fire in the Hollow," one of the nobles standing near Christian repeated. "Gadds Alley. An entire city block has already burned down."

"Well worth it," a drunken woman slurred back. "I'd burn half the city down if it meant getting rid of the Fetch."

Christian felt a pinch at his shoulder and realized that Niya was clutching it in a death grip, grinding the join of his armor. Her already pale face had now drained of all color, and her eyes were huge with fright.

"What did you say to me, Cleary?" Arla demanded, and the general, who had appeared from somewhere, muttered something in her ear.

"This city is made of wood, you say?" Arla began to laugh, then, abruptly, she slapped him. The entire assembly almost shivered in scandalized delight, but Cleary remained immobile, not even putting a hand to his face; Christian guessed that he had seen the Queen drunk a time or two before.

"I know what the Gut is built of," the Queen hissed. "Get the water; take it from my cistern if you have to. Just put out the fucking fire."

"Yes, Majesty," General Cleary said, and departed. Slowly, the party began to speak and move again, but stiffly, all mirth departed in the knowledge that the real excitement was elsewhere. The Queen had taken another glass of wine, and she drank defiantly, looking around as though begging someone to try to stop her. Behind Christian, Niya had collapsed back into her chair; he thought she might have fainted, but he did not want to call attention to the fact by trying to revive her. He caught a brief glimpse of the witch across the room, but then she faded from sight in the shifting of the crowd.

"Mace."

He looked down and found Niya, sitting up straight now, though her face was still white as salt. She grabbed his hand.

"Was it real, the fire? Tell me it wasn't real."

He opened his mouth, not sure what he meant to say, for in that strange moment, a lie seemed somehow kinder than the truth. But before he could choose either, the Queen began to scream.

All of the Guard moved at once, turning instinctively toward the Queen . . . all except Barty, who remained with Elyssa, and Christian himself. He surely did not belong here, because his first instinct was not to defend the Queen, or even the Princess, but Niya in her chair. He remained beside her, unmoving, observing almost coolly that the Queen had begun to beat at herself, her arms, the skirt of her dress. Her shrieks echoed across the room, and as the crowd watched in horrified silence, she crossed her arms and clawed through her sleeves, tearing crimson ribbons down her own biceps.

"The dress!" Givens shouted suddenly, springing forward. "It's the fucking dress! Get it off her! Now!"

Several guards, including Givens, converged on the Queen, grabbing the silky red material of her dress and tearing it from her body. But it did no good, for now the Queen hooked her fingers and began to claw at her own eyes, leaving bloody furrows beneath the sockets. The women in the audience began to scream, and as though the sound had given permission, a general stampede began, all of the nobles running in a herd for the double doors at the far end of the room.

"Barty!" Givens shouted, clutching one of the Queen's flailing arms. "Barty, get over here! And you, Coryn! Over here now! Send someone for Beale!"

With a last, agonized look at Elyssa, Barty went. Christian finally succeeded in sitting Niya on the chair; he thought of going to Elyssa, taking Barty's place, then decided not to, for she was in no danger. Thorne had gone to join the witch, who stood on the far side of the room. Elyssa, too, had moved toward her mother, but she had halted some twenty feet away. Now she watched the proceedings, her face a study in anxiety . . . but the anxiety was false. Christian knew it. Something else was in her eyes, crouched there like a child waiting behind a door, and in a single stunned moment, Christian identified it.

Glee.

The Queen had fallen now, her fall cushioned by the dozen guards who lowered her to the ground. Barty knelt and bent over her, pulling on thick leather gloves. Christian felt his respect for the old man increase. Barty had not rushed forward; he kept a cool head. The Queen's breathing was becoming labored now, devolving into great gasps that Christian could hear even across the ballroom. The crowd of guests had disappeared, and the double doors stood open, giving onto the wide, empty corridor like a gaping mouth.

"Contact poison," Barty muttered. "Neurotoxic; listen to her breath."

"Brenna can help her," Arlen Thorne announced. He had ventured closer, bringing the witch with him.

"Keep the albino back," Givens told him, drawing his sword. Barty was now examining the Queen's hands, her fingernails. With one gloved finger, he gently pulled up the Queen's eyelid.

"The Queen is dying," Thorne said. "Contact poisons may have timed delays, but they work quickly once activated. You cannot save her, but Brenna can."

"No," Givens said firmly. "Barty, can you mix an antidote?"

Barty shook his head. "I know this poison, milked from a Dry Lands cobra. The Cadarese call it the Burning Brand. But I would need my greenhouse, and more time than we have."

"What do we do?" Givens demanded. The Queen's harsh

breathing had begun to slow. One of her hands crept to her chest now, clutching the blue jewel that lay there, as a drowning man might cling to a rope.

"You have no time," Thorne announced. "Allow Brenna to try."

"No!" Christian shouted.

The rest turned to him, surprised. Christian had surprised himself. He had no doubt that the witch could do it, but he also had not forgotten what he knew of Arlen Thorne, who did nothing without reason, and certainly nothing for free.

"Hold your tongue, boy," Givens replied coldly. "Remember your place."

Christian did, though the disdain in the older guard's tone made resentment swell inside him.

I could help you, he thought angrily. *I could tell you all so much....*

He turned to check on Niya but found her gone, vanished from the chair behind him. The rise and fall of the Queen's chest was now almost imperceptible. She had begun to wheeze as well, an accordion sound so painful that it made Christian wince.

"There's no time," the Princess finally announced, moving forward. "We have to let Brenna try."

"Highness!" Givens snapped. "The witch is dangerous! She—"

"My mother is dying," Elyssa told him. "Will you stand over her and allow it?"

But the debate was pointless, for Arla's entire Guard had now drawn swords and planted themselves between Brenna and the Queen. Thorne himself, Christian noticed, had retreated all the way to the far wall, where he watched with the idle amusement of a man at a theatrical.

"Approach the Queen, witch, and I will cut you down," Givens told Brenna ... but only a moment later, he began to scream. Then they were all howling, all ten of the guards who had circled the

Queen . . . shrieking as they clawed at their own faces, their own eyes. Carroll leapt forward, meaning to run to them, but Christian grabbed him by the arm.

"You can't help them!" he shouted in Carroll's ear.

"Let me go!" Carroll cried, struggling against Christian's iron grip.

"You can't help them!" Christian repeated, shaking him. "They touched the dress! You can only die yourself!"

Carroll heard him this time; he stopped struggling and merely stood there, as though paralyzed. Still, he was the bravest of Elyssa's Guard, for the rest had already backed away from the Queen, from the screaming men who fell to their knees and tore at their own flesh. The sight of that, all of them rending themselves at once, was so bad that even Christian, who had seen a thousand deaths in the ring, could not watch. He kept his eyes fixed on the Queen, and so only he saw Brenna kneel beside her and peel the Queen's hand away from her sapphire, taking the jewel in her own fist.

"To the Princess!" Barty shouted. "Damn you all, snap out of it! To Elyssa!"

Christian whirled to see that Bowler and Webb, blinded in agony, had wandered dangerously close to the Princess, their hands outstretched. Christian drew his sword and moved in with the rest, forming a double ring around Elyssa. Kibb was on one side of Christian, Carroll on the other, and without discussion they pointed their swords outward, creating a ring of sharp points. Barty joined them a moment later, his face hard and set, shedding his gloves before he drew his sword.

Even for Christian, the next five minutes were very bad. Guards stumbled back and forth without direction, mindless, their howls echoing between the walls of the ballroom. Some called for their mothers, some screamed apologies to unseen ghosts. Eben died first, weeping as he buried the point of his own dagger in his belly. Brand bashed his own brains out, running himself into the wall again and again until his features were unrecognizable, and that was when Christian knew that it wasn't the poison, that no poison could do what he was seeing here. Bowler wandered up to the point of Christian's sword and then fell before him, clawing at his own throat, apparently intent on tearing it out. His fingers seized in death, their tips bloody and ruined, and he toppled to the floor.

Beside Christian, Kibb doubled over and began to vomit. Christian too felt sick, but he could not afford to entertain it. He was too busy watching Thorne ... Thorne and his witch, who now held the Queen's sapphire tightly in one hand, her eyes closed, a small smile playing across her lips.

CHAPTER 25

ON THE BATTLEMENTS

One should not lose heart at the onset of darkness. Being afraid is the first requirement of heroism, and certainly the only requirement of being brave.

—Greive the Madman

If there had been longer nights in the history of the world, Aislinn could not imagine them. Hours might have passed, or years, she could not say. The world had shrunken to the width of the castle roof, nothing but the loading and reloading of the enormous barrel that stood at the edge of the battlements . . . that, and the much trickier act of dumping it over. Aislinn had taken several burns now, blistered red patches on her arms and hands, and a dreadful welt on her left bicep. They had no doctor, but Lady Andrews's horse doctor had defected along with the rest of her servants, and he was able enough at surgery. Aislinn did not deceive herself about that welt, which would surely fester if left untreated. She would have to go and see the would-be surgeon.

If we live that long, she thought. The night must be almost over; a quick glance behind her showed an almost imperceptible lightening on the edges of the eastern horizon. But the force below would not relent with the light. Eamon had fled on Sunday, taking his kinsmen, and the army had first attacked on Tuesday, but Aislinn had no idea which day was dawning now.

Boom.

The infantry had begun ramming the back gate again. The steady vibration came straight up through the stone to thrum beneath Aislinn's feet. Between archers and oil, they had done very well, killing perhaps a third of the massed force below. But there were always more of them waiting out there in the darkness. They had not brought siege towers—*not yet, anyway,* Aislinn thought darkly—but they had a seemingly limitless supply of skilled climbers who tried constantly to scale the wall. Some ten feet beneath her, Aislinn heard an outraged cry as one of the parents hauled a child away from the window.

They want to watch, she thought. *Of course they do.* It had never occurred to Aislinn to think much about the fate of the children in this business; they were simply baggage, almost like provisions that the parents had brought along. Aislinn wondered when she had become so cold . . . she, who used to sing Bailey and Jory their bedtime songs and cuddle them before sleep.

All of your people are dead, and you wonder what has happened to you? They're dead, Aislinn, and now you're dead too.

"Aislinn!" Liam shouted, jarring her back to the battlement. He was wheeling the smoking barrel down the wall. In the end they had only been able to assemble four braziers on the roof, one for each wall, but Liam had found several wheeled platforms, which allowed them to move the barrels up and down the parapets, finding the points where the attackers had massed. Now, peeking over the edge, Aislinn saw the long shadow of the ram far beneath them, soldiers covering it like ants.

"Ready?"

Aislinn reached down and grabbed the base of the barrel, wincing as her burned fingers made contact.

"One, two, three!" Liam shouted, and Aislinn heaved with all of her strength, ignoring the agony in her palms, the sickening feeling of blisters bursting. As the oil crashed down, a chorus of voices howled in agony below them.

But they keep on coming, Aislinn thought bitterly. *We're fighting for something; we have a reason to die. What are they dying for?*

She couldn't imagine. Burned and bleeding men lay strewn across the hilltop at the base of the castle, but Aislinn suddenly realized that she had not seen any arrows launched from the lower windows in some time. They had finally run out. Eamon might have had some idea of a substitute, but Eamon was gone, fled while Aislinn slept. His cowardice had won out.

I don't mind dying, Aislinn thought, tightening the cloth around the wound on her arm. They had made a good fight of it, and she didn't mind dying, but she hated losing. She thought of Lady Andrews, once again riding her acres with her crop, and bared her teeth.

"Oil!" Liam called to the two men manning the brazier. "How long?"

"Ten minutes maybe!" one of them shouted back. "We're running low!"

"Volley!" someone cried from a window below. "Volley from the east! Get down!"

Aislinn dove for the base of the eastern battlement. Her burned arm thudded against the stone, and the pain was bad enough to make her emit a tiny shriek through her clenched teeth. For a moment black spots danced in front of her vision, and then she heard the clatter of arrows landing around them. Across the roof, someone began to scream. Aislinn looked up and saw that the sky was now a delicate pinkish violet over her head.

Dawn, she thought. *But it comes too late for us.*

"Riders!" one of the lookouts shouted. "Riders from the west!"

No, Aislinn thought bleakly. *No more. I'm too tired.*

But her mind came back at her, furious.

You got these people into this. Get up!

Aislinn rolled, carefully avoiding her burned arm, and darted to crouch behind the western wall. Peeking over the edge, she saw a vast shadow emerging from the mist that covered the fields.

"Reinforcements," Liam remarked, appearing at her shoulder. "Because we weren't overmatched enough."

Aislinn chuckled sourly. The sun was rising behind her, and now the light had spilled over the battlements to bathe the western slope, the fields of Lady Andrews's acreage . . . square plots, rectangular plots, the wide spread of ground that ruled a tenant's life, determined his future.

But we were free, Aislinn thought. *Even for a few months, we were free.*

"Aislinn," Liam murmured, his eye fixed to his spyglass. "Look."

Aislinn pulled her own spyglass from her skirts and socked it into her left eye, focusing on the approaching army. There was a line of horsemen in front, at least fifty riders, all heavily armored, but they were nothing to the infantry behind: thousands of dark-clad men.

It's over, she thought. *This is how it ends.*

But now one of the horsemen unfurled a banner, letting it fly in the brisk morning breeze. It whipped and snapped, and in the growing light, Aislinn saw an enormous orange circle, balanced on a flat field of blue: the sun, rising over water. And now, looking more closely, she saw that the infantry behind the flag were not soldiers, or even mercenaries, for they were dressed in rags. There were women down there, and children, and they carried not steel but iron and tin . . . pitchforks and scythes, the desperate tools of farmers.

Of rebels.

"Great God," Aislinn whispered.

And now a howl of fear echoed throughout the Tear battalions, for the leader of the horsemen had pushed back his hood, revealing a face so evil, so hideous, that even Aislinn gave a small shriek as she glimpsed it through her spyglass. Then she realized who he must be.

"Kelsea!" the leader cried, his voice carrying clearly in the morning air. "For Kelsea, and the better world!"

He raised his sword, and the line of horsemen roared in response as they charged, galloping forward into the massed might of the Tear army at the foot of the wall. Aislinn dropped her spyglass, feeling more laughter bubble in her throat, but honest laughter this time. Her arm was agony, and her blistered palms housed a hive of live bees, but Aislinn suddenly felt wonderful, as elated as that night when they had first taken this castle, marching in celebration . . . when it was all victory, and no blood had yet been shed.

"Liam! Liam!" she shouted in his ear, trying to make herself heard over the sudden clash of battle below. "It's them, Liam! It's the Blue Horizon!"

BOOK III

CHAPTER 26

THE TERRIBLE PRESENT

If contemporaries were reluctant to discuss Arlen Thorne, then they were even more reluctant to discuss his witch. Ask which head of the dragon was more fearsome, and there you have your answer.

—*The Early History of the Tearling*, AS TOLD BY MERWINIAN

Queen Arla twitched, her entire body shuddering on the bed. In the three months she had been asleep, her body had thinned until she seemed little more than paper. Brenna placed a gentle hand on the Queen's chest, just above the sapphire, and whispered inaudibly.

"What is she doing to her?" Barty asked.

"Removing the evil spirits that disturb the Queen's sleep," Thorne replied. "Brenna is a gifted healer."

With some relief, Niya saw that Barty believed this nonsense no more than she did. He turned to Elyssa, as though seeking arbitration, but Elyssa was not watching her mother at all, only admiring the sleeves of her new blue velvet dress: a gift from Mortmesne. The entire Guard had cautioned against accepting the dress, but Elyssa had overruled them, for the garment was expertly cut for pregnancy, rounded in the abdomen to accommodate the Princess's growing belly. Elyssa was not completely without caution, however, for she had ordered a hapless Keep servant to touch the dress before she wore it. As the bewildered girl plunged her hands into the deep velvet, her eyes closing in pleasure at the richness of the material, Niya's stomach had turned over. Elyssa, the old Elyssa, would never have done such a thing, thrown another woman into the pit to save herself, and so Niya had her final confirmation: the woman in the blue dress was no longer Elyssa, but someone else. All of them had underestimated the witch, from Barty on down, and now it was too late.

The Queen twitched again. Brenna made the same motions of calming her, but Niya could see the wild jumping motion beneath the Queen's closed eyelids. The Queen had been asleep for three months now, but it was not an easy sleep, for she moaned from time to time, her features twisting in pain. Initially, Niya had suspected the witch, but she could make no sense of that suspicion. Thorne could have no quarrel with Arla, for they charted parallel courses. Thorne's role in the Gadds Fire had never come out publicly, but Niya knew of it, as did anyone with the right amount of gold to spread around the Arvath. Were Arla conscious, she might have knighted Thorne for his deeds.

But Elyssa had done Arla one better, for Thorne now sat at her right hand. Niya chanced a quick glance at the blue-clad figure on the far side of the bed and found Elyssa smiling at her, such a malicious smile that Niya was sure Elyssa could read her thoughts. She tried to look away but could not, suddenly assaulted by the image that had taunted her for weeks: the Fetch wreathed in flame, his skin blackening and charring, his mouth wide in agony. Slick, feverish sweat broke out on Niya's forehead.

"Highness, the riots," Barty said, his voice urgent under the low tones of sickroom diplomacy. "We must make a decision today."

Elyssa turned to him. The image in Niya's mind mercifully faded.

"What is the situation at the storehouse?" Thorne asked.

Barty did not reply; none of the guards liked to answer Thorne. But Elyssa waved to Barty to answer the question, and so he did, though his mouth curled in distaste.

"More than two hundred looters. Colonel Bermond says the doors of the storehouse are still holding, but not for long. They'll be in before nightfall, but Bermond is looking beyond that. The Crown holds five storehouses in the Hollow, and Cleary thinks they'll soon be after them all."

"How many battalions do we have down there now?" Thorne asked.

Once again Barty hesitated, and once again Elyssa made a sound of cxaspcration and signaled him to speak.

"Four battalions. That's all Cleary says he can spare, with Essex and his contingent spread over the Almont as well."

"Shouldn't Essex have been back weeks ago?" Elyssa asked.

"Yes, Highness. Cleary says he's sent another battalion to investigate the delay."

Elyssa and Thorne turned to look at each other for a long moment. Niya didn't like these looks; she felt sure that the two of them were communicating somehow, speaking in silence. Barty's face had tightened; he didn't like it either.

"Tell Cleary to send in all four battalions," Elyssa said finally. "Any man found with his hand on Crown property will lose that hand."

Barty turned pale. "Cleary will take that order literally, Highness."

"Good."

"Majesty," Coryn finally ventured, stepping closer to Elyssa.

"The Queen needs proper medical attention. I beg you once again to let me summon a doctor."

"Coryn, I tired of this discussion months ago. Brenna has the situation well in hand."

"Majesty," Coryn murmured, then fell silent again, shooting a helpless look at Barty, who stood beside him. But Barty looked equally miserable. Niya found herself sorry for both of them, all of them. Most of the older guards had died the night of the Queen's party, but Elyssa had not replaced any of them. Despite the veteran presences of Barty and old Vincent the swordmaster, the Guard seemed so young now . . . too young to sort out what to do, let alone do it.

With a start, Niya realized that she was swaying on the spot. She was dizzy; she had not eaten breakfast that morning, or dinner the night before. It had once been her custom to dine with Elyssa, but those days were over; this new Elyssa wanted Niya nearby no more than she wanted to be there. She closed her eyes, trying to regain some hold on her balance.

A hand grasped her elbow, steadying her, and Niya looked up and saw Mace. His face was as impassive as ever, but in the next minute he had pulled one of his extraordinary feats of legerdemain, producing an apple from nowhere. He pressed it into Niya's hand, then stared at her, frowning, until she took a bite.

Who are you? Niya wondered. She asked herself this question constantly, but she knew better than to ask Mace himself. His past was like a wrapped box; one might not know the contents, but one could see the contours, spiked corners and vicious edges. He *was* a gifted fighter; one day he had showed Niya a clever trick of disabling a man with one hand pinned behind her back, and in return, she had showed him one of the entrances to the tunnels that beehived the walls of the Queen's Wing. Mace's clear delight in the discovery had baffled her; he had begun exploring the tunnels on his own and had already found several more entrances that even Niya had not known about. She didn't know where he found the time, not until Dyer enlightened her one day: Mace had a comfortable bed in the guard quarters, just like everyone else, but as far as the Guard could tell, he did not sleep.

The Queen had finally quieted now, her chest rising and falling in relaxed, natural breathing, and Brenna straightened with a satisfied expression on her face. Niya supposed the witch *was* keeping Arla alive, in some fashion or other, for Barty said she should have died. The Queen breathed—though she did not wake, or eat, or give any other signs of life—and the Christians among the Guard hailed that as a miracle, but Niya was no Christian, and she did not trust miracles. Elyssa had poisoned her mother, and beneath Thorne's expressionless face lay triumph, a sick triumph that only Niya—and perhaps Mace—could see. She sensed something terrible at work in this room.

"Highness," Elston said, poking his head around the door. "They're ready downstairs."

"Excellent," Elyssa replied, dropping the sleeve of her dress and turning back to them. Though the dress was cunningly tailored, nothing could hide the swell of her belly, now six months along. In her first rage of betrayal after the night of the party, Niya had thought of killing Elyssa; she was still Blue Horizon, after all, no matter how many of her companions were dead, and she had spent her adult life slaughtering anyone who stood in the way of the better world. But there had been no opportunity, for in the wake of the Queen's poisoning, Barty had tightened Elyssa's security to an impassable degree.

And could you really do that anyway? her mind demanded. *When she's carrying Gareth's child?*

Niya didn't know; she, who had once been so clear in her course, so certain of the right thing to do, now felt certain of nothing. She still believed in William Tear, in the Blue Horizon, but for what? Nearly fifty of her brothers and sisters had died in the Gadds Fire, and the remainder had dived deep underground after Elyssa had hired the Caden to hunt them down. There was no Blue Horizon anymore, only a collection of frightened mice, crouching in whatever holes they could find. The Caden were expert mousecatchers.

"Come along, all," Elyssa said lightly. "See the show."

Niya didn't want to go. She knew what awaited them on the Keep Lawn, and she could not face it again. But Elyssa would not let her plead off . . . not this new Elyssa, with the sick gaze of the witch glaring out through her eyes. Barty, too, looked unwell, his face pale and betrayed as he stared at Elyssa's retreating back.

Help us, William Tear, Niya prayed, as she followed Elyssa out the door and down the corridor. Nothing was permanent; Tear, who had watched the collapse of his great society, had known that as well as anyone. Even Elyssa's reign would fall one day, to be replaced by something better—or worse—and now Niya wondered whether the better world was even possible. It was the nature of humanity to cycle, to move from great to dreadful, utopia to terror. Even if they reached the better world, how could they possibly hold it against each new day's onslaught?

They went through Bowler's old quarters and emerged onto the balcony: a wide parapet that overhung the face of the Keep. The freezing air hit Niya like a slap, for now, in late January, the entire city was packed in snow. The first blizzard had come in early December, and although the city had greeted the snow with near ecstasy, the storm had come far too late to help the Almont, where famine was now laying waste. Elyssa no longer showed Niya the Crown reports, but Barty still saw them, and his summaries to the Guard stinted no detail. Entire Almont villages were in the process of starving to death, and in the out-Reddick, where winter always hit first and hardest, there had been scattered reports of cannibalism. Niya didn't like to believe these reports, but she had no reason to doubt them; in fact, knowing the army as she did, Niya thought it likely that such incidents were being deliberately underreported.

The Almont Coalition, realizing the dangers of the growing rebellion at this late date, had arranged for distribution of its members' hoarded stores. But that was a mere drop in the barrel, no match for the reaper who stalked the Almont. As the stores dwindled, slow starvation was beginning to creep its way into the city as well, with the poor suffering the worst, as always. The mob besieging the Crown storehouses was the first sign of open revolt, but it would surely not be the last.

Do they still think she's the True Queen? Niya wondered. The old Elyssa would have opened the Crown storehouses without a thought, given food to everyone. What did the city think of her now? With the Fetch dead, the Blue Horizon scattered, there was no one Niya could ask.

Leave, then, her mind whispered. *There's nothing for you in the Keep anymore, if there ever was. Why are you still here?*

Because she's not wholly gone, Niya replied stubbornly. *Not yet.* And there was another reason: the Fetch had given her a mission. His death changed nothing. The Fetch had told her to watch Elyssa, and Niya took orders from no one else.

Elyssa had moved to the edge of the parapet now. Niya tried to hang back near the doors, but Elyssa beckoned her forward, right to the edge. Niya forced herself to look down on the white expanse of the Keep Lawn, the enormous scaffold comprising five platforms, five nooses hanging down. Only three of the nooses were filled today; Niya supposed she ought to feel grateful for that, but she was beyond gratitude for anything, for she had already recognized Amelia's tall, thin form on one of the platforms, her dark hair spilling over her shoulders.

Elyssa's appearance on the balcony had clearly been the sign for things to commence, for now one of the soldiers stationed on the scaffold had begun to read some sort of announcement. Niya could not make out the words, but she didn't want to.

"What of the rest of them?" Elyssa asked Barty. "The plot against my mother?"

"Highness, we have found no evidence of any plot. The Blue Horizon are not—"

"No evidence?" Thorne broke in. "What of the poison? The signed confessions of the maids?"

"I do not trust those confessions," Barty replied coldly. "Those women had been with Queen Arla since her adolescence."

"And what of that?" Thorne asked, his tone amused. "Loyal maids are so hard to find."

Niya almost flinched. Behind her, Brenna emitted a low chuckle.

"The matter is proven," Elyssa announced. "My mother's maids laced the dress with poison, and they did so at the behest of the Blue Horizon. I want the man who dealt the poison."

"Highness, we cannot—"

"Cannot, cannot, cannot," she repeated softly. "Barty, I grow so very tired of hearing the same words out of your mouth."

Barty's mouth dropped open, his eyes wounded. Niya, unable to stop herself in the face of the old guard's pain, grasped his arm, leaned close to whisper in his ear.

"It's not her who speaks, Barty. You know it is not."

Barty drew a shuddering breath, then spent a moment mastering himself. "I will redouble the search, Highness."

"Do that," Elyssa replied, her eyes on the execution below. Then she grimaced, placing a hand on her belly.

"Stop kicking me, little heir."

Niya edged closer, unable to help herself. There was real

tenderness in Elyssa's voice; her eyes were soft as she looked down at the swell beneath her hand. It was always the child who seemed to bring on these rare moments, recalling Elyssa to who she was.

"She's a stubborn one," Elyssa remarked.

"She, Highness?"

"My little girl. She kicks and kicks."

"Is it you, Highness?" Niya asked suddenly, caution overborne by hope. "Are you still in there?"

Elyssa blinked, and then looked up at Niya, her face tightening into its usual cold lines.

"What?"

"Nothing, Highness," Niya replied, turning away. Tears had filled her eyes, but she did not want Thorne or his witch to see. Below, on the lawn, the soldier had finished reading, and now another man climbed the stairs of the scaffold, pulling a black hood over his head.

Thorne had moved up to stand on Elyssa's other side now, staring down at the scene on the lawn, his face betraying nothing, neither pleasure nor dismay. For a single, seemingly endless moment, Niya thought of pulling her dagger, shoving Elyssa aside, and burying the blade in Thorne's chest. She had never been so close to Thorne before, and she fingered the handle up her sleeve, considering. She might be able to reach him; they were only five feet apart. Of course, she herself would die afterward, but that might almost be worth it, might be—

"Barty! Don't!"

A low shriek echoed behind her. Niya whirled and felt her blood go cold.

Oh no, she thought. *No, no, no.*

Barty had wrapped an arm around the witch's throat from behind, and his other hand held a knife aimed at her jugular.

"Release her, witch," he snarled. "Whatever you have done to the Princess, you will undo it, right now. Or I will end you."

"Will you?" Brenna's voice was lilting, full of laughter . . . but her face was as cold as the winter moon. For a moment Niya thought she could even see the witch's bones, so pale that they shone nearly silver under the fine skin of her cheeks. Brenna's eyes seemed to blaze with white fire.

"Do you think I fear your knife, Captain?" she asked Barty. "I am a child of the Crossing, and I know each of you, better than you know yourselves. William Tear himself would fear me, if he could see me now."

Something snapped, as short and sharp as a twig underfoot. Barty fell with a howl, and Brenna darted away. Barty was groaning, clutching his knee; Niya began to go to him, but she was arrested by a cold voice in her mind: the Fetch, when she was no more than fourteen years old.

Diversion, Niya. Diversion is our most powerful weapon, for so much can be accomplished under cover of the noise.

And then: *The witch belongs to Arlen Thorne.*

Niya took a short, speculative look around the balcony. The Guard was busy, huddling over Barty as he writhed in pain. Elyssa had not moved, did not even seem to have noticed the uproar; she was watching the crowd. Brenna was leaning against the double doorway of the balcony, rubbing her throat. The witch might be invulnerable, but the witch was only a tool, and the man who wielded her stood just beside Elyssa, less than five feet away. In that single, seemingly endless moment while the guards fussed and clucked over Barty's wounded knee, Niya reached for her knife.

A low, venomous hissing rose behind her. Glancing backward, Niya saw the witch staring at her, her body tensed like that of a snake.

She sees me! Niya thought, horrified. *She sees every thought in my head!*

And now she realized that another figure stood beside Brenna: a dark figure, his skin blackened with burning. The only thing not black was his eyes, bright brown and horribly alive. As Niya hesitated, he began to totter toward her with outstretched arms.

No, she thought. *It's not him. He's dead. This is only her witchery.* Elyssa had succumbed, but it was precisely for Elyssa's sake that Niya could not. She shut her eyes for a long moment, calling up every ounce of her own strength, willing the dreadful apparition to be gone.

"Take hold, Barty," Coryn's voice murmured behind her. "This will be bad."

"Don't coddle me, boy!" Barty snarled. "Get it done."

Another snap, and Barty cried out. Niya opened her eyes and found, to her immeasurable relief, that the Fetch had vanished ... but so had the opportunity. Thorne had moved down the parapet, out of range. After another moment Niya released her dagger, pulling her hand from beneath her sleeve. Brenna settled back onto her heels, her eyes never leaving Niya's face.

"Have a care, Mistress Niya," Thorne remarked from the far end of the balcony. His gaze had not left the crowd, and now a small smile played upon his lips. "Death is never distant."

A loud crack echoed below them. Niya closed her eyes, willing herself not to look, but it made no difference, for she could see it behind her eyes, all of it: Amelia falling, her legs dancing, seeking purchase in the air and finding none. Niya could even hear her, though she was too far away to hear any such thing: gagging and coughing, and worse, cheering, the crowd roaring its approval as Amelia kicked and twisted. The witch giggled, and Niya suddenly understood that she was doing this as well, making Niya watch, forcing the images into her mind, the sounds into her ears, if for

307

no other reason than that Niya was desperate to shut them out. Amelia grabbed the noose, trying to claw it from her throat, and now Niya could not hold back the tears.

"Elyssa," she whispered. "If you're in there, please . . ."

But Elyssa did not seem to hear her. She was admiring her new dress again, running her hands over the blue velvet of the sleeves, swaying back and forth so that the skirt rustled against her legs. And now Niya understood, finally and for the last time, that there was no True Queen. There would be no better world, no shining future, only the terrible present: witchery, starvation, and the tall marionette in blue who stood at the end of the parapet, smiling pleasantly, as good people strangled beneath her feet.

CHAPTER 27

THE DEVIL'S CLUB

The sun told the moon they should play,
But the moon said no, they should hold,
For the sun's place was warmth and kindness,
And the moon's place was dark and cold,
But the sun persisted, longing for danger,
And the moon was compelled to proceed,
The sun ran screaming in terror,
The moon said, "A fine play indeed."

—Lost Rhymes of the Creche, FROM THE APOLOGIST'S APOCRYPHA

Christian had not known that he missed the tunnels. He had been so overwhelmed with the wonder of the Keep, the light, that for a time he thought that he would never tire of it. But now, ascending the stairs in the blackness, he realized that there was great comfort in the familiar, even if the familiar was poison, and that some part of him would always feel most at home here, surrounded by stone and wrapped in dark.

He had spent the three months since the Queen's collapse exploring the extent of the labyrinth that stretched inside the walls of the Keep. There were tunnels on nearly every floor, all of them joined by a none-too-stable staircase that towered at least several hundred feet in the hollow darkness between walls. Christian had seen many strange things in these tunnels: rats as big as small dogs; a strange discarded pile of high-quality oaken furniture; even, at one point, Elston and Kibb, embracing in a dark recess behind the guard quarters. They had been far too intent on each other to notice Christian, and he had slunk away without a sound. The frocks in the Creche condemned such things, but Christian, who cared little for God and even less for any frock, had decided that the incident was none of his business and resolved never to speak of it. He had never seen Elston or Kibb or any other guard in the tunnels again, and so he felt comfortable there, free from the scrutiny that hounded him in the Queen's Wing. When Elyssa had sacked Barty from the Guard, Christian had felt quiet relief, for Barty had always watched Christian like a hawk, clearly waiting for him to do something wrong. Barty had been foolish to attack the witch, but it had been a brave bit of foolishness, and it had earned Christian's respect. He had turned out, along with most of the Guard, to watch Barty leave the Keep: an old man, his shoulders slumped and defeated, limping across the drawbridge on his busted knee. His departure was a loss to the Guard, and they all knew it.

Christian supposed the punishment could have been worse; Elyssa might have chosen to have Barty tortured, or even executed. The younger Elyssa had supposedly loved Barty like a father, and Carroll believed that this Elyssa—"the old Elyssa," as the Guard referred to her—had spared his life. But Carroll had also explained to Christian that, for a Guard, exile was worse than death. Christian supposed there was something to that, for Barty had been spotted in any number of pubs in the Gut, where he was apparently determined to drink himself to death. Carroll's statement revealed much to Christian about this place and these men.

They feared loss of honor above all things, but that was only because they had never truly faced death. They were good men; Christian had even grown to like several of them, particularly Elston and Coryn, but he would never see the world as they did. They were of the Keep, but Christian was not and never would be. They all knew it as well, because even with Barty gone, the scrutiny had not abated.

Elyssa had appointed Carroll to take Barty's place, though no one understood why; Carroll was one of the most inexperienced members of the Guard, and surely had the softest heart of any of them. Christian and Carroll had a comfortable working relationship, bound not only by professional respect but by the unspoken memory of that night in the Creche. If Christian had been another man, he might even have said they were slowly becoming friends. But Christian was still on probation, not with a single man but with the entire Guard, all of them watching and waiting . . . Galen, Coryn, Dyer, Elston, even Carroll himself. What were they waiting for?

At the bottom of the staircase a single tunnel stretched underneath the moat and into the city proper. This tunnel allowed Christian to come and go at will, and he had spent much of the past month in the city, seeking information on Lord Tennant. Tennant was a fixture at Elyssa's court, but court was not where he did his black business. Latimer and his cohorts had been down on the third level of the Creche; they clearly knew the tunnels, and after days of tailing Tennant, Christian had hardly been surprised when the man ducked down one of the staircases that peppered the Gut. But he did not head downward, toward the Creche; instead, he went under the moat and up the stairs. Into the Keep.

Oddly, Christian's first thought as he followed the man up the staircase was not of Maura, or revenge, or even violence. Rather, he thought: *We must get these tunnels guarded.* If Tennant and his wretched friends could get into the Keep so easily, others would be able to as well. The tunnels were a liability, one that must be addressed.

It's almost as though you're a proper guard, his mind mocked. *You'll be reading books next.*

Christian frowned, for the reading was a sore spot with him. The rest of the guards no longer bested him with sword and knife; Christian came off the winner as often as he lost these days. Old Vincent the swordmaster was gone—he had quit in protest when Elyssa sacked Barty—but even with the inferior Venner now running the arms room, Christian was improving at a steady clip. One day, he knew, he would surpass them all at swordcraft . . . but he still could not read.

Carroll had offered to teach him, several times, but Christian had refused. He meant to earn his place here, and he felt that he could not bear to be any further in the other man's debt. He had tried to teach himself, using the notes that other guards left each other, but it was all wiggling lines and incomprehensible marks, and he finally ripped the notes to pieces, furious. Swords were easy; why must this be so hard?

He had been meaning to ask Niya for help, had only been waiting for the right opportunity. But he could not do it now, for Niya was unwell. Over the past weeks Christian had watched her face paling, her already-slight frame growing even thinner, the light fading from her eyes. He knew the source of her grief, and whenever he saw Niya staring hopelessly at Elyssa, as though waiting for a miracle, he found himself hating the Princess Regent, hating her with all his heart. Christian had not been in the Keep long enough to know the Princess they had all known, the True Queen who had defied Arla and caused riots in the Circus, but he did not think that Carroll's description of Elyssa had been exaggerated. Niya's grief, the grief of the Guard . . . these were too raw for him to doubt.

A foot scraped above him in the darkness, and Christian paused, tapping silent fingers on the banister. Tennant had left the staircase at the sixth floor, a level mostly reserved for servants' quarters and linen storehouses. The dim glow of his torch faded, then disappeared, and a few moments later Christian began climbing the stairs again. He exited at the sixth level, following the distant torchlight down a long, narrow tunnel. As the light vanished, Christian struck a match and lit the candle he carried in his belt. He always carried the candle on these expeditions, along with his guard kit, but he left his grey cloak behind. Whatever was going on in these tunnels, Thorne and Tennant were in it together, and so Christian understood the true nature of his purpose here: not guarding, but hunting. The grey cloak could have no part in it.

The tunnel was even smaller than he'd thought: barely wider than his shoulders, with a low ceiling that brushed the tips of his spiky hair. Behind the walls, Christian could hear the muffled sounds of machinery: the pumps and levers that ran the Keep's plumbing. The sheer size of this structure still managed to shock him at times, but not as often as it used to. A man could get used to anything; children of the Creche knew that better than anyone.

He turned the corner and found himself in a dead end.

Christian halted, staring at the walls. Tennant had certainly gone this way; Christian had seen the glare of his torch down here, not a minute before. He backed up slowly, rounding the corner again to see if he had missed some branching in the dark. But there was nothing. Christian turned one way, then another, running his hands over the walls, seeking whatever hidden door the man had used. But he found none of the tiny laced dots that bespoke the hidden exits in the Queen's Wing. Tennant had come down here and simply vanished.

He didn't vanish, Christian's mind returned calmly. *They're resourceful, these nonces. You must be resourceful too. Look around.*

Christian took a deep breath, held up his candle, and examined the stone walls around him. A dark smudge drew his eye, and he leaned forward, finding a tiny carving in the stone: the rising sun over water. So the Blue Horizon had even made their way up here. The image made Christian think of the tunnels, where the Blue Horizon had once liked to write their message large . . . but even that memory was dimming, growing distant. Some days he actually forgot, for long stretches, that he had ever been anything but a Queen's Guard.

Christian heard something.

Very faint; the sound of male laughter. It seemed to come from above his head.

Christian held up the candle, examining the ceiling, pressing here and there, looking for weaknesses as he went. He came back around the corner toward the dead end, still pressing, but he could find nothing, no crevices or other imperfections in the rock.

It's here, he told himself firmly. *I just have to find it.*

He began to examine the wall of the dead end. Again, nothing, only evenly laid stone. The candle guttered, and Christian blinked, for he had felt no drafts. After a moment's thought, he held the candle up again, watching it steadily, unblinking. Long seconds passed, and then the candle guttered again, not to the left or right but *downward*, as though that unseen draft had come from the ceiling. Christian looked up again but saw only stone. Frustration threatened to overwhelm him, but he forced himself to hold still. Another minute passed, and then he felt it: a breath of wind, blowing down onto his forehead. He reached up, feeling the top of the wall, and his hand slipped through the ceiling.

Christian stared at this phenomenon: his hand, vanished

through what appeared to be unbroken stone. Lifting his candle high, he saw that there *was* an opening there, barely wide enough to fit a man . . . an opening cleverly concealed. For the first time—but not nearly the last—Christian found himself wondering who had built this place.

Reaching higher into the opening, Christian found it: a protruding lip of stone, the first rung of a ladder. Christian doused his candle, tucked it back into his kit, and grasped the rung, pulling himself up into the hidden opening. It was tricky; he had to haul himself up, scrabbling against the wall for purchase, and he wondered how the slight arms of Lord Tennant had managed the trick. Perhaps there was some other structural help here, something Christian couldn't see. As he boosted himself up through the opening, he felt it for certain: a breeze, cool and dry against his sweaty brow.

He did not know whether it was his own eagerness, or the true span of time, that made that climb seem to last forever. The stone ladder might have had thirty rungs, or a thousand. Nothing seemed real, as though, rather than climbing through a hole in the ceiling, Christian had climbed through a hole in the top of the world, into a darkness so complete that there would never be any more light. But eventually the feeling disappeared, as Christian realized that he could see again, the clear outline of each stone in front of him. Somewhere above, there was torchlight, filtering down.

Cautiously, he climbed through a final opening and found himself in a long, broad corridor, lit with torches, which ended in either a corner or another dead end. The corridor was empty, so Christian pushed himself off the ladder and straightened, then winced as he saw the wall, where an enormous mural had been painted: a picture of a group of children at play, sitting on a floor among balls and jacks and dice. Above this pretty picture were three words. Christian could not read them, but he did not like the look of the script: swirling and sinister, painted in red.

He pulled his mace from his belt and began down the hallway, moving on tiptoe. As he neared the bend, he passed a pile of swords and cloaks, all of them thrown carelessly at the base of the wall that held the mural. Christian counted the swords carefully, found nine.

Laughter echoed again. Christian gritted his teeth, for the sound reminded him of the ring, where men went to drink and enjoy the thrill of combat from the cheap seats. Christian was high above the tunnels now, hundreds of feet in the air, but he smelled the Creche all over this place, a stink like nothing else on earth. He tightened his grip on his mace, squeezing it until his fingers felt as though they might shatter, and peeked around the bend.

For a moment, he was blinded by light. Glass and crystal seemed to sparkle everywhere, wineglasses and mirrors and even an enormous contraption hanging from the ceiling, innumerable candles strewn about its sides. Carroll had told him the name of such devices, though Christian could not remember it now. They were designed to light large rooms, and the room before him seemed nearly the size of the Queen's ballroom.

Everywhere Christian looked, he seemed to see children.

They were there, sitting on sofas and small cushions and men's laps. Some of the girls wore dresses, as grown women did: silks and satins in bright colors. Some of the boys were dressed as well, like pages or even knights. One small boy wore a miniature suit of armor. None of them were older than seven. Some of the littlest ones still wore nappies, and they walked or toddled freely around the floor.

Christian did not know how long he stood there, staring at the scene, trying to come to terms with it, to make it real inside his head. The men were all drinking, he saw; empty glasses seemed to sit on every available surface. Looking around for Tennant, Christian found him at a low bar on the left side of the room, pouring himself a whiskey. A naked boy toddled across the room, clutching a toy horse, and as he passed the group of men, one of them reached out and grabbed the boy, fondling his genitals for a moment before the child moved out of reach. Casual, this gesture, languid; the man touched the boy the same way another man might reach for his pint of beer. Across the room, a bearded man dressed in bright green velvet had his cock out of his trousers, and he leaned back in the cushions, a glass of wine in one hand and the other stroking himself. His eyes were fixed on a tiny girl who sat on the floor, playing with a doll.

It's a club, Latimer had said, that night down on the third level. *A club, for lords.* Latimer had not been ashamed, Christian remembered that quite clearly. He had not thought that he was doing anything wrong; his only concern had been in secrecy, and Christian suddenly understood how secrecy had allowed this little club to continue, to flourish, just as secrecy protected the Creche. The children in this room didn't look like Creche babies; they were too clean, for one thing, and all of them had fine, straight teeth. But then Christian heard Arliss's graveled voice in his mind—*straight teeth and unblemished skin*—and understood: these *were* Creche babies, handpicked by Thorne for this purpose. Christian recalled the mural he had seen in the tunnel, its paint cracked and desiccated with years. How long had this "club" been here?

It doesn't matter, his mind whispered. The words were firm and certain, rational as an advocate's, but lined with murder, cold murder like a fine layer of red silk. Thorne wasn't here, Maura wasn't here, but those facts didn't matter either. Deep in his mind,

Christian heard his own voice, speaking to Barty on that long-ago day of his test: *I'm tired of fighting for no reason. I would like to have some purpose behind it.* And Barty had believed him, never truly knowing what he had taken into the Guard. Christian killed; it was what he did, what he was good at, and for much of his life, that had been justification enough. But here, *here*, was purpose.

Reason.

The naked little boy saw Christian first; he dropped the toy horse and began to scream. That was good, for the rest of the children began to scream as well, jumping to their feet and fleeing, toward a broad doorway at the far end of the room. They would not see this, and a distant part of Christian's mind was pleased at that fact. As the children fled, the group of lords sprang to their feet, dropping their glasses. One of them began to say something, but Christian did not wait to hear it. He had not killed anyone in months, and at the sight of the group of men, their faces wide with horror—but not guilt; no, never that—something seemed to stretch and breathe inside him, some set of muscles long unused. He smiled wide, then began killing.

H e saved Tennant for last. The oily lord showed more rudi-mentary sense than the others, hiding behind the bar while Christian rampaged across the room, chasing shrieking lords into the corners. Several of them tried to reach the doorway, the pile of swords that lay in the corridor, but Christian was there before them, laughing and snarling, swinging his mace at one head after another, and each impact traveled through his chest like fire, turning everything inside him to light.

Only when all the rest were dead did Christian regain some bare sense of himself, enough to turn his attention to the balding man crouched behind the bar. Tennant squealed like a rat when

Christian hauled him to his feet. As he picked Tennant up and threw him on the bar, the man's silken shirt tore down both arms.

"Please," Tennant begged. "We didn't harm him. Or her. Whoever you're here for."

Christian nearly laughed; the filthy nonce thought he was an outraged father!

"Please! I have money. I can give you ten thousand pounds. Just let me go."

"Ten thousand," Christian murmured, leaning over him. "Perhaps. If you give me some information."

"Anything."

"Maura. Where is she?"

"Who?"

He hauled Tennant up and threw him across the room. Tennant landed on the floor with a crunch, howling as his shoulder popped neatly out of joint.

"Maura. The girl you nonces pulled from the Creche. The one with the pretty blonde hair. She's too old for your little stable here, so where is she?"

"Blonde hair," Tennant repeated, his gaze sharpening through the pain. "But she had no relatives, no one to come looking. Thorne assured us—"

Christian punched him square, breaking his nose.

"Please!" Tennant shrieked. "We didn't take her! We needed someone, but it was Thorne who found her! He found her and brought her here! We didn't even have to pay the fee for the club; Thorne said he would take care of that, so long as we remembered later—"

"Remembered what?"

"Debt, man! It's all Thorne wants, to collect noble markers and be able to call them in! He's piled up favors like a hoard—"

Christian bent down, wrapping his hands around Tennant's throat.

"For the last time," he said softly. "Where is Maura?"

"In the back!" Tennant replied, his voice a hoarse wheeze. He threw an arm toward the back of the chamber, the doorway that opened into another room. "Back there! We didn't harm her, I swear—"

But Christian had heard enough of the harm these men had not done. He tightened his grip on Tennant's throat, unmoved by the sounds the man made, the gasps and gulps that echoed throughout the silent chamber. When it was done, Christian turned and followed the direction indicated by Tennant's out-flung hand.

The doorway at the rear opened onto another cavernous room, but this room was as different from the room of light as could be. The walls were lined with small beds. Not cheap beds, Christian noted; the mattresses were thick, the covers made of soft wool. On one wall was a basin and a long flat piece of furniture that Christian recognized as a changing table; he had seen one in the Queen's Wing, in the enormous chamber adjoining Elyssa's, which was now being prepared as a nursery. A drawn curtain to his left indicated a toilet. Christian noted all of this in a quick glance, then forgot it, for the children had gathered around a tall girl in the center of the room, a girl with a wasted face and long, gleaming, white-blonde hair. She clutched the children close, staring fearfully at Christian, and an impassive part of him—the guard part—noted that she looked at least ten years older than when he had last seen her. Then her face softened in recognition, and she looked younger . . . almost like her old self.

"Christian?"

"Maura. You're alive."

She smiled. Christian lowered his mace, meaning to move toward her, but in that moment his nostrils registered the bitter-sweet smell in the air: morphia cooking. He stopped, looking around the room again, seeing it anew, an almost ghastly mirror of the enormous chamber being prepared downstairs for the royal heir. The floor was covered with soft toys. At Christian's feet lay a box of whittled animals. There were even a few hand-bound books sitting on a low shelf.

"This is where Thorne took you," he said flatly. "This place."

"It's a club. For nobles. It's—"

Maura stopped talking, a sudden flush spreading over her face. And now Christian saw the worst thing, the very worst thing: one of the thick, comfortable beds was much bigger than the others, not made for children at all, and on the nightstand beside the bed was a tiny crucible, a twisted spoon.

"They brought me here," Maura said, her voice rising in alarm at the look on Christian's face. "To care for the children."

"Care for them," Christian repeated, thinking of the way the dead men had stared at the children as they sipped their drinks. Anger began to coil inside him now, anger so black that he could not begin to imagine how to keep it in check. "I see."

"I do care for them!" Maura snapped. "Are you to sit in judgment on me now? You, Lazarus?"

Christian stared at her for a long moment, then asked, "The words on the wall outside. What do they say?"

"I can't read any more than you can!"

"But you know what the wall says."

Maura glanced in both directions, trapped.

"What does it say?"

"The Devil's Club. All right? The Devil's Club, that's what they call themselves."

"I see," Christian repeated, his voice deadly soft now. He stared at her, as intently as ever, but for the first time he did not see the girl he had loved since childhood, or even the tiny scrap of child who had taken his hand on the block.

He saw Mrs. Evans.

"I do them no harm!" Maura wailed. "I clean them! I put them to bed at night! I tell them stories!"

"*You whore them out!*" Christian shouted, so furious that he found himself backing away as well, lest he break every bone in her face with a single blow. Images flashed through his head, beyond his power to check: Mrs. Evans, her mouth smiling while her dead eyes rung up coin. Maura's shivering, naked body on the auction block. And then he looked down and saw the group of small children standing there, watching them, a terrible lack of wonder on their faces. They *were* beautiful, these children; a distant part of Christian's mind reckoned that they must have cost Thorne a fortune.

"I make it better," Maura whispered brokenly. "Afterward. I sing to them. I cuddle them. I remember how it was. I make it better."

Christian rubbed his temples, feeling his fingers slick with blood, wishing that he had never come to this place, wishing that he had fled the city, fled across the Almont, perished in the Dry Lands, anything else.

"You're a pimp," he told Maura, his voice flat and brutal. "You trade children for poppy. You're nothing."

He turned and strode away, leaving them all standing there, wanting no part of this, no responsibility. He had done enough. But he got no more than five feet before he saw it: a small symbol carved into the wall beside the double doors. Another sun rising over water, but this one was much more crudely drawn. The Blue Horizon had never been in this room; Maura, or perhaps one of the older children, had etched the picture, not knowing what it was.

The Blue Horizon has given you your life.

Christian looked up, seeing anew the slaughter in the large

room beyond the doors. Dead men lay everywhere, and the entire chamber had been painted in blood. Looking down, Christian found that he still had his mace raised in one fist; he had forgotten about it, ceased to feel it, as though it were just an extension of his hand. Arliss had given him the mace, and he had said something else too.

Do not waste it.

Turning, Christian looked back at the group of tiny children huddled around Maura, their hands clutching her skirts. Several of them were crying.

I only did half the job, Christian realized. He had gotten revenge for the children, but revenge would not help them now. They needed care . . . not Maura's twisted-spoon, morphia-drenched variety but *care,* the sort that no child in the Creche ever got. This business had been Christian's private war, and he had truly thought that he could keep it secret. But he saw now that he could not. He blinked, slowly and wearily, then lowered the mace.

"Keep them here," he told Maura. "Don't let them go into the other room; they shouldn't see it. I'll be back as soon as I can."

Maura nodded. Her eyes flicked left, toward the small plume of smoke that rose from the crucible, and in that moment Christian came within an inch of ending her life. He closed his eyes, opened them again, breathing slowly.

"Stay off the poppy," he told Maura. "Try to remember who you once were. You can do what you like as soon as we get the children out of here, but until they're safe, you keep a clear head. Do you understand me?"

Maura nodded again, swallowing. With a last glance at the group of huddled children, Christian turned and strode out of the room.

The way down was much faster than the way up, perhaps

because Christian knew where he was going now. He climbed down the ladder, lit his candle, and headed back toward the staircase. It seemed very important not to think about Maura, and so he would not allow himself to. The children in the room, they were what mattered ... and in that moment Christian felt the small boy on the auction block fall away forever, all loyalty to the past disappearing in smoke. He and Maura had been children, yes, but Christian suddenly understood, in a way he never had before, that the world was full of children.

We were not special, he thought, feeling a sting in the corners of his eyes. *We were only two threads in the tapestry.*

He reached the ninth floor, the tunnels that backed the Queen's Wing, and shambled through them, nearly breaking his leg in his haste. When he reached the hidden door that accessed the guard quarters, he opened it and found Coryn, Dyer, Elston, and Kibb. All four were off duty, sitting down at poker, and they stared at him in silence, taking in his red-spattered appearance with wide eyes.

"Help me," Christian pleaded, holding out his hands in a bloody appeal. He had meant to keep his life, his true life, separate from these topside men. He had meant to keep himself apart, but the children upstairs outweighed pride, solitude ... even contempt.

"I need help," Christian repeated.

The four guards stared at him for another long moment, then put down their cards.

CHAPTER 28

THE LESSON OF
LADY GLYNN

The Almont rebellion might have died quickly, but serendip-
ity saved it. The Blue Horizon had already made significant
inroads in the Almont, and volunteers sprung up in every vil-
lage. The rebels took castles in good proximity to the Mort
Road, and as they headed west, toward New London, more
and more nobles began to withdraw before them, pulling their
retainers and taking flight for city residences. These nobles
left behind significant provisions, which sustained the rebels
through the worst months of winter, allowing them to survive
the starvation that plagued the rest of the Almont. But Aislinn
Martin was not content with survival; she wanted equality
and redress. Thus did rebellion roll steadily onward, toward
revolution.

—Out of Famine: The Almont Uprising, ALLA BENEDICT

Have you thought of what you will say?" the Fetch asked.
"Say?" Aislinn returned absently. She was looking over an
inventory of Lord Marshall's stores, but it was a painstaking process; she was not a good reader. They had taken the Marshall
manse more than a week before, but there were not enough hours

in the day to sort everything out. Lord Marshall's stores were significantly depleted; he had been far less stingy with his tenants than had Lady Andrews. Aislinn felt a brief pang of regret; if she had only known, she might have let Marshall go. But it was too late now, for his head was already on its way to the Keep. Marshall's hoarded supplies would barely be enough to see Aislinn's people to New London; they would have to keep a tight belt. The Fetch's voice broke in again, annoying her.

"Have you thought of what happens when you stand before Elyssa, alone, without your people behind you?"

"I will demand justice."

"And what does justice look like?" he asked. "Distribution of the stores?"

"That, certainly. But the Crown's food will only hold us for a single winter. We need something more sustainable. We need land. Land of our very own, with no quotas or bailiffs. Our work should belong to us."

The Fetch laughed, and Aislinn looked up at him, annoyed. She was the leader here, the Fetch but a guest, but one would never know it from his attitude. His mask, a dreadful mixture of harlequin and devil, no longer frightened her, but it still seemed to mock.

"The Blue Horizon has been agitating for the same thing since before you were born," he told her. "We've gotten nowhere. The power of coin is too strong."

"You don't have enough people."

"You are very young, Aislinn. You see only your half of things, how wonderful it would be to own what you farm. Have you ever heard of a noblewoman named Lady Glynn?"

Aislinn thought for a moment. The name was distantly familiar, but she could not put her finger on it. She shook her head.

"She was Queen Arla's closest friend. A lifelong friend, so

trusted that Arla even brought her in to tutor Elyssa when she was young. But Lady Glynn was no noble. She was one of us."

"Blue Horizon?"

"Yes. And though I cautioned her that we must work gradually, she would not wait. She did what you propose. Five years ago, she freed all her tenants, forgave all their debt, and then took the final, unforgivable step of divvying up her family acres among them. She dismantled her own seat."

"A brave woman," Aislinn remarked, though she sensed where this story was heading. "And then?"

"Queen Arla was so furious at Lady Glynn that she stripped her of her title and threw her out of court. The lady hasn't been seen since. Lady Glynn's neighbors took it as a clear signal that the Queen would not protect her allotment of the land, and so they rode in to take it back. The tenants could have fled, but they fought. In the end, all of them were slaughtered."

"How many tenants?"

"Two hundred and ninety-eight souls."

"Well, there you are! We have nearly five thousand now, and more coming in every day."

"Numbers are not as important as you think they are, Aislinn. This kingdom has a vested interest in the tenancy system. Too many of the powerful profit from it, from the meanest lord all the way up to Elyssa herself. They cannot let it fail."

"I thought Elyssa was your True Queen," Aislinn replied acidly. "The one who saves us all."

The Fetch was silent for a long moment.

"We were mistaken," he said finally. "Elyssa has changed, become a greater tyrant than her mother ever was, and a viper sits on her shoulder. They will not be swayed by kindness and light."

"I'm not a simpleton!" Aislinn snapped. "I know she won't bend willingly."

"Then what is the leverage to make her bend?"

Look at us! Aislinn wanted to shout at him. *Look how many people we have!* But she didn't, for his question had disturbed her. What would she really do if Elyssa said no . . . if she refused to open the storehouses, let alone redistribute the land? Aislinn knew nothing of what moved such people. She would not know how to wheedle the Princess Regent, or even what more to say.

"Do you counsel me to retreat, then?" she asked. "Tuck tail and run back into the deep Almont, where there's no water and even less food?"

"Of course not. I do not counsel anything, for this is your rebellion. But if you are set on going to New London, you should go with your eyes open. You are true of heart, but heart will not win the Keep."

"Why not?"

The Fetch paused, clearly surprised by the question. But he did not dismiss it, or answer with one of those smooth witticisms that irritated Aislinn no end.

"There is no ultimate hope in revolution, Aislinn. The power of money is too great. And even in the handful of historical moments when a revolution initially succeeded, the revolutionaries invariably cannibalized their great achievement by turning into what they had once despised."

For a moment Aislinn could not reply, for his words had hit their mark, making her feel cold and hopeless. Then she thought of the full castle around her, and rallied. Their cause was different, for they were neither greedy nor corrupt. They wanted only what was just and right: each man owning his own land, his own efforts.

"I would have expected the leader of the Blue Horizon to be less of a cynic."

"Who says I'm the leader of the Blue Horizon?"

Aislinn stared at him. "But you are! All the stories . . ."

"Ah yes, stories. Always true." The derision in his voice made her flush. "As a matter of fact, I am not the leader of the Blue Horizon. Our leader is dead."

Aislinn blinked. "Why do you tell me this?"

"Because I want you to understand just how ruthless this new Elyssa Raleigh can be. Not so long ago, our leader was her lover, perhaps even her beloved. But when the time came, that did not prevent her from cutting his throat."

"I never heard of any such–"

"You did not, and you will not. This is one of the most tightly guarded secrets in Elyssa's Keep."

"Then how do you know it?"

"Because I can walk through walls."

She stared at him, unsure whether he was joking. She had heard the rumors about the Fetch, as they all had: that he was a magician, able to vanish from New London and reappear in the Almont, able to slip free of a noose around his neck. In the few months Aislinn had known him, she had never seen the Fetch do any magic, but he was not wholly ordinary either. The entire kingdom knew that he had burned to death in the Gadds Fire that had decimated a large section of New London, but here he sat. And Aislinn could not deny that there was something odd about him, an impression that he came of another world . . . or perhaps another time. The Fetch was not moved by the events of each new day. If rebellion was a game to him–and Aislinn often thought it was–then it was a very long game indeed.

"We must go to the city," she told him. "That's where the food is."

"Indeed you must. But do not think to find a warm welcome there."

"The city folk are starving. Surely they will welcome us."

"Likely they will. Can your people live on welcome?"

Aislinn scowled. No matter what argument she made, the devil always had an answer. She thought again of the castle around her, the people who had followed her from the deep Almont. Together, they had walked nearly a hundred miles and taken three castles. They had lost only sixty-seven people, and gained thousands more. How could they possibly stop?

"Sir."

The Fetch looked up, Aislinn over her shoulder. It was one of his companions, the wide one called Morgan.

"What is it?"

"Word from New London. A massacre beneath one of the Crown storehouses. More than forty people are dead, and some two hundred have lost–"

Morgan stopped and swallowed.

"What?"

"Hands, sir. The Princess Regent's orders, for thievery. She cut off their hands."

The Fetch turned back to Aislinn.

"You are determined in this?" he asked her, his voice weary. "You are utterly certain?"

Aislinn shot a glance at Liam, who sat silent to her left. He rarely offered his opinion, and never in the company of others, but if there was ever a time for him to gainsay her, it was now. But Liam said nothing, and Aislinn turned back to the Fetch.

"We will have the food, the land. We have earned it."

"Then we must help you, for we are the Blue Horizon." The Fetch smiled, but his eyes were sorrowful. "We take care of each other. We will gather our people and meet you before the New London Bridge."

Aislinn stood as well, and shook his hand. She did not like him, nor the fool's talk of his movement. But she had just added the entire Blue Horizon to the force she would bring before the Keep. They now had the numbers, if not the steel, to challenge the Tear army itself, and what was more, they had right on their side.

We can't lose, she thought.

CHAPTER 29

PROPHECY

Where did the Creche children come from? Some were unwanted, some runaways, some bastards sold outright. A few Creche nests even maintained breeding programs—for newborns themselves fetched a good price from childless nobility desperate for heirs—and the remaindered children were often sold back into the maelstrom. One way or another, the tunnels got the fodder they needed, and so the Creche continued from generation to generation, the Tear's great unexpiated sin.

—*Valor and Vice: The Troubled Reign of Amanda Raleigh,*
Emma Meadows

Thorne strode swiftly down the corridor, his feet rapping on the stone. His face was as immobile as ever, hiding his fury as a high hedge might conceal a house, but beneath his stoic's expression, a tempest raged. It was not enough that the rebels had defeated and humiliated two battalions of the Tear army. It was not even enough that they had now taken three castles and burned two more. The note in Thorne's hand had been delivered by a disheveled army major, beaten and starved, who claimed that the rebels had released him with orders to deliver it. Thorne had ordered the man thrown into the dungeons, but that had not assuaged his anger. The note was written in straggling, imperfect letters; only two sentences, but its meaning was plain.

We are coming to New London. We want the food.

The note was signed with an indecipherable scrawl, but the first letter was a large and decisive A. Thorne knew that signature by now—this was not the first such note he'd received—but this time, there had been a gift as well: Lord Marshall's severed head, stuffed without ceremony into a picnic hamper. Deep in his mind, Thorne showered Aislinn Martin with every curse he knew.

He rapped on the Queen's door, and Galen answered, giving him a long, cool look.

"The Queen is sleeping, Thorne."

"I only want to speak to Brenna," Thorne pleaded, swallowing his rage and making his voice as meek as possible. "I will be as quiet as a mouse."

Galen let him in, wrinkling his nose as Thorne went past. They hated him, the Guard, and they thought that such small gestures allowed them to keep their dignity. They thought that Thorne would care about being outcast . . . as though he had ever been anything else.

Still, he counted himself thankful that it was not Lazarus on the Queen's door today. The two of them seemed to have made a tacit arrangement not to speak of each other's origins, and that was just fine with Thorne, but it was not enough to allay his anxiety. Lazarus had been one of the most feared figures in the Creche, but that onetime brawling boy had now grown into something even more dangerous: the Mace, who had somehow found the Devil's Club and slaughtered nine nobles, four of them longtime clients of Thorne's. The entire kingdom was in uproar over the missing nobles, but neither the army nor the Caden had found any trace of them. Thorne could not reveal the Mace as a murderer, for to show anyone the hidden rooms would be to reveal Thorne's own complicity. And Thorne could not have done so anyway, for when he had made his own excursion to the eleventh floor, he had found the hidden entrance bricked and mortared.

Brenna had found the children easily, down on the lower floors of the castle, in the care of three masseuses who were barely more than whores. Thorne had no need to kill the children; none of his purchases had ever seen his face nor heard his voice. But the loss of the nobles was a blow, for he had been counting on their support. The Mace and the Guard, all of them had done this to him. Now he would have to start all over again, and he would have to be careful . . . so damnably careful. The Mace was always watching, and that should not have troubled a man like Thorne, who operated most comfortably in the dark.

But the Mace did not sleep.

Brenna was kneeling at the Queen's bedside. Above her, Elston loomed, watching her every move, but Brenna did not touch the Queen, only stared at her. Her face was frozen in an expression of utter concentration, but Thorne knew this was only for effect; Brenna could perform this particular trick in her sleep. He could feel the power in the room, a low line of voltage running between Brenna and the Queen, and thought it strange that the Guard could not.

"Five minutes only, Thorne," Galen told him. "Then you will have to—"

Galen stopped suddenly, his mouth rounding. Thorne watched with interest as both guards' faces slackened, becoming weak and malleable. Much of Thorne's early coin, the basis of the small fortune that he had now amassed, had come from people who were willing to pay heavy for even an hour of the forgetfulness that

Brenna could provide. Thorne himself was no dealer, but he had had plenty of truck with narcotics in his time; every pimp did, and seeing Brenna at work never failed to rouse an odd wish that he could somehow capture her talent, sell it in dose. With enough bottles, Thorne could rule the kingdom from an armchair, and he wouldn't need Elyssa or any of her feckless people to do it.

"They're sorted," Brenna told him. "Happy as lambs."

"Lambs don't stay happy for long," Thorne remarked. "What did you need from me?"

"The Queen," Brenna said, gesturing to the wasted woman on the bed. "There are signs. Troubling signs."

Thorne perched on the edge of the bed, staring at Arla's face. He had never been this close to her before, never noticed how pinched her mouth was, how sunken her eyes.

"What signs?"

"She murmurs in her sleep."

"I thought you said she couldn't speak."

"She can't," Brenna said. "I have her securely. Whatever is speaking is something else."

Thorne frowned, not understanding her words, but not liking them. He had little comprehension of the invisible world Brenna inhabited; was well content not to know, so long as it functioned as it should. He did not want to hear about phantom voices, only the future.

"What about the sapphire?" he demanded.

"I am making good progress."

"How long?"

Brenna glared at him.

"I'm only asking."

"You hear, but you do not listen. These jewels, they are difficult to know, as difficult as another person. Just when I think myself close to solving their mystery, they change heart. The Queen speaks in prophecy. She speaks of the True Queen. I can make no sense of it."

"Does she still suffer?"

"Every moment." Brenna looked up at him, her pale eyes questioning. "Do you want me to stop?"

"No. What of Elyssa's sapphire?"

"I am sorry, master. The Princess hides from me. She will not move."

Thorne's teeth clenched. He understood this no more than any of Brenna's other mysteries, but the upshot was the same: he was being balked. He paused for a long moment, then asked the question that worried him most.

"What of the baby?"

"Nothing."

"Elyssa's due in two months! How can that be?"

"I don't know, master!" Brenna replied, her voice rising in agitation. "The child is hidden! I do not understand it. It could be that the jewel hides her, but then it could be something else."

"Could be, could be," Thorne repeated, restraining a snarl. "The rebels are coming, and the entire damned city is waiting with open arms. I need certainty."

A chuckle came from the head of the bed, making Thorne jump. The Queen was smiling. Beneath her closed eyes, her mouth seemed to twist around her teeth.

"Why is she smiling?" Thorne hissed. "You told me she was in agony!"

"She is, master, I promise you!" Brenna leaned down, taking the Queen's sapphire in her hand. "Yet she speaks, and laughs, and smiles. . . . and the omens–"

"What omens?"

"I have been casting my bones. I see calm all the way to the horizon, but beyond, disaster. The Mace, the Fetch, these signs can end us."

"The Fetch is dead," Thorne returned calmly. "You yourself saw him walk into that building."

"So I did, master. But I have also seen him alive."

"The True Queen, the True Queen," Arla croaked suddenly, making them both jump. Her words were tuneless and hollow, utterly unlike the old Queen's iron voice. "We open the door."

"What is this?" Thorne demanded.

"I don't know, master." Brenna leaned forward and waved a hand in front of Arla's face. "What are you? Who are you?"

"I am the one who keeps the gate."

Brenna looked up at Thorne, and her eyes were full of such fear that Thorne felt himself suddenly unmanned, all of his carefully cultivated calm falling to pieces.

"Wake her up," he said abruptly. "We'll get the sapphire some other way. Wake her up now."

Brenna nodded and took Arla's sapphire in her hand, closing her eyes. But a moment later, she opened them again, looking down at Arla in confusion; confusion, and mounting horror. Arla began to chuckle again, a sound so monstrous that even Galen frowned, disturbed from his sleepless dream.

"The child is hidden, yes," Arla murmured. "But not from me. The stars rise."

"Wake her up!" Thorne hissed. Fear had slipped into him now, a creeping, helpless fear that he had never experienced once, not during all of Brenna's prophecy. "Wake her now!"

Brenna looked up at him, her face a picture of consternation. "Master, I cannot."

Arla opened her eyes. The irises were bright green, almost like emeralds; Elyssa's eyes, Raleigh eyes. They all had them, from Matthew Raleigh onward . . . but not Thorne. He had been robbed of those eyes, along with everything else.

"Arlen Thorne."

Arla's voice echoed, strangely hollow in the dead air of the sickroom. Her head turned, almost mechanically, to look at him, and Thorne fought the urge to flee the room.

"You will rise, Thorne, and become great. But your fall . . ." That deep, rich chuckle again. "Oh, your fall. Here the queen of spades, and there the victory of ships, and both of them wait for you."

"Shut her up!" Thorne snapped at Brenna. "Can't you shut her up?"

But Brenna had retreated to the far wall, sinking down against it, covering her ears with her hands.

Useless, Thorne thought. He suddenly hated her, this freak whose life was guided by that invisible, unseen world. In that moment he would have traded all of Brenna's gifts for a world that consisted only of what a man could see and touch.

"I know who you are, Arlen Thorne."

The hollow, otherworldly voice was gentler now, almost kind. Thorne closed his eyes, looking away, trying to master himself.

"Would you speak with her, your mother?"

"No!" Thorne snarled, for the question enraged him. He was no needy child, to demand reassurance and explanation! He had been less than a week old when the Queen's man had sold him for fifty-five pounds and a drink on the house. He had not been a child since.

Now a gentle touch stroked against his hand; Arla's fingers, and that was so unbearable that Thorne leapt off the bed and toward the door. He scrabbled at the handle; he felt that he could not get it open fast enough, as though the very door itself had turned against him now, just like everything else, defeat snatched from the jaws of victory—

Get hold of yourself!

The words were shouted deep inside his mind, from some deep core of self, the core that never broke, not even in childhood, at the worst times.

It's hallucination, only hallucination. Brenna's talk has gotten you all worked up.

Taking a deep breath, Thorne turned toward the bed. Arla's head was back on the pillow, her eyes closed in sleep.

Thorne stared at her for a long moment, feeling his heartbeat slowly return to normal, calm settling over him like a sheet. Once upon a time, he had admired this woman, admired her in spite of what she had done, or perhaps even because of it. He admired will, and the pimps who had bought him must have admired it as well, for they had named him after the old custom: Arlen, Arla's son. The Queen could have simply had him murdered, or exposed, but she had sold him into the Creche instead, and gotten a good price. Thorne could admire that . . . but it had been a mistake, all the same. Royal blood was royal blood, and there was no telling when it might come back to haunt you.

The child is hidden.

"Brenna," he murmured, putting a hand on the seer's shoulder, tugging her upward. She rose from the wall, her eyes bloodshot and unfocused.

"Master?"

"We must act," he told her. "Right away."

"Act, master?"

"The baby," he said. "We must get rid of it."

Brenna let out a shaky breath but nodded. After a moment she said, "It's late in the day, master. The Princess is some seven months along, and this is dark magic I will work. They may both die, Elyssa and the child."

"I will risk that," Thorne replied, pleased to find his voice level. "We will get the jewel some other way. Just get rid of the baby."

"Done."

He gestured toward the two Queen's Guards, who remained silent and dreaming above the Queen's bed.

"Let them wake in several minutes. Get back to your place."

He waited a moment while she wiped her face and straightened her dress. The guards might notice nothing, but it was better not to take chances. When Brenna was together again, he nudged her toward the bed, then went to the door.

"One thing more, Arlen Thorne," the Queen remarked behind him. Brenna gave a small shriek, and Thorne halted, his hand on the latch. Turning, he saw that Arla was now sitting up in bed, her green eyes fixed upon him.

"You crave certainty, Arlen. I can give it to you, but a single certainty, only one."

"What certainty?" he croaked.

"You will die screaming. I have seen it."

Thorne stared at her, momentarily startled out of his fear. All of the long years he had spent in the Creche, bought and sold, touched and degraded . . . it was almost comical, that she thought to frighten him now with words of fear, of pain. He was no longer a child, tethered by a strap of leather to an iron ring; now he was the man who held the leash. For a long moment Thorne hesitated, wanting to tell the woman on the bed about all of it, to make her understand the journey he had undergone . . . but in the end he found himself unable. He turned and fled.

CHAPTER 30

THE THIRD OPTION

Love does not consist in gazing at each other, but in looking outward in the same direction.

—Antoine de Saint-Exupéry (pre-Crossing Fr.)

M aura was dying.

They had installed her in the infirmary, which was usually used for guards. But no one was injured right now. Beale, the Queen's senior medic, had complained bitterly about taking care of a morphia addict, but Christian had dealt with that. Securing a bed for Maura had been easy. Watching her die was not.

"Christian."

Looking at Maura was not easy either. Christian found himself unable to forgive her, even now. He would never forget his first sight of that room, not if he lived for a hundred more years, and when Maura begged for morphia, pleading, sometimes even screaming at all of them, it was not her wasted face that Christian saw, but the room with the mirrors, the children. Morphia itself might be no great evil, but he could not forgive what morphia had done. What it had allowed.

Beale said that it was the withdrawal that was killing her. Her heart would already be weakened by the drug, Beale said, and she hadn't seemed to be in good health to begin with. Christian thought of telling the medic that she was a Creche child, then thought better of it. Maura was dying, and the reason didn't matter.

"Christian."

He looked down at her.

"Please," Maura whispered. "Just a little bit of poppy. Just to get me over."

Christian looked up at the medic, asking a silent question.

"This is the Queen's Wing," Beale replied stiffly. "Our morphia is for the Guard only, for medical emergencies."

"Oh, come on!" a voice said behind him, and Christian jumped. He turned to see Coryn and Dyer, standing just inside the doorway.

"No one has broken a leg or taken appendicitis," Coryn said, moving toward the bed with Dyer in tow. "We have plenty of morphia. What could one shot hurt?"

Little red flushes had appeared in Beale's cheeks. "I am Her Majesty's senior medic. I do not answer to you."

"This woman is suffering," said Dyer.

"Well, she is an addict. She brought it on herself, did she not?"

Coryn and Dyer looked at each other for a long moment. Then they grabbed the medic, one to each arm, and lifted him from his feet, propelling him toward the door.

"How dare you?" Beale cried. "I will tell Her Majesty!"

"Do that," Dyer muttered. "Much good it may do you."

Two more guards had appeared now: Cae and Kibb, who had been in the arms room, helping Venner sort through a delivery of armor. Venner needed the help, for new arms deliveries arrived at the Keep every day now. The rebels were coming; they had just crossed the Beth Ford, less than ten miles from the city, and there could be little doubt of where they were heading. The entire Keep was scrambling to prepare.

"What's going on?" Cae asked.

"The medic is taking a leave," Dyer panted, hauling Beale toward the door. Cae and Kibb moved aside quickly, clearing a path; Coryn and Dyer shoved Beale through, and Kibb slammed the door shut. Beale pounded for a few moments, but that was simply for form. Soon there was silence but for Maura's breathing, a slow and regular rasp.

"That old man," Coryn muttered darkly, digging into the supply cabinets in the corner until he came up with a vial of clear fluid. "Blows five ounces on a case of toothache, but not a pinch for this poor—"

He glanced at Christian and said nothing else, filling a syringe with a minute dose from the vial.

Christian looked back at Maura, feeling himself at a loss. They had helped him, all of them, the night he had discovered the Devil's Club. Together they had burned the bodies and sealed the laddered entrance, blocking off the cursed corridor forever. All sixteen of the children were downstairs now, tended by three Keep servants that Dyer swore could be trusted, at least until they found them homes. Christian did not question it, for what did he know of raising children, of tending to them? What would he ever know, beyond killing?

"You got topside, Christian," Maura whispered, smiling gently. "We both did."

No, Christian wanted to say. *You never got topside, nor did I. It's all a greater Creche, even this place.* But he could not, for his throat was suddenly tight, as though someone had locked it in a vise. He stared down at Maura, suddenly remembering all of those made-up birthdays, each with their own presents. Five-pence piece; raspberry tart; carved wooden horse; poached egg in a tiny carved cup . . . there had been so many of them, and he had never gotten Maura anything, not once. Topside or tunnels, he had not been able to save her. Coryn tapped the syringe, then injected Maura's arm, and almost immediately, her breathing began to ease. Her eyes drifted closed.

"What did Beale say?" Coryn asked, holding Maura's wrist in one hand.

"That she's dying."

"I hate that old buzzard, but he's probably not wrong. Her pulse is weak. Morphia is a vampire, and withdrawal is a bad death."

Coryn paused, looking at Christian speculatively.

"I could give her more, you know. A lot more."

For a long moment, Christian did not move. He had taken Maura's hand at some point, though he didn't know when. The rest had come closer, gathering around the bed, and as much as Christian wanted to see indifference in their faces, or even triumph, he saw neither . . . only honest sympathy.

"You've known her a long time," Kibb remarked.

Christian nodded.

"Since you were children."

"Yes." *In the tunnels,* he began to say, then bit down. They had not earned the right to know that.

"Christian," Maura whispered, her voice thin and reedy. Her eyes were still closed. She mumbled something else.

"What?"

"We got topside, but you don't know it. I know you. You don't think you should be here. Don't think you . . . belong."

Christian did not reply, aware of the guards listening around him. Did they know what topside was? He could explain away Maura's words later, perhaps, but if he could not answer her honestly, then he didn't want to answer at all.

"Belong," Maura whispered. "You should. Belong."

Coryn had readied another syringe now, filled it up. He tapped it, then looked at Christian, and after a long moment, Christian nodded. Coryn bent to her arm again.

"We were children together," Christian told them. "In the Almont."

The other guards nodded. Maura's breathing had begun to slow even further now; Christian could hear it, a dry wheeze.

"She lived on the next farm over."

They nodded again, their expressions solemn, carefully studied artifice in each face, as though they were a playing troupe miming tragedy instead of farce.

Are they mocking me? Christian wondered.

"Lazarus," Dyer said gently, almost kindly, as though Christian were a child himself. "Did you really think we didn't know who you were?"

Christian stared at him, stunned. But the circle of faces around him remained still. Maura's hand had gone limp in his, and they knew . . . all of them knew, and they hadn't revealed him. Why? Christian was suddenly tired, so very tired, of pretending to be someone else.

What if I was neither? he wondered suddenly. *Neither Lazarus nor Christian? What if there was a third option?*

He looked down at Maura, watching her breathing slow, the motion of her chest still and then stop. He hadn't been able to save her, not then and not now . . . but there were others. Other children.

"Mace!"

Carroll had appeared in the doorway, hurriedly buckling armor to his shoulder.

"I need you. Right now."

"Have a heart, Carroll," Dyer muttered. "His girl, she's—"

"I am sorry for your grief, Mace," Carroll said, and to his credit, he truly did seem sorry, his broad, open face filled with regret. Then he seemed to recover himself. "But I need you right now. It can't wait."

"What can't wait?"

"The Princess Regent," Carroll replied, and now, as he turned into the torchlight, Christian realized that his friend's face looked pale and sweaty, almost sick.

"The Princess Regent is in early labor, and it's gone bad."

CHAPTER 31

THE VICTORY OF SHIPS

The Red Queen of Mortmesne valued the Tear sapphires highly, though no one has ever known precisely why. The two jewels were passed down from Raleigh to Raleigh, in a ritual as detailed as it was ultimately meaningless, and despite their superstitious history, everyone—historians, the people, even the Raleighs themselves—thought the sapphires mere baubles, well-preserved trinkets of a decaying house. The Glynn Queen's reign demonstrated clearly that this belief could not have been more wrong, but the question remains: just how powerful were these jewels? How instrumental to the development of the Tearling as we know it today?

No one can say, save those who were in the room.

—*Red Queen, Black Queen: Roots of the Glynn Empire*, JESSICA FENN

A caesarean. It's the only way."

"A what?" Carroll asked, feeling foolish. He had been a Queen's Guard for nearly five years, a period of ongoing tutelage and testing that dwarfed the training for any other job in the Tearling. But here, in the birthing chamber, he knew nothing. Elyssa had been screaming for half the night, and Carroll had learned to appreciate these little lulls. It would not be long before the screaming started again.

"A caesarean," the doctor repeated, and then, not unkindly: "We will have to cut the baby out."

"You can do that?" Lazarus asked, and Carroll felt sudden relief, that Lazarus knew no more about birth than he did. None of them had been ready; the Princess was not supposed to go into labor for another six weeks, at least. But it was here now, and Carroll found himself wholly at a loss.

"I have done it many times," the doctor replied impatiently, "and we must act now. The Princess Regent is hemorrhaging, and the baby is in distress. If we delay longer, we may lose them both."

"Will the baby survive?" Niya asked. She was kneeling at the side of the bed, clutching Elyssa's hand. "Born this early?"

"Perhaps, perhaps not," the doctor replied tersely. "But I promise you, the baby will not survive in there."

Carroll turned to Lazarus, who looked helplessly back at him. Both of them would rather have been anywhere else, but Carroll, as Captain of Guard, could not escape, and he had brought Lazarus along, less out of a wish for his company than from the knowledge that Lazarus was the only one whose choice would not arouse envy among the rest of the Guard. Being present at a royal birth was no small thing, or at least that was the way they saw it, the men who were not in this room, who had no idea what it entailed.

At least a dozen lamps had been set around the bed, highlighting everything in grisly fashion: bloodstained sheets and torn linens. Elyssa's belly seemed almost impossibly huge beneath the sheet. The screaming had been bad, but there had been worse to contend with, much worse: the Princess babbling, talking to people who were not there, cursing in a voice that was not her own. Father Timpany had wanted to perform an exorcism, but Carroll had forbade him; a good thing too, for Niya looked likely to murder the priest every time he came near the birthing bed. At times Elyssa seemed almost herself again, the princess Carroll had known and respected in the old days, before the witch had come. But then she would lapse back into the present, her eyes as cold as chips of diamond.

I am the Captain of Guard, Carroll told himself again, as though repetition could make the thing real. Certainly nothing else had worked. On his last leave, Carroll had even tracked down Barty in the Gut, seeking advice, or validation, or perhaps forgiveness; he didn't know. But the former Captain had been dead drunk, in no mood for talk. For Carroll, the weeks since Barty's expulsion carried all the clarity of an early-morning dream, and now the dream had crossed fully into nightmare.

"Lady Glynn!" Elyssa screamed suddenly, her voice like broken glass. "Lady Glynn, help me!"

She arched in anguish, rolling dangerously near to the edge of the bed. Niya grabbed her shoulders, holding her down.

"Captain?"

Helpless, Carroll turned back to the doctor. There was no treachery here; this man had already birthed two generations of Raleighs, and despite a distant Mort ancestry, his loyalty was unimpeachable. This was a choice for Elyssa to make, but Elyssa had lapsed back into semiconsciousness. Niya placed a wet cloth on the Princess's forehead, her face oddly blank, as though she cared for a stranger.

"Mace?" Carroll asked, fighting to keep the edge of desperation from his voice. "What do you think?"

Lazarus looked from the doctor to Elyssa, then shrugged. "I say yes. What do we know of babies, or doctoring? Let the man do what he thinks best."

"And what if we lose the baby, or the Princess?"

"Then we hang."

The words were said without emotion, and even here, in extremity, Carroll could admire Lazarus for this quality: supreme detachment in the face of death. If the time ever came, Lazarus would do the right thing, even if his own life hung in the balance. Carroll was sure of it.

"Niya?"

"Yes," she said, without hesitation. "I've heard of this procedure; they do it in the brothels, when the baby will not come timely."

"Well, then—"

"You have not consulted Mother Church."

Carroll started; he had forgotten that Father Timpany was in the room.

"Perhaps we should consult Thorne," Father Timpany continued. "The albino might have some insight, or—"

"No," Niya said firmly, before Carroll could answer, and to his surprise, Lazarus joined her.

"She's right. The witch shouldn't be allowed within a mile of the Princess Regent, or the baby."

Father Timpany frowned, and Carroll cursed inwardly. The priest was Thorne's creature, for certain, just as every emissary from the Arvath seemed to be these days. Carroll had not needed Niya, or Lazarus, to tell him that the priest's advice could not be trusted, but the conversation would surely get back to Thorne.

"Time!" the doctor said tersely, filling a syringe. "Make a decision!"

"Do it," Carroll replied, as though the words were not his own but someone else's, speaking through his mouth. "Do what you must."

"I will put the Princess Regent under," the doctor said, moving swiftly to the bedside. "But you will need to hold her, all the same.

The pain will be great, perhaps great enough to cause her to move. She must not."

Carroll pinned Elyssa's left shoulder, Niya her right, while Lazarus took her legs. The doctor injected her, and almost immediately Elyssa began to quiet.

"Linens," the doctor muttered to the two midwives. "All you have. And get the needle and thread ready."

"This is ill-advised," Father Timpany muttered as the midwives scurried about the room. "Perhaps we should pray."

"Pray away, Father," Lazarus growled. "And tell us if He answers. There's a first time for everything."

Father Timpany paled with anger, but he did not quite dare to reply. He had to be here; it was one of the Keep Priest's many ceremonial functions, to certify the birth of the royal heir. But Lazarus had made no secret of his disdain for the Arvath, and even the priest seemed to understand the delicacy of his position in this room, for he turned and stormed back to the corner. Timpany feared Lazarus; they all did, even Carroll himself at times. Sometimes he believed that he and Lazarus were becoming friends, but just as often he wondered whether the fighter was even capable of friendship. He had civilized significantly since coming to the Keep, but there would always be something in his dark eyes that warned other men away, kept him apart.

"We will begin now."

The doctor knelt over Elyssa, but Carroll found that he was unable to watch; he stared at the blue coverlet instead. Lazarus would keep an eye on things, Lazarus, who had seen all of the world's horrors and found a way to live with that sight. Lazarus could stand and watch the end of the world.

He would have been a better Captain, Carroll thought, *even though he—*

But then Elyssa's right shoulder heaved beneath his hands, and

Carroll was forced to bear down, pressing so hard that he knew he would leave bruises. At the foot of the bed, Lazarus was straining as well, his scarred hands gripping Elyssa's shins. Niya cursed as she wrestled with Elyssa's shoulder, her face sheened with sweat.

"Hold her, damn it!" the doctor shouted.

Elyssa groaned, a soft sound that seemed to come from miles away. The room suddenly smelled of blood. Carroll shut his eyes, concentrating all of his will on holding Elyssa still.

Mum said I was too soft for the Guard.

Yes, she had said so. Carroll had not remembered those words in years, for his parents were dead. But now he wondered whether any of them were hard enough for this business. Long moments passed, a seeming eternity, until the doctor said, "There."

When Carroll finally worked up the courage to open his eyes, he found the doctor holding a tiny, bloodstained bundle.

"A girl," the doctor announced, passing the bundle to one of the midwives. "Clean her and get her warm; I will inspect her shortly."

The two midwives huddled over the new princess, unwrapping the cloth. Father Timpany moved in that direction, and almost immediately Niya left Elyssa's side to shadow the priest. Carroll looked to the doctor, saw the flash of a needle piercing bloodied skin, and turned quickly back to Elyssa, who appeared to be sleeping peacefully again. Her eyelids fluttered, as though she were dreaming, but that was all.

"The Princess Regent?" he asked the doctor.

"She should be fine," the doctor muttered, intent on his task. "Some blood loss, but not terrible. She will have a scar."

"Doctor!" one of the midwives screamed. "The baby! She's not breathing!"

Carroll jumped to his feet.

The doctor cursed. "The Princess must be stitched. I cannot come now."

"What do we do?" Carroll demanded, feeling shards of panic drive into his brain as he peered over Niya's shoulder and saw the small, still form lying there. Even Elyssa's death seemed a better outcome than this. "Doctor, what can we do?"

"Nothing," the doctor said. "The stitching must be done, or the Princess Regent will bleed out. I am working as fast as I can."

"Give her to me."

Carroll jumped. The voice had come from the head of the bed, so weak that it was barely more than a whisper. He turned and found Elyssa lying awake, her green eyes filled with tears.

"Niya. Give her to me."

"Highness?" Niya asked. "Is it you?"

"It's me. Give me my baby."

"No!" a voice shrieked, and Carroll jumped again. This voice, too, had come from Elyssa, but it was not her voice, nor even a woman's voice at all . . . thick and guttural, almost a bark. As Niya reached for the girl, the midwife moved to block her, but Niya shoved her out of the way and gently lifted the tiny form.

"No!" that thick, dreadful voice screamed from Elyssa's mouth. "No! No! No!"

The baby still wasn't breathing. Her blood-reddened skin had begun to darken to a bruised purple. As Niya approached the bed, Carroll saw that Elyssa was clutching her sapphire, trying to pull the chain over her head, struggling, almost flailing at it, as though restrained by invisible hands.

"Mace," Elyssa whispered. "Help me. I give you permission. Take it off."

After a questioning glance at Carroll, Lazarus leaned down and helped Elyssa pull the chain over her head. As it came off, more dreadful growls issued from Elyssa's mouth, threats and curses. In the corner, Father Timpany crossed himself and closed his eyes, clearly praying.

"Don't you dare, you bitch!" Elyssa's mouth howled. "Don't you dare!"

"I will!" Elyssa screamed back. "I will! I will! I will!"

She held out her arms, silently begging for the baby. But Carroll, utterly unsure now of what was real, or right, put out a hand, warning Niya back.

"Carroll," Niya murmured, tears in her eyes. "It's her. Really her. Look."

Carroll looked, and saw what Niya saw: beneath the pain-shriveled face, the old Elyssa, the princess he remembered, the girl who used to joust with Barty and write long treatises in support of the poor. She was here now, entirely here, and so he moved out of the way, allowing Niya to deposit the tiny creature into her arms. Elyssa stared at the baby for a long moment, tears working down her cheeks.

"My daughter," she whispered. "I see now. I see what we were waiting for."

She held up the necklace in one trembling hand.

"There is no time, Kelsea Raleigh," she said. "This is all we'll ever have, and you will never see me again. But you will perhaps remember this moment. This one gift. I give it to you."

She looped the chain gently around the baby's neck. Carroll was never sure what happened afterward, only a flash of blue light, so bright that he was temporarily blinded . . . and then, mercifully, the enraged wail of a newborn. Elyssa fell back against the pillows, her arms going limp, and the baby would have fallen off the edge of the bed if Carroll had not leapt to catch her. He looked at Niya, at Lazarus, in consternation, holding the infant close, wincing as she screamed into his left ear.

"Nothing wrong with her lungs, that's sure," the doctor muttered. "Get her warm, now."

Niya thrust some linens into Carroll's hand. Without thinking, he wrapped the cloth around the infant, struggling to avoid the sapphire. The night seemed weeks long, but when Carroll glanced at his watch he found that only four hours had passed. How could that be possible? He felt as though they had all climbed the highest peaks of the Fairwitch, all in one go.

"Captain."

The midwife Niya had shoved aside had crept close again, and now she timidly held out her arms.

"She needs to be bathed."

After a moment's thought, Carroll handed the baby over, and the midwife carried her to the small basin in the corner. The new princess screamed all the way through her bath, but once the midwives had swaddled her in clean linens, she quieted a bit, allowing the doctor to bend over her, examining her fingers and toes.

"Do we have a name?" Father Timpany asked.

"Princess Kelsea," Carroll replied. "You heard it yourself."

Father Timpany's face darkened. "That is a pagan name. The Princess Regent was in extremis; you cannot possibly expect her to—"

"It's the name she chose," Lazarus announced, moving in to tower over the priest, who blanched. Carroll felt a sudden, absurd gratitude.

"But the Holy Father has commanded first news. I must get back to the Arvath."

"Then go," Niya snarled. "No one wants you here."

"The Princess Regent is a faithful child of God," Father Timpany remonstrated, ignoring Niya entirely. "She cannot choose a name so wrapped up with the filth of the Blue Horizon—"

"She can do what she likes, Father." Carroll had never cared much for the priest, but now, seeing the deep fear in the man's eyes, he understood: Timpany was frightened. Had it been Elyssa, raving like a woman possessed? No, Carroll thought not. The priest–the Arvath–had been promised something here, and it had not been delivered. Father Timpany was afraid to go home. Carroll turned back to Elyssa's sleeping form on the bed, seeing her anew: the wan cheeks, the straggling blonde hair.

We couldn't save her, Carroll thought. The Guard had hatched so many plans among themselves: killing the witch, killing Thorne . . . Elston had even suggested enlisting help from the last of the Blue Horizon. But the witch was always in the way. In a mental blink, Carroll saw Barty lying on the balcony, his knee bent inward at an angle God had never intended. Who could fight against such power?

But we must, he thought. Thorne and his witch would not depart the Keep with the birth of the royal heir. Elyssa was lost, but now there was a child to consider.

"She named the heir, Father. It's done. Go and tell His Holiness."

Carroll turned away dismissively, beckoning Lazarus and Niya, both of whom followed him into the corner. Father Timpany did not depart, only huddled in an armchair and opened his Bible again.

"Mace," Carroll murmured, keeping an eye on the priest. "I want you to stay with the new princess at all times. You will be her close guard, at least until we come up with something else."

"Me?" Lazarus demanded. "What on earth for?"

"Listen to me," Carroll said, keeping his voice low. He wondered where the witch was right now, whether she was listening. "That baby is the heir to the Tear throne, and the Princess Regent is . . ."

He broke off. *Weak* was what he had meant to say, but that wasn't right. Since her mother's poisoning, Elyssa had been squeezing the kingdom with a fist of iron.

"Not herself," he finished.

"Am I being punished? Is this because of–"

"No," Carroll said quickly. "It's not because of the nobles, I swear to you. This is important, though I can't tell you why–"

He stopped, realizing that he sounded half mad himself.

"Am I to change nappies as well?"

"No," Carroll said, ignoring the bitterness in his friend's voice. "Niya will do that."

"What?" Niya demanded, just as outraged as Lazarus. "I'm no nursemaid!"

"No," Carroll said softly. "You are a member of the Blue Horizon."

Niya paled. Her eyes darted to the priest, who still read ponderously from his Bible, and then to Lazarus, where they rested in mute accusation.

"Yes, I told him," Lazarus murmured. "Not what you said, mind you, only what I suspected."

"You filthy–"

"I have no plans to tell anyone," Carroll cut in, forestalling the argument, "or to arrest you, Niya. We need you now."

"What, to dispense milk and clean up shit?"

Carroll narrowly restrained himself from slapping her, contenting himself with grabbing her shoulders.

"What do you think happened here?" he hissed. "You think it an accident that Elyssa went into childbirth two months early? Will you pretend that you didn't hear the voice of the witch from her mouth?"

Niya blinked.

"The baby is in danger," Carroll whispered grimly. "I know it, and you would too, Niya, if you could only look beyond your own pain."

"Elyssa is–"

"Elyssa is gone," Carroll replied firmly. "Did you think you were the only one betrayed? We must look to the future."

Niya did not reply, but she still looked mutinous.

"We must keep this between us," Carroll told them. "Not a word of what happened in this room. Thorne and the witch have been after the sapphires for months. Barty knew it; he told me before he left. The longer they think Elyssa still wears hers, the better. Our secret."

"And the Arvath's," Lazarus muttered.

"No," Carroll replied, glancing across the room at the priest. "Timpany may mean to tell the Holy Father everything, but he will have a long ride to think better of it. The Holy Father will blame him for not contesting the name, but if Elyssa was in entire control of her faculties, Timpany could do nothing; it is the Crown's choice, after all. Timpany is a craven; he will change the story."

Lazarus considered this, then gave a grudging nod. "I know little of the Arvath, but knowing men as I do, I'd agree with you. But this, Captain . . . guarding a *baby* . . ."

"I know." And Carroll did. It felt like a punishment. He looked around at the others in the room: midwives, Father Timpany, the doctor. Carroll trusted none of them.

But I trust Lazarus, he thought wonderingly. *Lazarus the murderer, Niya the traitor . . . I trust them both.*

"The Princess Regent needs sleep," the doctor's voice broke in. He had left the baby now and was crouched over Elyssa's bed, his hand on her forehead. "But I will stay, in case of complications."

"What of the baby?" Niya asked.

"Healthy and strong. Underweight, but such is not uncommon with those born early. With milk and care, she should increase quickly."

"Sir!"

Someone banged on the door. Carroll went to open it, drawing his sword. Elston's face filled the crack.

"What is it?"

"We found the Prince out here," Elston said, gesturing behind him. A low squealing punctuated his words. "Skulking behind the hangings. What should we do with him?"

Carroll thought for a long moment. "Boot him out of the Queen's Wing."

"You can't do that!" Thomas shouted, but his voice faded to a low *mmmph* as someone clapped a hand over his mouth.

"How's the Princess Regent?" Elston asked, casually, as though this was not the reason he'd knocked.

"Fine. She's borne a healthy heir. A girl."

"Ha!" someone called behind Elston: Dyer, Carroll thought. "That's ten pounds to me, lads!"

"Does she have a name?" Elston asked. "The baby?"

"Kelsea."

"But that's their word. The Blue—"

"I know." And for a moment, Carroll found himself longing to tell them about it, all of it . . . how for a single moment Elyssa had been there, with them once more. But once started, he knew he would not stop until he wept.

"Watch out for Thorne," he told Elston quietly. "Neither he nor the witch are to come anywhere near this room."

Elston nodded, though his throat convulsed in a nervous swallow that Carroll read easily: if the witch wanted to enter, how were they to stop her?

I don't know, Carroll thought, glancing involuntarily at the green door at the end of the corridor, behind which the Queen slumbered on and on. They could not even protect Arla; how were they to protect a helpless infant?

But we must, his mind insisted, irrationally but with perfect conviction. *We must.*

Carroll slipped back through the door and found the doctor perched over Elyssa's bedside, holding her wrist in one hand and his watch in the other. One of the midwives was rocking the baby, Lazarus close by, while the other tidied up the room. Under the baleful eye of Niya, Father Timpany sat in the corner still reading, his Bible open on his lap.

"Is the Princess Regent all right?" Carroll asked.

"Fine," the doctor replied. "I am only making the routine check."

Carroll stared down at Elyssa. She appeared dead to the world, but Carroll could not help hoping that she would awaken, see him, be herself. What would it mean if they could have her back, the Elyssa that was, the True Queen? What could they not do if she opened her eyes?

You're being as foolish as Niya, his mind chided. *You spoke the truth: Elyssa is gone.* Grief overwhelmed Carroll then, all the way down to his marrow. *You will never see me again,* Elyssa had told the baby, and the sorrow in her face had been too great to doubt. Tears welled in Carroll's eyes, and he blinked, dashing them away. Elyssa was gone, and now they must contend with what lay before them.

He moved to stand beside Lazarus, who was looking down at the new princess. She was swaddled in linen, but as Carroll approached, the midwife folded back the cloth so that he could see the baby's face: red-cheeked and angry.

"Sir," the midwife said quietly, "we must take the necklace off. The infant could strangle."

Carroll knew that she was right. No heir ever wore the jewel this young; typically, the firstborn did not receive it until the eighth birthday, a purely cynical delay to allow for medical problems, mental deficiencies, and other flaws to show. Barty had told him that an enormous ceremony had accompanied Elyssa's ascension to Heir Designate. A necklace on a newborn was dangerous, but how could Carroll dare take it off? The girl had been dead before their very eyes, until Elyssa had put the jewel around her neck.

Transferring ownership, Carroll thought. There was something in the old legends about that, wasn't there? The sapphires could not be taken, only given.

"No," Carroll replied quietly. "The Princess Regent gave her the jewel. It's not for us to take it off."

"But, sir—"

"No. Work around it."

Leaving Lazarus on guard, he collapsed into one of the nearby armchairs. The baby continued to mewl and snuffle, making tiny unsatisfied noises. One of her hands slipped free of the folds of linen, clenching as it waved in the air.

So much trouble for one scrap of girl, Carroll thought wearily. *Is she worth it?*

There could be no present answer to such a question, but the baby, Kelsea, replied all the same: mewling angrily, batting the midwife away, and shaking her fists.

CHAPTER 32

THE TRUE QUEEN

It's always the unbelievers who are easiest to convince. Doubters will always be doubters, but show me a staunch unbeliever and I show you the embryo of a fanatic. Men of science are the most vulnerable to that which appears before their own eyes, and their need for certainty can be directed anywhere . . . even toward God.

—*Lectures of His Holiness, Pius XX,* FROM THE ARVATH ARCHIVE

Niya was changing the baby.

She did not know how this had happened. She had been a pickpocket, a thief, a kidnapper, a murderess. Now she was a nurse. Niya had pointed out to Carroll the utter absurdity of these contradictions, but Carroll was adamant. She thought that Elyssa might gainsay him—Niya was still Elyssa's head maid, after all—but Elyssa was no longer a woman to argue with anyone. Niya wasn't even sure the Princess Regent had noticed she was gone. Elyssa was a different sorrow from that she felt for the Fetch, but no less powerful. Elyssa was lost for good, but Niya could not accept it. She kept on feeling as though Elyssa, the *real* Elyssa, would suddenly appear.

And then there was the name, Kelsea. Many in the Keep whispered that there had been some influence in the birthing chamber, some overreach by the Guard, and who could blame them? Since her mother's incapacitation, Elyssa had signed more than twenty death warrants for members of the Blue Horizon. Only Niya, Carroll, and Lazarus knew that in that last moment, the old Elyssa had been with them. Naming the baby had been Elyssa's last act as a member of the Blue Horizon, and Niya thought that Gareth would have approved. The child in her arms was both Gareth and Elyssa, and she was all that remained of either of them.

Is that why you stay?

Niya didn't know. The Princess who had placed the Crown storehouses under guard, who had ordered the Blue Horizon exterminated . . . that woman had betrayed them, and Niya could barely stand to be in the same room with her. But the Elyssa who had emerged since the birth was somehow worse: charming but vacant, as though the removal of the sapphire had somehow removed the last piece of her essential self as well.

Kelsea waved her tiny arms, batting Niya on the chin. She was an angry little thing, though she had odd periods of good temper that came and went. The sapphire had popped free of her swaddling clothes again; no matter how many times Niya tucked the jewel and chain in, they would not stay. But Carroll's orders had been explicit: the chain was not to come off.

Niya finished pinning the nappy and picked up the Princess, smoothing her tiny nightdress. The wet nurse had begun humming behind them, an oddly merry tune that annoyed Niya as well. What was there to be merry about?

The door opened, making Niya jump. But it was only Elyssa. Behind her came Carroll and Elston. Their expressions were carefully, almost studiedly blank, but beneath the blankness, Niya sensed consternation. At the sight of Elyssa, the wet nurse dropped into a low curtsy, but Elyssa barely noticed her, her eyes roaming the room dreamily. As she saw the baby in Niya's arms, an odd, empty smile appeared on Elyssa's face.

"My little princess! How is she today?"

"Fine, Highness," Niya replied, looking to Carroll and Elston for help. But they would not look at her . . . or even at each other. Mace was behind them, Niya noticed, peeking around the doorway. She tried to summon the anger she had felt toward him in the birthing chamber, but it was gone. His woman—a pro, or Niya was no judge, though she had gotten only one curious glimpse through the infirmary doorway—was dead, and even the Guard had been treading lightly around Mace lately, taking care with him. Mace probably wasn't aware of it, for he didn't know them as Niya did. But she had noted the contrast, and been moved, well past her anger. Mace noticed her looking at him and vanished from the doorway, back into the tiny antechamber that fronted the nursery.

"Would you like to hold her?" Niya asked, offering Kelsea toward Elyssa.

"No . . . no . . ." Elyssa replied. "I just came in to see that she was well. She eats enough?"

"Yes," Niya replied, though in truth, she didn't know. When Elyssa finally woke after the birth—a sleep of some eighteen hours, by Niya's reckoning—she had announced that she would not breastfeed the baby and demanded a wet nurse. But Carroll had already dispatched a servant, who had returned with several wet nurses, and Kelsea seemed fine with all of them. Niya supposed she *was* well fed, though it was difficult to tell with a baby so small.

But the wet nurses were not there for cuddles . . . nor, Niya thought darkly, was Elyssa. It was Niya who changed Kelsea's nappies, who quieted her when she cried. When the new princess had made clear her adamant refusal to go to sleep in her cot—or, truthfully, anywhere that she might safely lie down—it was Niya who dragged an enormous, comfortable armchair into the nursery and sat there with the baby every night, from dinner until dawn. Kelsea slept well enough, provided she had a warm body to cushion on, but Niya's back was beginning to ache from the long nights in the chair. She spent most of these nights brooding, turning over the pictures that would not leave her mind: Elyssa, contorted in agony, speaking in the voice of the witch; Amelia, falling endlessly from the scaffold; the Fetch, screaming as the Gadds Fire consumed him.

"That's good," Elyssa said brightly. "We'll be on our way, then. I have an appointment with my dressmaker at three. Perhaps tomorrow I'll come in for longer, play with her a little. . . ."

Elyssa reached out, and Niya felt herself instinctively recoil. But Elyssa was not trying to take the baby. Her fingers moved toward the sapphire, then drew back, as though burned. Her face twitched—in anger? Frustration? Niya didn't know—and then smoothed again.

"Look after her, Niya."

"Yes, Highness."

Elyssa gave her a little wave, then left the room. Carroll and Elston followed, Carroll shooting Niya a chagrined look as they went. As the door closed, Kelsea began to emit little squeaks, and Niya tucked her against her shoulder, rubbing her back. The Princess needed a proper nursemaid, but Carroll had refused to hear of it. In truth, Niya was beginning to wonder whether the Guard Captain was well. He had begun to look haunted, and she didn't think he was sleeping. He checked in on them constantly, poking his head into the nursery and vanishing just as suddenly. What was he looking for? Niya didn't know, and not knowing was maddening, far more maddening than the mess of nappies or the nights in the armchair.

The wet nurse had begun to hum again, the same sprightly

tune as before. Niya restrained an urge to hurl one of the baby's rattles at her. She sat down in her armchair, bouncing Kelsea gently on her lap. Sometime in the last two minutes, the sapphire had popped free again; Niya grabbed it, irritated, and then paused, giving the jewel a long, speculative look. Suppose she did take it off? She could tuck it away in a safe place—she had several—and give it back when the girl was old enough to wear it.

And when will that be? Niya's mind demanded for the thousandth time. *The Fetch is dead. The Blue Horizon is broken. Elyssa is just an empty shell. How long do you intend to stay here changing nappies? What are you waiting for?*

Niya frowned, staring down at the wriggling baby in her arms, unable to deny the truth: she had lingered too long. The rebels were coming, staggering their way out of the Almont, following the twisting line of the Caddell. The latest reports said there were nearly seven thousand approaching the city, and with the Blue Horizon finished, surely Niya's place must be with them? She stared down at Kelsea for another moment, then moved over to the cot. The wet nurse was here; if Niya put the baby down, the nurse would take care of her, at least long enough for Niya to pack some food, some weapons, and disappear. She could be out of here by nightfall, out of the city by morning. It was what the Fetch would have done . . . what he would have wanted her to do. Bending over, Niya set the baby down in the cot and made to let her go.

N iya."

She looked up, blinking, pulled to attention, every muscle in her body tensed. The light had changed; the room had changed. Vaulted ceilings spread high over Niya's head. They were in Queen Arla's throne room, but Arla was not there, nor

Elyssa, nor any of the servants or courtiers who hovered like flies. The throne room was empty . . . save for one.

"Niya."

The woman who sat on the silver throne was dark-haired, like Arla, but there the similarity ended. She was dressed all in black, and the Tear crown sat on her head. No one feature of her round face was remarkable, yet the total effect was curiously compelling. And now Niya saw that there *was* a similarity there: the green eyes, the Raleigh eyes, which pinned Niya as a child would pin a butterfly . . . and, beneath them, the sapphires, both of them, dangling from the woman's neck.

"Niya. Look at me."

And Niya looked, seeing further than she had ever imagined, not into past or present or future—for she understood now that these things were not fixed—but into the center. She saw the woman in black astride a pale horse, like Death himself; saw a tall, gaunt man with blond hair and silver eyes, standing on the prow of a ship; saw a flash of lightning and a fall of water. Now she saw a broad mass of humanity, their hands raised in jubilation before the stone face of the Keep; saw the fields of the Almont, their careful rows now covered with horses as well as farmers, not rail-thin scarecrows but healthy workers, tall and proud; saw New London, not a city of steel and guards but one of books and kindness and life . . . and now Niya blinked and saw once again the Queen on the silver throne, really *saw* her: grave and pale and sad. There were no friends in the room, no servants, no guards. The Queen was alone. All of the people she had loved were gone.

"The better world," the Queen whispered. "There is always a price."

"There is no better world," Niya told her. "It was only a story fed to us, like children at bedtime."

The Queen began to laugh . . . dark laughter, but not mocking, only bitter.

"Oh, there's a better world, Niya. I see it all the time. I *have seen* it. And we will get there . . . but you are needed."

"Who are you?" Niya demanded.

"I am the victory of ships," the woman returned calmly. "And you must wake now, Niya. Wake up."

Wake up," Niya murmured, blinking. She was back in the nursery, standing beside her armchair, with the Princess tucked comfortably in one arm and tears trickling down her cheeks.

"Great God," she whispered, her voice shaking, as she looked down at the baby: Kelsea. The victory of ships. But the baby only stared up at her calmly, and Niya suddenly realized that the room around her was oddly silent, that prickles had risen on the back of her neck.

She turned, and the wet nurse was coming for them, her eyes glaring, knife raised. Without thinking, Niya leapt backward, putting the bulk of the chair between them, cradling the baby's head against her shoulder to cushion the jerk. She opened her mouth to scream and found that she couldn't. Something had locked her throat.

The nurse darted around the right side of the armchair, moving in a low crouch. With both hands free, Niya could have taken her, even though the nurse was armed . . . but not while holding Kelsea. And there was no question that Kelsea was the target. As the woman rounded the chair, her pale gaze remained fixed on the tiny bundle in Niya's arms.

The True Queen! Niya's mind shrieked, though her mouth remained sealed. *Oh Great God, she's the True Queen and I can't save her! I can't speak!*

"Look at me."

Niya stiffened, for she knew that voice: deceptively warm and pleasant, a voice made for discussing the weather, even while kingdoms rose and fell.

William Tear, get me through this.

"Look at me," the wet nurse repeated, and Niya felt the pull of that voice, of a will even stronger of her own. With a tremendous effort, she turned away, cradling Kelsea in her arms. Mace was outside, he was *just outside the door*, but she couldn't even scream for help.

Make noise, then. Make a lot of noise.

Niya dashed away, clutching Kelsea, keeping her eyes from the nurse. As she passed the table full of toys, Niya swiped an arm across it, flinging wooden toys across the room to crash against the wall. She tipped the vanity glass that rested near the door, slamming it toward the floor, where it broke with a shattering crash of glass. Niya felt shards drive themselves into her stockinged ankles. She leapt over the wreckage, and as they landed near the door with a thud, the baby began to wail.

A hand grabbed Niya's shoulder, wrenching her around; Niya looked up and saw death in the woman's eyes . . . a cold, white death, and worst of all, not death for her. The nurse raised the knife and brought it down.

Something pushed past Niya, all armor and steel, sending her flying out of the way. She crashed against the wall, doing her best to shield the baby with her body. Kelsea was howling now; Niya longed to comfort her, but her throat was still frozen. She heard loud snarling behind her, an animal sound, and then a woman's shriek, cut off abruptly. The wet nurse crumpled to the floor, landing just before Niya in the field of shattered glass.

"Are you hurt?" Mace demanded. "Niya? Niya! Are you hurt?"

Niya shook her head, then realized that she could speak again.

The vise around her throat had loosened. Looking down at Kelsea, she saw that the baby was injured, a long scratch down her forearm... bloody, but not deep enough to be critical. Niya wrapped it in the excess material of the girl's nightdress, holding it tight.

"Thorne," she murmured, beginning to weep now, understanding how near disaster had been ... how close Brenna's instrument had come. "It was the witch, and Thorne."

Mace looked down at the dead woman on the ground, and with something beyond relief, Niya realized that she would not have to explain. She still didn't know what lay between Mace and Thorne, but he had clearly known the pimp well enough to believe her now, for he moved away without comment, shutting the door that led to the antechamber. The wet nurse's face had been obliterated; Niya turned Kelsea away, hiding the gruesome scene.

"What reason could Thorne have to attack the child?" Mace asked, his voice mercifully businesslike.

"I don't know," Niya admitted. "He means to move in here and rule the kingdom in all but name. Perhaps an heir threatens him?"

"Perhaps," Mace replied, helping her to her feet. "I always heard he had noble blood, and Arliss said he did, for certain."

"You know Arliss?" Niya asked, surprised. Then she wondered why she should be. Arliss knew everyone; that was part of his value to the Blue Horizon.

Was, her mind repeated sadly, as she carried the baby over to the armchair. *Was, Niya. Was.*

"I know him," Mace returned gruffly ... and then, after a long moment: "He saved my life."

"Arliss is a good man."

"He's a poppy dealer," Mace said. The words came out as profanity, but Niya checked her own angry reply, suddenly remembering the wasted woman lying in the infirmary, the lines of morphia etched into her face.

370

"If I were ever in trouble," she replied carefully, "I would go to Arliss. He deals poppy, yes. But I thieve, and you kill."

Mace looked at her sharply, and Niya was struck again by the strange mix of jade and innocence he represented. Did he truly think that she would not have heard?

She bent to inspect the wound on Kelsea's arm more closely. It was ugly and would need stitches, but not many; Coryn could do it. She wrapped it tight again, rocking the girl to quiet her whimpers.

"Arliss *is* a good man," she told Mace. "Once, when I was a girl starving on the streets of the Gut, he saw me and gave me an apple from his pocket."

Mace grunted. "The whole city is starving now. What does he give them?"

The better world! Niya began to snap, and then held her tongue. There was no better world; hadn't the Gadds Fire and Elyssa's fall proven as much?

Wake up, Niya. Wake up.

She blinked, then looked down at the baby again, seeing the green eyes, the blue jewel, the pink, stubborn face . . . all of the colors that would one day combine to make the tall, grave woman in black. The True Queen. She was come out of her time, yes, but not too late, not if they could be brave, not if they could–

"Take care of each other," Niya whispered. She looked up at Mace, seeing her friend of the past weeks, but even more: the man of that other life, the one who had burned in some cold darkness until he was tempered steel, a man who would never bend for his own safety, or even his own survival.

This is the man I need, Niya thought.

"Thorne doesn't take chances," Mace remarked. "If he wants the baby dead, there will be another attempt, and another. I'll talk to Carroll. We should increase her guard–"

371

"No," Niya told him firmly, for she had suddenly seen what to do . . . what *must* be done, if there was to be any hope for the future at all. "More guards won't keep her safe. We must get her out of here."

"Out of the Keep?" Mace asked. He, too, had clearly become a creature of the castle, for the bewilderment in his voice made plain that this solution had never occurred to him. "But where? Where could she go?"

"I don't know. Far away, where even the witch can't find her." Niya frowned, thinking of how many people roamed the Queen's Wing on a daily basis, all riddled with their own cracks, their own weaknesses . . . potential assassins, all of them.

"We must get her out of here," she repeated. "And we can't wait."

CHAPTER 33

THE VOICE OF THE ALMONT

Humanity extols victory. Battles won, legislation passed, tragedy surmounted ... of such moments is history made and fixed. No one wants to talk about the hidden cost of victory, the danger of overreach ... but that cost is there, all the same. Arrogance makes fools of us all.

—GREIVE THE MADMAN

There it is," the Fetch said, pointing down the hill. "The New London Bridge."

Aislinn had been prepared for the size of the city; she had heard tales about New London all her life, mostly from the few men from their village who had left to seek their fortune, and then returned after going bust. They had made the city out to be so extraordinary that Aislinn actually found herself a bit disappointed by the dark pile of stone that lay across the river canyon.

But the bridge was something else: several gigantic arches of white stone, their combined length at least one hundred meters, spanning the Caddell River. But the Caddell was hardly a river at all at this point, little more than a collection of puddles. Aislinn had not thought of the drought in the recent weeks, not since snow had begun to fall in the Almont, but now, at the sight of that vast, muddy riverbed, she felt a distant alarm. What if the next summer was as dry as the last? They would all die, the entire kingdom, from the highest noble to the lowest tenant.

No, Aislinn thought fiercely, looking up at the New London skyline. *It will rain. It must. We only have to get through to the next harvest, and there is enough food hoarded in this city to do that. We only need to get hold of it.*

The bridge was the easiest way into New London. They could go around the city, heading for the relatively undefended west side, but that would take an extra day. They had provisioned themselves from Lord Marshall's castle, but the provisions had run out several days before. Many of the men, particularly the ones with big feet, had been unable to find adequate shoe leather, and they had hiked all the way from the central Almont in cloth shoes. Now most of them continued barefoot, ignoring the frostbite that had begun to blacken their toes. These men could not afford an extra day's march, nor could Aislinn. More than seven thousand people waited on the hillside behind her, and they had come all this way on buoyancy. If they stopped or even slowed down, she feared that they would sink to the ground.

"Are there guards?" she asked the Fetch. "On the bridge?"

"Yes, for toll. The Crown charges one pound per head to enter the city."

"That's robbery," Aislinn muttered. "Visitors bring money into the city. What do they need with toll?"

"The Raleighs are not people to be content with less when they can demand more," the Fetch replied. "It's always been this way."

"Well, we don't have seven thousand pounds for toll. But we have seven thousand people."

Turning to the mass of humanity behind her on the slope—all of them silent, waiting for her judgment; they respected the Fetch, but did not trust him—Aislinn cupped her hands around her mouth and shouted, "Our labor has fed this city! Its food is ours by right! We go!"

They roared fiercely behind her, and Aislinn started down the hillside, Liam at her side. She knew he was there, without looking, just as she knew her right hand would always be beside her. Liam still carried the axe he had liberated from Lady Andrews's armory, and it was not a vanity weapon; Aislinn had seen him swing the axe enough times now, and he had even left several heads behind. In another life, he might have been a soldier, or a guard. Liam, Aislinn, all of them might have been so many things, had they not been born to the fields. The crop.

The bridge was fronted by a set of tables: a toll gate, and behind it stood several men in black cloaks. The army, Aislinn decided. The Fetch had no great opinion of the Tear army, but its soldiers carried steel, and presumably they knew how to use it.

"I'll go down and talk to them," she told the Fetch and Liam. "Just me."

"And me," Liam replied, in a tone Aislinn knew well by now; better try to shed an embedded tick than Liam in this moment.

"Come, then," she said, and headed down the hill toward the toll gate. She expected the Fetch to follow them as well, but he did not. Aislinn wondered at this, then realized it was for the best. She didn't need to use the Fetch as a crutch.

"Who approaches?" one of the soldiers cried from the table. "State your name and purpose!"

For a moment Aislinn thought of giving them her true name, then abandoned the idea, for what could a name matter? She was not important; not a single one of them was important. What mattered was the mass of them, their anger . . . anger powerful enough to overcome starvation and robbery, rape and murder. Powerful enough to bring them all here.

"I am the voice of the Almont," Aislinn replied. "I come to speak with the Princess Regent."

"Elyssa ain't about to let a filthy horde into her castle," one of the soldiers sneered.

"Not a horde. Just me."

Another soldier drew a knife, but Liam was immediately there, raising his axe. And Aislinn suddenly realized that every moment she spent at parley with these fools weakened her, gave them time to dispatch a messenger to the Keep, to call for reinforcements, to count her numbers. To put up obstacles.

But Aislinn would brook no obstacles. Leaving Liam to keep an eye on the soldiers, she turned and spread her arms wide, making a beckoning gesture toward the people behind her.

"Come on!" she shouted. "We're going in!"

For a long moment, she feared they would not follow. They were at the brink now, farther than any of them had ever journeyed, and Aislinn was suddenly certain that some of them would turn and run, infecting the rest with panic until they all fled over the hillside, back where they had come from. She had gone so far as to prepare herself for it when they began to move, an endless sea of torches walking, then running, down the hillside. One of the women from Haven, who had the best voice of any of them and had kept them marching on the long road through the western Almont, began to sing "It's Time to Cut the Corn."

Time indeed, Aislinn thought, turning back to the bridge . . . but they were alone. The soldiers had fled.

"Come on!" she shouted again, nearly delirious with triumph. As she led them across the bridge, the roar of their singing made the stone shake beneath Aislinn's feet, but she did not sing with them this time, for her eyes were fixed on the city ahead, the enormous black monolith that loomed before them, blocking the starlit curtain above.

The Keep.

CHAPTER 34

THE CHILD IS HIDDEN

We stood at a precipice. That we did not realize we stood there made no difference, for the earth is no respecter of ignorance, or even knowledge. Whatever we know, whatever we think, the ground may still crumble beneath our feet.

—Anonymous words, generally ascribed to William Tear

They were just wrapping up the baby when the knock came at the door.

For a long moment, Christian, Carroll, and Niya could only stare at each other. Technically, Christian and Carroll were on guard in the Princess's chamber; ever since the assassination attempt five days before, there had been two guards in the Princess's rooms at all times. To the outward eye, they had done nothing wrong. But they were already guilty, and in Carroll's eyes, Christian saw panic to mirror his own.

"Cover the baby," Carroll told Niya, then went to the door and opened it a tiny fraction.

"What is it?"

"The rebels, sir," someone replied; it sounded like Cae. "They're here, and they're filling up the lawn. General Cleary is asking for you."

"The general?" Carroll asked, bewildered. "What's he doing here?"

"I don't know, sir. Thorne's orders. Cleary's man said he's up on the battlements."

Carroll frowned. He looked to Christian, and they shared a grim, silent realization: nothing was going to go to plan.

"I'll be there in a minute," Carroll told Cae. He closed the door gently enough, but when he turned back to them, his face was pale.

"There's no time," he said. "I can't take her. Lazarus, it has to be you."

"What?"

"The general is asking for me. If I'm missed, then the game is up. Everything must look normal until morning. It has to be you."

For a long moment, the words meant nothing to Christian. The plan had been very simple; Carroll was to take Niya down, through the Keep tunnels and underneath the moat. Niya's knowledge of the city was extensive, but she did not know the tunnels well enough, and she certainly could not go alone, not with the baby in one arm. Once free of the Creche, she would depart the city and ride. Niya was a good rider, and they had chosen her a sturdy horse, now hidden downstairs, at the entrance to the tunnels. All of the supplies were in the saddlebags, including the map Niya was to follow; none of them had looked at it yet, in case one of them was taken before the fact. With Christian and Carroll on guard outside Kelsea's door, no one would know the baby was gone until the morning. Christian and Carroll might pay for their supposed negligence—perhaps even with their lives—but by morning it wouldn't matter, because Niya and the baby would be clear of the city, well on their way. Even to Christian's pessimistic mind, the plan had seemed workable, but now it had fallen to pieces before even begun.

"We could wait–" he began, but Carroll was already shaking his head, and with a sinking feeling, Christian knew he was right. They had chosen this night specifically because of the rebel approach; Elyssa had put Thorne in charge of dealing with the rebels, and it was the one time that he and his witch were guaranteed to be elsewhere. Christian didn't know what difference distance might make with a creature like Brenna, but even he had found himself comforted by the knowledge that she would not be in the Queen's Wing when they tried to smuggle the girl out. If they waited, giving Thorne and his witch the chance to get involved, then it seemed a good bet that they would all end up dead . . . or worse, like Elyssa. The Guard did their best not to discuss it, but Christian had seen the look in Galen's eyes–in Dyer's, in Kibb's, in Coryn's–when the Princess came into the room. All of them were hanging on as best they could, but they also seemed to share an unspoken understanding, a bitter acceptance of how precious little there was to hold on to. Elyssa was only a shell, and the Queen slept on and on. For men who had spent their lives steeped in the honorable traditions of the Guard, it was a miserable state of affairs.

Carroll had knelt on the bed again, helping Niya to wrap the baby in furs. It was late March, but the Almont was still frozen; warm clothing would be required, and Niya had already explained to Christian that a baby must be kept warmer still. Niya tucked the Heir's Jewel carefully inside the furs before binding the final layer.

"Lazarus," Carroll repeated. "You know the tunnels better than anyone, and you won't be missed until morning. You have to take Niya and go."

Christian cursed quietly. If anyone had ever told him that he would develop a hard core of obedience to a topside boy who couldn't even shave properly, he would have laughed. But the obedience was there. He didn't want to let Carroll down, and even more, he shuddered at the thought of Niya alone in the tunnels. When they had conceived the plan, she had protested that she could handle herself, that there was no need for an escort, she had lived in the Gut all her life . . . but Christian had argued her down. The Creche might run only twenty or thirty feet below the Gut's surface, but the distance was infinite. Niya would not make it through alone.

"I'm going," Carroll said, straightening from the bed. "I'll try to take as many of them as I can with me. Give it a few minutes, and you should have a straight shot to the Queen's chamber."

Niya nodded, lifting the fur-wrapped bundle from the bed. The baby had begun to make vaguely fussy noises, but as soon as Niya tucked her against one shoulder, she quieted.

"What of the second guard?" Christian asked suddenly. "The one meant to be on the chamber when you're gone?"

"I forgot to find a replacement. Surely the terrifying Mace doesn't need a backup."

Christian smiled unwillingly, surprised as ever by the strange mixture of innocence and deception that lurked behind Carroll's baby face. Christian had been in the Keep for only eight months, but he sometimes felt that his tenure as a Queen's Guard had been much longer, that lifetimes had passed since that long-ago day when he had stood staring at the rain. Even Maura's death had fallen away, so quickly that it bothered him; a good man, he felt sure, would have grieved longer. But whenever he thought of Maura now, he could not see her face, only the glaring room full of mirrors, the huddle of children.

"This is mad," he told Carroll. "Mad to the bone."

"I don't dispute it," Carroll replied, the ghost of a smile on his face. "But it's a greater madness to keep the girl here."

He held out a hand, and Christian clasped it without thinking.

"See her safe, Lazarus. Niya, luck to you."

And then he was gone, leaving Christian and Niya staring at each other. The Princess was asleep now, breathing in little snuffles and sighs. It was past midnight, and the Queen's Wing was silent around them.

It wasn't supposed to be this way, Christian thought. *I wasn't meant to be involved, not really.* He looked to Niya, but Niya wasn't looking at him; she was staring down at the Princess, her expression a mixture of love and awe. Niya was built to be a true believer, but Christian didn't have it in him. He didn't care about True Queens, or destiny. People mattered more than magic, and Christian was only in this business to protect the two of them, Niya and Carroll. Perhaps the child as well.

You have changed, Christian, his mind whispered, and Christian jerked in surprise, for the voice was not his own, but Maura's. He *had* changed, for certain; the question was how much. A racket rose outside: Carroll moving up the corridor, shouting orders, calling for guards to join him. Then there was silence.

"It's time," Christian told Niya, when a few minutes had gone by. "Let's go."

They crept down the corridor. All was quiet and still, save for the flicker and occasional snap of torches. When they reached the Queen's door, Christian knocked and, hearing nothing within, lifted the latch. Keeping Niya behind him, he moved inside cautiously, certain that he would see Elston there, or Cae, or, worst of all, the witch.

But he saw no one. Carroll had taken the Queen's regular guards with him, as promised, and the chamber was empty, save for the old woman who slumbered endlessly on the bed.

"It's safe," Christian told Niya, and stepped back from the doorway, giving her room to enter . . . then they both froze as a voice rang out down the corridor.

"You, maid! What are you doing in the Queen's chamber?"

Ever after, in Christian's memory, that few seconds stretched forever. Niya looked down the corridor, her eyes widening . . . and then she leapt through the doorway and slammed the door behind her. Without thinking, Christian reached out and shot the two thick steel bolts, one at his knee and the other at his head. Shouts echoed outside, running footsteps.

"They saw me," Niya told him. "Cae and Coryn, and they will fetch more."

Christian didn't know what to say. He felt the wreck of everything in this sudden turn of the world. But Niya didn't expect an answer. She was staring down at the baby now, her gaze calculating and—Christian would have sworn to it—resigned.

"They saw me, Mace," she remarked slowly, as though thinking things out. "But they didn't see you."

"What—" Christian began, and then, seeing her meaning: "No."

"It's you, Lazarus. It has to be. They've seen me with the baby. Even if I made it out, I could never come back. You have to take her, get her away."

"No. I can't."

"The bolts will keep them out, but not forever," Niya went on, as though he had not spoken. "One of us has to stay here, hold them off. If I do it, you may have time."

"No," Christian replied, but his stomach had already dropped at the grim certainty in her eyes. "You have to get out of here. They'll take you, torture you—"

"I have been tortured before," Niya countered. "They saw my face, don't you understand? One of us must be able to come back here, to have a place in the Keep. When the time comes for Kelsea to take the throne, the Guard must know where she is."

Christian cast around the room, as though he would find an alternative solution on the Queen's dresser, or perhaps leaning on the bedposts. He would fight a man and kill him without trouble, but this? Surely there must be a better way. But nothing came to him, only the echo of Niya's logic, impervious and inarguable. Barty had given Carroll the map, but it was still sealed. None of them knew the way. Outside the door, Christian heard the scrabbling of a blade against the wood, the muffled sound of men arguing. Whoever went must come back, but now Niya could not. Carroll was gone. He was the only one left.

Niya held out the baby, cradled in her arms, and after a long moment spent desperately seeking a way out, Christian took her.

"I don't know anything about little ones," he told Niya, hating the plaintive note in his own voice.

"Change nappies," Niya told him, without sympathy. "Give bottles. Learn."

"Christian."

They both jumped, and Niya let out a short bark of surprise. The baby murmured in sleepy confusion but did not wake. Christian looked around wildly, then bit his lip to keep from crying out.

Queen Arla was sitting up in bed, staring directly at him.

"Christian."

Her voice was nothing like the deep, imperious voice that Christian had heard so many times before the poisoning. Now it was harsh, high and raucous like a crow's, or the sharpening of metal.

"Christian, of the Creche. Mace, of the Queen's Guard. Come here."

But Christian did not move. He could not. His nerves told him that he was in the room with a ghost.

"Come here!" the Queen rasped.

Against his will, Christian felt his legs begin to move, as though he were a puppet. The door shook behind him as someone—Elston, likely, with his huge shoulders—tried to knock it down. But the tough oak held.

"Majesty," Christian muttered, kneeling down beside the bed. "Are you—"

"Be quiet," the Queen commanded, and Christian felt his tongue still. Her green eyes stared into his, unmanning him. "My time is short, and so is yours."

She reached out and touched the baby's forehead. Niya made a small sound of protest, but Christian could not begin to stop the Queen, not even if she intended violence. The fracas outside was forgotten; everything was forgotten. At the Queen's touch, the baby made a soft sound but still did not wake.

"My grandchild," the Queen murmured. "I have seen her, hidden and chosen. But I will never know her."

Now she reached beneath the furs, pulling the sapphire free from the girl's clothing, and placed her own sapphire beside it. Beneath the surface of each, Christian saw something move . . . and then it was gone. A trick of the light.

"I felt it," the Queen said, her voice wondering. "They call to each other, you know. I can feel them . . . so powerful, but they cannot fight the witch, not alone. She works on me, and in the end I will break . . . unless I act."

Withdrawing her hand from the baby, the Queen reached up behind her neck, as women did when they meant to fuss with their hair. But a moment later, she had lifted the thin silver chain, drawing it over her head. The sapphire came with it, tumbling down, and Christian realized that the jewel was actually glowing now, such a bright and clear blue that he could see the shadow of the Queen's hands against the coverlet.

"Are you loyal, Christian of the Queen's Guard?" she asked.

"Yes," Christian replied, not knowing in that moment whether he was answering truthfully or not. The baby in his arms seemed suddenly heavy, much heavier than she had before. The glow of the sapphire held him hypnotized.

"Then I have a task for you," the Queen replied. "Only a small task, perhaps, but kingdoms have turned on less."

She leaned forward, her arms so thin now that they seemed withered sticks against the bedclothes, and dropped the chain over Christian's head. The sapphire tumbled down his shoulder, but Christian caught it before it could hit the baby and wake her up. Without thinking, he tucked the jewel beneath his shirt.

"The witch must not have it," the Queen continued. "I give it to you, in trust for the child. Take her, hide her. The darkness is coming, but perhaps she will live through it. Go."

Christian blinked, wondering whether he was going mad ... but the racket outside the door was real enough. He looked down at the Queen again, but she had already fallen back to the pillows, her eyes closed. Her chest rose and fell, contracting in the deep, regular breathing they had all grown used to in the past months. The scene was so familiar that Christian might almost have been able to convince himself that none of it had happened at all ... but for the hard contours of the Queen's sapphire, lying against his chest.

Something heavy thudded against the door, and a moment later, the blow repeated, with a crunch of wood. They had found a ram.

"Go," Niya told him, pulling one arm behind her head ... stretching, Christian realized. Readying herself. He straightened, and his eyes went automatically to the hidden panel behind the Queen's nightstand. He had explored the length and breadth of the Queen's Wing now, and this was the best egress point, the closest to the great staircase. He wasn't even sure that anyone else in the Guard knew about it. If he acted quickly, they might still get away clean.

"Come with me," he said. "Come with me, you can hide."

"No," Niya replied, slipping a blade from her sleeve. She turned to him, her eyes grave, and Christian suddenly remembered who she was: Blue Horizon to the core.

"They will find the panel, Mace. It won't take them long. You won't make it out of here, not unless I slow them down. Go, now. Keep her safe, or you will find my ghost behind you with a knife."

Christian didn't move. Another blow landed, splintering the door, but still he hesitated, staring at the iron woman before him, the maid with the heart of a Guard.

"Go!" Niya shouted.

As if to counterpoint her order, one of the hinges splintered, giving way with a screech of metal. Christian's paralysis broke then; he leapt to the head of the bed, shoving the nightstand aside, and tapped the tenth stone up. The hidden door opened, and Christian darted through, then shoved it closed. Even through the stone, he heard the crash behind him as the Queen's door fell in. Working clumsily with the baby in his arms, he lit the torch Carroll had left, and then he was running, cradling the baby's head against his shoulder, heading downward into the dark.

CHAPTER 35

THE DROWNED MAN

One might think that Arlen Thorne met no true resistance until the advent of the Glynn Queen, but this is not strictly true. Long before the Glynn coronation, Thorne was balked ... only once, certainly, but in a matter so critical that it would eventually lead to his own downfall. In this respect, one might say that the first time paid for all.

—*The Early History of the Tearling*, AS TOLD BY MERWINIAN

A re we ready?" the master asked, for perhaps the tenth time. "Ready," Brenna replied, stirring her brazier and staring into its contents. There was nothing yet, but of course there should not be. The palm told certainties; the brazier was for surprises. Brenna expected none of the latter, for the master had planned this to perfection. She only wished to ensure his success.

They had hidden themselves in a room on the third floor of the Drowned Man, a pub that sat just on top of the rise where the Keep Lawn ended. The room commanded a good view of the entire lawn, and it sat high enough that one could see all the way down to the stinking circle of the moat. The publican had been one of the master's clients for years, and he asked no questions of them, not even when Brenna pushed back the hood of her cloak.

The rebels covered the Keep Lawn in all directions. Brenna sensed the master's contempt; she no longer wormed into his head on purpose, as she had done when they were children, but his thoughts were not hidden from her either. Now he was thinking how foolish the rebels were, how ridiculously anxious to march toward death. But another part of him, a younger part, was wavering, wondering what it would be like to be part of something, united to the whole. The master would never be one of those believers down there, singing and dancing and celebrating, and a rogue part of his mind could not help wondering how it would feel.

"You are vacillating, master," Brenna remarked, for this was one of her many functions: to keep the master on track. "It wastes energy. You will need all your focus tonight."

The master nodded, turning away from the window. As always, Brenna was struck by his austere face: so cold, and yet so beloved. She had been only a child when she chose him, but even then, she had been drawn by that coldness, that resolve, which had shown itself to Brenna in a series of mental pictures, so detailed that they almost had taste and smell.

This is the one, she had thought, in her frozen child's mind. *This is the one who will get me out.*

She looked back down at the brazier, stirring its gelatinous contents. The master had complained of the smell—like a sewage pipe in the Hollow, he said—but, as with so many things, he would complain once and then hold quiet. He needed her knowledge; it was part of their bargain. And the master had kept his end. They were out now, not only out of the stables but out of the Creche. The master had climbed high, and he had brought Brenna with him, every step of the way. Once the rabble on the lawn had been cleared away, the two of them would climb higher still.

Brenna stirred the brazier again, seeking movement beneath

the surface. When it remained lifeless, she took a quick moment to look out the window. There were so many of them down there: emaciated scarecrows with threadbare cloaks and falling-apart shoes. How they had managed to drag themselves across the Almont in the depth of winter was anyone's guess. They had come to speak to Elyssa, but Elyssa was now safely asleep in her bed; Brenna had made sure of it. Elyssa had given the master permission to handle everything.

And so she will, Brenna thought with satisfaction. *Now, and ever after.* They had not gotten hold of the heir's sapphire, and that, combined with the disaster at the nobles' club, should have spelled the wreck of all the master's plans. But now, quite by accident, they had something much better. On the throne sat a pliable girl, one who could not be bothered to think of anything more complicated than which earrings went with which gown. Manipulating her was like playing with a doll. The Queen would give up her jewel within the month, and tonight they would have the jewel off the child as well. Those jewels were the master's inheritance, and Brenna would be the one to procure them for him. With the sapphires in hand, the only obstacles standing in the master's way would be the wretched tenants, the tattered remnants of the Blue Horizon ... but now all of them were down there, packed tightly on the lawn. Brenna found herself staring at the scene below with a hunger so acute that it bordered on lust.

Any minute now. The master's orders had been explicit; even the Keep Guards couldn't fuck it up. *Any minute—*

Behind her, the bowl began to bubble: just one pop at first, then a series of tiny explosions. Reluctantly, Brenna turned back and leaned over the brazier, her eyes narrowing. Images formed beneath the surface, so scattered that at first they were meaningless: an archipelago of visions, one after another. The Queen's face, reposed in her endless slumber. The Blue Horizon bitch, the cursed child in her arms. The Captain of Guard, his face drawn in horror, the night sky black behind him.

Why does it show me this now? Brenna wondered, annoyed. *Why, when I have seen it all before?*

But now the child moved, her face blending and duplicating, from one dark island to another . . . the guard, the maid, the Queen. And now a final dark island broke the surface: the hated face of the Seven of Swords, blending with the child, holding her close as they sank beneath the surface, vanishing without a ripple. Panic erupted inside Brenna, nearly rending her chest.

"Master!"

He turned from the window, annoyed. "What is it?"

"We must go, master. Now."

"What?" Thorne demanded. "It hasn't happened yet. I told you–"

"Yes, you told me, master." She hated that she could not show him, could not make him understand how delicately the future balanced. "But we cannot watch. Come, we must go, now!"

"Why?" he demanded.

"The baby is gone."

The master's face darkened. "What do you mean, gone? I thought you had the Blue Horizon girl."

"It's not her, master." Brenna peered into the brazier again, but the surface lay undisturbed. There was no help there; she looked up at the master, despairing.

"It's the Mace, and he has disappeared. I cannot see him at all."

CHAPTER 36

IN THE QUIET

My esteemed colleague, Dr. Kerwin, posits that the Mace was a simple man, needlessly complicated by history. Nothing could be further from the truth. The Mace was neither a villain nor a hero . . . or perhaps he was. Not all heroism is simple, as the Glynn Queen herself would surely attest.

—LECTURE BY MICHAEL ARNOT, PROFESSOR EMERITUS OF HISTORY, UNIVERSITY OF NEW LONDON

The baby would not stop crying.

It was intolerable. She had stayed asleep on the long journey down the stairway and through the inner workings of the Keep, had even stayed asleep while Christian mounted his horse. But as they rode beneath the moat, a drop of water had landed on her cheek, and then the little brat had been off to the races.

The tunnels were as wet as ever, their walls slimed with mold that sparkled greenly in the torchlight, the air thick and damp in Christian's lungs. He had not missed the Creche, but he had forgotten how much it simplified things to know every inch of a place, to feel as though you belonged. He had forgotten how comforting it was.

The baby screamed right in his ear, and Christian hissed,

utterly maddened. The bundle in his arms could not be overpowered or reasoned with. He could not tell her that they were now in the Creche, where babies brought a premium. He could not tell her that silence was crucial. He had tried stopping his horse, even climbing down from the saddle to feed her milk from one of the bottles in the saddlebags, but the baby had knocked the bottle away into the dark, squalling. Christian had begun their journey with a torch, but the baby kept waving her arms, batting at it until Christian was afraid she would bring the flame down on top of them both. Now they rode along in the dim light provided by the occasional lamp on the walls. Christian had planned to light the torch again as soon as the girl fell back asleep, but now he wondered if that moment would ever come. With no light, they were moving very slowly, too slowly to outdistance pursuit. Above them, Mace could hear a distant thunder . . . the rebels on the Keep Lawn. Carroll had said that there were more than seven thousand of them out there: rebels and Blue Horizon.

Niya should have been with them, Christian thought, feeling a wound tear open inside him. He had left Niya there, left her to shoulder all the blame. If the Guard did not kill her outright, then she would die on the scaffold or in Welwyn Culp's dungeons. Niya had laid down her life, but Christian did not deceive himself that she had done it for him. Niya's sacrifice had been for the child in his arms, and so, scream as Kelsea might, Christian could not put her down.

Gradually, he became aware that they were being followed.

The footsteps were muffled, first distant and then close, their echoes both magnified and truncated, the way sound always was in the tunnels, nearly indiscernible under the baby's fury. He could not count the footsteps, but they were only two turnings away from Whore's Alley, and Alley raiding parties always went out in force. Christian knew this stretch well, right down to its echoes, and he judged that his pursuers were now less than a hundred yards behind. They did not need to slow to track him; the child's wailing could probably be heard in the Deep Patch. This was not how Christian and Carroll had envisioned it, or even Niya. In all their planning, the baby was never crying.

What else did we forget? Christian wondered, already feeling the futility of the question, the way it fell like a stone into unfathomable waters, unrecoverable. They were here now. Whatever else they had missed, there was no going back.

Coming around a corner, he felt a draft of warmer air. The wall had ended, and there was an opening, almost an alcove. Christian guided his horse in, then risked lighting a match. They were in a tiny, rounded room that must have been a guardhouse at one point. Next to the small opening he had come through was a thin sliver of wall, only two meters, not long enough to effectively hide a man, let alone a horse. He would have to fight.

Tucking the child in one arm, Christian pulled one leg from the stirrup and dropped to the floor. Impossibly, the baby screamed even louder when they had dismounted. Muttering a low curse, Christian lit a torch and set it in the bracket on the wall. Light spilled out into the tunnel, but that was no matter; those after him would have torches of their own. Already his mind had frozen, icing over with the welcome coldness of the fight. He pulled his mace from his belt, swapping the child over so that he could use his right hand, and at the sight of the weapon, the baby fell suddenly and mercifully silent.

"Lazarussssssss!"

The voice echoed in the darkness of the tunnel outside, slyly mocking. Christian's blood went cold.

Impossible! He could never have gotten down here in time . . . unless–

"Oh, Lazarussssssss!"

Unless he knew.

Thorne emerged from the darkness of the tunnel, the witch beside him. Brenna was hooded, her eyes hidden, but that was somehow worse: seeing only her white mouth, drawn up in a smile.

"Get back!" Christian snarled, turning to shield the baby.

"I think not," Thorne replied. He pushed back the hood of his own cloak, and Mace saw something that pleased him: Thorne was not as comfortable as his mocking tones would indicate. He had rushed to get here; his brow was wet with sweat, and though Christian could not be sure, he thought he saw a gleam of fear in the man's eyes.

"It was well conceived," Thorne told him, drawing his cloak aside to step over the broken wall. "And very nearly well executed. But my Brenna has foiled better-laid plans. The guards took the Blue Horizon bitch easily . . . using tricks you taught them, as it so happens."

"What of the rebels up there?" Christian asked, shutting the news about Niya away. "You were supposed to be treating with them."

"No need to treat with them," Thorne replied, a chilly smile crossing his face. "They're well in hand. The uprising is broken, and so is the Blue Horizon. My only remaining problem is that wailing brat . . . and you."

"Come on, then. I'm waiting."

"This needn't be difficult, Lazarus," Thorne said wearily. "You can't stand against Brenna; no one can. But nothing yet compels me to use her here. Hand over the Princess, and we can go our separate ways, pretend none of this ever happened."

"And what happens to the girl?"

"What do you care? As I recall, the welfare of children was never high on your list."

"What happens?" Christian repeated, ignoring the sting of Thorne's words. "What will you do? Hollow her out, like Elyssa?"

"Elyssa." Thorne smiled gently. "When she took off the jewel, we thought it was the end of everything, and now look at her! If I bought a painted marionette in the Circus, she would not perform half so well!"

The jewel, Christian thought. Yes, that had been the end of everything for Elyssa . . . and now he understood.

"You don't want the baby. You want the sapphire. Why? For the Mort Queen's bounty?"

"Ah, Lazarus. You think so small. Hand the little one over, and we can both forget about this moment. I will know you took the baby, and you will know I took the baby. We will each of us be safe. Elyssa will seek the child, yes, but Elyssa is malleable. She will not last long, and neither will the girl."

Reluctantly, Christian was forced to admit that Thorne was right. They had all known it: Carroll, Christian . . . even Niya, though she fought the knowledge like a cat. The child in Christian's arms was marked for assassination; even with all the might of the Guard, she would be lucky if she grew old enough to walk. She would certainly never make it to nineteen, to ascension. Thorne would make sure of it.

Then why? Christian wondered suddenly. *Why parley with me here? Why can't the witch just kill me and take her?*

"Think it through," Thorne murmured. "We both know these tunnels. Children disappear down here all the time."

We played right into his hands, Christian realized. Killing the baby up in the Queen's Wing was, if not impossible, then at least difficult. But down here . . .

"Think it through," Thorne repeated. "No one would ever know."

And that was the hell of it: no one would. Whether Kelsea

arrived safely or not, no one would know, at least until the girl's nineteenth birthday ... and who among them really believed that such a day would come to pass? Deep in his gut, Christian knew that Thorne was right: he could hand the noisy brat over and walk away clean. She would be just another Creche child, one of hundreds and thousands. Another thread in the tapestry. For a moment, Christian truly considered it—even afterward, he could never lie to himself and pretend that he had not—but then he blinked and saw the children in the mirrored room, some of them barely older than the girl in his arms. And on the heels of this image came Carroll's voice, so close that Christian could almost feel the Captain's breath in his ear.

Make no mistake, this is how you will be judged: on what you do in the quiet.

Thorne moved forward another few inches, holding out his arms. Distantly, Christian noted that he had a knife in his left hand. The knife was no danger to Christian ... but it wasn't meant for him.

"Be a smart lad," Thorne coaxed. "Give her to me."

I could. I could. She's dead already.

Perhaps, Christian. But does it have to be you?

A quiet sound came from beneath his chin. Looking down, Christian found the baby looking up at him, her gaze unblinking and strangely contemplative. Her tiny hand reached up, and Christian saw that she was straining for his mace. Instinctively, he began to jerk it away, and then stopped, for her fascination with the weapon was clearly the only thing keeping her quiet. The mace's points were sharp but clean of blood. He had never covered them in poison, as some men did with their blades. He could watch her, make sure she didn't hurt herself. And—

What are you thinking? Do something!

"Lazarus? Your answer?"

This is it, Christian realized. *The quiet, the place of judgment. And am I Lazarus, or Christian?*

"No," he heard himself say. "You won't have her."

"Dearest. Take him."

The witch pushed back her hood, locking eyes with Christian. He tucked the girl against him, trying to make his arm into a shield, knowing all the while the futility of it. All the old rumors were true. The witch could kill with a glance, turn a man's mind inside out and smile while she did it. He would die in the Creche; only as this knowledge tore through him, with unexpected pain, did Christian realize how badly he had wanted to end his life topside. He raised his mace, preparing to make a good fight of it . . . and then something happened that he did not understand.

He would not understand it for another nineteen years.

Brenna's smile slipped. She bit her pale lower lip, glaring at Christian as though she might bore holes into him, her icy eyes wide—

And nothing happened.

"No," Brenna whispered. "Oh, no."

"Dearest?" Thorne demanded. "What is it?"

"Oh, God. He has it. Hidden, both of them . . ."

"Has what?" Thorne grabbed Brenna, shaking her shoulders. "Has *what?* Make sense, damn you!"

"The jewels," Brenna whispered brokenly. "I cannot fight both of them, not unless I abandon you, master. I can't fight them both."

What is she talking about? Christian wondered. But then he felt it . . . burning, almost searing against his chest. He had forgotten the dreadful scene in the Queen's bedroom, the way her eyes had stabbed into him. The jewel she had hung around his neck.

"What is this nonsense?" Thorne snapped. "Take the child!"

"Master, I cannot."

Thorne slapped her, sending her reeling backward toward the

wall. Christian darted away, behind Fortune, placing the horse's solid bulk between himself and Thorne. He expected the baby to begin screaming again at any moment—was shocked, in fact, that she had not done so already—but she merely lay quiet in the crook of Christian's arm as he skidded across the mold-slimed floor, retreating from Thorne, who had begun to edge around the horse's flank, knife in hand.

"Are you Blue Horizon, Lazarus?" Thorne asked. "I can think of no other reason for you to be so stupid. So stubborn."

"One needn't believe in the better world to say no to you, Arlen." Christian said the name with relish, meaning it as an insult . . . but then he stopped, for his mind had finally made the connection, put two and two together.

"Arlen," he repeated. "Yes, I see. Cast off?"

The shot hit; for a moment Thorne's mask slipped, revealing much of himself.

"The past does not concern me, Lazarus. Only the future matters."

"Well, at least we agree on that," Christian replied, gripping his mace in one hand, tightening the other around the girl's squirming body. "Come on, then. No witches, no special tricks. Just you and me."

But Thorne remained still, his eyes assessing, and after a moment Christian smiled.

"You know I can beat you, don't you, scarecrow? Even with one hand tied."

"Master, please!" the witch moaned from the floor. It occurred to Christian that he might be able to kill Thorne in this moment, with the witch down . . . but to attack him would be to endanger the baby. And Christian would not do that.

"Master, I'm sorry!" Brenna cried brokenly, beginning to weep. "I love you! I didn't know!"

"Shut up," Thorne told her, and Brenna broke into a storm of weeping, rolling to cover her face, her bleeding nose. Christian found himself stirred by pity. The white woman on the ground did not deserve it, but what could one do but pity her . . . or any woman who loved such a creature as Arlen Thorne?

"We will find the girl," Thorne said quietly. "No matter where you take her."

"You will try," Christian replied, and though he meant to say no more, he found his mouth running on without him, as though another man spoke with his voice. "But you will have to come through me. I swear it."

"And what is your word worth?" Thorne demanded caustically . . . but beneath the sarcasm, his face had gone pale. The sapphire at Christian's chest burned and burned.

"I have watched you, Lazarus, more closely than you know. You have no loyalty . . . unless it be to the Creche itself. You're a fine figurehead for the tunnels. You know where all of us belong."

Bubbles in the ale, Christian thought distantly. Here was another Wigan, another great believer in the hierarchy of the Creche, the natural order; Christian only wondered that he had not seen it from the first. Thorne and Brenna were both Creche babies, likely sold in their first weeks of life, just as Christian had been himself, and they had each learned the great lesson of the tunnels: in a world where brutality was a constant, it was infinitely better to be the one holding the whip. Christian was struck with sorrow for the child Thorne, so long lost . . . but he did not confuse that child with the man who stood before him.

"Is this about your whore?"

Christian's hand clenched on the mace. Thorne was trying to draw him out, he knew it, and yet the draw was effective, for he moved forward a few inches, his feet scuffling of their own accord.

"Her name was Maura," Christian said flatly. "I know it was you who brought her to that place."

"And why not? The children needed a nursemaid. All the whore wanted was a steady supply of poppy, and I secured it. Who else had ever done so much for her, Lazarus? Had you?"

Great God, he means it! Thorne truly believed that he had acted the best part here, and in a flash of understanding, Christian realized that Arlen Thorne was just as dangerous as his witch, perhaps even more so. Brenna, after all, was only an instrument, but a man with Thorne's lack of conscience could justify anything.

"You took Maura," he said stonily. "But you will not have the child, not unless you come through me."

Thorne stared at him for another long moment, his eyes burning with sheer hatred, and something more pitiable: an impotent fury. Thorne did not just want the sapphire, Christian realized. He wanted to kill the child. More than that, he *needed* to kill her.

Why? Christian wondered again. *What has she done?*

And then: *What will she* do?

None too gently, Thorne pulled Brenna from the ground. Christian winced as he heard the tendons in the witch's elbow pop. Thorne got an arm beneath her and began hauling her toward the break in the wall. Christian thought they would simply melt away, but in the end Thorne himself was unable; he paused in the opening, turning his baleful gaze back to Christian.

"You will regret this, Lazarus. One day I will hold the power of this kingdom in my hands, and I will not forget."

"Good. Because I forget nothing either."

Thorne glared at him for another moment, and then he and

Brenna disappeared through the break. Christian waited several long minutes—he would never know how many—with the child clutched in one hand and his mace in the other, before he came to believe that they were really gone.

The horse nickered companionably as Christian touched her flank with one hand. He did so almost absentmindedly, staring down at the baby in his arms. She was going to start crying again, and he could not bear it. Slowly, fearing an explosion, he dug in his saddlebags for the other bottle. He offered it to the girl, turning the spout downward to suck. She drank greedily, and Christian was so relieved at the silence that he did not think to slow her down, only settled her in the crook of his arm and sat down among the rubble.

"What happened?" he asked the child. "What happened there?"

She did not answer, only watched him meditatively over the rim of the bottle. She was so small . . . Christian could not help thinking, again, of the children in the Devil's Club, their eyes wide with fright as they clutched Maura's skirts, as real to him as though they stood close by. And now it seemed to Christian that there was another figure here: a shadow hiding in the corner, or perhaps crouched in front of his horse, its dim silhouette flickering with the torchlight. Not Lazarus, this shadow, nor Christian, but an amalgam of the two: the Mace. He was not a good man, the Mace, but not a bad man, not by a long shot. He could not leave the other two behind, but—

But I need not bear them with me.

The baby had finished the bottle. Her eyes were drowsy, her face slackened.

"I know where we are, I think," Christian told her softly. "But we can't stay in these tunnels; you make too much noise, and Fortune makes us even easier to track. I'll need warm clothing for the journey. We'll have to get topside, but that's not an easy business on the north Creche. It's all ladders. How will we get you topside and get my horse out too?"

The girl was not interested in such matters. She closed her eyes, her mouth breaking wide in a tremendous yawn. Christian tucked her in one arm, grabbed his reins, and pulled himself back into the saddle. She was falling asleep right in front of him now, her eyes closing for longer and longer intervals. After a long moment's thought, Christian lifted her and clasped her to him, rocking her slowly, as he had seen Niya and Carroll do. The baby laid her head on his shoulder, digging her face into the side of his neck, and then wormed a small hand beneath the edge of his armor to find the warmth of his chest. Christian settled her firmly in one arm and took the reins in his other hand, unable to define what he felt, only knowing that he must move forward.

We are in the great quiet now, he thought, and then he shook the reins, guiding Fortune back out into the tunnel.

L ess than an hour later, he climbed a ladder. It was a slow process, for the baby was still tucked against his shoulder, sleeping soundly, and he could only use one arm. After some wrestling with the rungs, he reached the top and banged three times on the underside of a trapdoor. At the foot of the ladder, Fortune whickered.

"State your business!" a voice boomed from the other side.

"Open up, old man!" Christian growled softly. "Or I will break your other hip!"

There was a long silence. Then the bolt was drawn and the trapdoor rose, flooding the ladder with light. A silhouette loomed above him, but Christian did not flinch, for he recognized the set of those narrow shoulders, the tiny head with its wisps of flyaway hair.

"What have we here?" Arliss asked. "Have you become a father, boy? I could set every bookmaker in the kingdom on end with that one."

"I need help."

Arliss's silhouette considered him for a long, silent moment.

"Please," Christian added, and as he spoke the word, he felt something loosen inside him, some knot long tied.

"Another beating for the oddsmen," Arliss remarked. "Quite a day we're having."

Putting aside his pen, he reached down through the door. "Give me that child and haul yourself up, lad. We'll see what we can do."

Christian handed him the girl. Arliss tucked her against his shoulder with a finesse that spoke of some experience, then extended a hand.

"Well, come on, boy. Or do you want to stay down there forever?"

Mace climbed into the light.

CHAPTER 37

A STORM IN THE NIGHT

What we know of Arlen Thorne suggests sociopathy, or at best, a virulent narcissism. But that is only the benefit of hindsight. No one in the Tearling really knew Arlen Thorne, not until a single moment revealed him in his entirety.

—*Famous Traitors of the Tear: A Compendium*, EVAN CRAWFORD

Aislinn should have known that something was wrong when the drawbridge didn't open. They had been out there for more than an hour, their numbers steadily filling the lawn until there was no more room, and the last few were squeezed back onto the enormous boulevard. At the sight of the sea of torches around her, behind her, Aislinn's confidence had doubled, trebled. In the face of such numbers, Elyssa must appear; she would have to.

I learned nothing from my years with Lady Andrews, Aislinn thought ruefully. One gold-plated bitch was just like another. If Lady Andrews had had a moat and drawbridge, the rebellion would never even have gotten off the ground. Elyssa would not come out to treat with them; why should she? No, she would hide in her castle, waiting, testing their resolve.

Very well, Aislinn thought, staring up at the monstrous stone

405

facade before her. *We need a rest, and we are certainly well provi-sioned now. The entire city is behind us. We can wait you out.*

She sat down, feeling them all follow: Liam first, then those behind him . . . a vast wave of humanity, all settling to earth. The grass beneath her was slick with dew; Aislinn wiped her hands on her dress. She and Liam were no more than ten feet from the moat, a choice she now regretted, for the water smelled dreadful. Ais-linn ignored it, thinking of the city, the people behind her. They had emerged from the alleys, the hovels, their emaciated faces transported as they joined in, following Aislinn's people to the Keep. There were so *many* of them! Aislinn closed her eyes and tipped her head back, feeling a pure joy so acute that it made the stench of the moat fade into nothing. The stone facade of the Keep did not intimidate her any longer, for she felt certain that nothing could hold against them, not so long as they all stood together. Even the enormous silhouette of the scaffold behind her, black against the dark-blue sky, could not intimidate her now. The Crown must execute its traitors there, but her people were not traitors. They were demanding only what was right.

"Something's wrong," the Fetch said. He had reappeared beside her without warning, his masked face tilted upward toward the Keep. "I've been up and down the lawn now. There's no snow."

"What?"

"No snow on the ground."

Aislinn looked around, realizing that he was right. The entire city had been carpeted in snow, save only where foot and horse traffic had melted it on the streets. But the lawn was entirely clear.

"This is a huge patch of grass," Liam remarked. "It must take sunlight most of the day."

But the Fetch was not listening, still looking up at the Keep. "Do you smell that?"

"It's the moat," Aislinn replied. "The water must be putrid."

"That's not the moat." The Fetch was quiet for another moment, and then Aislinn heard his quick indrawn breath. "Get them out of here."

"What?"

The Fetch tore the mask from his head, and Aislinn had time to see that he was extraordinarily young, only half the age she had imagined. Then he grabbed her shoulders, shouting into her face.

"A trap! It's a trap, all of this! Get them off the lawn!"

Aislinn gaped at him for a long moment, wondering whether he was joking. The drawbridge was closed. Her people numbered seven thousand, more than the Tear army. How could it possibly be a trap?

"Get back!" the Fetch screamed, and now Aislinn heard the youth in his voice. The fright. "Get off the lawn! Now!"

But it was too late, for now a fearful scream rose from the sea of people behind her, hundreds of hands pointing into the air. Following their trajectory, Aislinn saw that a line of figures had appeared on the battlements far above. She could not see their faces, but all of them held strung bows. Even at this great distance, Aislinn could see the arrows, because the tips were alight, shimmering with flame.

"Get back!" the Fetch screamed again, but it was like trying to part the sea.

"Aislinn," Liam muttered. He had squatted down beside her to inspect the grass, and now he raised his hand into the light so that Aislinn could see his palm: glittering and slick with dew.

No, not dew, Aislinn realized suddenly, staring up at the Keep in sudden understanding, sudden horror.

Oil.

A man's voice shouted high above them, too distant to hear the words, and in unison the bows tilted downward, aiming the flaming arrows at the lawn.

"Run!" the Fetch screamed. "Get off the grass!"

But Aislinn's people simply stood there, staring upward, openmouthed. Even Aislinn herself stood frozen, unable to credit the sight before her, around her . . . the oil beneath her feet.

They wouldn't, she thought blankly. *How could they?*

Shrieks rose behind her, and Aislinn felt a wave of scorching heat at the back of her neck. Turning, she saw flames leaping high at the top of the lawn. They had already set the fire, trapping those at the back, cutting off their escape. If the entire Keep Lawn was coated with oil—and it was, of course it was—they would burn to death. All of them.

I could run, Aislinn thought. The moat was only ten feet away; she could run and dive into the water, holding her breath until the worst of the flame had passed. The soles of her shoes were slick with oil, but she might make it . . . and then she was sickened at herself. At least half of the people on the lawn were children. Aislinn might make it, yes, and so might the hundred or so other souls who stood at the front, closest to the moat. But what then? She could not save the rest, and so she merely stood there, staring upward, as the voice atop the battlements shouted its last command, as the bows unstrung.

All lost, Aislinn thought, in the instant before the arrows landed. *All lost, and how can that be? How can that be, when we worked so hard, when all we wanted was a just world? How can it end this way?*

There were no answers, only flame. Aislinn's dress went up first, and she heard them screaming around her, a world of nothing but screaming as the endless inferno tore across the grass and engulfed them all. She looked for Liam, but he had already fallen to the ground beside her, his skin boiling inside the armor he had picked out from Lady Andrews's armory, that proud day when they had marched inside, feeling themselves unstoppable, immortal with right. The flames rose higher and higher, tearing into the night sky—later on, farmers in the central Almont would claim they had seen the conflagration, even in Billingston, more than thirty miles away—but Aislinn understood, in her last moments of understanding anything, that it was not the height of the blaze that mattered, but the breadth . . . how it covered the entire lawn in seconds, taking them all, even the children, leaving nothing behind . . . no one to remember, no one to build.

CHAPTER 38

THE STRANGER IN THE CROWD

The dream was always running ahead of one. To catch up, to live for a moment in unison with it, that was the miracle.

—Anaïs Nin (pre-Crossing Fr./Cub.)

"Wake up, bitch! You have a visitor!"

Niya pulled herself from sleep, as though by inches. Waking was harder than it should have been; Culp had thrown her into a wall this morning—or was it last night?—and she had taken a bad blow to the head. Ever since, it seemed that all she wanted to do was sleep.

"Wake up, damn you!"

She opened her eyes to an odd sight: the underjailor, Kreb, setting a chair in the middle of the floor outside of her cell. The High Jailor, Peter, was rumored to be a decent enough man, but Niya was Culp's bird, and so she did not stay in the dungeon proper, but in the filthy rooms that had been sunken a floor below. Kreb was her jailor, and Kreb hated her like fire, for although he was clearly used to doing as he liked with the rare female prisoner in these cells, he did not dare to come inside Niya's cage. Culp was the only one who didn't fear her.

But Niya did not want to think of Culp.

"Here, Father. Here is our best chair."

If Niya had been more awake, she would have laughed at Kreb's subservient tone. Like every good Christian she had ever known, the underjailor wore a large wooden cross around his neck, and now he was nearly fawning as he ushered the priest toward Niya's cell. At the sight of the white robes, Niya rolled back over, closing her eyes.

"Fuck off, Father," she muttered.

"Shut up, bitch!" Kreb cried. "You'll mind your manners with the Father, or I will tell Culp!"

"Culp doesn't frighten me, you little shit. Or hadn't you noticed?"

But that was a lie, for the blank-faced interrogator *did* frighten Niya, long after she had thought herself done with being frightened by any man. That was nothing Kreb needed to know, of course. More than once, Niya had been grateful that Welwyn Culp did not like an audience for his art, for Kreb was just the sort to stand there, hard as a rock, storing up the images for later. Now the underjailor could only stare at Niya in impotent anger, his hand trembling toward his keys. Just as well. Culp intended to beat Niya down, and the ache in her head told her that he was slowly and surely making progress.

"Sit down, Father," Kreb said, his voice reverting quickly back to dog-slobbering obsequiousness. The chair creaked as the priest sat down, and Niya gave a large snore.

"I know Master Culp would like to have welcomed you himself, Father," Kreb went on. "But he's sleeping. It is very late."

"Indeed it is," the priest said, and at the sound of his voice, Niya's body jerked involuntarily. A better guard might have seen it, but Kreb was too busy falling all over himself; he noticed nothing.

"But we find that the early hours are the best time to attempt such redemptions. In the depth of night, these poor wretches see the dark gulf that awaits them."

"Of course, Father! Would you like some water or ale while you work? Or we have cheese—"

"Confessions are private, my son," the Fetch replied, and Niya could not help but admire his skill: perfect mimicry of the rich, compassionate tones of an experienced confessor priest, the very sort the Arvath would send for one final wheedle at a traitor's broken soul, so that the Church could announce yet another miraculous repentance and conversion. "Please leave us alone, so that I may do my best to save her corrupt soul."

"Yes, Father . . . yes, of course. I will be outside. Let me know if you need anything."

Kreb retreated, and Niya heard the low boom of the door that separated the cells from Culp's house of horrors.

"Great God," she whispered. "You're alive."

"I am not an easy man to kill."

"Good thing Kreb left when he did; I was worried he might piddle on your pretty robes."

"Me as well," the Fetch replied with a chuckle. But all humor vanished from his face as Niya rolled to sit up. Half of her face was sheeted with dried blood from the scalp wound she had taken yesterday. One of her thumbs and her third finger were missing. Her arms and legs were crusted with burns; Culp liked to play with flame. There were more bruises beneath the stained grey shift she wore, and they made it hard to sit up. But Niya did so, grunting, scooting backward so that she could lean against the wall.

"Welwyn Culp did this to you," the Fetch said flatly.

"Yes, but hopefully not for much longer; I think he is tiring of me. How did you get in here?"

412

"Why, through the front door, of course. Father Morrow, at your service."

The Fetch swept her a low bow, which made Niya smile. But his usually merry eyes were hard as flint, and now Niya saw that her injuries were not the only problem. The shadow that had always lain over the Fetch, that shadow that demanded that he take responsibility for all of the ills of the Tearling, was there, and darker than Niya had ever seen it. The Fetch looked like a man damned. Niya wanted to tell him that it was all right, argue him out of it, as she always did . . . but she was so tired.

I'm ready, she realized, wondering at her own calm . . . she, Niya, who had always fought like a cat when cornered! It had taken four Queen's Guards to subdue her in the end, including Elston, and Niya's only regret was the injuries she had dealt them: a broken arm for Galen, and a kick to Elston's jaw that had shattered most of his front teeth. She had hated hurting them, hated that they thought her a traitor, that they would never know why.

"What news?" she forced herself to ask the Fetch.

"Things go well," he replied. "The rebellion in the Almont is still strengthening. Our people have joined with them, demanding reforms. We have a good chance."

Lies, Niya thought. The Fetch was an excellent liar, but she had known him too long, and his tricks no longer fooled her. Something had happened, and if the Fetch would not tell her about it, then it could be nothing good. But she did not press him, for the shadow that lay over him was dark . . . so very dark.

"What else?"

"The little Princess is gone. Vanished without trace."

Niya blinked, coming awake a bit. The Princess . . . there was something she needed desperately to tell him. What was it?

"Your doing?" the Fetch asked. "The kidnapping?"

"And others'," Niya replied, racking her brain. Thinking was so hard now; she could not seem to remember anything anymore. Her eyes were trying to close again.

"Why did you come here?" she asked. "I'm glad you did, but why did you come?"

"To get you out of here, of course."

"Even you can't do that."

"Of course I can. But I mean to clean house first."

"House?" Niya asked, confused. Her head hurt.

"Nothing to bother you, Niya. Lie back down. Take a rest."

The old Niya would not have obeyed such an order, not even from the Fetch . . . but she was tired. So very tired. She lay down on the floor and closed her eyes, liking the feel of the cool stone against her bruised face.

"Jailor?" the Fetch called, his voice once again overlaid with the rich, satisfied tones of the career priest.

"Yes, Father?" Kreb nearly broke his neck opening the door.

"This poor creature has finally found God's grace, and agreed to confess her crimes. I suggest you fetch your master."

"Oh . . . oh! Yes, Father! I will wake him immediately!"

Kreb hurried away, and Niya heard the Fetch reseat himself in his chair. She wanted to look at him, but her eyelids were as heavy as anvils. She dozed in and out, for a period that seemed endless. She dreamed in this period . . . many dreams, and strange, full of sounds: a muffled scream, gagging. She was standing on a high hilltop, looking down at a river, and behind her a man begged for his life. A voice rang across the hilltop . . . a man's voice, but no man she had ever heard before. His words seemed almost part of the wind.

Niya.

"Niya."

A key rattled in the lock, jerking her awake, and then the Fetch was bending over her.

"Thank God. I thought you were dead."

"No." Niya coughed; her throat was dry, drier than she could ever remember. The Fetch handed her a dipper of water, and she drank deep, finishing the entire thing. "Not dead."

But you will be, her mind whispered, and now, suddenly, Niya remembered what had happened, what had brought her down here, what had kept her mouth shut as Culp beat her and burned her and even tore her hair out, taking piece after piece of scalp with it. She remembered everything, the crying baby in her arms and the tall, sorrowful woman on the throne . . . both of them one and the same.

"Help me up."

Outside her cell, Kreb lay sprawled on the ground, his throat cut. Culp lay nearby; Niya could not tell what had happened to him, save that he had no features anymore. The floor was sticky with blood.

"Thank you," she told the Fetch, meaning it with all her heart. "Now give me Kreb's knife."

"What?"

"I slew them. Give me Kreb's knife. That way, if someone should happen to come in here before you get clear of the Keep, it was only me who killed them, after you left. No one would suspect a priest, and you must leave here alive."

The Fetch stared at her for a long moment. Niya took pleasure in his careful scrutiny; even now, he did not mistake her words for nonsense or the distracted ravings of a lesser woman.

"Niya? What is it?"

"I'm going nowhere. My head feels strange. I can't stand up. I can't leave here, but you can . . . and you must."

"Why?"

Niya told him. Toward the end, her tale began to blur together, but the Fetch listened carefully, not interrupting. She wished that he had been there with her, had heard the grave woman in the crown, seen the outline of the better world. If he had only seen, then he could not doubt.

"Enough," he told her at last. "Enough. I understand. The girl must be watched, and guarded. But you need not have worried; I already have Howell on it."

"Already? Why?"

"Niya, who would you say fathered that child?"

"Gareth."

"Gareth, yes. Gareth, who had the sight. William Tear's sight."

Niya stared at him for a long moment, trying to think clearly, to ward off the waves of exhaustion.

"You think she has Tear blood."

"I think Gareth did. As for the girl, we'll have to see."

Tear blood. That meant something, but Niya could not come up with it, could not see the larger picture.

I'll think on it later, she decided. *After I sleep.*

"Get the knife," she told him. "Hurry up. I don't know when the guard shift changes."

The Fetch hesitated, and Niya raised her palms, a bit exasperated now. "What are they going to do? Kill me twice?"

But still he did not go, and now Niya finally understood.

"You came to kill me. So I couldn't tell them where she is."

The Fetch clearly had some thought of lying, for he did not reply right away. And then he paid her the highest compliment he had ever paid her in all of their long association, answering her with a nod.

"Well, you can kill me if you wish, but there's no need. I will die soon, one way or another. And I will not break."

The Fetch said nothing, merely looked at her. Niya thought there might be tears in his eyes, but she couldn't be sure. At long last he nodded, and went to get Kreb's knife. Niya leaned back against the wall again, feeling a headache begin its battering work against her temples.

I will die soon, she repeated to herself. But even that inevitability did not seem real.

"Here," the Fetch said, handing her the knife. Niya took it with her good hand, searching for a pocket . . . but of course the shapeless shift had none. She clutched the knife, looking up at the Fetch. Miraculously, there was not a spot of blood on his white robes; she supposed he must have taken them off at some point, then put them back on.

Niya.

She jerked awake; she had fallen asleep again . . . only for a moment, but long enough to once again hear that voice. Whose voice could it be?

"Thank you," she told the Fetch again, nudging Culp's body through the bars with her foot. "This is a great kindness. Now you should leave."

"I need not go yet."

But it was time. The Fetch knew it as well as she did. He backed away, straightening his robes, then turned to leave the cell. But Niya's question stopped him.

"Why did we fail?"

The Fetch stood silent for a long moment. Niya sensed that she had truly upset him, though she had not intended to.

"We didn't fail, Niya. We simply didn't win. History rules, not us. If we're lucky, we get an occasional star to guide us . . . but we didn't. Not this time."

"Do you think we'll ever reach it?" Niya asked sleepily. "The better world?"

"I don't know," the Fetch admitted, keeping his back to her.

"William Tear's better world required the Crossing, and that was an extraordinary event, one never duplicated. To get there again . . . it will take another extraordinary event."

"Keep her safe," Niya murmured. "Promise me."

"I will. You have my word."

Niya smiled. Relief seemed to bathe her, cool balm against her wounded heart. The Fetch opened the door, and she asked one last question . . . the question she had never asked him before.

"Who are you, really? Beneath the mask?"

The Fetch's shoulders rose and fell beneath the white robes. When he turned back, he looked not twenty or twenty-five but ancient, his face fallen into sagging lines of sorrow, like a man who had already burned through the best of his life.

"No one of importance, Niya. Only a man who must repair the gap. Sleep now."

She did.

The soldiers came in not long after . . . before the blood on the floor had dried, anyway. Niya woke when they began shouting at each other. They had locked her cell, and they did not dare to come inside; there were only two of them, and Niya still had a knife, after all. Finally, they decided to go upstairs and ask for guidance. Guidance did not take long; within perhaps thirty minutes, they came back again, and this time there were five of them.

"It's your lucky day, lassie," the soldier in charge said. "No time to train up a new interrogator, and the Princess Regent is tired of extending you hospitality. You're for the axe."

Niya nodded, a small smile creasing her face. If she hadn't been so tired, she might have whooped for joy, perhaps even cut a few capers.

I can sleep, she thought. *At last and finally, I can sleep.*

But though she was determined not to be afraid, all of her fine resolve left her as they ascended the stairs.

The smell hit her first, even before they had reached the first floor. It was like nothing Niya had ever smelled in her life: a meaty smell, half rotten. It got stronger as they exited the dungeons and approached the drawbridge, and then stronger still, until Niya felt that she would never be hungry again. The soldiers, too, were unwell; several of them looked decidedly ill, and all of them covered their mouths and noses.

Why the axe? she wondered suddenly. The scaffold on the Keep Lawn had taken so many Blue Horizon lives; why not Niya's as well? Then they moved out onto the drawbridge, and the view stopped Niya dead.

The Keep Lawn had turned black.

Burned, Niya thought numbly. The grass had burned in all directions, east to west, from the moat to the Great Boulevard. Niya could not see even a hint of green, and when she looked up to the top of the lawn, she saw that the facings of several buildings on the boulevard had blackened as well. Some areas of the lawn were still smoking, and it took Niya only a few steps beyond the drawbridge to realize that she was walking not on crisped grass, but charred flesh. She no longer felt tired, but wide awake, as though she had been slapped. Whatever had happened here had been terrible, so terrible that even the Fetch could not tell her the truth.

The scaffold was gone as well, probably burned to the ground. Niya had seen too many friends die there in the past months to mourn its loss, but as the soldiers led her forward and she glimpsed the squat black block with its protruding cup, her skin began to crawl. There was such an unrelenting implacability about that shape, somehow exacerbated by the fact that Niya's hands were bound behind her.

I should have done it myself, she thought, shivering in the early-morning air. *I should have slit my own wrists in my cell, while I still had the chance.*

There were no crowds on the lawn today; the smell alone was surely enough to keep even the most hardened gawkers away. Only two figures stood beside the block: a priest and a headsman, hooded in black. Both of them had clearly just been roused from sleep, for the priest's robes were wrinkled, and the headsman leaned tiredly on his axe. The axe had been used for someone else, Niya saw, and recently. Bits of flesh still caked the blade. Many good men and women had died out here in the past months; the smell was horrendous, and the axe was worse, but Niya tried to comfort herself with the thought that those shreds of flesh were perhaps the remnants of someone she had known, shared community with, admired. She was Blue Horizon, and the Blue Horizon took care of each other, even in death.

The priest—a real priest, this one—began to read from his Bible. Niya didn't listen. She had meant to keep her eyes closed, but she found that she could not help looking behind her, up at the stone facade of the Keep. Were they watching? Elyssa, Thorne, the witch, the Guard . . . had any of them come to see her die? Niya looked out over the blackened lawn again, trying to understand, to decrypt what had happened . . . but thinking made her head hurt. She wondered where Mace was, whether he had cleared the Creche, the city walls. Perhaps he and Kelsea had perished in the tunnels. Perhaps it had all been for nothing.

No, she thought fiercely. *I don't believe that.* They had played and lost, as the Fetch had said, but even loss was not permanent. Niya would not see the better world, but it did not follow that there would be none. It was the great gift of humanity, after all: to hold to hope, even when all torches went out.

After what seemed eons, the priest finally stopped babbling about God and closed his book. The soldiers took Niya's arms, shoving her roughly to her knees and bending her over the block, and Niya suddenly realized that a crowd *had* gathered to watch her die . . . a huge crowd, so many that she could not count them all. She craned her neck, straining to glimpse their faces, as the soldiers pinned her back and the headsman moved to stand beside the block.

I know them, Niya thought, staring at the crowd. And then, a moment later: *Great God, I know all of them!* There was Gareth, there Amelia, there Dylan, there old Maeve, there Lila and Marco . . . even Danny the Prince, who had died years before, killed during his first raid in the Gut. All of them were here, yes, but now Niya's attention was caught by a single man: a stranger, standing at the forefront of the crowd. She could not see his face clearly, and that was odd, for all of the other faces were so clear to her . . . so clear, and so well-loved. The sun was about to break the horizon, and the morning was bright and cold, but still she could not see the stranger's face.

Niya.

"May you repent your treason and your sins," the priest intoned behind her, "and in such repentance find God's forgiveness. His everlasting kingdom."

That brought Niya back, enough to allow her to snarl at the priest, "I don't need your kingdom, old man, or your God. I am Blue Horizon. There's a better world out there, so close we can almost touch it."

The soldiers shoved her down again, pushing her face into the cup of ice-cold stone. Niya squinted, trying to see the stranger, but all she could see was his general outline: tall, taller than the rest. The sun broke the horizon, and the first rays gleamed off the top of his blond head.

"May God have mercy on your soul."

The axe rose above her; Niya heard it clearly, the susurration of air, the headsman's intake of breath as he hefted it high. But the fall seemed very long, so long that she had time to look up at them, all of them, her friends, her brothers and sisters; time to remember every word the True Queen had spoken in that vaulted room of stone; time to look out across the city and the Almont beyond, to the horizon of the Tearling, this kingdom to which Niya had given so much . . . in the end, everything. She even had time to examine the stranger, the faceless man who stood at the head of the crowd, and in the moment before the axe bit, Niya realized that she did know him, after all: a tall blond man with eyes so bright they seemed almost silver, and it was the eyes that Niya recognized, eyes that had looked across the void and seen the better world, the land beyond the Crossing. The world for all of them. Niya opened her mouth, wanting to speak to him, even just to call him by name . . . and then she realized that she didn't need to, that he had heard her already. The axe met stone, a resounding crack that echoed across the vast length of the Keep Lawn, and the last thing Niya saw was the eastern horizon, that deep blue line that might hide anything at all, even a better world.

Niya reached out and touched it.

AND AT THE END

A SONG OF THE GUARD

All the darkness in the world cannot extinguish the light of a single candle.

—Francis of Assisi (pre-Crossing Ital.)

It was nearly dawn and pouring rain when Mace dismounted and knocked on the door of the cottage. At his chest, the baby made a loud yowling noise, voicing her anger that the ride had stopped. He had rigged the sling to guard her from the rain, which had been falling steadily since they left New London, but it had also allowed him to ride much faster with both hands on the reins, and the girl had been delighted, making happy little sounds for much of their journey. Now Mace jiggled her a bit, to ward off the inevitable tantrum, and knocked again.

Barty opened the door. He had clearly just woken; his eyes were rimmed with red, and he wore only trousers. He stared at Mace for a long, surprised moment, then spoke in a rusty wheeze of a voice.

"Thought you'd have quit the Guard by now, lad. Gone back to your boxing, as it were."

"You knew as well?"

"Think I'm stupid? Of course I knew. Carroll's a young fool, but his heart is good. He'll make a fine Captain, once he grows up a bit." Barty's expression sobered as he looked over Mace's shoulder. "Where is Niya? Carroll told us she would be coming."

"She didn't make it."

Barty raised his eyebrows, but Mace did not elaborate. After a long moment, Barty gestured toward the baby at his chest.

"Is that her? Elyssa's daughter?"

"Yes."

Barty bit the inside of his cheek. "Can I hold her?"

Mace handed the girl over, surprised to find himself a bit reluctant. In the three days they had been on the road, he had grown used to the small scrap: her scrunched-up face, her waving arms, the astonishing volume of her screams when Mace slowed his horse. Even changing nappies had not been so terrible as he had imagined.

"Come in, lad, come in," Barty told him. "You're wet through."

Mace went inside, dropped his saddlebags, and pulled off his sopping cloak, hanging it on one of the pegs near the door.

"Barty?"

A woman had appeared in the hall. She was tall and forbidding, this woman, with hawklike eyes and whitening hair. Mace did not know her by sight, only by reputation, but all the same, he thought he could have picked her out of a crowd in the New London Circus: Lady Glynn, the tutor, who had brought fear to the entire Queen's Wing in her day, who had lost her title when she redistributed her lands. Lady Glynn, whom everyone had believed dead.

"Will you join us for breakfast, lad?" Barty asked.

From the corner of his eye, Mace saw the old lady's mouth pinch; she did not like him. Most people did not . . . and they would not, Mace thought. Those who had accepted him—Carroll,

Niya, Arliss—were the exceptions, and there would not be many of them. Perhaps it was better so.

"No," he replied. "But I could use some food for the journey back."

"Help yourself, lad. Kitchen's through there."

But Barty did not look at Mace as he spoke; all of his attention was riveted on the baby. He was taken with her, Mace thought, and he made a mental note to tell Carroll when he got back to the Keep. Carroll had grown attached to the girl, and it would ease his mind to know that Barty cared as well. Niya, too, would want to know—but Mace closed his eyes, putting that thought away. Early yesterday morning, he had thought he heard Niya's voice, but the sound had vanished abruptly when the baby began to howl for her morning bottle. Mace told himself that it had only been a dream, but the idea did not rest easy in his mind.

"Bring that child in here, Barty," Lady Glynn ordered. "Before she catches her death of cold."

They took the baby into the living room, and Mace went on to the kitchen.

He was pulling meat and cheese from the icebox when the sapphire at his chest began to burn. Mace had forgotten all about it; if the jewel had not spoken up, he likely would have gotten all the way back to New London with the damned thing still dangling beneath his shirt.

Setting the food on top of his saddlebags, Mace pulled the necklace off and took it into the living room, a small, comfortable area in which every available surface appeared to be covered with books: books stacked neatly in piles on the floor, books lying on tables, even a few stacks balanced precariously on the arms of the sofa. Mace noted the books without judgment; such things were not for him, never would be, but perhaps they would serve some-one else.

"Here," he said, holding out the sapphire to Barty.

"The Queen's Jewel?" Barty asked, raising his eyebrows. "I saw the other one; it's hers by right. But where did you get that?"

"Couldn't begin to tell you." Mace held it out, dangling it above them, and it was Lady Glynn who finally took it.

"It's for the baby. When she's old enough."

Lady Glynn nodded, tucking the jewel away in her pocket.

"Well, goodbye," Mace said awkwardly. "Perhaps we'll see each other again."

"Nineteen years," Barty replied, chortling. "When you're sprouting grey hair, and all your muscle fallen into flab."

"Fuck off, Barty."

"Watch your mouth!" Lady Glynn hissed. "She will hear you! Even a baby can learn."

Barty sobered, looking abashed, and Mace backed away, rais-ing his hands in a gesture of surrender.

"Goodbye, Barty," he said. "Thank you."

"Same to you, lad," Barty replied, and this time Mace was sure of it: tears in the old man's eyes as he looked down at the girl. "This is a gift beyond price."

With a nod to the terrifying Lady Glynn, Mace retreated into the hallway, packed and fastened his saddlebags, and then donned his cloak and gloves. Half of his mind was listening to the mur-mured conversation from the living room, but the other half was miles away: in New London, in the Keep. *We got topside*, Maura had told him, and Christian had not had the heart to correct her. But where was he now? The sight of Barty's foolish grin as he bent over the baby had brought up an old sting, one that would never heal. It was grief for Maura, as it always would be, but now Mace's grief had broadened to include all of them . . . even himself, perhaps: the children of the Creche, children who had never been held, whose first cradles were stone floors, who slept wrapped in rags. Who would sing to them? Who would fight for them? Who would put an end to it?

Barty had begun crooning to the girl now, singing a song of the Guard, and Mace paused in the doorway for a moment, listening, watching the two people on the couch: Barty, already besotted with the child, and Lady Glynn, observing the two of them with a severe eye. Mace wondered at their relationship, the bond that could weld two such distinct people . . . but it was beyond him. They would take care of the Princess, do the best they could; the rest would be up to the girl herself. Bidding a silent farewell to the little mite, Mace grabbed his bags and slipped out the door.

Fortune was still waiting where he had looped her, beneath the eaves in the front yard. Mace tied his bags, then pulled himself up, looking around as he did so. It was a good cottage: comfortable and well fixed and private, hidden deep in the forest, far from any road. The girl might be safe here, at least for a time. As Mace reined the horse around, he saw Lady Glynn standing at the front window, watching him through the driving rain. He raised a hand in farewell, and the lady surprised him by waving back.

I will never stop being a killer, Mace thought, and knew it for simple truth. Whether by birth or raising, the delivery of death was woven into his very bones. *The darkness is coming*, the Queen had said, and Mace knew that she was right. Elyssa, the real Elyssa, was gone, never to return. Arlen Thorne and his witch now held the strings.

You did not make this tangle, Wigan whispered inside his head. *You are obligated to nothing.*

That was true as well, so true that Mace's hands jerked on the reins, drawing Fortune to an abrupt halt in the pouring rain. He had rescued the children in the Devil's Club, delivered the Princess to safety; his debt to Carroll was paid. He could still abandon this, shed his grey cloak and fade away into the vast anonymity of the Tearling. He was a big man, not afraid of hard work, and such men could always begin a new life.

But Mace couldn't, because he still had an obligation. No debt, this, nor even an oath, but rather a compact. *Do not waste it,* Arliss had said, and he would not. The Creche would always be inside his head, but suffering was not exclusive to the Creche; the shadow of indifference lay over the entire kingdom, protecting cruelty, seeding sorrow. Mace closed his eyes and saw Maura, holding out a crudely woven bracelet in her child's fist: the sun rising over blue water, a pretty picture from the tunnel walls. Neither of them had had the faintest idea of what that sunrise represented, but now he did, and he suddenly felt himself one with all of them: Lady Glynn, Niya, Arliss, even the nameless multitude who had burned in the Gadds Fire or dangled from the gallows.

"But you *are* with us, Mace. Didn't you know?"

Niya's voice was so close, so real, that Mace jerked in surprise, glancing around. But there was no one, only the driving rain around him, the endless shadow of branches against the lightening sky above his head. For a moment, something seemed to brush his cheek. Mace saw no one, but he didn't believe that no one was there.

After a few minutes, he spurred Fortune and headed southeast, toward the Keep. Toward home. Niya said nothing else, but she did not need to, for Mace had already realized that she was right: he *was* with them. He was with all of them. He was Blue Horizon, and as the knowledge crystallized inside him, Mace suddenly understood, as though for the first time, the magnitude of what he had left behind in that cottage, the weight of the future. And he knew that come hell and death, nineteen years from now he would return along this same path, still seeking the future, the better world . . . still seeking Kelsea.

He didn't know what he would find, but he knew that he would remember the way.

ACKNOWLEDGMENTS

At least half of the credit for this book must go to my editor, Maya Ziv. It took several false starts and months of hard work and arguing to get the book moving in the right direction, and I never once heard a reproach. This book was a collaborative effort; I wrote it, but Maya midwifed it, and it belongs to her as much as it does to me. A lovely lady, Maya Ziv.

The very luckiest authors get a literary agent who is also family. Thank you, Dorian Karchmar; you know why. Thanks also to Alex Kane and Laura Bonner at William Morris Endeavor, Hannah Feeney and Alice Dalrymple at Penguin Random House, and Simon Taylor and Imogen Nelson at TransWorld. Last but not least, a big thanks to Miranda Ottewell, whose attention to detail holds the Tearling together.

To Shane and George, I owe something beyond thanks. Our little family keeps me going, and writing, through the worst days and the hardest times. I literally don't know what I would do without you both, and I love you dearly. To Jayne Meadows, as well, I owe a deep debt of gratitude; I could not have finished this book without her help. Deb, Christian, and Katie: you are far away, but never far from my thoughts when I think about the world as I wish it could be.

Every time I write about the Tearling, I am compelled to thank my father, Curt Johansen. Long before I understood much about politics, my upbringing had already shaped my conception of the world, and it was my dad who raised me to always think of the little guy, to never let the small cruelties be forgotten in service of the big picture. The little guy is under siege now—in the Tearling and everywhere else—and every year I understand a bit more how lucky I am to have a parent who knew it, and who made sure I did too.

On a related note: as I thank my readers most of all, I want to say a word about resistance. We have now reached yet another crisis point in our history. The many labor and suffer to support the luxury of the few; open bigotry has become quotidian; desperate people seeking safety are brutalized; erosion of the separation of church and state is costing more and more lives. Fascism is rising, and even in a nominal democracy, fascism has a particularly pernicious ability to discourage resistance. I resist in fiction—it's the only thing I know how to do—but that's nothing; there are people who resist in the real world, though it takes bravery I don't possess and can barely conceive of. I like to talk the talk, but there are plenty of people out there walking the walk, and this book owes a debt to all of them. When we finally get back to Kelsea (not too long now, faithful reader, I promise), I will have many more shining examples to work with. There's a better world out there; I still believe it, even now, and nothing is irretrievable. So let's turn this shit around, shall we?

ABOUT THE AUTHOR

Erika Johansen grew up in the San Francisco Bay Area. She went to Swarthmore College in Pennsylvania before attending the celebrated Iowa Writers' Workshop, where she earned a Master of Fine Arts degree. She eventually became an attorney, but she never stopped writing. Her debut was the international bestseller *The Queen of the Tearling* – the first novel in a remarkable trilogy. This was followed by the acclaimed *The Invasion of the Tearling* and *The Fate of the Tearling*.

Erika now lives in the UK.